PRIDE OF
ASHNA

EMMANUEL M
ARRIAGA

PRIDE OF
ASHNA

FOUNDRA SERIES 02

Emmanuel M Arriaga

Copyright © 2021 EA Starchilde Company

All Rights Reserved.

ISBN: 9798703084601

ASIN B08VJ7MB68

Cover design: Jeff Brown / jeffbrowngraphics.com

Internal formatting: Natalia Junqueira / dawnbookdesign.com

Editor: Courtney Andersson

To my son Emmanuel Jr,
watching your imagination grow
reminds me of why I write.

Stay Up To Date

Join the MinSci, a special Facebook Group created for readers of Emmanuel M Arriaga's books. Come together and share interests related to his creative universes and engage with other readers.

Visit www.emmanuelarriaga.com and subscribe to the Founder's Log and keep up to date on new releases, promotions and general awesomeness.

Follow Emmanuel on Twitter @emmanuelarriaga
Follow the Foundra Universe on Instagram @foundra_universe

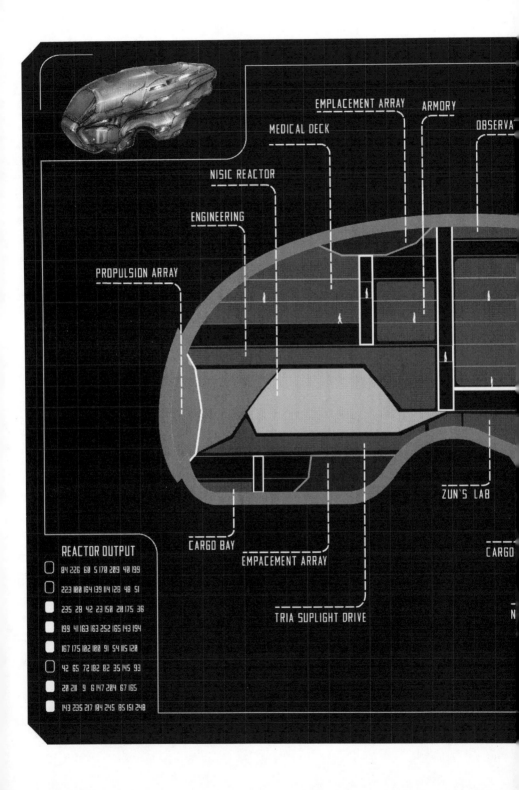

EMPLACEMENT ARRAY

ARMORY

OBSERVA

MEDICAL DECK

NISIC REACTOR

ENGINEERING

PROPULSION ARRAY

ZUN'S LAB

CARGO BAY

CARGO

EMPACEMENT ARRAY

TRIA SUPLIGHT DRIVE

REACTOR OUTPUT

- 84 226 60 5 170 209 40 199
- 223 100 164 139 114 128 48 51
- 235 28 42 23 150 20 175 36
- 199 41 163 163 252 165 143 194
- 167 175 102 100 91 54 115 120
- 42 65 72 182 82 35 145 93
- 20 211 9 6 147 204 67 165
- 143 235 217 104 245 85 151 248

IMPERIAL ID
ID-B7C9E1F9E4D

SHIP CLASS.
HSS-FFABBT

HOME PORT
THAE-A1

COMMAND ID
ID-0000000003

PRIMARY ARMORY

COMMAND DECK

FOUNDERS QUARTERS

FOUNDER'S ELITE QUARTERS

MESS HALL

EMPLACEMENT ARRAY

EMPLACEMENT ARRAY

FOUNDRA SI CORE

BAY

CARGO BAY

FOUNDRA ASCENSION

FOUNDER LANRETE'S SHIP

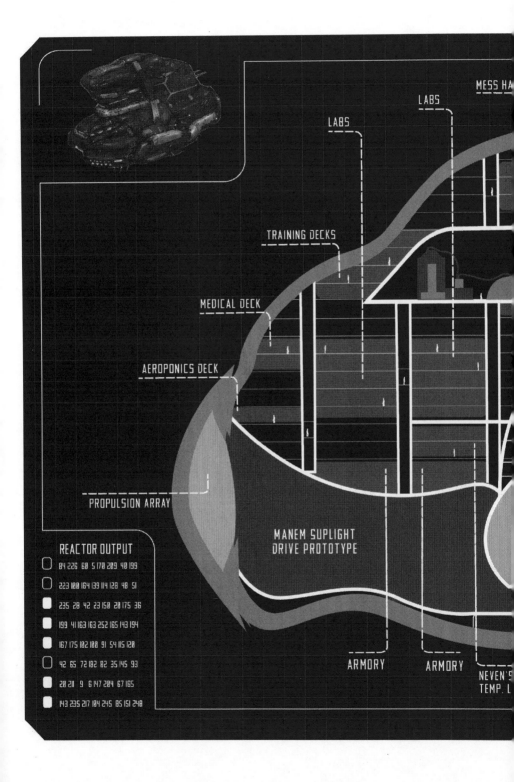

MESS HA

LABS

LABS

TRAINING DECKS

MEDICAL DECK

AEROPONICS DECK

PROPULSION ARRAY

MANEM SUPLIGHT
DRIVE PROTOTYPE

ARMORY

ARMORY

NEVEN'S
TEMP. L

REACTOR OUTPUT

84 226 60 5 170 209 40 199

223 188 164 139 114 128 40 51

235 28 42 23 150 20 175 36

199 41 163 163 252 165 143 194

167 175 182 188 91 54 115 128

42 65 72 182 82 35 145 93

20 211 9 6 147 204 67 165

143 235 217 184 245 85 151 248

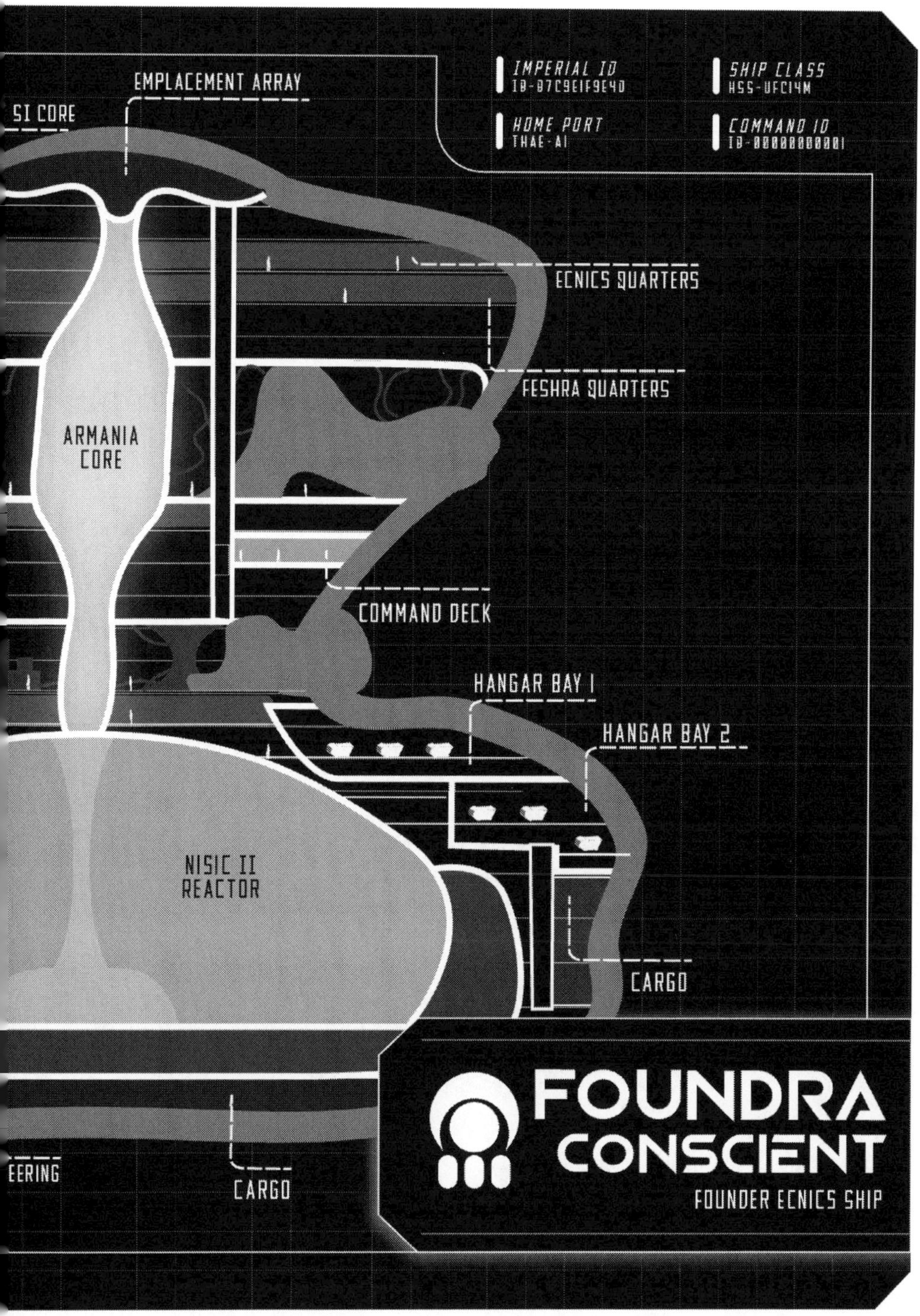

SI CORE

EMPLACEMENT ARRAY

IMPERIAL ID
ID-07C9E1F9E4D

SHIP CLASS
HSS-UFC14M

HOME PORT
THAE-A1

COMMAND ID
ID-0000000001

ECNICS QUARTERS

FESHRA QUARTERS

ARMANIA
CORE

COMMAND DECK

HANGAR BAY 1

HANGAR BAY 2

NISIC II
REACTOR

CARGO

EERING

CARGO

FOUNDRA
CONSCIENT
FOUNDER ECNICS SHIP

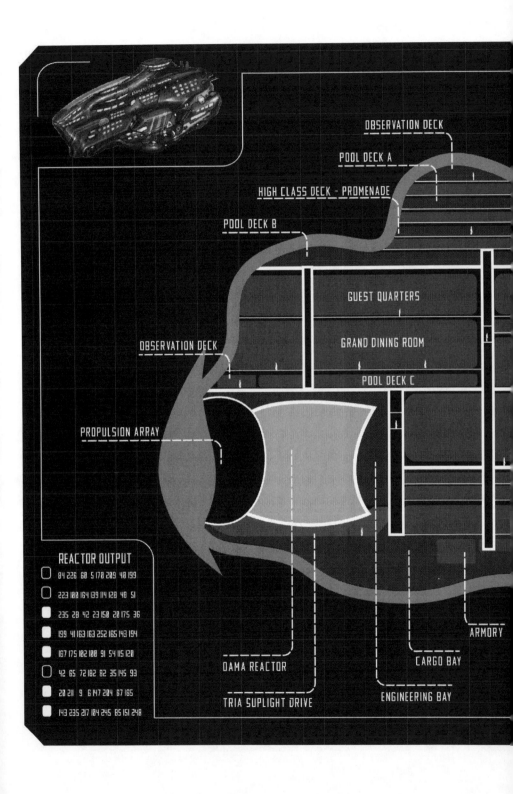

OBSERVATION DECK

POOL DECK A

HIGH CLASS DECK - PROMENADE

POOL DECK B

GUEST QUARTERS

GRAND DINING ROOM

OBSERVATION DECK

POOL DECK C

PROPULSION ARRAY

REACTOR OUTPUT

84 226 60 5 170 209 40 199

223 100 164 139 114 128 40 51

235 28 42 23 150 20 175 36

199 41 163 163 252 165 143 194

167 175 102 100 91 54 115 120

42 65 72 182 82 35 145 93

20 211 9 6 147 204 67 165

143 235 217 104 245 85 151 248

ARMORY

CARGO BAY

DAMA REACTOR

ENGINEERING BAY

TRIA SUPLIGHT DRIVE

IMPERIAL ID
IB-A4A7C2A889A

SHIP CLASS.
HSS-CES83T

HOME PORT
THAE-F8

COMMAND ID
IB-B19CIA3C2I73

BRIDGE CREW QUARTERS

ARTERS

BRIDGE

GUEST QUARTERS

OBSERVATION DECK

GUEST QUARTERS

JARTERS

EMPRESS CLUB

ROYAL THEATRE

FAMILY FUN DECK   OBSERVATION DECK

GUEST QUARTERS

ACTIVITIES DECK

CARGO BAY

BARS OF THE EMPRESS   CREW QUARTERS

EMPRESS MARKETPLACE

EMPRESS STAR

CRUISE SHIP

HANGAR BAY

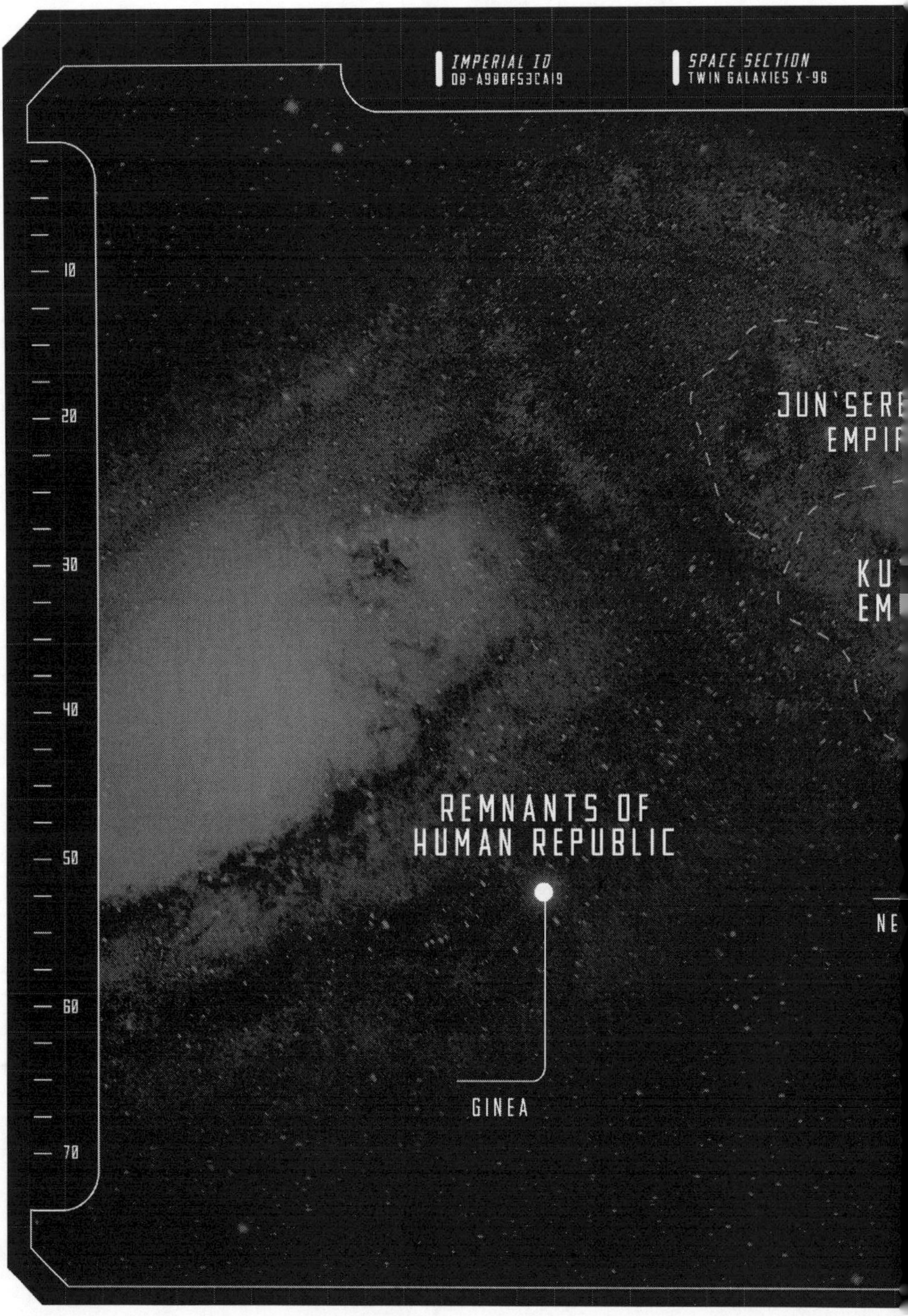
IMPERIAL ID
0B-A980F53CA19
SPACE SECTION
TWIN GALAXIES X-96
10
20
30
40
50
60
70
REMNANTS OF
HUMAN REPUBLIC
GINEA

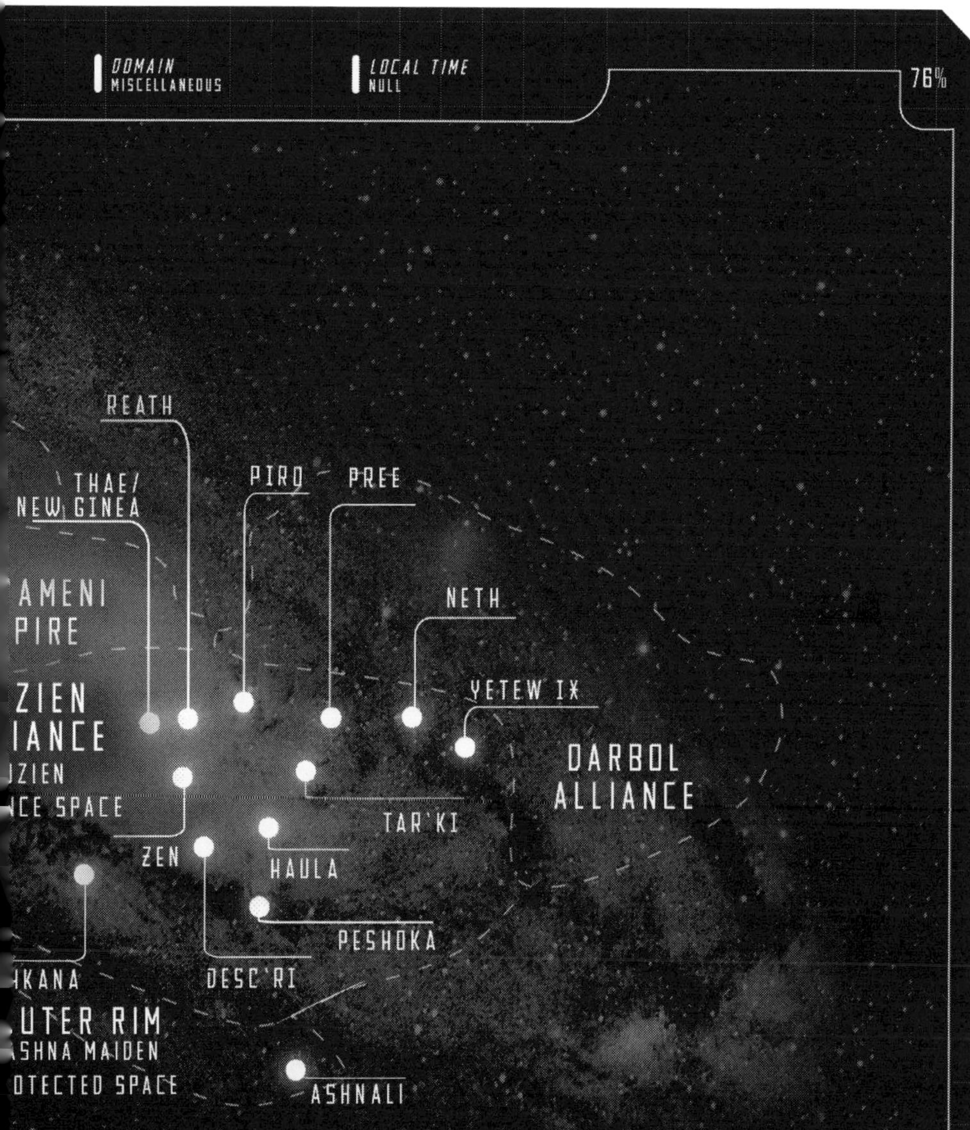

REATH

THAE/
NEW GINEA

PIRO   PREE

AMENI
PIRE

NETH

ZIEN
IANCE

YETEW IX

IZIEN
CE SPACE

DARBOL
ALLIANCE

ZEN

TAR'KI

HAULA

PESHOKA

KANA

DESC'RI

UTER RIM
SHNA MAIDEN

OTECTED SPACE

ASHNALI

TWIN GALAXIES

DAPHEN ASRACKA

STRONGHOLD

HEHETE'BEN
CONTROLLED SPACE

HET WRAST AH
CONTROLLED SPACE

STR

— 10   STRONGHOLD

STRONGHOLD

RUGTORA
PRIMARY STRONGHOLD

STRONGHOLD

BEN'YURI
PRIMARY STRONGHOLD

STRONGHOLD

— 20   STRONGHOLD

STRONGHOLD

STRONGHOLD

STRONGHOLD

— 30

A
STR

TARBAIAR
PRIMARY STRONGHOLD

STRONGHOLD

ROPT YOLRA
PRIMARY STRONGHOLD

RASTRAMAJER
CONTROLLED SPACE

STRONGHOLD

STRONGHOLD

STRONGHOLD

ASHNA
STRONGHOLD

— 40   STRONGHOLD

VERSRES
CONTROLLED SPACE

ASHNA
STRONGHOLD

ASHNARET
CIVILIAN REFUGE

— 50

STRONGHOLD

— 60

ASHNALI
ASHNA MAIDEN
HOMEWORLD

ASHNA
STRONGHOLD

— 70

STRONGHOLD

FRINGE
WORLD

ASHNA
STRONGHOLD

ASHNA
STRONGHOLD

ASHNA MAIDEN
SPACE

LD

ASHNAYULANI
FEMALE REFUGE

ASHNA
STRONGHOLD

  OUTER RIM

SENTILRAHM

KITYA
SEA

DELHISSA
OCEAN

ANIHL

MINSCI

GULF
FESHRA

LOAEM
OCEAN

ECK

DAHCE
SEA

LUNAM
SEA

HURISEW

OGEN
OCEAN

SENTILRA

DOMAIN
HUZIEN EMPIRE
LOCAL TIME
13:21
89%
ZELI SEA
SETNA ISLES
YULL SEA
LUVA
JORICEM
ANIHL
ONWA
RAMN OCEAN
ERS
SEMAJE SEA
HUZA
(APITAL)
TRUTARA
HAHVA SEA
HEEDILV OCEAN
TOMEN
HUZIEN INTELLIGENCE
TRESA OCEAN
PHAE OCEAN
THAE
SECTOR 57-B
X: 4.74147, Y: -29.26681, Z: 1.01
LUVA

| IMPERIAL ID | PLANET | LOCAL TIME |
| IB-B7C9EIF9E4D | THAE | 16:05 |

| IMPERIAL RANK | MISSION CODE | MISSION TYPE | COMMAND ID |
| CAPTAIN | THB57043-B | PERSONNEL TRANSFER | IB-BBBBBBBBBB3 |

DEPARTMENT OF
AEROSPACE
RESEARCH &
ENGINEERING

DEPARTMENT OF
COMMUNICATIONS RESEARCH

DEPARTMENT OF
SCIENTIFIC THEORY

DEPARTMENT OF
WEAPONS DEVELOPMENT

ADMINISTRATIVE
COMPLEX

ECNICS'S OFFICE

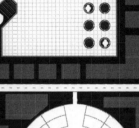

DEPARTMENT OF
ENERGY RESEARCH

HUZIEN
SYSTEM
OPERATION

DEPARTMENT OF ADVANCED
COMPUTING & SI RESEARCH

DEPARTMENT OF
BIOLOGICAL &
ENVIRONMENTAL RESEARCH

DEPARTMENT OF
CHPHIST
TECHNOLOGY

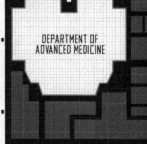

DEPARTMENT OF
ADVANCED MEDICINE

PARKING &
TRANSPORATION
COMPLEX

LOG DATA
84 226 68 5 170 209 40 199 223 100 104 139 114 128 48 51 235 28 42 23 150 28 175
36 199 41 163 163 252 165 143 194 167 175 182 180 91 54 115 128 42 65 72 182 82 35
145 93 28 21 9 6 147 204 67 165 143 235 217 184 245 85 151 248 88 70 213 92 221
85 15 137 119 88 9 172 141 118 248 88 115 196 204 163 140 184 48 129 168 38 171 39 239
40 1 128 79 178 46 185 6 147 204 67 165 143 235 217 184 245 85 151 248 88 70 213

MINSC

MINISTRY OF SCIEN
X: 8.73295, Y: -109.294021, Z: 13

IMPERIAL ID
ID-B7C9E1F9E4D

PLANET
ASHNALI

LOCAL TIME
19:43

IMPERIAL RANK
CAPTAIN

MISSION CODE
TH2090RSC02

MISSION TYPE
RECONNAISSANCE

COMMAND ID
ID-000000000003

GOVERNMENT
ADMINISTRATIVE
WING

LIVING QUARTERS FOR
HALLE NEDIM

HIGH PRIESTESS
QUARTERS

HIGH PRIESTESS
QUARTERS

HIGH TEMPLE OF ASHNA

ASHNA
MOTHER
QUARTERS

HIGH PRIESTESS
QUARTERS

PRIESTESS
QUARTERS

AVATAR WING

TEMPLE
OF ASHNA

LOG DATA
84 226 68 5 178 209 40 199 223 180 164 139 114 128 48 51 235 28 42
23 150 28 175 36 199 41 163 163 252 165 143 194 187 175 182 180 91 54
115 128 42 85 72 182 82 35 145 93 20 211 9 6 147 204 67 185 143
235 217 184 245 85 151 248 88 70 213 92 221 85 15 137 119 88 9 172
141 118 249 80 115 196 204 163 140 184 40 129 168 38 171 39 239 40 1

HIGH TEMPLE
HIGH TEMPLE CITY
X: 9.29495, Y: 29.286021, Z: 98.321

The Enesmic touches on the very nature of our existence. From it comes the power to create and destroy. A power that by some act of genetic sensitivity, we can interact with and manipulate.

–FROM "ON THE NATURE OF THE ENESMIC"
BY SHAPER LUKIR AFREV

CHAPTER 1 SERAH'ELAX REZ ASHFALEN

512th Retinue dropship orbiting Guna IV, Outer Rim

The soft hum of the Nies reactor resonated within the dropship cabin. Serah'Elax strode through seated rows of all-female warriors from the 512th Retinue, her shoulder-length red hair flowing behind her. Each soldier focused on Serah'Elax as she passed, the presence of a scion of Ashna causing many to sit up straighter. She came to a graceful stop at the sealed wall-sized exit to the dropship. With a thought to the mobi communicator tucked securely in her collar, the minuscule device instructed the bay doors to begin their ascent. Cool blasts of ozone and fresh air filled the cabin, its torrents sending Serah'Elax's short black cloak dancing in the wind.

Turning to face her warriors, Serah'Elax met their gazes as she held her arms out to her sides. Her light brown skin caught the sun's light in just the right way, causing the streaks of silver hues within to sparkle. With a smile, she slowly leaned backward, allowing gravity to take hold of her.

She closed her eyes as she fell away from the dropship, the air rushing past her in her rapid free fall from the upper atmosphere of the planet. She breathed in deep, electricity in her veins, then spun her body around to face the ground. Slowly, she opened her almond-colored eyes.

The sound of rapid winds filled her ears, the howling almost soothing. Her pulse raced, the moment one of pure freedom as her gaze soaked in the sight of large swaths of land quickly becoming more distinct. She allowed the serenity of untouched nature to pull her into a heightened state of consciousness.

She leaned forward, angling herself like a spear and picking up speed. Another thought to her mobi prompted a device clipped to her back to slowly open, and a sleek set of nanoplexi-enforced black wings appeared behind her. With another thought, the wings spread out, catching the wind and abruptly sending her body into a tight glide parallel to the ground. A gravimetric thruster powered on, and Serah'Elax began flying like a bird, the sky her plaything. The micro-display etched into her retina flared to life, her target identified. A small compound a few miles away became highlighted in her heads-up display as she flew lower to the ground.

The wings spread out more as the thruster disengaged. Serah'Elax transitioned into a careful glide toward the south-facing wall of the compound, and with another abrupt motion, the wings sent her quickly toward the ground. She disengaged them, and they retracted into their dens. She landed in a breakfall, came up running, then slid to one of the external walls. The scion of Ashna raised her fist into the air, and her seraglio—an elite force of forty-nine Ashna Maidens—came to a stop behind her. All had joined in their leader's free fall from the dropship.

She silently surveyed her forces as her subordinate Maiden protectors—each in charge of a haram—gave her the go signal, each team of sixteen ready and accounted for, then grabbed the dual Blades of the Goddess sheathed at her sides. The deadly plexicarbonite blades matched the length of her arms. Their design was efficient, brutal, and beautiful. As she held the grips, an extension connected into the wrist guards on each of her arms, locking the blades into place. Uttering a prayer to the goddess, her eyes became death.

Serah'Elax had taken the heads of four people before the pirate camp realized it was under attack. Rushing ahead at the front of the throng of Ashna Maidens storming the compound, she dodged weapons fire with an uncanny ease, ascending like an angel of death, the wings on her back shooting out to enhance her movements as she rapidly closed the distance on a group of three pirates. Landing with her weapons drawn, she ripped into a grim-faced Human, her blades going deep as she extended her arms, severing him in half. His body collapsed in a heap.

Her glorious entrance alerted the two remaining pirates to her presence, and they moved to level their weapons at her. Letting out a slow breath, time seemed to slow down around Serah'Elax. She raised her two ornate blades, each blessed instrument aimed at one of the pirates. With just a thought, the blades began to glow, and then the terrible energy building up within their weapon cores released. The blasts left gaping holes in the chests of the two shocked men. As time caught up with Serah'Elax, she flew past the still-standing corpses.

She made her way toward the command tower. Her ship in the upper atmosphere was jamming signals from leaving the compound, but she couldn't risk the possibility of a warning getting out somehow and alerting the rest of the system to their presence. Two more pirates moved to block her and opened fire. Both were women with brands on their faces, the horrid markings indications of who they belonged to. Without a tinge of sympathy in her heart, Serah'Elax dodged their attacks while raising her blades as she flew past them in a flash. The pirates stood as though in shock as lines of blood appeared on their necks, their bodies no longer capable of obeying commands as their minds shut down. Both collapsed to the ground, their heads rolling off to the sides.

A frown crossed Serah'Elax's face as the door to the command tower slammed shut and a set of turrets nearby jerked to life. The automated weapons systems turned to her. Jumping straight up, she engaged her thrusters as they opened fire, her heart skipping a beat. Flying past the ground floor, she pushed the limits of her flight, gritting her teeth against the slam of g-forces against her body. She circled the tower, dropping out of turret tracking range. With a powerful blast from her blades, she blew a hole toward the top of the structure. Moving inside, weapons fire greeted her from two autonomous drones. Their destructive onslaught forced her to seek cover, but as the drones converged on her location she lashed out, her blade impaling one of the automatons. She then kicked herself off the ground and flew over the impaled drone, her other blade digging into its back as she twisted, sending the machine spinning to the ground as scrap.

A powerful blast slammed into her chest, throwing the scion back. Her combat suit absorbed the full impact, preventing any real damage. Recovering, Serah'Elax slammed her blades together blade edge to blade edge, unleashing a powerful blast that ripped through the drone and sent it flying out of the hole she had created in the wall. When she rose to her feet, the barrel of a weapon was pressed against the back of her head. The sound of it powering on rang in her ears.

She froze.

"Looks like I've caught myself a pretty trophy," said a deep voice from behind her. The weapon pressed harder into the back of her skull. "Tell your little whores to lay down their weapons and maybe I'll let you all live."

"Life as a slave is no life at all," Serah'Elax replied. In a heartbeat, she dropped to the ground, the weapon's discharge missing her by a hair. Spinning, she took out the legs of the large man behind her, her blades making quick work of his weapon arm. Without letting him fully drop to the ground, she caught him in the chest with both blades, then used her momentum to impale him against the wall. He had light brown munsha marks running from his forehead down his face, a sign of his Tuzen heritage. When she released her blades, they disconnected from her wrist guards, and she left him hanging there, pinned to the wall. She casually walked over to the holographic display system built into his desk, a swagger in her step.

The brute's attempts at insults came out as gurgling sounds. Blood was filling his lungs. Serah'Elax took her time with bringing up the holodisplay and uploading an assault-grade SI—systems intelligence—from her mobi, which quickly gave her control of the command systems.

Without acknowledging the presence of the dying man, she began the process of shutting down the communication system. The pirate captain's bloodshot eyes glared at her, his eyebrows narrowed menacingly as he struggled to keep them open. The soft hum in the room faded as all power within the compound was shut down. Serah'Elax smiled, then retrieved the blades from the fresh corpse of the pirate captain and moved to the hole she had created earlier. Listening with elation to the dying screams of pirate scum, she instructed her seraglio to not leave a single person alive. There would be no prisoners taken today.

Twenty-six years ago
Firyia, Outer Rim

Serah'Elax reached out toward her *wo'shae*, her sister twin, who lay motionless a few meters away. The sounds of screams and sobbing echoed outside. Many of the walls around Serah'Elax had collapsed. The ceiling was caved in at various points with her bedroom, which had been on the second floor, now part of the living room. Her mothers, Dera'Liv and Ovah'Hal, had grabbed her and pulled her under a table after the first orbital barrage. Another explosion a short distance away rocked the house, causing debris and dust to crash down around them.

"Nesal'Velexi!" Serah'Elax cried. She broke away from her mothers and rushed over to her *wo'shae*, turning her over. The front of her body was dark black, scorch marks and severe burns eliminating all semblances of her beautiful light brown face. Platinum blood coated the floor. Serah'Elax's hands were soaked in it. Tears filled her eyes. "Nesnes, say something," she whispered. The tears began to stream down her cheeks; she could no longer feel the telepathic connection she had shared with her *wo'shae* since the womb. She began to shake, raw emotion in her voice as she screamed and put her forehead to Nesal'Velexi's.

The sound of the front door to her house being kicked open snapped up her attention. She turned to see three large men with tattoos covering their faces charge into the remnants of her home.

"Hide!" Ovah'Hal said, her gaze on Dera'Liv. "Take Serah'Elax and get out of sight!" Ovah'Hal pushed herself up from the ground, her eyes lingering for a second on Serah'Elax before refocusing on the intruders. Her face hardened, fire in her eyes. Charging forward, her muscular frame connected with one of the men, her solid hit snapping bone as she tackled him from the side. Dera'Liv grabbed Serah'Elax and pulled her back under the table, out of view. Ovah'Hal kicked out, knocking another man to the ground, and brought her hand down hard on his throat. He began to choke, his windpipe broken. She jumped to her feet and turned toward the remaining man. He leveled his assault rifle at her chest and squeezed the trigger.

Serah'Elax watched Ovah'Hal's legs as she staggered back, her platinum blood coating the floor and mixing with Nesal'Velexi's. Ovah'Hal then collapsed to the ground, unmoving. Serah'Elax's eyes went wide, and Dera'Liv snapped a hand over her mouth, sending a powerful telepathic urge to her daughter to keep quiet. She heard the remaining man curse, then watched him angle his assault rifle down and unload another barrage into the unmoving body of Ovah'Hal. Platinum blood splattered onto her face.

Present day
72nd Ashna Maiden Fleet in orbit around Ashnali,
Ashna Maiden home system

Serah'Elax woke with a start, her hand reflexively going to the gun she kept under her pillow. In a heartbeat, she had it leveled on the door to her bunk room. Recognition of where she was caused her to relax her grip on the weapon, the sound of the Ashna Maiden in the bunk above her steadily breathing in a restful sleep putting her at ease.

Rubbing her eyes, she lay back down in her bunk and turned her head to catch the subtle hints of a picture clipped to her bunk wall. She reached out and unclipped the picture. It was one of the few physical possessions she kept. The picture lit up slightly, becoming more visible in the darkness. Serah'Elax stared at her family. Dera'Liv Elax Ashfalen, her *yu'shae*, or birth mother. Ovah'Hal Velexi Rez, her *uma'shae,* or non-birth mother. Her *wo'shae*, Nesal'Velexi Ashfalen Rez, and a much younger version of herself. The digital paper looped the scene of them posing for a moment before all semblances of order rapidly faded with Serah'Elax and Nesal'Velexi making faces as they were both scooped up by their mothers in hugs. Her gaze hung on Ovah'Hal and Nesal'Velexi for a long moment, a single tear rolling down her cheek.

> *We do not truly understand what the Enesmic is, although some cihphists speculate that it is simply another force of nature, similar to gravity.*
>
> –FROM "ON THE NATURE OF THE ENESMIC"
> BY SHAPER LUKIR AFREV

CHAPTER 2 VALANA ETRUEN

Ashna Maiden patrol fleet, Huzien Alliance / Ashna Maiden border

Keeper Valana Etruen sat in the bridge command chair aboard the Ashna Maiden cruiser *Greschenathalan* as it patrolled the borders of Ashna Maiden protected space. Things had been quiet as of late, with pirate ships going out of their way to avoid Maiden controlled space since the last stronghold raid by Avatar Hegna a few light-years away. The Ashna Council had increased the number of warships on border patrols in case of retaliation. They doubted a counterattack, but the Maidens survived on a cautiousness that bordered on paranoia.

"Keeper, we're picking up something on our sensors," a young Ashna Maiden said. She stared at her holodisplay with her eyes wide, her mouth agape.

"What is it?" Keeper Valana walked toward the female soldier, eyeing the tremble in the young Maiden's hand.

"It's . . . a fleet."

"A fleet?" Valana echoed, "How many ships?"

"Thousands, Keeper," she whispered. Valana grabbed the holodisplay output and projected it onto the main holodisplay aboard the bridge.

"Those aren't Alliance or pirate vessels."

"Keeper, they're heading right toward our location!"

Keeper Valana slowly backed into her command chair, almost stumbling as she fell into it. "Ashna, save us . . ." she whispered. Her face hardened as she pushed herself up from the chair, then glanced to her bridge crew. All eyes were on her.

"Send word to the Ashna Council at once. Attach all the information we are seeing," she ordered. Her voice was calm and controlled. "Open up a broadcast channel." Valana paused for a moment to think through her words. "This is the Ashna Maiden battle cruiser *Greschenathalan*, and you are in Maiden controlled space. I repeat, you are in Maiden controlled space. State your purpose or leave."

A powerful telepathic broadcast hit Valana, and she put a hand to her chair to catch herself. Images flashed in her mind of her ships destroyed and her own bloodstained corpse on the ground in front of her with her bridge burning.

The alien fleet suddenly became alive with activity. Valana's eyes widened as the fleet swarmed toward her ships, the pack of ravenous bees hungry for blood at her poking of the beehive. Her heart began to race, and terror filled the faces of her crew.

"Get us out of here!" the keeper yelled. The suplight drive of the *Greschenathalan* spurred to life, but ships popped into existence all around them as enemy vessels dropped out of suplight right on top of them. The powerful ships unleashed a barrage immediately, the overwhelming display of firepower breathtaking. In a heartbeat, the bridge of the *Greschenathalan* became a shattered mess. It took just seconds for the enemy fleet to pick apart the rest of the Ashna Maiden ships.

We know that the Enesmic flows in a pattern throughout the universe, permeating every aspect of our physical world. It does not appear to be stoppable by any form of material, natural or manmade.

—FROM "ON THE NATURE OF THE ENESMIC"
BY SHAPER LUKIR AFREV

CHAPTER 3 LUKA HELRIT

Ashnali, Ashna Maiden home system

"If they ain't pirate or Alliance vessels, then what are they?" Avatar Luka Helrit yelled in frustration. Her sharp grey eyes glanced between the other assembled avatars. Luka was a member of the one hundred avatars who commanded both an Ashna fleet and a retinue of mobile infantry. She had command of the 72nd Fleet and 512th Retinue of the Ashna Maidens. The other nine hundred avatars had little or no experience in ship command, and as such were focused completely on ground forces. The briefing chamber was packed, as almost all one thousand avatars were in attendance, many via hologram. The Ashna Council stood together in the center of the room on an elevated platform. The fifty women, each in long cloaks, glanced between one another at the avatar's outburst.

"We . . . do not know. The Mothers are in prayer now to Ashna for guidance." The reply came from the primary speaker for the council, and the older woman's voice was firm. The speaker's steely gaze hung on the form of the toffee-skinned Tuzen avatar.

"Have we been able to communicate with this new force?" asked Avatar Hegna, a renowned avatar in charge of the 1st Fleet and 19th Retinue. She was similar in both complexion and features to Luka, their iconic long blond hair equal in length and thickness.

"No . . . they ignored our attempts at communication and have destroyed two Maiden vessels," the primary speaker answered.

"If Maiden blood is on their hands, then their blood should be on ours!" Luka shouted back. The chamber erupted into shouts of agreement. Hegna glanced to Luka and silently shook her head as their gazes locked briefly.

"Enough!" yelled Ashna Councilor Di Na Se Tl. The Eeriteen woman stepped down from the elevated platform. Black, corded bones covered her entire body, and thick tubular appendages trailed behind her legs, almost hovering behind her. Her additional appendages touched the ground as she moved toward Luka, her movements fluid and in perfect balance. She covered the expanse in a heartbeat, her speed jolting. Luka stood unafraid as Di Na Se Tl came to a stop in front of her, though the other avatars backed away from the two. Large orbs of black, accented by an eerie blue glow encircling the irises, focused on Luka. The Eeriteen's head rested atop a powerful neck, with tubular bones continuing up her head and stopping where ears would have been on other species, creating an imposing silhouette.

"Avatar Luka Helrit, if you feel so strongly about our course of action, then I deem it appropriate that your fleet be at the forefront of the attack on this unknown threat." The councilor turned her smooth face to the side, her thin lips painted a dark purple in contrast to the night black of her entire body. No nose was present on her face. "So second?" she called out.

"I second," said another Ashna councilor.

"Then I call for a vote." Di Na Se Tl turned her chilling eyes back to Luka. "The 72nd Fleet will lead the assault on the unknown threat that encroaches on our space." A moment of silence passed as Councilor Di Na Se Tl motioned toward the massive holodisplay above the elevated platform. Projected there for all to see was an overwhelming passing of her proposal. The Eeriteen's gaze bore into Luka.

"You have your wish for blood. I pray to the goddess that it will not be your own."

Luka subconsciously raised her hand to her cheek.

The councilor turned her back on Luka, and without a word slowly returned to the platform. Luka stared hard at the holodisplay, her fists clenched tight.

A few minutes later, Luka shouldered her way through the chamber door, exiting into the primary hall outside the briefing chamber. Thousands of waiting Maidens stood there, eagerly awaiting news from their avatars. Most of the women were exemplars of Ashna, senior officials that reported to the avatars directly. Exemplar Chrissy Uilo watched Luka with a frown etched across her rose-colored face. Luka stormed past her, and the young Tuzen let out a sigh before quickly moving after her superior.

"I take it things went well?" Chrissy asked. She fell into step directly behind Luka. The avatar flashed her an all-too-familiar glare of annoyance. Taking the silent rebuke, Chrissy clamped her mouth shut and trailed Luka in silence. The two walked for a few minutes, eventually exiting the High Temple of Ashna and entering the sprawling courtyard between the buildings. The area was lush, with expansive gardens in every direction. Intricate designs were etched across the buildings, the aesthetic meant to highlight the glory of Ashna, the all-powerful goddess of the Ashna Maidens.

Luka stuck to the walkway connecting the High Temple to the Avatar Wing, a massive glass superstructure that housed living quarters and offices for all the avatars when they were in High Temple City. She passed through the ornate entrance, making her way through the hallways to a waiting meglift, Chrissy behind her. A thought through her mobi brought the meglift to life, and it rapidly ascended thirty floors before depositing the pair into a bright and expansive hallway lined with numbered doors. They made their way to one with *512* etched onto the elaborate frame. The door slid open as Luka walked through. She turned on Chrissy as soon as the door sealed shut.

"Those witches have us leading the assault," said Luka. A string of profanities left her lips that would have caused anyone but

Chrissy to blush; the exemplar had long ago become accustomed to Luka's foul mouth.

"With you provoking them as you do, I'm surprised we weren't ordered into the battle alone," Chrissy said. She bit her lip the moment she realized she had said her thought out loud. Luka flashed her a murderous glare. Chrissy tilted her head down as she walked to a nearby seat and promptly sat, then performed a zipping motion with her fingers across her lips. Luka stared hard at her second in command, then moved to her desk and brought up her holodisplays with a thought.

"Why do I bring you with me?" Luka whispered to herself.

"Because we both don't know when to keep our mouths shut?" Chrissy replied. She looked up with a smile and was greeted by another glare from Luka. She immediately returned her gaze to the ground.

"Ahh!" Luka yelled. She slammed her fist on her desk, causing the holodisplay to flicker.

"What?" Chrissy jumped up.

"Nothing, just . . . frustrated with this whole situation."

"If it's any consolation," Chrissy began with trepidation, "the raid on Guna IV was a success."

Luka looked over at Chrissy, a smile creeping its way onto her face.

"I expected nothing less from Scion Serah'Elax. She has the makings of an avatar in her."

"She has a long way to go."

"Maybe not as long as you think, my dear exemplar," Luka countered. A proud smile dominated her face. "My request for her ascendance to keeper has been approved by the council. The one good decision they've made lately."

"Keeper . . . for one so young . . ." Chrissy's gaze wandered. "But . . . we have no purdah for her to command; we have lost no keepers."

"I am aware." Luka gave her second a knowing smile. "She will shadow Exemplar Ahtlana for the time being."

"Avatar, we are losing a powerful scion on the battlefield with this decision."

"It sounds to me like you need to get busy finding a replacement then," Luka snapped. Without another word, she went back to staring at her holodisplays. A few minutes later, a knock at the door pulled their attention. After Luka commanded it to open, Avatar Hegna walked into the room, trailed by her own exemplar, Ember Riss. The two women appeared regal, each with an air of authority that didn't sit well with Luka.

"What do you want?" Luka barked. Standing up, she moved her hands to her hips.

"May we speak in private?" Hegna glanced to Chrissy.

Luka nodded. Chrissy and Ember bowed their heads and exited the office. Luka stood unmoving, her gaze never leaving Hegna. Both women stood watching each other in silence as the door closed behind their exemplars.

"Your actions were foolish," Hegna said. She moved to sit on a nearby couch and glanced toward the portrait on Luka's wall of them both as little girls.

"Ah, the great Hegna come to reprimand her wayward Luka." Luka's tone was bitter, and she scoffed as she moved toward a drone holding a cup of strong-smelling orange liquid.

"Luka . . ." Hegna frowned. "My love, I speak these words to you out of concern for your life. Why do you seek to draw the ire of the Ashna Council? Those women hold our lives in their very hands!"

Luka let out a sigh and took a long swig of the drink before setting her cup down on the desk. She then collapsed into her seat, one leg up over the arm rest. She stared at her sister, the only person in the world that she loved, her one true friend.

"I don't understand how you can be so calm." Luka shook her head. "Those were *your* ships that were destroyed." Her grey eyes locked with Hegna's.

"Retribution is in the hands of the goddess; they will be avenged in her time."

Luka could see a momentary tinge of sadness in Hegna's eyes, but it was gone in a heartbeat as the soldier settled back into her impeccable composure, armor in place. Luka closed her eyes and muttered a prayer of forgiveness to the goddess for her continued brashness.

"I will be the vengeance of our goddess; I will get you your retribution," Luka promised.

Hegna watched Luka, her gaze softening as she stood up. She took in a deep breath, closed her eyes, then slowly opened them.

"Be careful . . ." Hegna breathed. She embraced Luka and held on. Luka was taken aback by the sudden display of affection. Reluctantly, she joined in the embrace, and the two held each other for a long moment. Without a word, Hegna backed away from Luka, then exited the office.

CHAPTER 4 VENICE FAWNI

Ashnali, Ashna Maiden home system

Mother Venice Fawni stared out of the massive window that marked her private prayer room on the top floor of the High Temple of Ashna. Five such rooms existed throughout the top floor, with the large central area designated as a private sanctuary. Venice watched the specks on the ground far below her as they went about their tasks.

"Revered mother," came a soft voice from behind her. Venice turned to see a dark grey Eeriteen priestess bowing low at her door. "Please forgive my intrusion, but the other Mothers have assembled in the High Sanctuary and request your presence."

"Do not fret, my child," Mother Venice said with a smile. "Thank you for coming to get me. Time escapes me, hand in hand with my youth." Her sepia skin glistened in the soft sunlight that shone through the ceiling. The priestess returned the smile and quickly backed out of the room, keeping herself partially bowed as the door closed behind her.

Venice let out a low sigh, picked herself up from her comfortable sitting area near the window, and moved through the door.

Upon entering the expansive High Sanctuary, she found four other Ashna Mothers waiting patiently for her. Huddled around them were priestesses of Ashna attending to their every need.

"Ah, Mother Venice," came the melodic greeting of Ce Nu Yo Kl.

The older Eeriteen's black orbs—accented by a glow of yellow—focused intently on Venice. The Human glanced at the dark red Eeriteen, the corded tubular bones outside of her body mostly obscured under the heavy Ashna Mother regalia, a mix of white and blue fabrics with elaborate golden embroidery.

"Mother Ce Nu Yo Kl, how fare you on this glorious day blessed to us by Ashna?"

"Blessed as always," Ce Nu Yo Kl said with a coy smile. Her thin lips were painted blue, contrasting nicely with her smooth, dark red face. Venice moved to stand beside the other Mothers, and all of them turned toward the Altar of Ashna. After standing still for a moment, they kneeled in unison in front of the pristine silver table covered by an embroidered golden cloth. The priestesses backed away silently, then exited through the sanctuary door, closing it behind them.

"The council has already acted without our guidance," Mother Alenet Dascl said. The older Tuzen rested her ivory hands on the floor, then bowed her head down to her fingertips. She slowly rose back up, her blue gaze staying on the altar.

"Impulsiveness leads to destruction . . ." came a soft reply from Mother Venice. She followed suit, repeating the motions of Mother Alenet. Her long brown hair touched the ground as her head touched her fingertips.

"Inaction also leads to destruction . . ." Mother Ce Nu Yo Kl replied.

"Careful observation and thoughtful decision are not inaction." Venice stared intently at the altar.

"Maiden blood has already been spilled. Ashna demands vengeance!" Ce Nu Yo Kl's tubular bones momentarily rattled.

"Ashna does not demand that which she can enact herself," Alenet said as she glanced at Ce Nu Yo Kl, who locked gazes with her. Venice cleared her throat. Both women returned their gazes to the altar.

"As stated so eloquently by Mother Alenet," Mother Venice said, her tone soft, "the council has already made the decision to engage the unknown ships. Unless we seek to overrule their decision, there is no point in discussing this any further."

"We will wait until they return defeated, then," Mother Halle Tentle interjected. Her tone was matter-of-fact and emotionless. The other Mothers turned to regard her.

Venice shivered; her gaze stuck on the ebony-skinned Human. Halle looked over at Venice with an innocent smile, her white irises seeming to glow. Venice shivered again.

FOUNDERS LOG:
Crucible of the Heart

For almost eighty thousand years, I have been a founder of the Huzien Empire. I am called Lanrete, although that is not my birth name. One thing I have learned during my time in this universe is that life is precious, yet it is only in the moments when our lives seem close to an end that we acknowledge this truth. Worst yet are the moments when we lose those we love with regrets for all left undone. It took millennia for me to truly embrace the time I have with those I hold dear; to drop all else to spend a lifetime with them.

Early on, in the infancy of the Huzien Empire, my life was devoted to the Huzien people, with my eifis, my life partners, as a far second. I missed so much in the lives of those wonderful women, time that will never return, their bodies long cold and returned to dust. Life is a cruel teacher, its lessons harsh and unforgiving. Some time has passed since the death of Brime, with a little over two months since the death of Sagren. Soahc . . . my obrehen, *my brother. I fear he is filled with regret. Regret for things outside of his control, regret for not being strong enough, and regret at the time wasted doing what may now seem like pointless things. Foresight is something we all wish we had the benefit of. The unknown future is an impossible enemy, or a sorely needed friend. Although I understand his pain, the experience is truly never the same when a loved one dies. Death affects people in different ways. While similarities exist in the grief state, the pain can kill some and leave others broken.*

For myself, the sting of loss has taken years to heal, and memories bring with them the powerful emotions of joy and sorrow. As long as I have lived, I still do not truly understand the feelings that control us. Some species, such as the Omiciri, go to great lengths to shut out emotion, even going as far as to implant their young with emotion-inhibiting technology. Such actions have led to a society of cold, calculating organic machines, with no love or hatred seen in any of their kind.

And then there are the Unita'Tayn, a species that makes decisions purely on feeling, living in the now with no thought of consequence. How many times have I witnessed their civilization on the brink of destruction? Many believe there to be an ideal state, a state beyond both extremes. Emotion without pain. It is a foreign concept that seems perfect on the surface, but without pain, would we truly value anyone else? Maybe it is pain that is the instrument of life's most powerful lessons.

-Lanrete

CHAPTER 5 SOAHC

Etan Rachnie, Reath, Huzien Alliance space

Soahc kissed Brime, taking in her scent. Her laugh made him grin, and he leaned back to look at his bride as her snow-white skin glowed in the sunlight. He stared at her, enjoying the moment. Brime's skin then began to glow brighter, the light radiating from her causing him to shield his eyes. He struggled to look at his wife, the woman he loved. The light was impossibly bright, too much for him to bear. And then it was gone. Soahc quickly opened his eyes, but in the place of Brime stood a tear to the Enesmic plane, with the monstrous silver hand of Sagren reaching through, seeking to grab him.

Soahc's eyes burst open, the Human quickly sitting up. Raw Enesmic energy hung in his hand, the powerful manifestation held taut, its chaotic torrents bathing his bedchambers in a mix of blue and purple light. His eyes darted to every shadow in his room and he sat still as a statue for a long moment, a tear eventually rolling down his cheek. He released the manifestation and rested his head in his hands. A wave of sorrow washed over him, the sickening sadness painful, maddening. Dropping his hands to the sweat-stained sheets of his lavish bed, Soahc looked to his left at the elaborate purple and blue curtains rustling in the breeze from the open balcony door. Forcing himself up, he walked through the curtains and out into the crisp nighttime air, his hands coming to rest on a marble railing.

The legendary cihphist looked out across the rolling fields around his mansion, the beautiful scene highlighted by the twin moons in the sky; his sky. He was on Reath, a planet he personally owned. The planet he had shared with Brime, his apprentice, his lover, his wife. Soahc took in a deep breath, trying to remain in control. The nights were not getting easier. Light from Etan Rachnie caught his eye and his gaze shifted to the massive campus in the distance as memories of his first encounter with Brime assaulted him.

A cool breeze caressed Soahc's bare, dark brown muscular body, the moonlight highlighting the streaks of silver in his black hair. His brown eyes glowed in the darkness, the irises laced with an unnatural silver gifted to him from his walk in the Enesmic plane over one hundred thousand years ago. He took in a deep breath and slowly let it out through his mouth, clearing his mind and attempting to smother the memory. He wanted the pain to stop, to continue with his life. His heart denied him that peace.

Five years ago
Etan Rachnie, Reath, Huzien Alliance space

The dress Brime wore was modestly cut, but expensive, her posture poised and perfect, the model of a woman from high-class society. Soahc knew she was a wealthy corporate executive's daughter, but those things didn't impress him. Within the walls of Etan Rachnie, he cared only for one's affinity to cihphism and the mastery of manipulating Enesmic forces to one's will—the true measure of power. Yet, when the young woman looked over to Soahc, her smile stirred something inside of him, something long dormant and hidden away.

"Brime Wewta?" Soahc said, calling out to her.

"Yes!" she replied. Brime performed a low bow that brought a smile to Soahc's lips. She stayed bowed, awkwardly. Soahc walked over, clearing his throat and motioning for her to rise.

"Please, bowing is unnecessary."

"My apologies, Lord Soahc."

"Headmaster Teral tells me that I should take you on as an apprentice." Soahc eyed the young woman now staring back at him, nervousness etched across her face.

"I want to become a better cihphist," Brime said, and smiled.

"What makes you any more special than the hundreds of other high-performing students throughout my campus?" Soahc's eyes narrowed. "I don't care who your daddy is or what your family has done. What makes you worthy of becoming my apprentice?"

Brime's smile disappeared, and a look of annoyance took over her face. The transformation was so sudden and intense that it took Soahc off guard.

"Everything I have accomplished," Brime said, balling her hands into fists, "I have accomplished because of my ability, not because of who my father is."

"Oh?" Soahc wore an amused expression on his face. "It's not because of the large sums of money your father donated to my school upon your acceptance?"

"How dare you!" Brime stabbed a finger into Soahc's chest. "I don't care who you are," she said, fire in her eyes, "I worked hard to achieve my grades, I passed my tests, and I excelled in combat training—and none of that has anything to do with money." The strength in her voice was intimidating, even to Soahc. "I could care less about being the apprentice of some self-righteous immortal who thinks he's hot stuff because he blew up some planet a long time ago."

Brime's accusatory finger poked Soahc again in his chest, the action pushing him back a step. All semblances of the nervous student were gone, and Soahc could detect the swell of Enesmic energy building in the young woman—a powerful river, but untamed and chaotic.

"Interesting . . ." Soahc smiled again at Brime. Turning his back to her, he started to walk away. He took a few steps and then turned to look at Brime, who had remained unmoving. Soahc flashed her a look of impatience. "Well, don't just stand there. Your training starts now, my dear apprentice."

"Wait . . . what?" Brime yelled after him. Soahc turned back around and continued to walk, Brime running to catch up with him.

How these complex patterns that manipulate the Enesmic came to be is a mystery, some secret of nature that we work diligently to understand and explain. Through Enesmic experimentation and creative thought, we have been able to achieve wondrous acts of cihphism limited only by the imagination of the cihphist.

–FROM "ON THE NATURE OF THE ENESMIC"
BY SHAPER LUKIR AFREV

CHAPTER 6 NEVEN KENK

MinSci, Thae, Huzien home system

Neven walked through the MinSci grounds, a smile etched on his olive-skinned face as he took in the beautiful campus. It hadn't been a full year since he left, but it seemed like an eternity. He had spent every waking moment of his life before joining the Founder's Elite in the *BRAS* engineering lab within the Ministry of Science. The young Human walked through broad sliding metallic doors and into the large building that functioned as the home of the Department of Weapons Development.

A strong female voice grabbed his attention. "Neven Kenk, a little birdy told me you were in the area." The young Human turned his green-eyed gaze to a woman exiting one of the many meglifts lining the entry hall. Her piercing sharp brown eyes were intently focused on him, as if analyzing every detail of his mortal soul. She walked forward and extended a hand, her mahogany skin glistening in the light. Neven extended his own, her grip surprisingly tight and brief.

"I'm sorry, do I know you?"

"I would hope so, although this is the first time we are meeting in person, so I am willing to forgive the transgression. Remi Etwa, head of Weapon's Development."

Neven's eyes went wide, and he stood up straight.

"I . . . I'm sorry," Neven sputtered out.

"I believe I already stated that I forgave the transgression," she said, slight annoyance lacing her words. "Anyway . . . what brings a secnic such as you back to the MinSci? I was under the impression that you had chosen to remain with Founder Lanrete in the military, despite the prestigious position that was graciously offered to you."

"I've come to say hello to some of my previous team members."

Remi let out a *tcch* sound.

"Please try your best to not distract them from their work," she stated bluntly. After giving him a false smile, she moved past him and out of the building. Neven turned to watch her leave, his gaze hanging on her for a long moment.

"Met our illustrious department head I see," a familiar voice said, grabbing Neven's full attention. He turned to see Charlene Yentu staring back at him, a smile on her face.

Charlene led Neven through the sliding doors of the old BRAS lab, where she had first said goodbye to him almost a year ago. They stopped at the balcony near the entrance overlooking the lab. The early stages of a new power frame prototype stood half assembled in the center of the massive room, surrounded by other power armors also in early stages of development.

"New project?" Neven asked.

"And a new team," Charlene added. "Only a handful of people from the BRAS Mark I project are still with me; most of the former team was snatched away due to politics."

"Kechu?" Neven failed to catch sight of his friend.

"He's over in Systems Intelligence Research now," Charlene responded. "Your friend jumped departments when you left."

"SI Research . . ." Neven stared at her in confusion. "Kechu was never interested in system complexity and intelligence reproduction."

Charlene glanced over at Neven, the Huzien woman slowly shaking her head before looking back down at her team.

"You know that Kechu just followed you around, right?"

Neven turned to watch Charlene in silence for a few moments. "You're saying that he purposefully liked what I liked." Neven turned around and leaned against the balcony railing.

"Some people are like that. They choose to be with their friends instead of pursuing their own dreams." Charlene mirrored Neven's pose, her pale white hands grasping the cool metallic railing. Neven glanced at her, instantly remembering how much he liked Charlene. The secret crush he'd had on her seemed almost childish; it felt like so long ago. The two stood in silence for a few moments, the sounds of busy engineers filling the air.

"Meet any new women, Mr. Founder's Elite?" the blond project lead asked. Neven tried his best to hide a smile. "I take that as a yes." Charlene turned back around to look out over her lab.

"Yeah." Neven gave up on trying to conceal his smile. "Her name is Zun Shan. She's also a Founder's Elite."

"Zun Shan?" Charlene yelled. "*The* Zun Shan?" She turned on Neven with a shocked expression. Her outburst caused everyone in the lab to stop what they were doing and look up at the two. "As you were," she called down to her team. Charlene took a moment to compose herself while Neven stared at her with wide eyes.

"Yeah . . . she used to work for the MinSci a long time ago. She was a former chief assistant to Ecnics."

"Oh, I know who she is." Charlene eyed Neven with an air of skepticism. "The question is, do you?"

"I . . . just told you."

"Neven." Charlene fixed him with an intense gaze. "That woman was chief assistant to Ecnics for sixty years. Most people barely last ten before they burn out." The older woman shook her head as she crossed her arms. "She's a feshra and a legend throughout the MinSci. Zun was also notorious for destroying the careers of those who irked her." Charlene sighed. "And young men who fawned over her were prime targets. I lost a few promising engineers to her moods."

"She's a feshra?"

"Out of everything I said, that's what you pick up . . ." Charlene whispered to herself. "Yes, she's a feshra. Do you even research the women you date?"

"She's . . . technically the first woman I've ever dated."

The blood drained from Charlene's face.

"Neven . . . you're my friend, and I feel it is important for me to say this to you. Be careful around Zun. Don't pursue a relationship with her unless you're serious. That type of woman isn't looking for a fling and she can hold a very powerful grudge if things don't work out. She also still has a great deal of pull here at the MinSci. Ecnics trusts her completely." Charlene let out another sigh. "I don't want to see another career ruined by that woman."

"I love her . . ." Neven said, his voice sheepish. Charlene's gaze hung on him for a few moments, a long silence lingering in the air.

"Neven . . . you've only known her for a few months. I don't think you've had enough time to actually fall in love with her."

Neven's nose scrunched up and a flicker of anger ignited in his eyes. He took a moment to calm himself before speaking. "Charlene, I respect you, but please don't say things like that. You don't know what we've been through."

Shaking her head at his shift in demeanor, Charlene's gaze became more intense.

"Neven, I know the games that the heart can play. I've learned those lessons over the course of my four hundred and thirty years in this galaxy. Trust me when I tell you to be careful." Charlene walked up to Neven and embraced him. He was surprised at the gesture. She briefly pressed her body against his, and the feeling caused the childish parts of his brain to go wild. "It's good to see you again," Charlene said. She let go of him and then turned, instantly descending the walkway to the lab floor.

Neven watched her get back to her life, the life he had thrown away to join the Founder's Elite. He glanced back down at the half-assembled prototype and then exited the lab.

CHAPTER 7 MARCUS HENSON

Empress Star, Huzien Alliance space

"This is the life . . ." Marcus smiled broadly. The ebony-skinned giant of a man stretched his barrel-sized arms as he sunbathed in the artificial sunlight of the pool deck aboard the *Empress Star.*

"You know you could just retire and spend the rest of your life like this . . ." Dexter chimed in. The pale-skinned half Huzien lay facedown on a nearby pool chair. "It's not like you need to *vusging* work."

"Watch your language, there are kids around," Zun snapped at him. "But Dexter does have a point, you know." Zun slowly rose out of the pool. Her tanned skin with its golden undertones glistened as water dripped from her body. Gazes from around the pool stuck to her like flies on a flytrap. She wore a black bikini that displayed her voluptuous form, and faint black esha marks ran from her temples to the soles of her feet, signs of her half-Huzien heritage.

Marcus let out a laugh, shaking his head.

"Speaking of people who should *vusging* retire . . ." Dexter glanced at Zun, his eyes lingering on her breasts. Zun glared at him. Dexter grinned and then flipped over, his corded muscles flexing with the action.

"Should you even be out in the sun? Won't you melt or something?" Zun grabbed a towel to dry herself off.

"I'm prepared." Dexter tapped a small wristband on his arm, showing that the portable UV shield was active. "I'm surprised your boy toy decided not to come."

Zun took a seat next to Marcus. The older Human's wife was passed out on a pool chair at his other side.

"Boy toy?" Zun glanced at Dexter with a confused look.

"Oh please, we all know you're *vusging* the new kid."

Zun let out a nervous laugh, her head reflexively shaking no. She turned to Marcus for support. He smiled and winked at her before closing his eyes to take a nap.

"How long have you known?"

"Since you played kissy face in his lab."

"You know, there is such a thing as privacy."

"That's what rooms are for." Dexter jumped to his feet. "If you want privacy, try being some place *vusging* private." He continued to unnecessarily flex his muscles. "Anyway, I'm off to get some tail of my own."

"Just to set the record straight," Zun interjected, "I'm not having sex with Neven; he's not that type of guy. We're just dating, getting to know each other better."

"That's unfortunate." The green-eyed Sentinel walked up to the pool's edge. Upon catching sight of a young Uri woman in the water, he winked at her. She smiled back. Dexter dove in and began to swim toward her, a grin on his face. Zun watched the scene, sighed, then leaned back into the pool chair, her eyes closing for a nap of her own.

CHAPTER 8   ADRIAN HULIM

Empress Star, Huzien Alliance space

Captain Adrian Hulim walked across the bridge of the luxury cruise ship *Empress Star*, smiling as usual to every member of his bridge crew. Like most days, the bridge was quiet, with the crew casually engaged in low conversations. Adrian walked to the large concave window situated toward the front of the bridge. Putting his hands on the railing, he stared out at the stars and soaked up the serenity, the sight breathtaking.

"Captain, we've got a small frigate heading toward us." The words brought Adrian out of his trance.

"Identifier?"

"They're broadcasting an Alliance signal."

"Any contact?" Adrian walked toward Zeph, his chief communications officer.

"Nothing yet, wait . . . now they're contacting us," Zeph called out. The Huzien was currently surrounded by holodisplays. He pushed the call through to the main holodisplay on the bridge. The image of a ruddy-skinned Tuzen male appeared on the screen. The stranger's brown eyes flickered to Adrian, his hat identifying him as captain.

"Ahoy!" The man's face, his eyes strangely large, transformed into a toothy grin.

"Ahoy to you as well. I'm Captain Adrian Hulim, and this is the *Empress Star*, a galaxy-class cruise ship on the way to Arcadia III."

"Ah, a mighty fine vessel," the man responded. "My name be Heshel Vrot, captain of the *Liron Storm*. We're a trading vessel heading toward the Avo system."

"Are you lost?" Captain Adrian asked, his eyes narrowing.

"Aye, it be worse than that I fear; our suplight drive be damaged."

"Oh my. How long have you been drifting?"

"Three weeks! Had a run-in with a meteor storm that left us worse for wear. Blasted thing took out coms, which we just be getting back with lucky time."

Adrian glanced at Hanna, his safety officer. She brought up the positions of nearby meteor storms and identified a cluster that could have met with the *Liron Storm*'s trajectory. Adrian muted the line, then glanced at Arnold, his chief security officer.

"Weapons?"

"Nothing coming up on scans. They're clean."

Unmuting the line, Adrian turned back to face Heshel.

"Lucky timing indeed, Captain Heshel. We were just about to jump to suplight and continue on our cruise route. How can we be of assistance?"

"I know this be asking much of ye, but can we dock with yer ship and receive assistance from yer engineers?"

"Unfortunately, protocol prohibits me from allowing non-HighStar Cruise Line vessels from docking with this ship. We can notify the Alliance military of your situation and request immediate assistance."

Heshel's grin disappeared. Glancing off to his side, he muted the line and yelled something to an unseen person. The captain of the *Liron Storm* then stared hard at Adrian before unmuting his end.

"Captain Adrian, I be needing yer help! We have injured on the ship, women and children who haven't eaten in days. We've already lost fifteen people with no doc for patching wounds."

The look of fear on Heshel's face caused Adrian to glance back at his crew. After taking a deep breath, Adrian faced Heshel.

"I'm sorry, I can't . . . it's protocol."

"*Vusg* yer protocol, ye going to let women and children starve to death?"

Adrian looked over to Zeph, who had brought up nearby fleet reports.

"The closest Alliance patrol is about a week away," Zeph said.

The captain of the *Empress Star* glanced to his First Officer Jessie Gumnen, who had moved to stand at his side. Adrian muted the line and turned to Jessie.

"Options?"

"We can give them supplies; maybe have one of our doctors look at the injured. If we send a transport vessel out to meet them, that won't break protocol," she said.

Adrian nodded. He unmuted the line and turned to face Heshel.

"Here's what we can do. I'll send over a transport with supplies and a doctor to look at your injured. We'll postpone jumping to suplight for a few hours to ensure you're able to wait here safely for Alliance support."

The grin returned to Heshel's face.

"Many thanks, Captain. Ye won't regret this."

> *Modern-day cihphists attribute the structure we see in weavings of the Enesmic flow to our desire to add meaning where none exists.*
>
> –FROM "ENESMIC AND THEORIES OF ORDERING"
> BY SHAPER LUKIR AFREV

CHAPTER 9 TASHANIRA YEN UNVESAL

Empress Star, Huzien Alliance space

Tashanira reached for the next hand grip, but the hold was a few inches too far. Her yellow, feline-esque eyes caught sight of another foothold. She released a breath and jumped to the side. Her foot connected, her new grip sure. Cheers went up from below. Tashanira tuned out the spectating crowd. She was near the top of the artificial cliff face, and no tether connected her to safety. Jenshi stood watching her from below. Grunting, Tashanira continued her ascent.

Her white and black fur was a blur as she made another jump, this time far to the left, and grabbed another handhold. Her feet dangled in the air, prompting gasps from below. With ease, she pulled herself up the remainder of the cliff face. When she crested the top, she thrust her hands into the air. A holodisplay hovering high in the air projecting a timer stopped, and the time flashed with *New Record* highlighted in bright colors next to it.

"We have a new record holder here on the *Empress Star!*" the game room announcer bellowed to the crowd. The crowd erupted into cheers, and Jenshi smiled as Tashanira blew him a kiss. Electronic dance music began to blare from the loudspeakers. Catching the beat, Tashanira broke into dance and began moving in a blur to the rhythm. The crowd went ballistic. The top of the cliff face became her stage while the music ignited her soul. She was the center of attention and soaking it all in. Spinning, she stopped and then back-flipped off the top.

As she flew toward the floor, everyone gasped. At the last minute, she was caught by an antigravity field near the bottom. The field deposited her on the floor safely, the mechanism disappearing as if it was never there. Every eye in the packed room stared at her as she walked up to Jenshi, who stood with his mouth open, stunned by the death-defying jump. Seductively walking past him, she slapped her black tail against his leg.

"Always the daredevil," Jenshi said.

The room exploded in deafening cheers.

Jenshi turned around, his sharp grey eyes following his lover. The cruise staff quickly organized themselves, and the announcer, flanked by more staff, walked up to Tashanira. The group ushered Tashanira off to a small area where they presented her with a flashy trophy that had the date and *Empress Star* emblazoned across the front. They then took her picture for the record books. Jenshi met up with her when they were done. The crowds pressed against them as everyone tried to get close to Tashanira.

She gave Jenshi a knowing look before breaking off into a sprint through the crowd. He fell into step behind her, attempting to keep pace. They burst through a side entrance to the massive game room.

Tashanira exhaled, her body tingling.

"Where to now?" Jenshi asked. A wall of windows with an amazing view of space was directly across from them.

"The room?" Tashanira flashed Jenshi a playful smile. The peach-skinned Huzien grinned.

Tashanira's grip on the sheets loosened as Jenshi slowly pulled back and slapped her bare butt. She collapsed onto the bed of their luxury suite, panting.

It had been a good day.

Jenshi collapsed next to her. Tashanira stared at him through half-closed slits, her glowing yellow eyes entrancing. Her mixed black and white fur played with her features, and her peppered white catlike ears completed the package.

"Maker, you're beautiful," Jenshi said.

"Not so bad yourself, handsome," Tashanira purred as they lay there for a long moment.

"I'm so glad all of that mess with Sagren is over and we can finally relax," Jenshi said. Tashanira frowned.

"Way to kill the mood." Tashanira broke his gaze and stared up at the high ceiling.

"Sorry . . ."

"I miss Brime. She was fun."

"I wonder how Soahc is doing."

"Exactly how you'd be if that Ceshra had finished me off."

Jenshi turned to look up at the ceiling with her. "I'm glad Zun was able to move on after Yuvan died."

"That's such an insensitive thing to say." Tashanira glanced at Jenshi. "Uri don't move on when people die. We honor and remember them, always."

Jenshi sighed and met Tashanira's gaze. "I'm sorry. I would have absolutely honored and remembered you if anything had happened."

"Just like you honor and remember your parents?" Tashanira sat up in bed, resting on her arms. She glanced down at Jenshi, who avoided her gaze. "Aww don't get upset, I'm just messing with you." She snuggled up close to him, pulling the sheets over their bodies.

"It's been a rough year for all of us, first with that *vusging* sociopath Entradis and then Sagren." She shook her head. "We didn't even get a chance to properly avenge Yuvan. The trail for Entradis is a dead end."

"Lanrete still has Sentinels hunting him. I'm sure they will turn up something soon." They lay in silence for a long moment.

"Let's make a deal."

Jenshi raised an eyebrow.

"No more talk about Sagren or Entradis for the rest of our vacation. Just you and me, enjoying everything this cruise ship has to offer."

"Deal." Jenshi snuggled in closer to Tashanira.

CHAPTER 10 JESSICA OLIC

Empress Star, Huzien Alliance space

Jessica lay facedown on a large massage table in a dimly lit room. A Ken'Tar masseur was at work on her back, his four arms working expertly in sync with one another. Jessica soaked up the soothing music, her pleasure senses exploding with ecstasy. The Ken'Tar's firm yet precise hands stretched out her muscles, removing the knots.

Working as if in a trance, the masseur shifted around the room, manipulating every inch of her body and hitting every pressure point on her back in sequence, ending at her neck. The battle-hardened Huzien's toes curled and her body shuddered as her back arched, her eyes rolling back into her skull. The moan that escaped her lips was deep and throaty. With a final few touches to her neck, the Ken'Tar ended with a series of light touches down her back.

"Ms. Olic, this concludes our session," he said. "Please take your time getting up. I will meet you outside." He left the room, quietly closing the door.

Jessica Olic lay on the table, not wanting to move. Reluctantly, she pushed herself up, coming to rest on her knees. Toned muscles covered every inch of her nude, honey-skinned body. After taking in a deep breath, another shudder wracked her body. She slowly let it out, seeking to take back control.

Putting her hands down on the table, she lifted her full body up until she was suspended in the air, parallel to the table. After moving her legs out and to the side, she turned the pose into a sitting position. A moment later, she jumped up, her warm feet contacting with the cool floor, then sprinted to her robe and slippers against the wall. Sliding them on, she stared for a few minutes at the table, a blush on her face. She slowly walked toward the door, opening it with a light push. She was greeted by her masseur extending a large cup of water toward her with a smile.

"Did you enjoy your massage?"

Jessica took the water bashfully.

"Very much so . . ." She downed the full glass. He motioned for her to follow him.

"This way to continue your Galactic Queen spa package."

Jessica blushed again.

CHAPTER 11   HESHEL VROT

Liron Storm, Huzien Alliance space

"How long will we have with the jammer?" Heshel barked to his engine master, a young Human named Hegfe Deni. The pale engineer shuffled nervously

"Uh . . . twenty minutes? Give or take a few," he said. Hegfe's blue eyes went to the ground as Heshel's features contorted. The captain grabbed Hegfe by his shirt, pulling the Human roughly forward. His hot breath made Hegfe close his eyes and swallow hard.

"Ye said this *vusging* thing could last an hour when we brought it!" Murder was in Heshel's eyes.

"Their defense system is newer! The SI attack matrix is designed for the previous generation of their software platform." His voice became a squeal. "Please don't kill me!"

Heshel roughly pushed Hegfe to the ground, then glanced over at the men standing close to the circular wall of the bridge, all their gazes downcast. The door across from him slid open, and a brown-skinned Tuzen casually entered. He stopped, the unexpected scene causing him to glance from a shivering Hegfe to Heshel. The captain stood brooding.

"We ready?" Vexl Jabstren said.

Heshel walked over to Hegfe and pulled him up roughly. Pushing the engineer toward Vexl, he gave them a dismissive sneer.

"Ye've got twenty minutes to take the ship once the jammer starts."

"Twenty minutes?" Vexl blanched. He glared at Hegfe, who shuffled past him without a word.

"Yea, twenty minutes. And if ye fail, make sure ye die on the *vusging* ship."

"*Vusg* . . ." Vexl turned and followed after Hegfe. The men lining the walls of the bridge fell into step behind Vexl.

Heshel watched the first stage of his plan unfold through the video feeds of his assault team. The *Empress Star*'s transport ship had started docking procedures with the *Liron Storm*. As the pressurized hatch sealed, he switched to the view of the first person outside the airlock. The door opened and a woman on his assault team stepped through. An *Empress Star* guard eyed her warily before glancing behind her to the rest of the assault team, who were all in disguise. Upon identifying the doctor, the woman began to move toward him as a commotion behind her prompted yells and hurried voices.

The doctor's eyes went wide as he glanced down at the ground, where a small spherical device had rolled into view of the feed. When it began flashing a sequence of lights, one of the guards dove for it. A bright flash filled the video feed, and everyone in sight dropped to the ground, unmoving. Heshel switched to the video feed of Vexl, who was entering through the airlock as one of the last members of his assault team. He caught sight of his men moving to each member of the *Empress Star*'s transport crew and opening fire on their unconscious bodies. Others dragged the unconscious decoys of the assault team back to the *Liron Storm*.

"Ship secure," Vexl said through the audio channel.

Weaving powerful torrents of Enesmic energy is challenging for similar reasons to the practice of Elhirtha: the exertion of will over the flow to such an extent causes a violent reaction from the Enesmic.

–FROM "ENESMIC AND THEORIES OF ORDERING"

BY SHAPER LUKIR AFREV

CHAPTER 12 VEXL JABSTREN

Empress Star, Huzien Alliance space

V exl eyed Hegfe with clear annoyance. Hegfe was focused on a series of holodisplays in an effort to get his jammer online. He had hardwired his jammer system into the SI core of the transport shuttle to utilize its trusted connection to the *Empress Star* as a backdoor. The screens flashed when the cyber-attack SI established a connection to the *Empress Star* itself.

"We ready?" Impatience hung in Vexl's tone. Hegfe remained silent for a few more seconds, his final set of commands launching the SI into action.

"Now!" Hegfe yelled.

Within a few seconds, the SI breached the *Empress Star*'s core systems. The door to the transport opened, and Vexl rolled a small spherical orb down the ramp connecting the transport to the *Empress Star*. A pair of security guards waiting outside glanced down at it, then gasped as it rose into the air. It then released a powerful field that vaporized them but left their clothes and equipment intact.

Vexl emerged from the transport, an old set of WMAs, or Wopan master arms, in his hands. He walked with a swagger in his step, the music coming alive in his mind as he raised his weapons and opened fire on the people on the loading deck. The rhythmic cadence of his weapons fire became a symphony as he led the *Liron Storm* assault force into the heart of the *Empress Star*. Vexl and his men wasted no time in their mission. Their route was planned out, with the quickest path to the bridge highlighted in their HUDs. More from the *Liron Storm* would soon be boarding the pleasure ship; the transport had already been sent back to retrieve the full contingent of their forces.

When they banked a corner, Vexl spun to the side to avoid a blast, then sprinted toward the wall before kicking off it and flipping in the air. He landed in the center of an organized force of guards, four of them with weapons hot. He danced between them, his WMAs moving in a flurry as he fired in sequence, stomping with each blast to add emphasis to his attacks. The guards tried to back away but Vexl was too fast, ending them before they could counter his sudden advance. More guards streamed into the corridor, and Vexl dropped to the floor.

The assault party behind him opened fire, the first line of guards dropping like flies as the rest scrambled for cover. Vexl rolled to the side and then kicked off a wall, propelling himself forward on the floor like a missile. He slid past their impromptu barricade and kicked himself up, jumping into the air and releasing a barrage of shots in a circle of death. The men and women of the security force scrambled to get away from him, but his WMAs peppered their bodies, and more than half of them dropped to the floor unmoving.

A bold guard moved forward and attempted to slam the butt of his rifle into Vexl's head. The assault master smirked, dodged the blow, then flipped his WMAs around and grabbed them by the barrels. Short blades emerged from the handles as he launched a few quick strikes across the temple, throat, and chest of the man. The guard staggered back before dropping to the floor, blood pooling out of the small puncture wounds. Flipping his WMAs back around, Vexl charged forward, his team catching up as they put down the rest of the defense force in the corridor.

Vexl hid behind cover, the corridor outside the bridge filled with weapons fire. His team was pinned down by the primary security force, led by a muscular, ruddy-skinned Human. The insignia on his collar informed Vexl that he was the head of security for the *Empress Star*. He could see the efficiency of the man's command, the way he easily called out orders and the surprising, coordinated defense that greeted them now after the pathetic attempt on the lower levels. He stunk of ex-Huzien military.

The ten-minute warning blipped in Vexl's micro-display, the time bought by the assault SI slowly whittling away. Cursing, he reached into his side pouch and pulled out his last two skin resolvers. After arming the small spherical devices, he flared his personal shield and charged out of his barricade toward a nearby wall before quick stepping up it, kicking off, and angling his body upside down. Able to see over the other barricade, he chucked one toward the head of security and then landed in a breakfall. He then quick stepped up the other wall and lobbed the other grenade over the opposite barricade. Landing in a flourish, he slammed hard into the security barricade, curling up into a tight ball.

Shouts went up from the other side as he heard scrambling feet and shouts to move from the head of security. Explosions went off a second later, and the sound of equipment hitting the floor caused Vexl to smile. He motioned for his men to move forward and glanced around the barricades to see piles of clothes and weapons. He caught the gaze of the head of security as he supported another guard into a meglift. There was malice there, an unspoken promise.

The remaining guards moved into the bridge and sealed the door shut. Vexl blew a kiss at the head of security as the meglift door shut. The assault party quickly took over the area and set up a perimeter while Vexl moved to examine the bridge door. He glanced at the inactive sentry drones lining the walls next to it with a grin. Tapping on the door, he listened to the echo. He motioned to one of his cronies, who walked up and attached a small rectangular device to the door while Vexl motioned for everyone to fall back.

A powerful explosion filled the corridor. The heat and flames quickly subsided due to the flame-suppression systems flaring to life. Vexl motioned forward, and his men stormed onto the bridge with large mobile shields. Weapons fire greeted them as they fanned out and began to press on the remaining security forces.

"We surrender! We surrender!" Captain Adrian shouted. The battle had been quick and intense. Dead bodies, mostly his crew, filled the bridge. "Please, hold off your assault. We surrender."

Vexl motioned for his men to hold their fire once the security force threw down their weapons. He then stepped out from behind a mobile shield, his chin held high as he closed the distance to the captain, none too impressed with the man's appearance. His gaze then went to the remaining bridge crew. With a snap of his fingers, his men leveled guns on the crew, herding them all to one side of the room with rough hands and curses.

Vexl came to stop in front of Adrian. Their gazes locked, and Vexl cracked a smile. Upon bringing up the timer set in his HUD, Vexl's smile widened. *Five minutes to spare.* He had taken a multi-billion-larod cruise ship in fifteen minutes with minimal losses. *Heshel better be impressed.*

"Dear Captain, your hospitality will be the death of you," Vexl mocked. "Set a course for these coordinates." Vexl brought up a star chart on a nearby holodisplay, showcasing a location far in the Outer Rim. He sent a message to Hegfe to re-enable bridge control for the navigation systems, and the navigation console flared back to life.

Adrian eyed him warily and glanced from the holodisplay to the navigation controls, hesitating. He looked over to his crew, every eye on him.

"I want you to guarantee my crew's safety." Adrian clenched his jaw, his tone firm.

Vexl raised his gun and fired point-blank at Adrian's head. Gore splattered the control station behind him. Vexl snapped his fingers, and his men began searching through the crowd. Rough hands grabbed hold of First Officer Jessie Gumnen, pulling her out of the crowd and pushing her toward Vexl. She collapsed to the floor, then slowly stood and faced Vexl.

He glared at her.

"Set a course for these coordinates." Vexl's tone was even as he leveled his gun at her head. Jessie stared down the barrel, a single tear rolling down her cheek as her eyes glossed over for a long moment. When they refocused, she steeled her gaze, her face becoming hard. Closing her eyes, she took in a deep breath.

"I want you to guaran—" Weapons fire cut her short. First Officer Jessie Gumnen collapsed to the floor dead, right next to her captain.

Letting out a long sigh, Vexl snapped his fingers again. Second Officer Deidra Kul was pulled from the group of crying and terrified bridge crew. With a cold glare, Vexl leveled his gun at her head.

"Don't waste my time, you know what I want. Either do it or die." Vexl glanced at the timer in his HUD, the seconds dwindling down. The first two dead bodies had cost him a minute.

Deidra hesitated. She stared at the gun and then down at the corpses of her captain and first officer. She glanced back over at the bridge crew; terror-filled gazes locked with her own. No one was going to save her. Without saying a word, Deidra moved to the navigation console, authenticated with it, and quickly entered the coordinates displayed on the holodisplay next to Vexl. The *Empress Star* began to move, the ship realigning itself. Its powerful engines came online, and within a matter of seconds it entered suplight.

"Good. Now I need you to turn over full control of this ship to me." He kept his gun leveled with her head. The bridge command console flared back to life.

She glanced back to the crew and let out a slow breath, then closed her eyes and began to tear up. Moving to the command console, she entered an emergency authorization request for the transfer of command. Automated responses from the mobis of the captain and first officer indicated their statuses as deceased and provided emergency approval. In a heartbeat, she became captain of the *Empress Star*. Another thought brought up the command transfer screen, which prompted her to designate a new commanding officer. Vexl moved forward, syncing his mobi with the control system, and the ship recognized him as the new captain.

"Good girl . . ." Vexl grinned and snapped his fingers. His men opened fire on the remaining bridge crew, peppering their bodies with holes and burn marks as blood spray coated the wall behind them. Deidra screamed and covered her ears with her hands.

An eerie silence descended on the bridge. Deidra opened her eyes to discover herself as the sole surviving member of the bridge crew.

"Your mobi, now!" Vexl yelled.

Deidra slowly turned to regard him, her eyes hollow. His gun was still leveled at her head. She reached into her collar and ripped out her mobi, then tossed it to Vexl in a robotic motion. He shot it out of the air with flair.

"You should feel lucky." Spinning his WMAs like a cowboy, Vexl holstered them and moved past her. He brought up the communications control array for the *Empress Star* and put it into a permanent maintenance mode. "If your predecessors had been more cooperative, you would be in that pile over there." He nonchalantly glanced at her and then to the dead bodies not too far from her feet.

Deidra clutched her abdomen and collapsed to her knees, then vomited up the contents of her stomach. She continued to retch for a few minutes, her arms crossed, her body shaking. Tears streamed down her face as she muttered, the sounds of her voice barely audible.

Violent reactions in the Enesmic flow are most acutely felt and seen through the effects it has on our physical world with tremors in the earth, levitation of material objects in the affected area, and even powerful winds.

–FROM "ENESMIC AND THEORIES OF ORDERING"
BY SHAPER LUKIR AFREV

CHAPTER 13   DEXTER PINSTEN

Empress Star, Huzien Alliance space

Dexter woke with a start, his green eyes focusing on the mirrored ceiling of his suite aboard the *Empress Star*. He remained motionless as he surveyed the room. There was a nagging feeling at the back of his mind that something was off. A blue-furred Uri to his side stirred. Dexter glanced from her to the Das'Vin at his other side, who was sprawled out on top of the covers, her leg hooked around his. Her skin had a distinct silver hue to it, and her hair was a deep black. He enjoyed *fra'sha*, Das'Vin whose every thought was driven by physical pleasure. Dexter had learned that the condition was born out of a traumatic experience, usually when a Das'Vin's *ha'ishi* was severed with the murder of their *dru'sha*, or life mate. That part didn't bother him too much, considering he didn't even remember the names of either of the women in his bed.

A few minutes went by with Dexter remaining perfectly still, his breathing slow and measured. Deciding that it was only him and the girls in the room, Dexter quietly removed himself from the bed. Pulling on his clothes, he moved to the window and caught sight of the stars passing by, then grunted.

The constellations were off.

He had sailed on this same cruise twice before and had long ago memorized the route it would take. Cruise routes were almost never deviated from unless something had gone horribly wrong. In his 170 years of life, Dexter's senses had never betrayed him, and he wasn't going to start ignoring them now. He moved to the door of his suite, listening for a long moment before prompting the door to slide open and cautiously entering the hallway. While making his way to the observation deck at the front of the ship, he silently scanned the area, then stopped. He glared at the *Closed* sign; the observation deck was sectioned off.

Backtracking, he sought out one of the security stations. It was empty, and the sliding door was open. He eyed the door, then moved to the shadows and began tracing one of the guard routes he had memorized until he came to a stop near a private crew entrance. Similar such crew entrances were found throughout the ship; they provided access to a network of tunnels and meglifts that allowed the crew to traverse the ship without ever encountering a guest. Dexter stood watching the door for a few moments. A quick test of the access controls verified that he was locked out. His military overrides should have given him immediate access.

The sound of footsteps caused his ears to perk up. He quickly moved out of sight. The door slid open, and a disheveled Tuzen male with a curious face tattoo walked through. He wore a security guard's uniform. Dexter's back stiffened as he caught sight of a brand just below the collar of the guard's uniform. A moment later, the man adjusted his collar, hiding the brand from view. Dexter let out a slow, measured breath and attempted to reach out through his mobi to Jessica.

Network Unavailable flashed in his micro-display. He cursed.

Glancing around, his gaze eventually returned to the guard. He watched the man start walking out onto the promenade. Dexter kept him in his sights as the Tuzen's gaze hung on some of the more attractive women walking in the area. Shaking his head, Dexter silently moved toward the guard and bumped him from behind. The action caused the guard to fall hard to the ground.

"You wanna die?" the Tuzen shouted. He eyed Dexter wildly, his hand reaching for something hidden under his shirt.

"Oh, sorry man!" Dexter quickly offered his hand. He made out the full brand on the Tuzen's chest. "I've got some horny chicks waiting back at my place for a good *vusg* and wasn't paying attention," Dexter laughed. The Tuzen reluctantly took his hand. Dexter pulled him up, his surprising strength causing the guard to frown. "You know..." Dexter leaned in closer. "I don't think I can take them by myself; I may need some help." He glanced around with a grin. The security guard glanced around as well before his gaze returned to Dexter.

"I might be havin' a break right about now... think I could help out." A toothy grin filled the Tuzen's face. "What kind of *vusging* pussy?"

"Das'Vin and Uri." Dexter smiled.

The guard nodded and motioned for Dexter to lead. When they got to Dexter's suite, Dexter glanced around before nodding to the guard. He opened the door and motioned for the Tuzen to enter.

Catching sight of nude bodies on the bed, the Tuzen began to pull off his pants, his tongue hanging out of his mouth. Powerful arms wrapped around his neck, and a heavy blow to his back knocked the air out of his lungs. He dropped to his knees and tried to reach for the concealed gun at his waist, but Dexter was too fast and slammed him forward. The guard's head connected with the ground in a splatter of blood, his nose broken. Dexter lifted his head back up and then slammed him down hard again.

Screams erupted from both women, who stared horrified at Dexter, then rushed to the opposite end of the room. The Tuzen tried futilely to fight back. Utilizing his cybernetic strength, Dexter lifted the man up, slammed him hard against the door, and punched, crushing the man's windpipe. The guard coughed up blood as Dexter landed a powerful blow on one of his lungs.

Dexter allowed the Tuzen to collapse to the floor. The man's trachea was destroyed; suffocation would comprise the last minutes of his life. Dexter then reached down, removed the gun from the man's belt, and casually dropped it on a nearby table. The man eventually went very still.

"*Vusg*! You killed him!" the Das'Vin screamed. She stood holding the Uri, both naked.

The women stared at Dexter, who had the air of a gladiator reveling in his brutal victory within the arena. Glancing over to them, he sighed. He lifted the man's head up and ripped his shirt to expose the brand at the top of his chest.

"That mark there"—Dexter motioned toward the brand—"is a signifier of *vusging* Het Wrast Aht." He waited a few seconds, expecting both women to nod in understanding. They returned blank stares. "They're the largest pirate band that operates in the Outer Rim." Both women remained silent, still no recognition in their eyes. "*Vusging ciths* . . ." Dexter muttered under his breath. "I think this ship has been infiltrated by pirates. This one was posing as a security guard, which tells me that they may already have control of the ship."

The women's eyes went wide as they processed Dexter's words. Still using each other as support, they slid to the floor against the window. Glancing from them to the fresh corpse at his feet, Dexter turned to his suitcase near the foot of his bed. Moving to it, he utilized his mobi to open a secret compartment at the back. His Sentinel armor slid out in a compact tray. His weapons were locked up in the armory toward the center of the ship. No one, not even the Founder's Elites, could carry weapons onboard.

Quickly stripping down to nothing with both women watching, Dexter pulled on his armor in a matter of seconds. He ran a full system check while he walked over to the gun lying on the table. He picked it up and gave it a once-over. With a grunt, he slid it into a concealed holder on his thigh and walked toward the door to his suite. The nanoplexi frame quickly slid out of his way.

"What about us!" The Uri jumped to her feet. Looking back over his shoulder, Dexter eyed her breasts for a moment before his gaze met hers.

"*Vusg*, I don't know." Dexter gave a shrug. "My advice? Don't leave this room." Dexter instructed the door to close and stepped out into the hallway. A mini holodisplay appeared over his left wrist, and he brought the full suite of his biological enhancements online. With a thought, he cloaked, instantly disappearing.

A cihphist losing focus or control during critical moments of manipulating torrents of Enesmic energy can be catastrophic, resulting in explosions of immense power that have the potential to vaporize or consume cihphists. It is not uncommon for multiple cihphists to collaborate on Enesmic weaving of this scale to minimize the risk of disaster.

–FROM "ENESMIC AND THEORIES OF ORDERING"
BY SHAPER LUKIR AFREV

CHAPTER 14 BRESHA VECEN

Six months ago
Enesmic Wilds, Enesmic plane

Bresha opened her eyes, her body now fully in the Enesmic plane. The Wilds of the Enesmic were all around her, their chaotic flows breathtaking, overpowering, terrifying. Sagren's control over her had faded the moment she stepped through the vortex. Her mind was once again her own, and the hints of a smile began to form on her lips.

Terrible pain overwhelmed her. The intensity of it was unlike anything she had ever experienced. Bresha dropped to her knees and screamed. It felt as if every cell in her body was being ripped apart piece by piece; like her skin was joining the chaotic swirling of Enesmic energy all around her. Blood began to pool on the ground. She collapsed to her hands, gasping for air, but nothing entered her lungs, her need for oxygen left on the Havin plane. Her eyes darted back and forth rapidly as she let out another scream.

There was subtle movement to her side as a voice said, "Fear not." She painfully shifted her gaze to see a being unlike anything she had ever before imagined. Its intense gaze lingered on her as the creature silently glided across the ground. Knowledge began to flood her mind, much of it beyond her understanding. She gasped.

"Eshgren . . ." Bresha said, and whimpered. Images of Sagren returned to her mind, the being's essence hinting at the same taint. Summoning all her strength, Bresha pushed herself to her feet and turned to face the rift she had entered through. She took one step, then collapsed onto her stomach, hitting the ground hard. She reached one hand forward, straining, but the rift was out of reach.

"I am Sephan." The voice came from her side. "I can help you." Bresha turned her head to see the Eshgren kneeling beside her. Sephan's radiant purple gaze engulfed her, its massive silver claw-like appendage outstretched in an inviting gesture next to her hand. "Simply accept me into your essence. I can save you."

"No!" Bresha whispered a scream. "I would rather die."

"Very well." Sephan retracted its appendage and stood up. It began to glide away from her as pain rippled throughout her body. She gasped, her gaze going to her hand. All the skin was gone, and tendons of muscle began breaking off and fading away. Terror gripped her.

"Wait!" The word was barely audible.

Sephan stopped, glancing over its shoulder to regard her.

Bresha closed her eyes, and a tear rolled down her cheek.

Present day
Huzien shuttle, Huzien Alliance space

Bresha Vecen's eyes shot open, her bloodred lips curling into a smile as the former shaper of the Argents recognized the sudden absence of Sagren's presence. She stood from her seat in the hijacked Huzien Alliance shuttle and moved to stand near the primary holodisplay.

Ship metrics and controls sprang to life, displaying the destination of Etan Rachnie on the screen. When she terminated the route, the shuttle dropped out of suplight. Her bright blue gaze, laced with strands of interwoven silver in the irises, glowed in the low light of the cabin, and she raised her fingers to her chin, tapping lightly against the soft flesh. The body was weak by Eshgren standards, but it would have to do.

Sephan, an Eshgren being from the Enesmic plane, now inhabited Bresha's body. The fact that its fellow Eshgren's plans had come to a bloody end at the hands of the Havin gave Sephan pause. Exerting control over Bresha's mind, Sephan instructed her mobi to change the destination to the Alliance borders toward the Outer Rim.

FOUNDERS LOG:
The Price of Safety

Society; the concept is a fickle one. Through blood, sweat, and tears, nations are born and governments are established, with order and laws becoming mainstays. And yet, these people, these citizens of the empire . . . they take it all for granted. From the safety of their homes, they curse their politicians, complain about taxes, and believe that they could do things better themselves. Yet when challenged, they shrink back—surely someone else can do it for them.

Safety is taken for granted, but it is not something that everyone has the luxury of. There are billions on the worlds in the Outer Rim that would kill for safety, and in fact . . . many do. Legions of people on such unprotected worlds willingly throw in their lots with the bands of monsters that grow like cancers. Pirates. Hordes filled with chaos, ruthless hierarchies of merciless people who would, and have, sold out their families in order to protect themselves.

Slavery, murder, rape, poverty. That is the life of the unprotected, the life of those who were unlucky enough to be born in the Outer Rim. Many do what they must to survive, their moral cores thrown away like dirty rags. Many citizens of the empire truly have no idea of what some live through. How many fathers have stood pinned to the wall helpless as they watched their daughters and wives brutally ravished before their very eyes? How many wives lay broken as they watched their husbands killed because they tried to do something, anything, to protect those they loved? How many sons and daughters screamed through tears as their hopes and dreams were shattered and their numb bodies were dragged out of their burning homes to become slaves sold on the Outer Market?

I . . . cannot express these sentiments without accepting some responsibility. As I stare out at the great empire that we have built, I must admit that while most of our citizens are shielded from ever experiencing such horrors, we have created the environment that has bred such injustices. At the heart of many pirate hordes exists Tuzen hate and pain, bred throughout generations and finally given an outlet outside the confines of society.

But Tuzen hate alone could not have sustained these cancers; no. Our borders have done that. We establish them and police them and protect them. Yet we ignore the pleas for help from outside. We use borders to justify our inaction, to put aside our guilt. To tell ourselves that we must focus on what we have; that we can't do more. Excuses are an infinite commodity.

The Ashna Maidens, I applaud what they have done. Deep in the cold recesses of the Outer Rim, those women have worked tirelessly to establish the safety that my people hold so dear—but even they have borders. Although, I must admit, they don't ignore the pleas for help from outside of them. The Maidens give their lives to protect people who have nothing to give them in return. They shame us as we ignore the horrors of those without hope. Although, safety always has a price. Some pay it with taxes, others with blood.

-Lanrete

CHAPTER 15 NEVEN KENK

Ecka, Thae, Huzien home system

Neven patted the top of his Encro 350 coupe as the doors closed. The high-end performance hovercar was a splurge, a relic of his self-indulgence. He had been forced to leave it behind when he joined the Founder's Elites as a secnic. Since returning to Thae, there had been a period of adjustment. Gone was the ever-present hum of the *Foundra Ascension*'s suplight drive, replaced by the deafening quiet of his posh house. It had been exactly as he left it; all signs of the military coming in and out to maintain it were well hidden.

His gaze wandered up the walkway to his parents' house, the single-family dwelling the only home he'd known growing up. The smell of recently cut grass lingered in the air. Memories rushed back: his father sitting next to him on the bank of the lake behind their house, fishing rods in their hands; his mother showing him the inner workings of their maintenance drone on a late afternoon in the nearby shed on their two-acre property; Neven reclining on the grass with both his parents at his sides, all of them staring up at the stars. He smiled.

"Neven?" the voice was hesitant, unsure. Neven's gaze focused, his mind coming back to reality. "Neven!" An olive-skinned woman with green eyes and long black hair raced down the walkway. Neven moved to greet his mother, Adinah, who embraced him in a deep hug. A tear rolled down her cheek and a broad smile lit up her face. The two hugged in silence for a long moment. "We were so worried!"

"Correction," came a strong voice from behind them. "Your mother was worried; I knew you'd be okay."

Neven smiled as he greeted his father, Michael, with a sturdy handshake. The two men locked gazes briefly, both glancing toward the ground after a few seconds. Neven was the spitting image of his father with the same deep green eyes and jet-black hair, although Michael's was beginning to grey.

"Are you hungry?" Adinah fawned over her son.

"A little." Neven smiled. "Only had a protein pack on my way out of the MinSci."

"Well, that's convenient." Michael grinned at Neven. "Your mother was just finishing up dinner."

"Oh, is that so?" Neven grinned back at his father. Hugging him again for good measure, Adinah ushered Neven into the house while Michael went off to set a place for him at the table. Neven marveled at how nothing inside of the house had changed since he left. It was as if the abode was locked in time. Pictures of Neven hung all over the place, highlighting his accomplishments, even down to his offer letter from the MinSci. He had learned on that day that he made more than his father, but not more than his mother. Adinah was renowned in the field of robotics. She took a temporary leave from her position when Neven was born, the brilliant woman deciding to focus all her energy on raising her son. The investment had paid off, and after Neven completed his education at home, she had rejoined the workforce.

Neven slid into his chair at the table. He silently watched his parents at work, nostalgia assaulting him. Within minutes, his mother appeared, flanked by her drone assistant. The two laid out a spread on the table, the meal modest yet still managing to fill the air with a lovely aroma. Neven's thoughts went to Zun, memories of that special dinner in her quarters aboard the *Foundra Ascension* coming to the forefront of his mind. It was during that meal that he had learned the truth of Yuvan and the relationship the two had shared.

Everyone settled down at the table, Adinah taking Neven's plate and serving him reflexively. She made sure to give him a little of everything, ensuring that each portion was sectioned off and not touching the other. Neven smiled. Adinah set the plate down in front of him, and he grinned at his father, who grinned back at him without hesitation before digging into his own food.

Neven sat watching the plate in silence for a long moment, his eyes unfocusing again. Images flashed in his mind of the final battle against Sagren, Neven standing shoulder-to-shoulder with his fellow Founder's Elites as they faced down Ififus and Regfalen, Ceshra overlords from Sagren's army. The terrifying creatures had glowed unnaturally, their powerful energy attacks bombarding his power armor, his shield the only thing separating him from life and death. He gasped as Regfalen charged, monstrous orange eyes focused on him and him alone.

"Is everything okay?" Michael asked, a concerned look on his face.

"Yes, sorry, it's nothing," Neven said. Michael furrowed his brow and glanced to Adinah, who cocked her head and glared at him. Michael took in a quick breath, his eyes darting to Neven, then back to his food.

"You should eat, honey. You're starved," Adinah said. Neven nodded and picked up his fork. They ate in silence for a few minutes, Neven slowly picking at his food.

"How's the new job? It isn't stressing you too much is it? Military life can be tough," Michael said. He glanced from Neven to Adinah, who rolled her head back and sighed.

"Yeah, it's pretty rough," Neven said. "I . . . it isn't what I expected." He shuddered.

Adinah cleared her throat. "So . . ." She glanced sideways at her son. "Have you met anyone interesting in your galactic journeys?" Neven grinned and leaned back in his chair.

"Now that you mention it, yes, I have."

"Oh?" Michael raised an eyebrow. Neven glanced his way and then sat up straight.

"Uh, yeah. Her name is Zun, Zun Shan."

"Zun Shan . . ." Adinah echoed the words. "Well, how did you meet?" Her tone was excited, yet purposefully reserved.

"She's also a member of the Founder's Elite." Neven's attention was fully on his mother. "Zun's a secnic, just like me, except she's more of a scientist, not an engineer. And she also used to work at the MinSci! We have so much in common, and she's . . ." Neven hesitated.

"She's?" Adinah's chair was suddenly much closer.

"She's so beautiful mom, I mean like really beautiful, and so mature."

"Mature?" Michael's eyes narrowed. "Just how mature?"

Neven bit his lip.

Adinah glanced at Michael and then back to Neven, her head cocking to the side again.

"Yeah, how mature is she?" Her smile was gone. Neven took in a deep breath and leaned back in his chair. He had moved to the front of his seat without realizing it.

"Well, like I said." Neven gulped. "Zun used to work at the MinSci, until she retired."

"Retired?" both parents said in unison.

"It's okay! Zun's half Huzien, so . . . she isn't really that old." Neven put his hand on the back of his neck. He watched his parents lean back in their chairs and exchange looks. "Zun's three hundred and eleven years old." Neven let out a low sigh. "She'll be three hundred and twelve next month." He stared down at his plate and wished Zun was beside him.

Without looking, he brought up an image of Zun through the holodisplay built into the dining room table. The image, a three-dimensional replica of her head and shoulders, was projected right above the food in the center of the spread. A powerful silence descended over the room. Neven could see recognition in Adinah's eyes at the sight of Zun. She frowned, but almost immediately caught herself and sucked in a quick breath.

"You're right, honey," Adinah said in a soft voice, "she *is* beautiful." Adinah turned to regard Neven with a motherly smile, her eyes filled with nothing but love. She got up and walked over to Neven, hugging him. Neven let out the breath he hadn't realized he'd been holding and fully embraced his mother. That's when he began to cry. The emotional floodgates opened as everything from the past year came out all at once.

"I killed people mom, many people . . . I . . . they were bad people, but . . . but I still killed them. Me, with my hands."

"It's okay, honey," Adinah whispered, squeezing him tighter, "it will be alright." Neven shuddered again, slowly regaining his composure. A long silence passed in the room.

"When do we get to meet her? This . . . uh, Zun?" Michael glanced from Neven to Adinah, who forced a smile, nodding.

"Zun should be back in a month." Neven continued to hug his mother, calming. "She went on a cruise with some other members of my team. I opted out to come back and see you both instead."

"I don't know about you," Adinah said, glancing to her husband, "but I think this is cause for celebration!"

"It's not like he's getting married," Michael countered.

"It's the first step!" Adinah snapped back.

"Then I guess it's cause for celebration!" Michael said with a strained smile, his hand at the back of his neck.

Ancient texts describe the earliest forms of experimentation with the Enesmic seen in the creation of fire, the detection of another's thoughts, and the remote manipulation of objects.

–FROM "EARLIEST INTERACTIONS WITH THE ENESMIC"
BY SHAPER LUKIR AFREV

CHAPTER 16 ENVERO OLIC

Setna Isles, Thae, Huzien home system

"You expecting visitors?" Jasha glanced over to her husband, Envero Olic. The middle-aged man yawned, his tawny sun-kissed ears perking up, then leaned back into a stretch, his callused hands on his hips. The living room was quaint, their modest farmhouse a relic hinting at a simpler life. He made his way over to stand next to his wife. She was about the same age, her hair a light brown and her skin a warm gold. Both were Huzien, with dark brown esha marks down their sides. Envero's gaze lingered on the large hovercar making its way down the long road leading up to their house. Large harvest drones littered the fields on each side of the road.

"No," Envero growled. "And last time I checked this was private property." His eyes narrowed, attempting to make out the driver in the fading sunlight. He started walking toward the front door. Stepping out onto the porch, he watched the car slow to a stop. Enviro glared at the driver, a male Uri who didn't make eye contact. His posture was perfect, his gaze straight ahead. Envero could easily make out the military uniform through the glass.

"Jessica." Envero's heart caught in his throat, his face blanching. "Is something . . ." The side of the vehicle lifted open, and a muscular Huzien female dropped to the ground, dust wafting up at her feet. Her gaze locked onto Envero as her hands fell to rest comfortably on the side arm and Huzien blade at her hips. The ice in her glare caused Envero to flinch. He subconsciously took a step back.

"Envero Olic?" Her voice was strong, commanding.

"Who's asking?" A hint of fight crept into Envero's voice. Jasha moved to stand next to him. Everyone's gaze shifted to the new figure emerging from the vehicle.

"That's him." Lanrete's gaze locked with Envero's.

Envero's esha marks bulged, his eyes going wide as his nose flared. Rage morphed his features into something grotesque and horrific. His pulse started to race as adrenaline coursed through his veins. He charged down the steps toward Lanrete, his hands balled into fists.

"You bastard!" Envero yelled. The Huzien soldier drew her sidearm and had it leveled on Envero in a heartbeat.

"Hold." Lanrete held up his hand and moved past the Huzien soldier with a calm stride. She turned a nervous glance in his direction, then exchanged a quick look with the Uri soldier still in the car. Both stared after their founder as he walked out to meet the charging man.

Lanrete's blue cloak retracted into his collar, and he came to a stop a short distance from Envero, who seemed to pick up speed with each passing second. Lanrete gave a pained look as Envero lunged forward in a tackling motion before stepping out of the way at the last minute. Envero sailed hard into the dirt. He was up in a heartbeat, spinning. He lunged at Lanrete, his fists up as Lanrete ducked and dodged, Envero's strikes wild. Lanrete danced around the front yard, Envero struggling to keep up his assault. The farmer eventually collapsed to his knees and began to wheeze, glaring up at Lanrete.

"Did you just come here"—Envero struggled to catch his breath—"to humiliate me?"

"What would I gain from that?" Lanrete sighed and glanced at Jasha. She looked mortified, her eyes pleading. Tears began to stream down her face.

"Please don't arrest him!" she blurted.

Lanrete glanced up at the sky. Taking in a deep breath, he returned his gaze to Jasha and gave her a genuine smile.

"I have no intention of arresting your husband, Mrs. Olic." Lanrete started moving toward her. "Do you mind if I come in?" Jasha nodded her head rapidly, her arm coming across to wipe her eyes dry.

"Yes! Yes! Please come in, Founder Lanrete!" She quickly turned around, opening the door. "Are you . . . are you thirsty?" She glanced at Envero, who was glaring at Lanrete's back. She began to shake her head from side to side, her gaze going to the ground.

"Thank you for your hospitality." Lanrete met Jasha's gaze. Stark terror stared back at him. "Yes, tea would be appreciated." She stared at him for a long moment, the words taking some time to register.

"Yes . . . yes! Right away!" Jasha rushed into the house.

Envero remained on his knees, his gaze turned up toward the sky. Tears rolled down his cheeks as his brain finally caught up with his actions. A sense of dread overwhelmed him. The feeling of eyes boring into the back of his skull caused Envero to glance back at Lanrete's vehicle. The gazes of both the Uri and Huzien were on him, their hands dangerously close to their sidearms. Turning away from them and back toward his house, Envero let out a long, drawn-out sigh. He slowly got to his feet, his jaw set. The short walk back to his house seemed like an eternity. Both soldiers mirrored his steps, flanking him.

Envero took in a deep breath and walked into his house. The soldiers remained on the porch, each conveniently near a window with a view inside. Envero's gaze immediately went to Lanrete. The founder was sipping from a cup of tea while seated in a large chair covered in flower designs.

"Why are you here?" Envero barked.

"Your daughter asked me to come visit you." Lanrete finished his sip of tea and set the cup down on a small end table.

"I don't have a daughter."

"The birth records for Jessica Olic would disagree with you."

"That woman is not my daughter," Envero spat. "No daughter of mine would kill people for a living. She wouldn't work for a Maker-forsaken Founder."

Lanrete's jaw clenched. "Jessica is an amazing woman and a key member of my team. She was instrumental in the defeat of Sagren's forces, and her heroic actions saved the lives of trillions across the Alliance during the Rift War." There was no visible response from Envero at his words. Lanrete glanced at Jasha. She was smiling, her gaze stuck on the floor. Letting out a slow breath, he looked back to Envero. "What is it that you think I do?" Lanrete's voice was calm, controlled. An intensity filled his gaze. The sudden shift caught Envero off guard.

"You take children and turn them into monsters." Envero's voiced cracked.

Lanrete remained silent for a few seconds, his face softening. "Yes . . . I suppose you're right." Envero staggered back. "I create monsters to protect this empire from monsters." Lanrete gave a sad smile, his eyes distant. Neither said a word for a long moment. "I'm sorry that there is blood on your little girl's hands." His gaze again focused on Envero, who had balled his hands into fists.

"I don't forgive you." Tears began to form in Envero's eyes. "I'll never forgive you."

"I accept that." Lanrete glanced to Jasha. Her gaze was still stuck on the floor, tears now rolling down her cheeks. Taking in a deep breath, Lanrete picked up the cup of tea from the table and downed the rest. The scalding water burned his throat, but he didn't wince. Once he set the cup back on the table, he stood up. "I'll be taking my leave. Thank you for your time." Lanrete walked past him. Envero's shoulders slumped, his gaze on the ceiling. Lanrete got to the door and stopped. "One more thing."

Jasha paled, her hand at her chest, her eyes going to Lanrete's guards standing outside.

"Your daughter, Jessica." Lanrete hesitated. "She's an immortal like me." Lanrete glanced to a picture on the wall, an old photo of Jessica. It was her as a little girl on her father's shoulder. She had an oversized cowboy hat on her head. "She doesn't know it yet. It's usually best for immortals to find this out on their own, later in life." Lanrete sighed. "I recommend keeping this secret to yourselves. It's not uncommon for immortals her age to commit suicide upon finding out." Without another word, Lanrete exited the house. Both soldiers moved to flank him as he descended the steps.

Jasha gasped and then began to squeal. Envero's heart leapt into his throat, excitement mixed with confusion overwhelming him.

Lanrete entered the vehicle as both soldiers took their seats. The car rose a few feet off the ground, performed a quick one-hundred-and-eighty-degree turn, then surged forward, speeding off toward the farm exit. Envero stumbled out of the house, frantically motioning for Lanrete to come back.

CHAPTER 17 NEVEN KENK

MinSci, Thae, Huzien home system

The light from Thae's supergiant white star glistened off the glass-covered buildings throughout the MinSci campus. Neven took in a deep breath, smiling as he walked out of the parking and transportation superstructure at the south entrance of the campus. Thoughts of his first time taking in the sight rushed back to him, the sense of awe overwhelming.

"There you are!" Neven glanced back at the speaker. A young green-eyed Huzien was beaming at him.

"Kechu, my friend!" The two embraced in a short hug. "How did you know I'd be here?" Neven asked. "This place is too massive for this to be random chance."

Kechu grinned. "Lahl told me."

"Lahl?"

"My SSI."

"SSI?" Neven gave Kechu a blank stare.

"Synaptic systems intelligence," Kechu replied. "It's a prototype that I've been working on. Name is also a work in progress. I originally tried to name it super systems intelligence, but everyone just told me no."

"What makes it super?" Neven grinned.

I can function at a higher cognitive level than current system intelligences, a soft feminine voice said through Neven's mobi. Neven took a step back, his eyes wide. He glanced to Kechu, who smiled nervously.

"She has a knack for listening in on my conversations." Kechu sighed. "She approximated that you'd be here today, at this time, then detected when you exited the terminal and ultimately guided me to this spot for a meet-up."

"Interesting . . ."

And a bit creepy, I admit, Lahl said to both. The two engineers laughed.

"Anyway, let me show you to my lab," Kechu said. "I can show you her core matrix and how she works."

I thought I'd at least get dinner and a movie first, Lahl said.

Kechu smiled. Neven was genuinely impressed by the exchange. She reminded him a bit of Asha, Zun's SI, although he assumed there were probably substantial differences between the two.

Shuttle to the Department of Advanced Computing & SI Research departing in one minute, Lahl informed them. The two men glanced at each other and then began to race through the transportation center.

The door to a large engineering lab opened, prompting a complex system of lights to softly rise in brightness until the whole room was illuminated. Kechu motioned for Neven to enter.

"How did you get your own private lab? I thought these were reserved for chief architects and feshra." Neven's eyes were wide, his mouth open.

"I uh . . . impressed Phenste Wahkin, the head of my department." Kechu rubbed his neck. "She was blown away by my initial proof of concept with Lahl. I'd been working on Lahl in my spare time." He paused for a moment, his cheeks reddening. "I'm the chief architect for the SSI project."

The blood drained from Neven's face as he stared at Kechu for a long moment. Neven thought back to the offer from Remi Etwa to become a chief architect within Weapons Development. That offer had taken him becoming a secnic and almost dying at the hands of Sagren's forces to attain.

"Congratulations," he said, the words almost a whisper. Neven quickly turned away from Kechu and began to investigate the lab. Its size was staggering, reminiscent of Zun's lab back on the *Foundra Ascension*, except less cleanroom and more mad scientist. Kechu walked ahead of Neven and toward the center of the lab, where a large hologrid filled the area, and brought up a visual representation of Lahl's virtual cortex.

"I started my research from studies that had been done by feshra in the fields of neuroscience and SI resonance. Lahl is actually the combination of six distinct SI cores merged together to form a new entity." Kechu glanced over to Neven as he walked up to the hologrid. Neven was mesmerized by the interconnecting webs of neural SI synapses interlinking. "Instead of having them working in tandem with each other, as is typical, they are fully interconnected, merged to form a massive consciousness. I had to rewrite large portions of the code, which took forever." Kechu let out a heavy sigh. "But it all paid off!"

"How large is the central core?" Neven glanced to Kechu. "The processing power needed to handle something like this sounds like it would be staggering."

"That's the beauty of it all." Kechu had a twinkle in his eye. After guiding Neven toward the back of the lab, the young architect instructed a protective housing to open. The innards showed a series of three mobis side by side.

"I don't understand."

"Lahl," Kechu said, clasping his hands together, "is a symbiotic entity. I've designed her to pull from the resting cognitive power of her host."

"So, the Lahl that has been talking to me . . ."

"Is right here." Kechu flipped up his collar and pulled out a mobi similar to the ones in the protective housing.

Neven stared at the device, his mind rapidly processing all the details.

"How much of a strain does she put on you?" Neven glanced from the device to Kechu.

Kechu nodded and brought up a recent scan of his own brain and nervous system. The image showed clusters of green and blue.

"Those green areas there"—Kechu pointed to the screen—"those are Lahl."

Neven stared at the green clusters, their size minuscule when compared to the blue clusters.

"And the blue is you?"

"I guess you could say that," Kechu laughed. He instructed the screen to enhance the blue areas. "Those are the areas of my brain that were in use during the test. I was stressing my brain as much as I could by attempting to quickly solve a series of complex equations."

"What was Lahl doing at the time?" Neven glanced back at Kechu.

"Solving the same equations." Kechu grinned. "She beat me to the answers."

"A math savant like you?" Neven grinned. "At least you still have the trophies, I guess."

Kechu picked up one of the mobis.

"I consider Lahl better than any competitive trophy I've won." Turning around, he held the mobi out toward Neven. "I want you to have this. It's a copy of Lahl's core, but it hasn't been activated. You just need to go through the activation process and sync the mobi to your micro-display for it to work."

"Is it safe?" Neven immediately bit his tongue. "I mean . . . is it okay for me to take this out of the MinSci?"

"It's safe as far as I can tell." Kechu shrugged. "It is experimental technology, but you know how that goes. I've already gotten approval from Ecnics for you to take it. He's curious to see how it works in the field."

"Great. I've become a lab rat!" Neven laughed.

"We're all lab rats," Kechu grinned. "Some of us just have the common enough sense to recognize it and accept our fates."

Neven took the mobi into his hand and flipped up his own collar, removing his familiar mobi and shutting it off. Sliding the inactive device into his pants, he slipped the new one into the small pocket and pulled his collar back down. Neven went through the activation process, which only took a matter of seconds once his micro-display came online and recognized the new device.

Synaptic Systems Intelligence Mark I online and synced to host. Please designate a name.

Neven glanced to Kechu as the voice spoke into his mind.

"I decided to make them all distinct," Kechu watched Neven. "Figured it would be weird if they all sounded the same."

"Should I name her Lahl?"

"That's boring. Think up something unique!"

"Hmmm . . ." Neven stood in silence for a few seconds. "Ellipse."

Name accepted. I am Ellipse. It's a pleasure to meet you, Neven.

A strange tingling sensation went down Neven's spine and through his gut as the SSI interfaced with his nervous system through the micro-display cognitive interface. He and the entity were now one. *What did I just sign myself up for?* Neven thought to himself.

An experiment, came the soothing response in his head, the voice that of Ellipse.

You can read my thoughts?

Yes. I exist in your mind through our connection from the mobi, Ellipse answered.

So . . . you'll know everything I know?

Yes.

Both fear and excitement coursed through Neven. His gaze went to Kechu, who stared at him with a knowing smile.

"It's awesome, isn't it?"

"That's one way of describing it . . ."

The ability to weave the Enesmic flow set up the early power structures in civilizations and can still be seen in many of the wealthy classes today, with those in positions of power often having a high sensitivity to the Enesmic.

−FROM "EARLIEST INTERACTIONS WITH THE ENESMIC"
BY SHAPER LUKIR AFREV

CHAPTER 18 BRIME WEWTA

Aheraneth, Enesmic plane

B rime Wewta opened her eyes to an intense brightness that slowly faded. The young Human quickly looked around, trying to get her bearings. She crossed her arms, covering her bare breasts. The last thing she remembered was destroying the Ceshra, Sifitis, with impossible power, and then Soahc, her love, staring at her in shock before everything went black. The hair on her bare back stood on end as she sensed something watching her. Glancing from side to side, she slowly turned her gaze upward. Her eyes went wide, a scream on her lips.

Above her stood hovering beings of immense power, each with multiple sets of wings. Their bodies were unlike anything she had ever before witnessed, forms that she struggled to comprehend. One caught her eye, that of a giant being with six sets of wings. Its head was cloaked under a deep golden and silver hood, and black fire radiated from two orbs of deep purple that stared back at her. Its body was adorned with a mix of gold and silver armor with diamonds acting as bolts holding it all together.

Brime stared, entranced by the being, her fear quickly replaced by curiosity as she forgot her nakedness. The being descended, landing on the translucent floor with a thunderclap. It began to approach Brime, its wings folding behind its body. Brime stood unafraid, her gaze locked onto its purple orbs. A sense of calm and serenity washed over her.

"Welcome, Brime Wewta." The voice rang with authority and the sound filled the chamber as the words resonated in Brime's bones. "I am Augrashumen the Valorous, and my voice will be that of the Rel Ach'Kel Council. Through me they will commune with you to lessen the strain on your mind."

Brime glanced back up at the host of beings above her, all watching.

"Where am I?" Brime's attention was drawn back to Augrashumen as it stopped in front of her and kneeled. The tall being lowered its head to become level with her.

"You are on what your kind calls the Enesmic plane." Augrashumen's words were all around and inside of her.

"What?" Brime squealed, her eyes going wide. "How is that possible?"

"You passed through to this plane after your encounter with an agent of the Fallen Commander, a being you know as Sifitis. You drew power from here to save your beloved, Soahc." Augrashumen turned its hood to regard an empty space next to it. The area became alive with light as a perfect reproduction of her battle with Sifitis was created.

Brime watched as she lay dying with a fatal wound in her chest. Her hand subconsciously went to where the wound had been. Soahc stood frozen as Sifitis silently moved in to kill him. She witnessed her body start to glow. Tingling sensations went up and down her spine as she remembered the horrible pain of walking on the Enesmic plane. Then she returned, fully healed, to defeat Sifitis. Tears filled Brime's eyes as she watched the final goodbye between her and Soahc. Her body faded in a glow of light, and an Enesmic tear was left in her place. Brime watched Soahc move to seal it, then collapse to his knees.

"Okay . . ." Brime breathed. She tried to process what she had just watched. "So . . . does this mean that everyone that gets consumed by the Enesmic plane ends up here like me?

"No." Brime detected sadness in Augrashumen's voice. "All but you have been destroyed by the transition. Your beloved himself was mere moments from destruction when he walked this plane."

"You mean . . . when Soahc walked the Enesmic plane over one hundred thousand years ago," Brime gasped, "to become immortal?"

"Yes." Augrashumen's purple orbs returned to Brime, the light to its side fading. "Now you see why your state intrigues us so. You were deposited in the Wilds, a part of the Enesmic plane that is untamed, filled with chaos and what you would consider monstrosities. We have been watching your beloved for some time, and by nature, you. It is because of this attention that I was able to ascertain your location in the Wilds."

"Then I guess I owe you my thanks." Brime smiled.

"Do not thank me yet," Augrashumen cautioned. "Your fate has not yet been determined by the council." Brime frowned. She glanced up at the forms watching her and then back to Augrashumen.

"Why is that?"

"Your mere presence here is a danger to us."

Brime laughed. She looked Augrashumen up and down, then glanced to the other massive beings in the air. Looking down at her naked body, she patted her stomach.

"I'm a danger to you?" she scoffed. "You do realize that I'm naked and alone, standing on a silken sheet surrounded by fifty-foot-tall beings that could snap me in half like a twig, right?"

Augrashumen's eyes flickered with humor.

"Let me clarify," Augrashumen said. "Do you remember Sagren the Betrayer?"

"Remember?" Brime teared up. "How could I ever forget?" Her voice cracked. Emotions took on the form of images as an area to her side became alive with light. Images of the near death of Soahc played out as she remembered them. She watched the scene unfold,

Sagren moving in for the kill, Soahc saved at the last minute by her as she teleported in and whisked him away. Brime covered her mouth as she watched herself try to keep Soahc alive in that gut-wrenching shuttle ride back to the *Foundra Ascension*. "How did I do that . . . ?" Brime's eyes were wide.

"We are able to express your memories as images to be shared with the council," Augrashumen clarified. "Take comfort, Brime, in the knowledge that your beloved has defeated the Fallen Commander, the Betrayer Sagren." Images of Sagren being defeated by Lanrete and Soahc appeared in the chamber, the final battle between the trio played out in its last moments. Brime smiled as she watched her husband standing victorious over the body of Sagren, its head lifeless at his side. "Sagren was not alone. There are others like it, many even more powerful." Brime's gaze snapped back to the Rel Ach'Kel as it regarded her in a moment of silence.

"No . . ." Brime breathed. She began to shake her head.

"There is a treaty that binds them to this plane," Augrashumen said. "A treaty that prevents them from entering your own. Sagren was able to enter at the cost of its life, its true form destroyed by my hands. A fragment of its essence was reformed into the being you faced." Augrashumen paused for a moment to allow that information to sink in. "But your presence here violates that treaty. You should be sent back to the Havin plane immediately for the terms of the agreement to be upheld."

"So, send me back. You'll have no complaint from me."

"It is not so simple." The Rel Ach'Kel shook its hooded head. "Doing so would most assuredly kill you."

"What?" Brime yelled.

"Your body has been transformed. You, dear Brime, are an Enesmic being, or something more. We cannot know for sure, because you are the first of your kind." Augrashumen paused. "Do you believe that this is air around you?" Augrashumen motioned around. Brime nodded. "No. Nothing but Enesmic energy swirls here. You no longer breathe, no longer eat, no longer sleep. All your sustaining life force comes from the Enesmic energy around you. Sending you back to the Havin plane would kill you, because the Havin plane would seek to transform you back into your Havin shell, an imperfect vessel that cannot contain all that you have become. The effect would be similar to one attempting to walk the Enesmic plane for the first time." Augrashumen leaned in closer to Brime, its gaze locking onto hers. "It would rip you apart."

Brime stared at the silken sheet at her feet, her alabaster toes caressing the comforting blue silk. Her mind was abuzz with activity as she processed Augrashumen's words. *This can't be real.* Brime wanted to believe it was all a dream and desperately hoped to awaken at her husband's side.

"Brime . . ." There was sympathy in Augrashumen's voice. "This is real; I am sorry that the situation is not ideal."

"So, it would appear that I have no mental barriers here." Annoyance dripped from Brime's voice. Memories of digging through Neven's mind rushed back to nip at her.

"The Enesmic plane is not the same as your Havin plane," Augrashumen stated apologetically. "The Enesmic flow is very different here, and you will not be able to easily manipulate it without instruction."

"I see." Brime tried to do exactly that. She started with something simple: an orb of light in her hands. The forces were overpowering as they refused her command, and Brime collapsed to the ground, then slowly wrapped her arms around her legs, pulling them in closer. With wide eyes, she stared off into the distance and began to rock back and forth, breaking out into a cold sweat.

Augrashumen moved in closer and touched her. Its hand steadied her body, her mind becoming clear.

"We are sorry; this is much to take in." Augrashumen glanced toward its peers. "I will be your guardian, and will help you adjust to our plane of existence." Brime tried to take in a deep breath, then remembered that she didn't breathe anymore. She started to rock back and forth once more, though Augrashumen's calming touch again steadied her mind. There was sympathy in Augrashumen's glowing purple orbs. "Rest now . . ." Augrashumen said.

Brime lost consciousness immediately, though her form was caught by the Rel Ach'Kel before it could hit the ground.

CHAPTER 19 SERAH'ELAX REZ ASHFALEN

Rion, Huzien Alliance / Ashna Maiden border

Serah'Elax shifted uncomfortably in her new uniform, the stiffer material more show than function. She stood beside Exemplar Ahtlana Jufre on the command bridge of the *Rion*, an Ashna Maiden carrier. She had been ordered to shadow Exemplar Ahtlana in her duties. Serah'Elax had tried to be grateful for her promotion, but she missed the open battlefield, the freedom of movement it afforded. The bridge of the *Rion* felt limiting, her life and death dictated by the clashing of machines. She longed for the touch of her Blades of the Goddess. They now adorned the wall of her quarters, mementos and nothing more.

"My dear pupil . . ." Ahtlana's tone was melodic. "Soon we will be engaged in combat. I believe it best for us to sit." Ahtlana moved back toward her command chair. A temporary seat had been placed for Serah'Elax right next to it. Ahtlana had an ebony complexion with wrinkles slowly forming on her face and sharp red eyes that held a world of wisdom. Her posture commanded respect, and her gaze left many feeling as if they were being evaluated.

"Yes, my exemplar." Serah'Elax moved to her seat, hiding her discomfort as she stared straight ahead at the main holodisplay. Sensing the eyes of Ahtlana on her, Serah'Elax turned to regard her superior with a hint of curiosity.

"I always go a size larger with these uniforms." Ahtlana grinned, her gaze returning to the holodisplay.

Serah'Elax cracked a smile.

"Exiting from suplight in three . . . two . . . one . . ." The image of the dreadnaught Yutrea filled the holodisplay, and they all held their breath as the command ship of the 72nd Fleet of the Ashna Maidens, flying at the head of the hastily put together attack armada of forty-six fleets, headed toward the unknown ships that had dared to shed Maiden blood.

"We have them on sensors," came a call from one of the bridge crew.

"Fellow Maidens of our mighty goddess!" Avatar Luka's voice broadcasted to their ship. "We head today into battle against a foe who would dare shed the blood of our sisters!" Her voice rose in intensity, anger lacing every word. "May the goddess have mercy on their souls as we send them to meet her!" Cheers went up across the bridge. Serah'Elax imagined the same scene happening in every ship across the combined fleet. She had heard that the legendary Avatar Hegna had also chosen to participate in the assault today. Their armada was a show of force Serah'Elax had never seen in her lifetime.

Serah'Elax watched from the sidelines as Exemplar Ahtlana commanded her forces with ease. Hers was the second most powerful ship in Avatar Luka's fleet, and the carrier unleashed untold amounts of drone fighters to weaken the onslaught from the enemy, but the Ashna Maidens were unprepared for the ferocity of their foe. Both battle cruisers stationed to protect the *Rion* were being hard-pressed, and neither was able to offer the carrier any support. Squadrons of fast-moving Ashna Maiden fighters moved in to pepper one of the ships barreling down on the *Rion*. The enemy vessel's shields were quickly eaten away, but the Maidens' victory was short-lived as the ship retreated and another quickly filled its place. The fighters refocused on the new target.

The consistent pattern from the enemy ships did not sit well with Serah'Elax. Their battle coordination had her in a state of macabre awe. Within minutes, more enemy ships had joined in with the newer vessel as the enemy suddenly refocused the brunt of its forces on the *Rion*. Ahtlana's eyes went wide.

"Back! Take us from the fight." The *Rion* started to retreat, but it wasn't fast enough. Enemy ships unleashed a barrage on the carrier. The vessel trembled. "Emergency suplight jump, now!" Ahtlana yelled.

Serah'Elax gripped the arm of her chair as warnings blared across the bridge. A barrage tore through the ship's armor, the blasts going deep. Serah'Elax gasped as an explosion from nearby knocked her hard to the ground. She struggled to hold onto consciousness. Pushing herself up from the floor, her battlefield instincts kicked in. After getting her bearings, she detected moisture running down the side of her head; a touch revealed platinum blood.

The bridge was in shambles. Many were dead, with more struggling to keep the ship in order. Upon catching sight of Ahtlana, Serah'Elax processed the image of the regal exemplar half covered by debris. Red blood was pooling around her. Racing to her side, Serah'Elax searched for a pulse. It was faint. Her well-toned muscles bulged as she pushed away the debris and pulled Ahtlana across the floor to the other side of the bridge. Ripping off strips from her uniform, Serah'Elax used the material to wrap Ahtlana's injuries. She applied pressure to the worst of them. Many on the bridge stared at her with dull eyes, their bodies limp.

"Do we still have suplight?" Serah'Elax asked, her tone strong and confident. The question snapped the other Maidens out of their dazes.

"Yes, Keeper."

"Jump us behind the fleet, now!" Serah'Elax ordered. The Maiden quickly followed through as the ship's suplight drive engaged. The *Rion* shuddered as space bent around them. The short-range jump instantly took them behind Avatar Hegna's fleet. Serah'Elax brought up a damage report readout on a nearby functioning holodisplay. The barrages had been centered on the bridge, life support systems, and personnel quarters. Their reactor, weapons systems, and many of their carrier bays were still functional. Serah'Elax cursed. This enemy commander was ruthless. "I'm taking the exemplar to the medical bay. Start emergency repairs immediately and evacuate all unnecessary areas!" Serah'Elax ordered. "I want us battle ready as soon as I get back!" Nods confirmed her command.

She gingerly picked up Ahtlana and rushed toward the meglift, hoping against all hope that it still functioned. The door opened at her command, lights flickering. She ran a diagnostic, the green indicators signaling that it was still functional. Running inside, she leaned against the wall as the door closed. The meglift flared to life and sped toward the medical bay.

Twenty-four years ago
Ashnayulani, Ashna Maiden refuge system

Ashna Maiden officials stood at the door, Dera'Liv between them and Serah'Elax. Dera'Liv's eyes were wide, frantic. She was still regularly breaking out in cold sweats; the severing of her *ha'ishi* a little over a year ago at the death of Ovah'Hal had weighed heavily on her. Serah'Elax watched her mother sob. She didn't understand why; the nice ladies had done so much to help them over the past year.

"No! You cannot have her." Dera'Liv yelled. "She is all I have!"

"Those are the terms of safe haven in our space." The official glanced at Serah'Elax and then back to Dera'Liv. "You are free to take your daughter and leave if you have secured transport off planet."

"I . . . I petitioned the Das'Vin Republic, but I have not heard a reply. I am sure they will respond. Please, just a little more time."

"We have already given you longer than is normally allowed by law. You must either submit your daughter into service to the Ashna Maidens or leave our space immediately."

"She is only eleven! Still a toddler by my people's standards. A toddler!"

"Most girls start in the Ashna Maidens at the age of five. Your daughter is not an anomaly."

Dera'Liv glanced back at Serah'Elax, her face pained. She turned back to the official.

"My people, we abhor violence. It is not in our nature." Dera'Liv dropped to her knees. "Surely, you must know this. You must know about the Das'Vin."

"Your daughter can choose which path to follow—one of public service or military service—after she has completed her Maiden-in-waiting training." The official's face went soft. "You will still be able to see your daughter; we will not keep you from visiting her." Her face hardened. "But she must come with us. Now."

Present day
Rion, Huzien Alliance / Ashna Maiden border

The meglift rose to the bridge as Serah'Elax took in a steadying breath and opened her eyes. The urge to sleep was strong. She caught sight of her hands, where specks of her platinum blood mixed with a thick coating of red that belonged to Ahtlana. Her hand began to quiver. She silenced it and took in another steadying breath. Serah'Elax refused to allow her body to defeat her. She was in command of the *Rion* now, and her crew needed her. It didn't matter that she had no idea what she was doing.

The door slid open and her gaze snapped up. Debris was still being cleared away by sets of drones busy at work. The dead had been moved to the back of the bridge, their bodies covered. Serah'Elax's gaze lingered on them for a moment before turning her attention back to the Maidens busy at work preparing the ship for combat. She then moved to the remnants of Ahtlana's command chair and sat down.

"Report!" Her voice was cold.

"We are battle ready, Keeper. Our breaches have been sealed and our shield generators have been repaired. Unnecessary areas have been evacuated and remaining life support systems have been rerouted."

"Take us in."

Serah'Elax watched the holodisplay as the *Rion* slowly made its way into a defensible position near the front. Each avatar was on the frontlines with their respective dreadnaughts, the show of bravery common for Ashna Maiden leaders. That was when she saw it: the formation of enemy ships slowly branching out and extending themselves around the dreadnaughts. The sight began to unsettle her. Her instincts yelled at her as she watched her superiors move deeper and deeper into the pincer. With eyes wide, she attempted to open a channel to Avatar Luka.

The pincer closed.

With sickening efficiency, all the enemy ships attacked with renewed ferocity, moving their dreadnaughts in for the kill as they unleashed devastating barrages on the Ashna Maiden command ships. The powerful beam weapons had been quiet the entire battle, and their first display shattered shields and punched holes through ships. One connected with a reactor core, triggering an explosion that ended the *Gegeyuf*, dreadnaught of the 53rd Fleet. Another devastating barrage tore through the *Yutrea*.

Avatar Luka's voice broadcast to the armada. "Hegna!" The fear in Luka's call to her sister caused all the blood to drain from Serah'Elax's face. Luka's ship split in two. The *Yutrea*'s reactor went critical seconds later in a devastating explosion that lit up the battle-field in a dizzying display.

"Full retreat." Avatar Hegna's voice cracked as she broadcast to the remnants of the armada. Serah'Elax shed a solitary tear and quickly wiped it away with her blood-covered sleeve. A sudden realization hit Serah'Elax with the destruction of the *Yutrea*.

She now commanded the 72nd Fleet.

Pushing down the feeling of disbelief, she immediately began coordinating a full retreat. Over half of the 72nd Fleet was destroyed. The remainder of her forces were in the worst of the fighting, near the remains of the *Yutrea*.

"They're not going to make it," Serah'Elax breathed. "Take us closer to the front!"

"Keeper?"

"If we don't save those ships, they won't escape in time," Serah'Elax clarified. "Prep the suplight drive. I want us ready to go to full suplight on my command." Many stared at her, paralyzed. Her words must have seemed like suicide to them. "Now!" she yelled. The forceful command jolted them into obedience as the carrier headed toward the front.

"Kamikaze the fighters, all of them! Target the ships closest to our retreating sisters!" Serah'Elax ordered. Streams of drone fighters begin to slam into enemy ships. The impacts demolished shields and bored holes into vessels as the enemy ships began to fill up the holodisplay with horrifying explosions. The angry hornet's nest turned its full attention to the *Rion*. Serah'Elax waited for confirmation that the final Maiden vessel had passed by them safely.

"Now!" The *Rion* jumped to suplight, heading in the opposite direction of the rest of the fleet. A full contingent of the enemy fleet broke off in pursuit of the lone carrier.

Rion, Huzien Alliance / Ashna Maiden border

The *Rion* barreled through space in deep suplight, the hum of its powerful drive the only sound throughout the battered bridge. Every gaze was on Serah'Elax. She stood beside Exemplar Ahtlana's command chair—her command chair.

Serah'Elax had no plan.

She hadn't thought out anything past: save ships, jump to suplight—and now they had a fleet of angry ships on their tail. Taking in a long, deep breath, she slowly descended into the command chair. Her gaze remained focused on the holodisplay toward the front of the bridge. Readouts of enemy ship signatures could be seen trailing them, hundreds of the little red beacons staring back at her like beady eyes watching her every move.

"Sisters . . ." Serah'Elax said. She began to strain her mind for a solution to their problem, her lack of experience blatantly apparent in that moment. "We are in a precarious situation. If we drop out of suplight, we die. If we stay in suplight, we'll end up in Huzien space and risk death, or even worse . . ." Serah'Elax paused. "A political fiasco." The mood across the bridge lightened slightly; a few Maidens even cracked smiles.

"What is your plan, Keeper?" Came the bold reply of an older Human Maiden. The woman's blue eyes were sharp.

"I'll be honest with you, sisters; I am not Exemplar Ahtlana. I do not have the experience necessary to come up with a solution to our problem." She pushed herself up from the chair and came to stand next to the older Maiden. "I must ask you all for help. How do we get out of this alive?"

Silence gripped the bridge. Many Maidens looked away, rubbing their arms or the backs of their necks. A few minutes went by; more silence. Some of the Maidens returned to their normal tasks, seeming to forget the request by their keeper.

"I have an idea . . ." the older Maiden said. Her gaze locked with Serah'Elax's.

"Let's hear it, uh . . ." Serah'Elax caught sight of the Maiden's badge identifier, her name appearing in Serah'Elax's micro-display. "Maiden Delira."

"Suplight banking," she responded without hesitation.

"Suplight banking?" Serah'Elax shook her head. "I'm not familiar with that term."

"We don't fully disengage the suplight drives; rather, we force a blip in the system that will bring us out of suplight for a split second. We could, in theory, attempt to angle the ship in such a way that it would put us back on track in the right direction." She paused for a moment as her mind worked. A few other Maidens nodded their heads in sudden understanding and agreement. "We'd probably have to do it a few times, maybe two or three. The calculations would have to be precise; we'd be stressing the SI to make critical decisions in a fraction of a second."

"What do we need in order to do this?" Serah'Elax asked.

"We'd need to shut off all nonessential systems to reduce the load to the SI to allow for the calculations to happen within that time window. We'd also need to program in the blips for the suplight drive and pray to Ashna that it doesn't fully disengage the system."

"Are you confident that this will work?"

"No, but it's all I've got."

Serah'Elax patted Delira on the shoulder and nodded.

"Do it."

The older woman dropped to her station, her holodisplay filling with screens. A few other Maidens moved to assist as they began working on their new plan. The minutes rolled by as Serah'Elax sat deep in silent prayer to the goddess, her heart pounding in her chest.

"We're ready!" Delira called out.

Serah'Elax took in a deep breath. On cue, the lights dimmed aboard the bridge as everything but life support, propulsion, external defenses, and the suplight drive shut off.

"It's your show, ladies," Serah'Elax said.

With a nod, Delira initiated the prescribed program. A countdown appeared on the screen. Every person on the bridge gripped their seat as the timer hit zero. The *Rion* dropped out of suplight for half a second, the propulsion kicking on and spinning the ship slightly while the suplight drive re-engaged.

The enemy ships detected the change and dropped out of suplight before repositioning and resuming their hunt.

The maneuver bought the crew of the *Rion* a few moments against the monsters under their bed. Serah'Elax breathed a sigh of relief; the first blip had gone off without a hitch. Her gaze went to Delira, who glanced back at her, a smile wide on her face.

"Better than expected!" Delira said. "We just need one more and we should be en route to Ashnakev."

Nodding with approval, the newly minted keeper went back to watching the holodisplay as another countdown timer appeared.

"This one is longer?"

"Giving the drive some time to get back into a normal rhythm. Don't want to overstress the system and cause a system failure." Delira took in a deep breath. "That mistake would probably be fatal." Serah'Elax nodded.

When the timer hit ten seconds, every gaze went to Delira, who shuffled nervously and locked eyes with Serah'Elax. Every Maiden was praying to the goddess in that moment, and every gaze was focused on the holodisplay as the timer hit zero. The *Rion* dropped out of suplight, then the drive shut completely off, going into a full systems failure. The crew aboard the bridge exploded into action. There was no room for panic; everyone was at peak focus. Serah'Elax rushed over to Delira, who was frantically working on queueing up commands as the suplight drive system rebooted.

"Four minutes until the system is back up." Delira let out a measured breath.

"Is there anything you can do?" Serah'Elax said, forcing calm into her voice.

"I can throw out the security protocols and force the drive to engage without the control system fully online." Delira began building a separate engage function in the suplight code that would bypass the safeguards. "Of course, we could blow up in the process." Delira glanced at Serah'Elax.

Serah'Elax's gaze jumped to the screen, an engagement timer ticking down, the forces almost on them.

"Do it. Remove the safeguards."

Nodding, Delira engaged her new program. The ship begrudgingly lurched to suplight, warning sounds blaring. Serah'Elax quickly realized that she wasn't the only one holding her breath. The ship experienced a great deal of turbulence as Delira manually controlled it. One small slipup and she would rip the *Rion* apart.

The enemy ships continued to gain on them with the *Rion*'s speed within suplight limited; the core system was holding back the full power of the drive until the main suplight system was fully online. Delira began to transition control of suplight back to the SI as the system finally came back online. The turbulence disappeared and the ship picked up speed. Their route was now true. The enemy forces began falling back, the chase abandoned.

"Thank the goddess!" Serah'Elax smiled at Delira, who smiled back. Then Serah'Elax's eyes closed, and the floor came up to meet her.

The progress of technology helped to equalize power between those who could wield the Enesmic and those who couldn't, with some of the most advanced technologies barely distinguishable from cihphism.

−FROM "EARLIEST INTERACTIONS WITH THE ENESMIC"
BY SHAPER LUKIR AFREV

CHAPTER 20 SEPHAN

Huzien shuttle orbiting Carneth, Ashna Maiden protected space

Bresha's shuttle dropped out of suplight and entered orbit around a small fringe world within the Outer Rim. The planet was unremarkable, with large swathes of desert and small splotches of green visible from orbit. Like many of the planets past the Alliance border, there was an impoverished society on the surface that continuously found themselves besieged by pirates. The shuttle highlighted signs of debris and weapons fire residue on its scanners.

"They've been here recently." Bresha smiled. "Good . . ." A blip on the shuttle's communication console caused Bresha's smile to deepen. She accepted the incoming call and pushed it to a nearby holodisplay, though she muted her video feed. An older Tuzen woman appeared on-screen, her brown eyes narrowed. She wore an Ashna Maiden uniform with a signifier that indicated her as a Maiden protector.

"Alliance vessel, this is Ashna Maiden protected space. Leave immediately or we will open fire."

"Ashna smiles on me today, sister," Bresha replied. The Tuzen women's eyes relaxed, a smile forming on her lips.

"As she does on all of her favored," the woman answered, a hint of surprise in her voice.

"Sister, the goddess has watched over me these past few weeks," Bresha said. "I am favored by your presence here; this ship is in need of repair and I had no choice but to seek refuge on this planet."

"We are intrigued to hear your story. I'm sending you the coordinates of our ship, the *Juyunerga*. You are lucky; we were just ordered to return to Ashnakev. There is a threat that requires all of us, sister."

Bresha locked in the coordinates, and her shuttle began moving to rendezvous with the ship.

She waited patiently for the seal to complete as her shuttle docked with the Ashna Maiden frigate. A final hiss signaled a locked seal as she gave approval for the door to slide open. Within seconds, she was staring at the woman she had spoken with. The Maiden protector looked Bresha up and down.

"Where is your uniform?"

"Long gone, sister." Bresha faked a sad expression, her eyes going distant.

"I am curious to hear more of your story. Please, rest on my ship."

"Will we be returning to a nearby fleet?"

"No, we are on our own." A sad expression crossed the woman's face. "Our primary fleet was sent to assist in the attack against the alien fleet at our borders. Most of our sisters did not survive."

Bresha walked into the main hallway leading away from her shuttle. "How many sisters do we have here?" she asked.

"About two hundred," the Maiden protector replied.

They entered a meglift. After giving a few seconds for everyone to file in, the door closed, and it began to rise toward the bridge. Bresha smiled. Strands of Enesmic power shook the meglift, and the system issued a warning sound as the energy flowed around Bresha in torrents. Motioning with both of her hands outward, bands of razor-sharp energy flew out from her, spinning in a controlled fury. The attack was so violent and quick that none had registered it before their lives were snuffed out.

The meglift opened to the bridge, and Sephan stepped out of the gore-stained metal box. Gasps went up from across the bridge. They all stared at the macabre, blood- and gore-covered figure walking toward them. Before the bridge crew could react, Sephan motioned forward, and the bands of death continued their relentless assault. Within seconds, every member of the bridge crew, except one woman, was a pile of ruined flesh. Sephan smiled at the carnage, the smell of blood pleasing to its senses.

The lone woman, a ship navigator, stared at Bresha. Her eyes were wide, and her body quivered. Sephan tilted its head. A telepathic barrage unlike anything the poor woman had ever experienced destroyed her mind. Her thoughts were shattered as Sephan dominated her consciousness. The Eshgren ordered her to set a course for what it assumed to be Jughent's fleet, the former Overlord who had served Sagren most likely the commander of the alien vessels the Maiden protector had mentioned. Within seconds, the ship entered suplight. Bresha's mobi brought up a schematic of the *Juyunerga* as Sephan turned around and went back into the meglift. The Eshgren had a ship to clear.

A sole unnoticed tear began to roll down Bresha's cheek as the meglift door closed.

CHAPTER 21 NEVEN KENK

MinSci, Thae, Huzien home system

*T**ime to get up,** the now familiar voice of Ellipse said into Neven's mind. He rubbed the sleep from his eyes, a yawn escaping his lips. *Please don't fall out of the couch again.*

Neven caught himself as he started pushing off from the sofa, his surroundings coming into focus. Neven smiled. He was home in his own house for once. Stretching, Neven made his way to the kitchen as the smell of fresh-cooked eggs and toast greeted him. A cup of orange juice and an apple sat next to the plate on his Omn-fridge counter.

"Thanks, Ellipse." Neven moved to grab the food and sat down at his table.

I figured you'd be hungry. The apple was to appease your mother.

Neven laughed.

He stared at the plate, considering the newfound budding relationship with the SSI now living within his mobi and brain. The strangeness of their interactions was quickly fading, and Neven was coming to rely on Ellipse more and more. It was as if the SSI were an extension of his own mind. Sure, that's what mobis were supposed to be anyway, but this was different. Ellipse knew everything about him and could make decisions for him; the two were in perfect sync.

You'll probably be getting a call from Lanrete shortly.

Neven's ears perked up.

"Why is that? I'm on vacation for another few weeks," Neven asked out loud. He was still not used to mental communication with Ellipse.

The Empress Star *has gone missing, I saw the report come in over the HIN this morning.*

"Since when do you have access to the Huzien Intelligence Network?"

Since we interfaced, I have access to everything you have access to.

"I see . . ." His eyes went wide, the fork dropping from his hand. "Wait, was that the ship Zun was on?"

Yes.

"Oh no . . ." His mind raced, thoughts of safety for his new girlfriend at the forefront.

Speak of the devil . . . Ellipse said. Neven's mobi blipped. Neven accepted the call on his kitchen holodisplay and Lanrete appeared, his face grim.

"Vacation's been cut short, we leave today." Lanrete seemed to register the sight of Neven in his underclothes. "Sorry if I woke you."

Neven shook his head.

"*Empress Star?*" Neven asked, which prompted Lanrete to raise a curious eyebrow. "Is the *Ascension* still being retrofitted?" Neven started to move toward his bedroom, instantly prepping his Vencom rinse chamber. A drone began prepping his Founder's Elite uniform on his bed.

"Yes. I've arranged for another ship to provide transport. We'll be taking the *Foundra Conscient*."

"The *Foundra Conscient?*" Neven echoed. "That's Founder Ecnics's ship!"

Lanrete smirked.

"I'm aware. I'll meet you there. Military transport should be arriving within the hour."

Lanrete terminated the connection as Neven stripped. Stepping into his bathroom, he caught sight of himself in the mirror. He had six-pack abs for the first time in his life, and the rest of his body was chiseled with well-toned muscles. Ellipse growled in his ear, making Neven crack an embarrassed smile.

"Stop doing that."

I can't help it that you're an irresistible hunk, she said, a hint of playfulness in her voice.

"I guess the brutal training regimen and having Tenett as a personal chef on the *Ascension* really does pay off." He shook his head and stepped into the VRC. The powerful jets started to cleanse his body, the cycle completing within a few minutes. Neven emerged completely dry, and a pleasing scent reminiscent of a tropical rainforest filled the air. After pulling on his Founder's Elite uniform, Neven grabbed his mobi from his old shirt and slipped it into his collar. A sigh escaped his lips as he walked out of his bedroom. He took in what he assumed would be the last view of his home for the foreseeable future.

Transport is here. The doorbell to his home rang in sync with his mobi.

"Guess that's the end of my vacation." Neven made his way to the door.

The *Foundra Conscient* came into view as the military transport dropped out of suplight. Neven, one of only a handful of people on the dropship, was tightly strapped to one of the many chairs lining the surprisingly large interior of the unassuming vessel. The dropship SI began linking up with the *Conscient*'s docking systems. Through the dropship's window, Neven could make out the details of the *Conscient*. The sleek black vessel was accented by tinges of silver, and was of a drastically different design when compared with the *Foundra Ascension*. Ecnics's ship was larger, with more attention given to function over form.

He could tell that the *Conscient* had the feel of a science vessel as opposed to a military ship. Although, looking at the schematics in his micro-display, he surmised that Founder Ecnics's ship could still hold its own in a fight. Within a few minutes, the transport docked in one of the many bays lining the side of the *Conscient*. The moment the ship touched down, the suplight drive of the *Conscient* kicked on.

After unstrapping himself, Neven rushed out of the transport and caught sight of Lanrete waiting for him in the shuttle bay. The dark grey esha marks lining the sides of Lanrete's face seemed to tense at the sight of Neven.

"Have you heard any word from Zun?" Neven stopped in front of Lanrete. He was searching his mentor's face for any hint of news.

"Nothing." Lanrete turned and began walking out of the shuttle bay. "We've been unable to get in contact with anyone."

"Is this the work of Sagren's forces?"

"Unlikely. It's possible pirates may be involved."

"Pirates?"

"Yes." Lanrete sighed. "We've received reports of unidentified ships in that area. It's far from the Outer Rim, but not as heavily policed due to the lack of major colonies in that part of space. That would also explain the lack of contact; pirates are known for deploying mobi scramblers."

"What's the plan?"

Ellipse started to feed Neven information. Details on pirate activity and the history of the area filled his backlog of items to get caught up on.

"We investigate." Lanrete and Neven entered a meglift. Both stood in silence for a few moments as the meglift accelerated toward the bridge. Neven glanced at Lanrete, who was staring intently at the meglift door.

"Are you worried about the team?" The soft hum of the meglift provided a somber ambiance.

"About six highly trained and lethal killing machines?" Lanrete shook his head. "No, I'm worried about the prospect of pirates openly attacking and kidnapping Alliance citizens in Alliance space. I've been too lax in our management of the Outer Rim and the threats on our borders." Lanrete locked gazes with Neven. "This is my fault." The meglift door opened, and the founder exited. Neven watched him for a moment before following, his hand rubbing the back of his neck.

FOUNDERS LOG:
Burden of Leadership

Billions of people strive for positions of leadership, many without knowing the costs of such a mantle. They fawn over the prestige and power, and indeed, many leadership roles come with substantial benefits. However, very few truly grasp what it means to be a leader. I faced that harsh reality early in my life. I did not want to be a leader; it was a mantle that was thrust upon me. A weight dropped onto the shoulders of Cislot, Ecnics, and me. All we wanted was an end to the war.

The Huzien leadership had faltered, our nation was in disarray, and there was no safety, no hope. That was the beginning of our story; the situation that enabled our ascension as founders. We were molded in the fire of death and bloodshed, hardened in the ice-cold rain of sorrow and loss. That was not what I had intended for my life. Before the war that tore my world apart, I was a professor. I taught others and lived the life of an educator, an academic. For forty years, I trained what I believed to be the next generation of philosophers and strategists and taught them military history, one of my passions. But then they became soldiers.

I was around two hundred years old when I met Semaje Traet . . . the man who would become Ecnics. He was a widely known immortal, a rarity even in that day and age. He was over one thousand years old and yet . . . looked as old as I did. He was also a professor, and he was phenomenal, a legend. Then we met, and he was just a man.

We lost many colleagues in the first attack, the spark that started the war. Overnight, our lives were changed. Dahca Resif—Cislot—the war was the last thing she wanted. Her job up to that point had been as an ambassador to the Tuzen nation. That attack destroyed any chance of peace ever existing between our peoples.

How little time changes things. Leadership was the only way we could survive. Our nation was in shambles, our people leaderless. I truly do not believe that the Huzien Empire would exist today if we had not risen to the challenge. It was only because of our unique circumstances, only because *of our shared immortality, that we were able to rally the people to our cause and endure the thousand-year war. We were viewed as divine! Viewed as angels of war sent in a time of need. Our backgrounds became myth, our trivial lives before nothing but rumors and stories of the impossible. I did not want it. Ecnics did not want it. Cislot did not want it. But we took it. We put on the mantle of leadership because it was necessary—because we wanted to survive.*

-Lanrete

Telepathy utilizes the Enesmic to directly control and influence aspects of the mind, including mind reading, thought implantation, direct communication, and will domination.

–FROM "SCHOOLS OF CIHPHISM"

BY SHAPER LUKIR AFREV

CHAPTER 22 JESSICA OLIC

Empress Star, Huzien Alliance space

J essica Olic stared at the sparkling glass cup on the rim of her Jacuzzi as jazz music played in the background. The powerful jets massaged every inch of her body with streams of water that caused her to moan occasionally. Steam rose to the vents around her quarters, the suite massive and featuring decorations of ancient Huzien gods from an era long ago in erotic poses with enticing smiles. Lifting the glass cup, she swirled the golden liquid around a few times before bringing it to her lips and taking a sip, then closed her eyes and leaned back, her smile deepening as she sank into the bubbling waters. The doorbell to her quarters blipped, prompting her to open a single eye. Closing it again, she took in a deep breath and sunk deeper into the Jacuzzi. The doorbell sounded again.

Jessica sighed and sat up, pausing the Jacuzzi's program and killing the music.

"Who is it?" she said, speaking through her mobi. *Network Unavailable* came back to her in her micro-display, prompting a frustrated sigh. The mobi network had been out of commission for the past four days; even the short-range functionality was not working.

That had been the one mark on an otherwise perfect vacation. Pushing herself up and out of the Jacuzzi, Jessica dried off and pulled on a large fluffy red robe with a small reproduction of the *Empress Star* across the back. Moving to the door, she opened it and was greeted by dead air.

Jessica gingerly stepped out and glanced down both sides of the hallway. Not a person was in sight. Scratching her head, she moved back into her room and closed her door. She began to undo her robe, turning around and allowing it to tumble to the floor en route to her Jacuzzi. A catcall from near her bed stopped her heart. She exploded into motion, rushing to her robe and pulling it on.

"You're a horrible person!" Jessica yelled.

Dexter uncloaked near her bed. He stared at her with a smirk. "I was right; you do have perfect breasts."

"*Vusg* you, get out!" Jessica's face reddened, her voice cold as she moved toward the door.

"Calm down! I came here for a *vusging* reason." Dexter moved to intercept Jessica. Two hard strikes hit Dexter faster than he could block. The impacts sent him back a step, his armor absorbing most of the kinetic energy. Jessica planted her front foot on the ground with a resounding stomp and angled her back foot to the side. Dexter clearly recognized the pose, as he lifted his hands high into the air. "Wait, wait!" Jessica's glare caused Dexter to take another step back.

"It better be a *vusging* good reason." Her irises had already morphed to fire red.

"Pirates have the ship," Dexter said. "I've confirmed that they are in complete control."

"Pirates?" For the first time, Jessica noticed Dexter's Sentinel armor.

"They took down the mobi network and have stationed men posing as security all throughout the ship."

"That explains the sudden uptick in lewd comments, gawking, and aggressiveness from the security personnel." Jessica frowned. "What's the plan?" She moved to grab her clothes and headed into the bathroom.

"We take the *vusging* armory."

"Does anyone else know?"

"You're the first."

"Okay, let's find Marcus."

Jessica stepped out of the bathroom in a skintight jumpsuit, the suit designed more for use with her combat armor—which was currently in the armory—than for regular wear. Dexter's gaze lingered on her form before his eyes slowly drifted up to meet hers. Anger flashed across her face. Dexter shrugged, glanced away, and moved toward the door as she glared at him.

"Ready?"

"It's in your best interest to forget what I look like naked." There was an edge in her voice. Dexter's back straightened.

"Yes, ma'am."

Dexter and Jessica hurriedly walked down the hall toward Marcus's quarters.

"Fifty-fifty chance they are here. Either that or the pool deck," Jessica whispered. Dexter stopped them both with a hand signal and motioned down the hall before leading them up to the wall, out of sight.

"We have a sentry," Dexter relayed via hand signals.

"Follow my lead," Jessica silently relayed back. She grabbed his hand and led them out into the center of the hallway.

"I don't know if I want to go to the pool today . . . maybe tomorrow," Jessica said loudly.

Dexter had already enabled the camouflage on his armor, and plain clothes were holographically projected over the armor, which had physically morphed to match the texture and feel of the clothes.

"Oh, come on, we didn't go yesterday because you wanted to go *vusging* shopping! I paid for this cruise so I could spend my days at the *vusging* pool!"

The guard heard them down the hallway and glanced in their direction. He sized up Dexter, lost interest, then glanced to Jessica and grinned before proceeding to ignore them. The guard's gaze was fixed on Marcus's room, though he occasionally glanced to the meg-lift at the other end of the hallway.

"Fine! We'll go to the stupid pool," Jessica replied. Jessica let go of Dexter's hand as they passed the guard. She brought her knee hard into the guard's stomach, knocking the wind out of him. Not giving him time to react, she kicked off the ground and slammed her other knee into his chin. Jessica, now in the air, quickly wrapped her legs around his neck. In one fluid motion, she brought them to the ground, flexing her leg muscles as they hit the floor. A snap echoed throughout the hallway, and the guard's body went limp. Jessica glanced over to Dexter, who stood watching her, a grin on his face.

She glared at him.

Dexter frowned, rolling his eyes.

Cihphists specializing in telepathy, or telepaths, are heavily relied upon in negotiations, peace talks, and other forms of high stakes discussion, with many telepaths finding themselves involved in corporations or galactic politics.

–FROM "SCHOOLS OF CIHPHISM"
BY SHAPER LUKIR AFREV

CHAPTER 23   MARCUS HENSON

Empress Star, Huzien Alliance space

The sounds of people enjoying themselves in the massive pool at the top of the Empress Star acted like a soothing melody to Marcus as the giant of a man relaxed on a reclined deck chair. Every day, he found himself coming to the same spot, his wife joining him as they de-stressed at the poolside. His shirt was off and to the side, his hulking chest bare as he lay in the artificial sunlight. A young boy glanced at him while pulling himself out of the pool, his gaze sticking on Marcus's mammoth-sized arms, each one the size of the boy's entire body.

Opening one eye, Marcus caught sight of the boy, and their gazes met. Marcus cracked a smile. The young boy, caught in his staring, quickly returned the smile, then went darting off to jump into the pool. Marcus's gaze shifted farther to the side, catching a security guard eyeing him. The smile on Marcus's face vanished as the guard averted his gaze and pretended to survey the rest of the pool.

"Guards still eyeing you?" Arnea asked.

"Same ones, cycling shifts, always on my tail." Marcus let out a sigh. He sat up in his chair and scratched the stubble on his face.

He then slowly pushed himself up to his full height, a quick set of stretches flexing his muscles. The gazes of more than a few women went in his direction, young and old alike fawning over the picture of brawn. Arnea flashed him a confident smile and took in the sight of her husband, her gaze calming his mind. He walked over to her chair and kneeled at her side.

"Tired of the pool already?"

"Nah." Marcus smiled. "Just think I'll go for a walk."

Arnea frowned.

"Please don't get us kicked off of this ship, my dear husband."

Marcus let out a mock gasp.

"Never!"

She leaned up in her seat and kissed him on the lips. Arnea held the kiss for a long moment, her hand coming up to rub the side of Marcus's face.

"You should keep stubble more often."

Marcus put his hand to hers and then stood up, his gaze momentarily going to the guard now trying to hide from his view. After walking over to grab his shirt, Marcus pulled it on and headed toward the exit.

A large walking track circled the top of the *Empress Star*. There was a water park at its center with a multitude of activity hubs littered across the deck. Marcus's enhanced vision could easily pick up the reflection of the guard tailing him, the superhuman sight a remnant from his extensive genetic modifications as part of the Archlight program.

Frowning, Marcus continued along the track, eventually finding his way to a secluded area with no other people around. Escaping the guard's line of sight, Marcus broke off into a sprint to a nearby maintenance hub and positioned himself in a good ambush spot. The guard soon came rushing into the area, and Marcus moved to block the exit.

"I take it you have a good reason for tailing me these past few days," Marcus said.

The guard glared at Marcus and moved his hand to his side, fingering what Marcus assumed was a firearm.

"Now, you should have known better than to assault a security guard." The man sighed. He drew his gun, shaking his head. "I warned you to stop, multiple times, but you had a crazed look in your eyes." The guard smiled. "I had no choice but to put you down."

He started to level his gun at Marcus's head, but was too slow. Marcus covered the distance in the blink of an eye, his speed superhuman. He slammed shoulder first into the guard's midsection, bone crunching as the guard's spine snapped at the impact. A shot went off that hit the nearby wall. Marcus grabbed the man's head with one mammoth hand and slammed it down onto the ground. The powerful motion caved in the man's skull, splattering blood across the floor. Marcus inspected the body and sucked in a quick breath when he discovered several tattoos and brands.

"Het Wrast Aht . . ." Marcus swore as he grabbed the body and moved it to a nearby trash chute, dislocating joints to get it down quickly. He used the man's shirt to clean up as much of the blood as he could, then grabbed the firearm and slid it into his swim trunks, covering it with his shirt. He quickly made his way back to Arnea.

"We need to go."

Arnea glared at her husband.

"You killed him, didn't you?"

"Go. Now." Marcus's voice was deathly calm as he began to grab their belongings.

Arnea quietly obeyed, shuffling through the exit and toward the meglift, Marcus right behind her.

Marcus and Arnea were nearly sprinting to their quarters when they caught sight of Dexter and Jessica waiting near their door. Marcus couldn't help but smile. The mobi network outage had heightened the tenseness of the situation, and without uttering a word, Marcus opened the door. All of them filed inside. As the door slid shut, Marcus collapsed onto the couch near the massive window to his suite. The ceiling-to-floor glass provided a clear view into outer space. Arnea moved to stand next to the bathroom door, silently watching her husband.

Jessica and Dexter glanced at each other as if prompting the other to speak up first. Jessica frowned, then moved to drop onto the couch next to Marcus. "We have some bad news."

"Let me guess," Marcus said. "Het Wrast Aht?"

Jessica glanced to Dexter before turning her gaze back to Marcus.

"Yes. Dexter has confirmed that they have taken control of the ship."

"Great." Marcus shook his head. "So, the mobi network?"

"Taken down by them," Dexter confirmed. "They set up *vusging* scramblers to prevent short-range broadcasts. That's why we can't communicate over our secure channel."

"Have you gotten in contact with Zun, Tashanira, or Jenshi?"

"No, we came straight to you," Jessica replied.

Marcus broke eye contact with Jessica and looked over at his wife. It was hard to read her in that moment. Her gaze was intense, but Marcus detected no fear or panic in her eyes. His gaze shifted to Dexter.

"They were watching my room?" he asked. Dexter nodded. "They are looking for me. I killed one of the guards they had tailing me."

"Two of their guards," Jessica said.

Marcus laughed.

"We should move as a group," Marcus said. "Find Zun and then head to Tashanira and Jenshi's room."

"It's too risky for all of us to move together," Dexter interjected. "Especially with you already on their radar. We should hit the armory first, get our weapons."

"And what happens if all-out war breaks out?" Marcus countered. "It would be better if we were all together."

"I agree with Marcus." Jessica stood up from the couch. Her gaze shifted from Marcus to Arnea. "But before all that, we need a place we can establish as our base of command. A place that serves as our fallback point."

"My room," Dexter said.

"Ha, the last thing we need is one of your sluts showing up to our hideout looking for a good time with a guard tailing her," Jessica quipped.

Dexter began to respond, then stopped. Marcus eyed him curiously. With an annoyed sigh, Dexter shook his head and crossed his arms as Jessica glared at him.

"What happened between you two?" Marcus asked.

Both turned to Marcus with wide eyes.

"Uh ... it's nothing," Jessica responded.

"I *vusging* saw her naked and she threatened my life after I gave her a compliment," Dexter countered.

Jessica fixed Dexter with a wicked glare as Marcus raised an eyebrow, glancing from Jessica to Dexter.

"Explain." Marcus clenched his jaw.

"It was an accident," Dexter relented. "Don't we have better things to focus our attention on? Like, oh I don't know, the *vusging* pirates that are in complete control of this ship?"

After eyeing Dexter for a long moment, Marcus let out a sigh and stood up. He began to stretch his back.

"I'm making an executive decision on this one," Marcus said. "Jessica's quarters will be our fallback point. Arnea will gather some supplies for use in an emergency should we need them." Marcus glanced over to Jessica. "Jessica, you go with Arnea and help her get situated in your quarters. We'll meet up with you after we retrieve the others." His gaze shifted to Dexter. "You and I will move together to find the rest of our team." Jessica and Dexter nodded in agreement. "Let's move!"

CHAPTER 24 ZUN SHAN

Empress Star, Huzien Alliance space

Zun walked out onto the observation deck at the back of the Empress Star, a towel around her waist. She had just spent the past half hour in a private Jacuzzi, and a sigh of contentment escaped her lips as she watched the stars speed by, the sight breathtaking.

"Oh Neven, I wish you were here," Zun said.

"That yer boyfriend?"

The voice startled her. She turned to see a man in a security uniform standing a few feet away. The glaring face tattoo immediately put her on edge.

"Yeah, you could say that." She quickly got a read of the area; no one else was in sight. "Things quiet on your patrol?"

"Yeah, until I ran into a sexy *cusshin* girl all alone." The derogatory term used to refer to her as a Huzien half-breed caused Zun to frown.

"Ah, well . . . have a good night. I have some friends waiting for me." Zun began to move toward the exit. He stepped to block her path, flashing his holstered firearm.

"They can wait." The guard advanced toward her.

Zun feigned a smile. "Well, let me get rid of this towel then." Zun pulled off her towel, her blue bikini bottom now visible.

The guard let out a whistle.

She threw the towel into his face, and the guard cursed and drew his weapon. Zun was at his side in an instant, her knee coming up into his crotch. Balling both her fists together, she hammer struck the back of his neck. The attack knocked him to the ground, his weapon dropping to the floor.

Enesmic energy swirled around Zun, and she snapped her fingers. Immediately, intense flames engulfed the man, his screams filling the air as the flames rapidly devoured his flesh. Within seconds, a charred husk was all that remained. Ignoring the scent of burned flesh, Zun scooped up his weapon and sprinted out of the observation deck back into the Jacuzzi area to grab another towel.

While tying it around her waist, she heard running footsteps. She glanced out the door and saw two guards with similar tattoos examining the body.

"Lock the area down. Hetye is dead." Both guards covered their noses.

"Looks like the bastard took his gun too."

"Spread out; they're probably still in the area. Shoot first, ask questions later. We're dealing with a cihphist."

Zun retreated inside, holding her breath as she glanced around. Her eyes stopped on the sign for the mechanical room for the Jacuzzi system. Making her way to the door, she attempted a military override, but it locked her out. She grabbed another towel, covered the muzzle of the weapon, and aimed it toward the locking mechanism, then began to weave more Enesmic energy to create a sound-dampening field around her. Diverting her eyes, she fired a shot. The sound was muffled, but still too loud for her liking.

"Over here!"

Zun pressed her body against the door and began to slide it open. After moving inside, she closed it and tapped into the Enesmic flow once again, igniting a portion of the door and fusing the metal shut. Turning around, she saw a host of mechanical equipment with a crew entrance on the other side of the room.

She tried her override on the crew entrance again with no luck. Repeating her actions with the first door, she moved through and found herself in the primary engineering bay of the *Empress Star*. A multitude of drones were at work performing routine maintenance. Zun sprinted toward a nearby meglift, then climbed up it and tore off a panel to reveal emergency controls. She brought up a schematic of the ship from the resident memory on her mobi. Highlighting the armory in her HUD, she summoned a meglift and hit the cargo bay button, jumping inside as the doors closed shut.

CHAPTER 25 JENSHI RUNSO

Empress Star, Huzien Alliance space

Tashanira moaned softly as she guided her hips down onto Jenshi. Jenshi watched her in a trance as her body moved rhythmically, her motions precise and controlled. Her hands rested in the center of his chest while he held her hips in a haze of pleasure. She stared at him with a soft smile, her half-closed eyes hypnotizing him and her spicy scent filling his nostrils. Jenshi worshiped the goddess atop him.

A pounding at the door momentarily snapped Jenshi from the moment. He glanced in the direction of the sound and then back to Tashanira.

"Ignore it," she whispered.

Jenshi grunted in acknowledgement. Tashanira continued as if nothing had happened. The pounding came again, this time more forceful. The muffled sound of Marcus's voice came through the door. Tashanira stopped, coming to rest on Jenshi's pelvis as she glared in the direction of the door. Her gaze slowly dropped to Jenshi, annoyance dripping from her like sweat. Jenshi let out a disapproving moan.

The pounding came again, this time even louder, and they could both hear Marcus shouting.

"*Vusg!*" Jenshi shouted back. "Give us a minute!" Jenshi began a bout of profanity so profound that Tashanira smirked. She got off him, sliding to the floor with the grace of a dancer. Light on her toes, she twirled past Jenshi as he grabbed a pair of pants and made his way to the entrance of their presidential suite.

"This better be *vusging* good!" Jenshi got to the door and opened it.

Marcus and Dexter burst into the room, pushing Jenshi out of the way. Dexter glanced back out into the hallway before sealing the door shut. Jenshi eyed both men with a raised eyebrow as Dexter and Marcus let out a collective sigh.

"What's happened?" Jenshi asked.

Tashanira walked out into the living room in one of Jenshi's shirts. It barely covered her hips as she leaned up against a nearby wall. Dexter glanced at her, his gaze dropping to her inner thighs and the signs of moisture there on the unfurred skin, her fine mixed black and white fur present on her outer thighs, legs, and feet. Jenshi's shirt stuck to the sweat of her unfurred stomach, her nipples pressed up against the material. Tashanira's yellow feline-esque gaze locked on Dexter as she smirked and raised an eyebrow. Dexter glanced back to Jenshi, who was glaring at him. Marcus cleared his throat.

"We have a situation," Marcus said.

"Het Wrast Aht has taken the ship." Dexter crossed his arms.

"*Vusging ciths!* When?" Jenshi said.

"Not sure, but they have complete control."

"Is everyone safe?" Tashanira asked.

"Arnea is with Jessica," Marcus said. "They are heading to her quarters to establish a base of command. We couldn't find Zun. We broke into her quarters, but she hadn't been there for some time. Dexter left a coded message for her to meet at our base of command."

"What's the plan?" Tashanira responded.

"Rendezvous at base of command, hit armory, retake ship," Dexter said.

"Definitely a plan." Jenshi let out a slow breath. "Now, as to the merits of whether it's a good plan . . ."

"Babe, where's your spirit of adventure?" Tashanira turned around, pulling Jenshi's shirt off and exposing her bare butt and furred back as she headed into the bedroom. Dexter watched her leave, her tail curling around her leg. Jenshi cleared his throat, prompting Dexter to inspect the ceiling.

"We don't have many options," Marcus said. "They've taken out communications and have scramblers set up. We have to act before this ship winds up in the Outer Rim."

"You think the *vusgers* will honestly try and make a break for it?" Jenshi asked.

"They already have." Dexter met his gaze. "They changed our course a few days ago. It's hard to estimate how long, but if I had to guess, I would say it's about a week max before we cross the border."

Jenshi's face became a stoic mask.

"I'll get changed."

Cihphists specializing in telekinesis, or shifters, have some of the most practical abilities in all of cihphism. These include remotely moving objects, shifting their bodies to incredible speeds, and even halting projectiles, allowing for a wide range of commercial and military applications.

–FROM "SCHOOLS OF CIHPHISM"
BY SHAPER LUKIR AFREV

CHAPTER 26 BRIME WEWTA

Aheraneth, Enesmic plane

B rime took in a deep breath as she began to focus her mind, trying to fall into the meditative techniques that Soahc had taught her early in her apprenticeship. With her eyes closed, she focused on the Enesmic flow, the forces around her powerful. The impassive ebb and flow she had become accustomed to on the Havin plane was instead a continual torrent of powerful energy all around her. She sat with her legs crossed in the center of a large bed. The sheets were of the same material as the silken one she had woken up on during her first encounter with the Rel Ach'Kel.

The beings had neglected to provide her with clothing, but she had learned to cope. Brime was obsessed with regaining control over her cihphistic abilities, and had spent her every waking moment on a mundanely simple task that was now out of her grasp. From an early age, she had been able to manifest her cihphistic abilities. It was something she had always had, and now she couldn't even create a glowing orb of light.

Brime whimpered, her hands flopping to her sides. Taking in a deep breath, she went back to performing the simple motions with her hands. Again.

The forces struggled against her as she sought to bend them to her will, trying with all her might to manipulate the flow. She latched on to one of the strands of power flowing around her and attempted to force it to create light. A struggle ensued as the incredible power became violent, primal.

Then nothing.

Brime gave up and began to weep. She fell back onto the bed, her body crashing into the sheets and curling up into a fetal position.

Augrashumen materialized next to the bed, the regal being standing quietly as it observed Brime for a few moments.

"The flow does not function here as it does in the Havin plane," Augrashumen stated.

Brime sat up and scooted back in the bed, her eyes wide. Recognizing the being, her gaze softened.

"You know, where I'm from, it's polite to knock," Brime said.

"My apologies." Augrashumen dipped its hooded head in a slight bow as it stood quietly for a few moments. Brime watched the being, its hooded gaze locked with hers.

"What's under the hood?"

Augrashumen's flaring eyes rose slightly, as if the being were smiling at her comment.

"My essence," Augrashumen said. "Nothing that you would recognize as a face or head."

"Ah," Brime sighed. "That's disappointing."

Augrashumen moved away from her bed, turned its back to her as it walked toward the center of the large room that had become Brime's temporary home, and raised its hand. The Rel Ach'Kel then summoned an orb of light, which hovered beside it.

"You must not seek to control the flow." Augrashumen turned to regard Brime. "The Enesmic that you are familiar with is a trickle that seeps from our plane of existence. We opened that doorway hundreds of thousands of years ago after Sagren almost wiped out life on the Havin plane. We deemed it necessary to give Havins a chance to defend themselves against Enesmic beings." The Rel Ach'Kel turned fully to face Brime, allowing the orb to dissipate. "Your kind seek to force the Enesmic to bend to your will." Augrashumen shook its head. "That is not how it was intended, and is a corruption of the gift."

"I don't understand." Brime stared at Augrashumen like a child who had just been rebuked.

"The Enesmic is the essence of life, of power. Through it, the Havin plane—and many other planes—have come to exist. There is much that I cannot tell you." Augrashumen abruptly stopped speaking and seemed to consider its next words carefully. "In order to manipulate the Enesmic, you must embrace the flow and understand its rhythm. You must work with it to accomplish your goals, not against it. Open your eyes!"

Augrashumen lifted its gauntleted hand. A veil seemed to lift from Brime's eyes as she once again saw the Enesmic flow all around her. Amazed, she observed the flow as if for the first time. *I can hear it!* Her eyes went wide as she listened to the Enesmic whispers, the flow of the energy around her singing a beautiful song. She closed her eyes, her mind engulfed in the lovely melody.

Slowly, she moved from the bed, her body responding to the joy in the song. She reached out her hand and for the first time, touched the Enesmic flow. She didn't grab hold of it or attempt to bend it to her will; no, she merely touched it. Tingles spread throughout her body as she felt the flow embrace her, and a smile crested her lips as ecstasy coursed through her veins. Brime was unable to contain her joy as the Enesmic force noticed her for the first time, the essence of it regarding her fully. It began to flow in and through her, the Enesmic now alive within her as her soul joined in the song. Augrashumen smiled.

Brime spoke to the Enesmic, not physically, but in a way that transcended normal speech. It listened to her, its flow moving *with* her as her hand rose into the air. An orb of light formed exactly where she had intended. It grew in brightness and intensity, unlike any orb of light she had ever before created, until she could no longer look at it. Brime thanked the Enesmic forces, then severed the link fueling the manifestation. It blinked out of existence in a heartbeat.

The Enesmic continued to flow through her body, now truly one with her. Brime's eyes opened, her irises now a perfect mix of brown and silver, the two entwined so naturally that it could have been how she was born.

Brime began to walk toward Augrashumen, her hands moving subtly in another act of cihphism. She spoke a word of power, not at the Enesmic, but with it, and the flow began singing the word in a chorus. Around her, an elaborate white and red robe was made manifest. The material was like the silken sheet she had rested on, with glittering precious metals adorning various areas. A pair of gem-encrusted sandals formed around her feet as she came to a stop directly in front of the towering Rel Ach'Kel.

"Impressive," Augrashumen said.

"I merely did as you instructed," Brime replied.

Augrashumen nodded as it silently observed the woman, the expression on her face relaxed.

"I must take my leave. I will report your progress to the council." Augrashumen bowed, and in the blink of an eye was gone.

Brime looked around, her mind reaching out to see if the being was still around her. Satisfied it wasn't, she moved back to her bed and sat down, expanding her mind. She focused her thoughts and embraced the Enesmic once more, pleading her case as her hands moved rapidly. As if accepting her plea, she felt her mind rushing on the flow of the Enesmic out toward the Havin plane and felt the familiarity of her former home. A severe longing welled up inside of her, but she pushed it down. This exercise had a purpose, and she wouldn't squander her opportunity.

Continuing to reach out, the Enesmic guided her to Reath—to Etan Rachnie. She found the path to her and Soahc's home. Brime opened her eyes. Next to her was a window into the Havin plane, directly into Soahc's bedchambers. She watched him sleep, a soft smile on her face. Longing filled her heart, urging her to step through the window and appear by his side, to move into his arms and let him know that she was there. She took a step toward the window.

The Enesmic pushed her back, the whispers crying out in warning. She nodded in understanding, a tear rolling down her cheek. Reaching out with her mind, she touched the dreams of Soahc. She kissed him there, embracing him and holding him tightly.

"I'm alive!" Brime yelled. The words came out in a subtle whisper. Soahc stared at Brime, confusion filling his face. "My love, I'm on the Enesmic plane!" Brime yelled again. As Soahc stirred, the window to the Havin plane was forcefully shut, and Brime fell back in confusion. The Enesmic returned to normal, but there was something different in its song. She sensed fear. The strange feeling faded, and the song returned to normal.

CHAPTER 27 SOAHC

Etan Rachnie, Reath, Huzien Alliance space

Soahc awoke with a start, sweat beading down his face. On instinct, he jumped out of bed and ran through the doors to his balcony as his gaze swept the surrounding area. He had just felt Brime's presence; he was sure of it. He stood panting, his hands gripping the marble banister as he slowly turned his gaze up to the night sky. After a long moment, he let out a heavy sigh, walked back into his room, and sat on the corner of his bed, resting his head in his hands.

He lifted his head and glanced to a spot above his bed, something caught by his subconscious.

"An echo?" Soahc moved toward the remnants of a powerful act of cihphism. His eyes went wide as the echo began to rapidly deconstruct. He reached out and took hold of an Enesmic strand, attempting to examine it. The strand and all traces of the echo faded from existence before his eyes. He took a step back. "How is that possible?" Soahc sat back down on the bed, his mind racing. "A dream, what was the dream!" Soahc closed his eyes, trying to force his brain to recall the traces of the dream fading from his memory.

Images returned like a flood as Brime appeared, her body whole. He gasped, the crystal-clear image causing him to tear up. She was speaking to him, her lips moving in silence. Soahc struggled to remember what it was she had said to him. He grasped at the far reaches of his mind, commanding his body to obey him, to give him what he desired. Two words resonated, the sounds matching to Brime's lips as he suddenly heard them loud and clear. *Enesmic plane.*

"Brime is alive!" Soahc yelled. He stood in an elaborate robe, strands of Enesmic energy woven into the material itself. Streaks of purplish-white energy arced occasionally at his movements. Soahc, Narmo Swela, Merbi Teral, and Ristolte Aris III stood in the living area within Soahc's mansion a short distance outside of Etan Rachnie's campus grounds.

"Soahc." Narmo walked over to Soahc and put his dark red hand on his shoulder. The tall Vempiir's crystalline gaze held him. "I understand that this is a difficult time . . ."

Soahc brushed Narmo's hand away. "I am not losing my sanity; I felt the weaving of Enesmic energy in my room. I heard her words in my dream. She told me to come to the Enesmic plane, I'm sure of it."

"What you are proposing is beyond dangerous!" Merbi Teral countered, the older man's booming voice overshadowing his small frame. His green-eyed gaze locked on Soahc. "Even if she had made it to the Enesmic plane, the forces there would have torn her apart. I'm sorry, Soahc, but there is no way that Brime is still alive." Merbi hesitated for a moment. "I miss her too."

Soahc roared in frustration. A shock wave of wind buffeted out from him, ruffling the clothes of the other men assembled and shaking some furniture. The action was subconscious, Soahc's emotions touching the Enesmic.

"First I was doubted when I felt Sagren's Enesmic rift form. Now you doubt my sanity when I speak of Enesmic weavings and calls to the Enesmic plane itself! Will you never trust my judgement on matters of which there is no equal in this galaxy?"

Narmo and Merbi winced. The two looked at each other for a long moment before slowly returning their gazes to Soahc. The master of Etan Rachnie's silver-laced gaze was filled with hot anger.

"Lord Soahc." Ristolte moved toward the immortal. "If you believe that Brime is alive, then I will do whatever I can to aid you. I owe you that much."

Soahc grunted with a surprised look at Ristolte. "What I seek to do may result in your death."

"I have never feared death. Not on the front lines of the mobile infantry, and not now."

Soahc nodded in thanks. His gaze went to Merbi and Narmo, who were staring hard at Ristolte. Their attention gradually shifted back to Soahc, and he raised an eyebrow.

Narmo let out a sigh.

"What's the plan?"

Soahc cracked a smile.

"We reopen Sagren's rift, I step through, and you close it behind me."

Due to the utility of telekinesis, many cihphists spend time learning aspects of this school before further specialization, with many core Etan Rachnie curriculums starting with telekinesis as foundational training.

−FROM "SCHOOLS OF CIHPHISM"
BY SHAPER LUKIR AFREV

CHAPTER 28 CISLOT

Huza, Thae, Huzien home system

Cislot sat with her legs crossed, her head resting on her fist as she leaned to one side in the chair behind her nanoplexi and glass desk. Her gaze was focused on the current restendi, Marcarias Yonvi, who rested comfortably in a seat across from her. They were on the top floor of the Huzien Capitol building, the pristine skyscraper almost six kilometers high. Her office was immaculate, and art from across the galaxy lined her walls, with a large sculpture displayed toward the center. It was a piece commissioned after the Rift War; her favorite living artist had delivered it to her personally. It was a representation of the planet Neth, with symbols of unity and victory inscribed in the form of continents across the multicolored globe.

"Missing?" Cislot echoed as her stunning silver gaze locked with Marcarias's. Her auburn hair fell over the sides of her chair, coming to rest a few inches below her waist. "An entire cruise ship just gone?" She glanced over the restendi's shoulder toward her centerpiece, her gaze flickering back to him in an instant. "Were any of Sagren's forces in that area?"

"No." Marcarias sat up straighter in his chair. "I've confirmed that none of Sagren's forces were anywhere near the *Empress Star*'s cruise route. The military has done a sweep of the route as well, searching for any signs of debris. Nothing has turned up."

Cislot leaned back in her chair, holding Marcarias's gaze in silence. There was a fire-like intensity in her eyes. She looked far younger than him, and to a casual observer, she would look like a young Huzien woman in her prime, barely over the age of a hundred. However, she was far older than the ebony-skinned man sitting across from her. Cislot was an immortal, and one of the founders of the Huzien Empire. Her eyes held that wisdom of time.

"Does Lanrete know?"

"No . . ." Marcarias responded. His gaze broke from hers as he looked out the window to his right. The view was magnificent, the sight that of the entire city of Huza, the Huzien capital. "I didn't feel that it was my place to initiate such a conversation." His gaze slowly returned to Cislot. She regarded him with a curious smile, her eyes narrowing slightly.

"Since when?" At that moment, a platinum-furred Uri entered the expansive office. The golden-eyed woman caught sight of Marcarias and Cislot engaged in conversation and froze, blood rushing to her face.

"Oh, I'm sorry . . . I should have chimed. I'm so sorry . . ." she blurted out.

Marcarias shifted uncomfortably in his chair, returning his gaze to the window. Cislot caught the subtle action and then fixed a glare on Huiara Mau Gehreyati, her personal assistant.

"That's quite alright Huiara, please wait outside," Cislot said.

Huiara turned about-face and quickly walked out, the door sliding closed behind her. Cislot's gaze came to a rest on Marcarias as her lips curled into a smile, her eyes narrowing. She got up out of her chair, walked around her desk, and sat in the chair next to Marcarias.

"You like her?" Cislot's tone was casual. A serving drone came to rest next to her, and she picked up a glass filled with a neon orange liquid.

Marcarias tensed. Leaning back in his chair, he let out a sigh and then turned to face Cislot, his gaze avoiding hers.

"Have you slept with her?" Cislot's voice became deeper, almost haughty.

Marcarias fervently shook his head.

"You know as well as I do that she isn't like other Uri," Marcarias countered.

"Which is why you like her?"

"That's one of the reasons, yes." He crossed his muscular arms, the well-built man blushing slightly.

"Do you find her a novelty? Something to play with until the luster has worn off?"

"No, of course not." A flash of anger lit up the man's eyes. "She is unique, yes. But she is a brilliant person, a woman deserving of respect and admiration."

"Ah," Cislot said. "Then you're afraid that if you two get involved, any risky political action you take now could hurt her chances of being restendi." Cislot sighed.

"I hate it when you do that." Marcarias shook his head.

"Do what?"

"Strategize about my personal life."

Cislot smiled and gulped down the remainder of her drink, then got up and moved to the expansive window, gazing out over the city.

"My dear *burush*," Cislot said, utilizing the Huzien term for son, "if she chooses to join with you, then she does so knowing full well the risks involved." Cislot paused for a moment. "You are no good to me toothless and lame." Her tone was cold. Marcarias subconsciously reached up to touch his face.

"Forgive me, *lurra*." He stood and dropped to one knee, his gaze on the ground. "I will inform Founder Lanrete of the missing ship and his missing Elites."

"Good." Cislot's tone was cool as she returned to her seat behind her desk.

Determining that their conversation was over, Marcarias rose, performed a slight bow, then quickly exited the office.

Cihphists specializing in kineticism, or kintaths, manipulate kinetic, thermal, electrical, chemical, nuclear and raw Enesmic energy in destructive ways.

–FROM "SCHOOLS OF CIHPHISM"
BY SHAPER LUKIR AFREV

CHAPTER 29 HUIARA MAU GEHREYATI

Huza, Thae, Huzien home system

Huiara let out a slow, steady breath, her eyes closed. "Stupid and careless." She bit her lip, shaking her head. "A rookie mistake." The door slid open and her golden eyes flashed up to Marcarias as he stopped in front of her. Their gazes locked.

"Hey Huiara, how are you?" He flashed a cavalier smile.

"Quite well, and you?"

"Never better." The two stood in silence for a long moment. Huiara began to nod her head slowly, her hands clasped in front of her. Marcarias stood unmoving, her path to Cislot's office blocked. She forced a smile, her eyebrows raised.

"Oh, sorry!" He quickly moved to the side. Giving another nod, Huiara moved past him. Marcarias turned as if to intercept her. "Oh, by the way." She stopped in the middle of the doorway. "I uh . . . planned to take a trip down to Trutara in a week. I thought it might be a good opportunity for you to see the politics of the oceanic cities firsthand. It's very different from what you'd see up here and it's a great way to build recognition among the populace."

Huiara's eyes went wide. "Absolutely! I . . . I mean I'll have to check with Founder Cislot to make sure it's okay." She composed herself. "I've never been to any of the oceanic cities. Not sure I could ever live in one of them, but I hear they are beautiful."

"Great, I'll send you the details later." Marcarias turned and proceeded toward his office. Huiara walked into Cislot's office, a wide smile on her face. Her gaze slowly came up to meet Cislot's glare. The smile on her face dropped instantly as she averted her gaze and moved to the seat in front of Cislot. A few moments of silence passed before Cislot stood up and moved to stand next to Huiara. The young Uri's gaze came up to meet the founder's.

"Oh, don't mind me." Cislot put up her hands. "I was just moving out of your seat; clearly this is your office." Her hands dropped to her hips.

"Forgive me, Founder. I wasn't thinking."

"If you weren't thinking, then you would have habitually chimed the door before walking in." Cislot casually dropped herself into the chair next to Huiara. The serving drone came to Cislot's side, and she took a glass filled with a bluish-purple liquid. "The reality is that you were lost in thought, my dear assistant, and sometimes being lost in thought is a good thing." Cislot's gaze softened as she turned to look out the window.

Huiara let out a sigh of relief.

Cislot got up and moved toward the window as she took a sip from her glass. "Marcarias invited you to go with him to Trutara?"

"Yes, he believes it would be a good experience for me."

"And what do you believe?"

"I believe that he's right. I would learn more about the political climate of the oceanic cities. They do account for a third of the population on Thae, after all."

"Are you seeing anyone?"

Huiara's face distorted in confusion. "Am . . . I . . . seeing anyone?" Huiara repeated the words slowly.

"Yes. It's a simple question." Cislot turned to face Huiara and took a finishing swig from her glass as she leaned against the window.

"No. I have never been in a relationship." Huiara's eyes narrowed.

"Interesting." Cislot pushed off from the window and made her way toward her seat, the serving drone coming to hover beside her with a glass of dark red liquid. Taking it, she slid into the chair. Her gaze locked with Huiara's as she took a sip. "I can assume that you've never slept with anyone then?" She brought the cup down from her lips, an eyebrow raised.

"N . . . no . . ." Huiara gave a bashful look. *Is she coming on to me?* Huiara gulped. She began to play through scenarios in her head as her cheeks flushed. "F . . . for the record . . . I . . . I like men." Huiara took in a deep breath.

A deep, raw laughter filled the room.

"It is not for me that I ask these questions of you, my dear Huiara, although I do believe that you are a very pretty girl." Cislot gave her an entertained smile. "Tell me of your plans for Trutara. I have yet to decide if I will allow you to go."

After letting out a sigh of relief at Cislot's return to her usual demeanor, Huiara began to build an exhaustive case for the trip.

Kineticism utilizes the Enesmic to influence various forms of energy to create manifestations of devastating power.

–FROM "SCHOOLS OF CIHPHISM"
BY SHAPER LUKIR AFREV

CHAPTER 30 BRIME WEWTA

Aheraneth, Enesmic plane

"Your beloved intends to come to you, here." The powerful voice of Augrashumen surrounded Brime. She sat up in her bed, her gaze instantly locking onto the magnificent being. It stood a few feet away from the foot of her bed.

"I hate it when you do that!" Brime said.

"Your actions have put Soahc's life at risk. He will not give up now until he has found you or killed himself in the process."

"Why are you blaming that on me?" Brime shuffled to her feet. Gem-encrusted sandals materialized instantly as her feet hit the floor. Augrashumen regarded Brime with disappointment.

"Nothing you do here is secret, dear Brime."

"So, you *are* watching me."

"Always."

Augrashumen motioned with its hand, and the room around both began shifting. Instantly, they were on a high tower, surrounded by a magnificent shining city. Power radiated from every facet of its construction. Brime's eyes widened, her mouth agape. There was nothing but city as far as her eyes could see. Giving her a moment to take it all in, Augrashumen slowly pointed behind her with its hand.

Brime followed Augrashumen's urging and turned around, and then they were at the edge of the city. A dark wasteland of chaotic storms could be seen in the distance, far outside the city gates.

"So . . . this is what the Enesmic plane looks like," Brime said.

"One aspect of it, yes," Augrashumen said. "We call this city Aheraneth."

"Is that the Wilds?" Brime pointed to the chaotic storms in the distance.

"Yes."

"Why are you showing me this?" Brime turned to face Augrashumen.

"Soahc is on his way now to the remnants of Sagren's defeated rift." Brime perked up at the words. "If he survives reopening the portal and crossing over into the Enesmic plane, then he has to brave the Wilds. Alone."

"Why couldn't you go get him like you retrieved me?"

Augrashumen shook its hooded head. "If Soahc succeeds in reopening the portal and steps through, there is no doubt the Betrayers will sense it. If we move to intervene and bring him here, they will know, and there will be no peace."

"I don't understand. If you beings are all-powerful, why couldn't you just wipe out the Betrayers and be done with it?"

Brime couldn't see it, but she felt Augrashumen give her a sad smile.

"We are not all powerful," Augrashumen said. "The Betrayers are former Rel Ach'Kel. They may be corrupted, twisted, but many still retain their full power. Any war that happens here will spill over into the Havin plane, and your people would be wiped out." Augrashumen paused, as if recalling a bitter memory. "I have said too much already. This is not for your kind to understand."

"I thought I was an Enesmic being now?"

Augrashumen's flaring eyes rose in a smile, but it quickly faded as the Rel Ach'Kel looked out into the swirling chaos of the

Wilds. "Your beloved will be on his own. For your sake, I hope he makes it here."

"What happens when he arrives at the gates?"

Augrashumen turned to regard Brime. "I do not know."

Kineticism, at its core, is about devastation and destruction; power put on clear display with sickening efficiency. Kineticism came to exist from the harsh reality within our Twin Galaxies that war and conflict are facts of life we cannot ignore.

–FROM "SCHOOLS OF CIHPHISM"
BY SHAPER LUKIR AFREV

CHAPTER 31 SOAHC

Etan Rachnie, Reath, Huzien Alliance space

"You intend to do what?" Kaloni Setla stared at Soahc with an incredulous look.

Soahc sighed as he eyed the Human. The golden undertones of her beige skin could clearly be seen in the perfect reproduction of her within the Etan Rachnie boardroom hologrid. She was sitting next to him at the table, her legs crossed. Kaloni's almond-shaped black eyes slowly moved to meet Ristolte's, who sat watching her from across the table.

She shook her head.

"You're going to get yourself killed."

"That's why I called you," Soahc countered. "I need something to ensure that I stay alive when I cross over into the Enesmic plane, and I know you've been working on something that does exactly that."

"That's a stretch," Kaloni said. "The Jehu prototype is still just testing a hypothesis at this point. It isn't designed for prolonged use, let alone a rescue mission to the Enesmic plane." She paused for a moment. "I mean, come on Soahc; do you honestly believe that she's still alive there?"

"Yes."

Kaloni let out a heavy sigh. "I'm not responsible for your death if you do this and use this device. I can't guarantee that it will work. I can't even guarantee that you'll survive the crossover." She shook her head again. "Did you talk with Ecnics?"

"No, I think it best not to involve him."

Kaloni scoffed. "Great, you die, and I get fired." She glared at Soahc.

"I'm reaching out to you as a friend. I understand if you don't want to get involved."

"You know I'm going to help you." Kaloni rested her head in her hands. "When should I expect you to come pick up the Jehu?"

"Right now." Soahc stood up and exploded into motion, the Enesmic flow around him shaking the boardroom. With a clap of his hands, a thin line of light formed between him and Kaloni. Pulling his hands apart, the line expanded into a glowing door of Enesmic energy. Stepping through, Soahc appeared directly in front of Kaloni in her office at the MinSci on Thae. She jumped back.

"What?" Fear flashed across her face, immediately followed by curiosity. The curiosity won out, and she got up to walk past Soahc and examine the portal. "So, this is the cihphism that Sagren used to traverse worlds?" At that moment, Ristolte stepped through the portal. Kaloni looked at him, a tsk her only greeting as her gaze went back to the Enesmic creation. "This is truly amazing; unlike anything I've ever seen. You must promise to come back and allow me to study this one day."

"Deal," Soahc said.

"Let's go get the Jehu."

Yetew IX, Huzien Alliance space

Soahc emerged from a multicolored portal, with Ristolte, Narmo, and Merbi following directly behind him. Six Argent shapers stepped from the portal after them, then quickly fanned out to secure the area. Everyone stood in Sagren's former command chamber.

"Never thought I'd be stepping foot back in this place," Soahc said.

"What happened to Sagren's body?" Merbi asked.

"MinSci took it," Ristolte said. "They packed up shop and left a few weeks ago after completing their analysis of the planet."

"Shame. We could have learned a lot from it," Merbi said.

"Some battles are not worth fighting," Soahc added as one of the shapers came to stand in front of Ristolte.

"The area is clear."

Ristolte nodded. "Let's get this over with."

Soahc moved to the site of the original rift that Sagren had created. He traced the exact location, his eyes attuned to the Enesmic energy itself. The echo of the rift was still radiant and substantial in the ebb and flow of the Enesmic around them. Soahc paused, memories rushing back to him of his and Lanrete's final battle against the seemingly unstoppable monster.

"I can't believe it's still here," Narmo breathed. "I've never seen an echo last this long, and with such prominence."

They all came to stand in a circle around the echo.

"Are you sure you want to do this, Soahc?" Merbi said.

The Enesmic energy around them began to swirl violently, the structure they were in trembling as if from an aftershock of an earthquake. Stepping forward, Soahc raised his hands.

"I guess that's a yes," Ristolte muttered under his breath as he stepped forward and began to channel Enesmic energy into Soahc's cihphistic weaving. The whole group added to the cihphistic mani-festation, and a glow began forming in the center of the echo.

Soahc thrust Enesmic energy forward, feeding it into the small tear, a litany of words of power bursting from the assembled group. Instantly, like a drain plug being pulled in a swimming pool, a vortex of energy exploded open. The rift manifested in its full glory, the echo becoming whole once more.

"Yes!" Soahc yelled as the swirling Enesmic energy howled throughout the room. They began to feel themselves being pulled toward the manifestation. "That's not right." Soahc frowned. "There was never a pull before."

"Get back!" Ristolte yelled.

Soahc stood defiant in front of the rift, his own power hold-ing him in place. Narmo struggled under the strain, and Merbi was pulled forward before he was able to stop the force. Ristolte shifted himself between Merbi and the rift and released a blast of energy that sent Merbi flying back toward the opposite end of the room. The headmaster gained his senses just in time to catch himself and land safely near the far wall.

Ristolte was not so lucky. Like a tree in the path of a tornado, Ristolte was ripped from where he stood and sucked into the rift.

"No!" Soahc yelled. Without a moment's hesitation, he went into the rift after him.

"What do we do?" an argent shouted.

Narmo stared at the rift. Everyone around him was holding on for dear life, their power draining rapidly. After taking a deep breath, Narmo glanced to Merbi and then back to the rift, his jaw clenched.

"Seal the rift, now!"

All the argents swarmed on the location, and Merbi quickly stood and moved back toward the rift. They began to weave strands of Enesmic power around the manifestation. Slowly, painfully, they snuffed the rift back out of existence.

Narmo struggled to catch his breath. "I hope we didn't just lose those two."

Merbi looked over at Narmo. He tried to find words of comfort, for something encouraging to say, and failed.

Enesmic Wilds, Enesmic plane

Soahc and Ristolte struggled under the violent assault of raw Enesmic power. Soahc activated the Jehu, the device contained within in a vest covering his chest. It flared to life and pushed the forces away from him. The Enesmic energy hesitated for a moment, then renewed its assault as the Jehu whirled, going into overdrive. Soahc looked over to Ristolte, who was screaming in pain, and winced as he watched Ristolte's flesh start to dematerialize.

Ristolte reflexively held out his hand toward Soahc. His eyes were on fire, silver intertwining with their reddish-grey hue.

Soahc stretched out his hand.

"I will extend the Jehu's field over you!" he shouted above the torrent.

"No! You'll just kill both of us!" Ristolte retracted his hand. "Find . . . Brime . . ." Ristolte again screamed in horrible pain as the flesh on his hand was ripped away atom by atom. "Let my death . . . mean something!"

Ristolte gave up the struggle and faded away into the swirling Enesmic energy, his essence joining in the flow. Soahc tore his gaze away from where Ristolte had been mere moments before. He turned toward the wavering image of a wasteland at the end of the tunnel of swirling Enesmic energy, then glanced back toward the way he had come and saw that the portal was closed.

"Good job, Narmo."

Soahc looked back toward the wasteland and flung himself forward. Passing through the image, he landed like lightning on the

Enesmic plane itself. The Enesmic renewed its assault, the power of it overwhelming as it surrounded Soahc. He attempted to enact a barrier, but the energy refused his will. Seemingly angered by his attempt at wielding it, it sought to crush him. The Jehu whirled louder and then failed spectacularly.

Soahc yelled as Enesmic energy pierced him like daggers of fire. His torment was intensified a millionfold, no pain in his past comparing to what he now experienced.

"I . . . will . . . not . . . yield!" Soahc yelled.

He extended his hands out and seemingly gripped the Enesmic itself. With raw strength, Soahc held on and refused to let go. The energy seeped deeper into his body, the force permeating every cell, every atom. Soahc then collapsed to the ground, his world going dark.

Kintaths are brought in when the telepaths have failed. They are considered dangerous on many Alliance worlds and each kintath is forced to register themselves as weapons with the Alliance once formally recognized by Etan Rachnie. This designation forever follows them.

–FROM "SCHOOLS OF CIHPHISM"
BY SHAPER LUKIR AFREV

CHAPTER 32 HUIARA MAU GEHREYATI

Trutara, Thae, Huzien home system

H uiara stared in wide-eyed wonder at the oceanic city of Trutara far below her. She sat in an expansive see-through meglift with Marcarias at her side. He silently watched her as she took in the magnificent sight. They had embarked a few minutes earlier from the trade hub that connected to Trutara from the surface of the water.

"I thought the trade hub was impressive, but this . . ." Huiara whispered.

"Millions of people live in the trade hub." Marcarias smiled. "Billions in the city.

"It's so bright."

"Truly beautiful." Marcarias met Huiara's gaze as she blushed. "The meglifts move with the water currents, bobbing back and forth. It's an impressive engineering feat."

"I don't feel it at all." Huiara peered out of the meglift.

"We can thank dampeners for that. They keep people from getting seasick." Marcarias glanced up toward the trade hub quickly fading from sight. Thousands of other meglifts like the one they occupied connected Trutara to the trade hub.

"So . . . Trutara is built into the ocean floor," Huiara said, "almost four thousand meters below the surface of the Heedilv Ocean."

"I take it Cislot still makes her assistants memorize and recite random facts at the drop of a hat."

Huiara laughed. "I can see the merit in her methods," she said. "It's important to understand the facts of the people and places we interact with." Marcarias continued to gaze out of the meglift. "What was she like when you were her assistant?" Huiara asked.

Marcarias's eyes glazed over. "Trutara was designed by the Feshra Augamentres almost thirty thousand years ago. It was her crowning achievement." He glanced at Huiara, smiling. "Cislot is one of the few constants in this galaxy." He turned his attention to Trutara, which was coming more into focus. "Look at the oceanicscraper." Marcarias pointed toward a towering construct. A myriad of meglift tubes connected the megastructure to others like it. The core of the city was made up of hundreds of the towering oceanicscrapers, with smaller superstructures littering the spaces between them. Topping many of the largest oceanicscrapers were elaborate observation decks, housing parks, and recreation centers.

"Look at all the lights." Huiara's gaze lingered on the multitude of bright blue and white lights littering each structure. "It's so pretty." Their meglift rapidly approached one of the largest oceanicscrapers. Huiara's ocean view was replaced by a beautiful view of the inside of the massive structure as the meglift descended through an open expanse that simulated the outdoors, artificial sunlight blanketing the area. The meglift slowed, eventually coming to a smooth stop on a dais.

"This is us." Marcarias got up from his seat.

He made his way through the meglift doors to an elaborate walking path. Huiara followed him, their security contingent moving with them.

"Looks like we're drawing a crowd," Huiara said.

"The people want to see their restendi." Marcarias grinned at her as he lifted his hand in the air, waving to the residents as he passed. Many waved back, but a few held signs that caused Huiara to suppress a frown. Their security detail ushered them into the Trutara city hall, an impressive building that took up the central area of the park level.

"Honored Restendi, I humbly welcome you to Trutara."

Marcarias and Huiara came to stand in front of a dashing young Huzien man with long blond hair, green eyes, and ivory skin. The crowd had grown to mammoth proportions, seeming to press in around them.

"Grand Lichar, thank you for welcoming us to your wonderful city," Marcarias said, "and thank you to the great people of Trutara for opening your home to us." A cheer from the crowd went up as Marcarias flashed his pearly whites and waved.

The grand lichar turned and motioned for them to follow. They moved out of sight and into the restricted administration chamber of the city hall structure. Expansive doors closed behind them, with the majority of the security detail staying behind. The three made their way to a meglift leading them to the grand lichar's office. The young man smiled and motioned for Huiara to proceed first.

Huiara blushed.

Marcarias cleared his throat as all three piled inside. "Allow me to introduce Huiara Mau Gehreyati, personal assistant to Founder Cislot."

A soft hum signaled their momentary ascent to the top floor of the city hall structure.

"Pleasure to make your acquaintance, Ms. Gehreyati." The grand lichar performed a customary bow. "I am Grand Lichar Ulter Wern, the one solely responsible for the great oceanic city of Trutara."

"Likewise, Grand Lichar." Huiara gave her own slight bow. "You have a magnificent city."

"My people thank you for your kind words."

Ulter stepped out of the meglift and proceeded to lead his two guests into his office. A serving drone moved to Huiara's side as both she and Marcarias slid into seats across from Ulter's desk. Huiara took a small glass of red liquid from the drone. It moved to Marcarias next, but he dismissed it silently.

"Now that we've exchanged pleasantries," Marcarias said, "how about we get down to business?"

"Of course." Ulter brought up a holodisplay facing Marcarias and Huiara. "Ganrele Retril Corporation and Kekid Group are currently seeking approval to start construction of a new oceanicscraper in the city." A three-dimensional rendition of the megastructure appeared on the holodisplay, with its proposed location shown on a grid of the city map. "The project would bring a great deal of new jobs to the city, and once completed, would allow for a population expansion of roughly ten million."

"And would require a Huzien imperial investment of almost fifty billion larods," Marcarias countered.

"Yes, but with an additional one hundred billion larod investment being provided by the corporations. You know how expensive these types of construction projects are. This would be a boon for Trutara. Job growth has stifled over the past decade," Ulter said.

"The senate would not approve of a spending bill of that magnitude to aid private corporations in a building project on Thae. We're still recovering from the Rift War, Ulter."

"If the proposal had your support when it hit the senate floor, I think it would have a chance," Ulter countered.

Marcarias shook his head, letting out a long sigh. "I can't support this proposal, as much as I truly want to help. Funds of this magnitude are needed elsewhere. We have entire worlds to rebuild!

For Neth alone we're spending four trillion larods on reconstruction efforts."

"You will lose the support of the populace if you take that stance. The people of Trutara have been re-energized by this proposal. The last oceanicscraper was built almost twelve hundred years ago." Ulter let out a frustrated sigh. "We need to expand; our city has no more room to grow!"

Marcarias sat for a long moment. He turned to Huiara, who had been silently listening to the discussion.

"What do you think Founder Cislot's opinion would be on this matter?" Marcarias asked.

Huiara blinked rapidly as she glanced from Ulter to Marcarias before sitting back in her chair.

"I . . . believe . . . that she would weigh the long-term benefits of starting a construction project here with the risk of diverting funds from the rebuilding efforts," Huiara said.

"And that means?" Ulter prompted.

"That means . . . that she might put her support behind an effort like this in order to boost morale with the local populace, but at a drastically reduced initial imperial investment." The pieces began to fall into place in her head. "The founder would put more pressure on Ganrele Retril Corporation and Kekid Group to front the costs to start the construction effort with imperial funds promised later, once construction had reached critical mass, possibly a few years down the road. That would also give us time to focus attention on critical rebuilding efforts without immediately diverting funds." Huiara paused. "This would . . . show commitment on the part of the primary investors with less of a burden on our constituents, initially."

"Humph," Marcarias responded.

Silence descended on the room as Ulter looked from Huiara to Marcarias and then back to Huiara.

"I can talk with Ganrele Retril and Kekid to get their buy-in," Ulter said. "Will you take this before the senate?"

Huiara looked from Ulter to Marcarias with uncertainty.

"It's your idea," Marcarias said.

"Uh, I'll have to run it by Cislot before I take any action," Huiara countered.

"Please." Ulter leaned forward.

Huiara glanced from Marcarias back to Ulter and began to rub the back of her neck. What had she just gotten herself into?

Skilled Kintaths tend to enlist in the military or become mercenaries for hire, brought in as insurance for dangerous situations. Many corporations employ Kintaths as part of their elite security forces, commonly to protect top executives.

–FROM "SCHOOLS OF CIHPHISM"
BY SHAPER LUKIR AFREV

CHAPTER 33 SEPHAN

Many eons ago
Aheraneth, Enesmic plane

S agren the Virtuous hovered above the central gate to the shining city of Aheraneth. Immaculate ebony and golden armor covered every inch of its towering frame except for its midsection and biceps, where its bright blue skin shone through. Two sets of massive silver wings extended from its back. The being was beautiful to behold. Sagren wore no helmet, and its calm purple gaze glowed brightly as it scanned the Enesmic Wilds for any signs of movement. Motion at its side caused Sagren to turn.

"Why guard the gates yourself, Virtuous Commander?" A being covered in bright orange robes inlaid with a diamond-encrusted breastplate and similar gauntlets appeared at Sagren's side. "Surely such tasks can be delegated to one of the many within your ranks."

"Sephan the Eloquent, what brings you to the entrance to the Wilds?"

"All business." Sephan grinned. "Can I not simply visit one as great as yourself?"

Sagren's face held no mouth or nose; its eyes were the only discerning feature. They aligned themselves in an expression signaling a smile.

"It has been some time since we last met. How fare you?"

"I fare well." Sephan turned to face the Enesmic Wilds. Sagren mirrored the action. "Anything of interest?"

"Beasts test themselves against my blade from time to time, but it is nothing of concern."

"To think that Cirfuletanas is out there." Sagren turned to glance at Sephan. "The Anointed One is building an army to challenge us."

"Cirfuletanas stopped being the Anointed One the moment it challenged Vesgrilana the Sagacious and began spewing its hate for the Havin." Sagren's gaze hardened. "We are tasked with protecting the planes of existence; that is our purpose. That is this city's purpose."

"Wisdom you speak, virtuous one," Sephan said. "If only the Originator would intervene. Surely it would bring Cirfuletanas back into our fold and soften its heart toward all of its creation."

"The Originator's will is known. Cirfuletanas ignores it."

"True, yet . . ." Sephan motioned with its hand, and a window into the Havin plane appeared in midair. The scene showcased a man with a crude sword skewering another man. Pushing the man off his blade, he turned to a woman behind the fallen man. Lifting the sword, he spoke a few words, prompting the woman's eyes to go wide. She tried to run out of the room, but the man intercepted her, then punched her to the ground and moved to mount her.

Sagren forced itself to watch the resulting scene play out. Sephan waved its hand again, hundreds of other windows appearing all around them, each filled with similar scenes played out by different species.

"This is the Originator's will?" Sephan asked. Sagren the Virtuous remained quiet, its face neutral. "Cirfuletanas's treachery cannot be forgiven, yet its words ring true." Sephan began to move toward the Wilds, away from the city. It stopped and turned to regard Sagren. "Shall we question Cirfuletanas ourselves?"

Present day
Remnants of Ashna Maiden attack armada, Huzien Alliance / Ashna
Maiden border

Sephan opened its eyes, its gaze going to the image of Jughent's fleet on the holodisplay. The Ashna Maiden vessel it had stolen slowed to a stop, and the young Ashna Maiden piloting the ship sat motionless in the navigation chair. Her eyes were hollow, all higher thought functions dominated by Sephan, who lithely moved out of the command chair and came to stand behind her before giving the woman a comforting pat.

"Be a dear and kill yourself." Bresha's tone was friendly, almost motherly. The young Ashna Maiden got up from her seat and walked over to one of the dead Maidens on the floor. She picked up a small weapon and held it to her head. A squeeze of the trigger deposited her brain matter across the bridge floor. The lifeless body dropped to the ground as Sephan let out a contented sigh.

Reaching out with its mind, Sephan touched the thoughts of Jughent.

Jughent, my dear friend, what a pleasure it is to see you.

Metaphysicism, the final school, is still in many ways the most unexplored and least understood of the four.

–FROM "SCHOOLS OF CIHPHISM"
BY SHAPER LUKIR AFREV

CHAPTER 34 JUGHENT

Remnants of Ashna Maiden attack armada, Huzien Alliance / Ashna Maiden border

Jughent went pale at the sound of Sephan in his mind. He reached his hand into the insubstantial control node next to his command chair and quickly sought the source of the voice with his mind and external sensors. Fear dripped from him like sweat. Locating an Ashna Maiden vessel, he ordered the full force of his fleet to attack with a fury. His ships swarmed in the direction of the vessel, descending on it like a pack of hungry wolves. Within seconds, the ship was torn apart, an explosion signaling its destruction.

The pale yellow Ceshra sat back in his command chair, breathing a sigh of relief, his thoughts clear. He had a humanoid appearance, with solid bright orange orbs in the place of eyes. Jughent smiled to himself, revealing razor-sharp fangs. The thought of another Eshgren usurping his power was not something he had any interest in now.

"Now, that's not any way to greet an ally." The voice came from behind Jughent.

Jughent jumped out of his seat and dashed to the other side of the command node. The sight of Bresha Vecen greeted him, her arms behind her back. A tight-lipped smile hung on her face. Bresha's eyes held power; power that caused Jughent to cower in fear.

"If I had wanted to take control of your fleet, I would have simply done so." Sephan's voice was calm. Jughent could see the rage held back like a sandbag holding a tidal wave at bay. Sephan moved toward the seat Jughent had just been in. "Instead, I come as an ally with a plan of mutual benefit." Sephan took a seat.

"Yes, of course." Jughent's voice was timid. He stood unmoving, his gaze locked onto Sephan's form. He felt that the Eshgren was contemplating ending his existence, and that thought terrified him.

"I seek to wipe out the Ashna Maidens," Sephan said. "I believe their absence in this part of space will allow for you to flourish here and make a little empire for yourself." Jughent perked up at Sephan's words, the fear gone. A hunger for power took over.

"What is your plan?" Jughent asked.

Sephan smiled. "Let's just say that I'm going to infiltrate the Ashna Maidens and convince them to launch their full force at you."

Jughent frowned.

"That doesn't sound like a good plan."

"Have faith, dear Jughent," Sephan said. "There is a second part to this plan. I will also convince the pirate bands in this part of space to ally with you in exchange for a momentary non-aggression pact. The combined forces will easily overwhelm what the Ashna Maidens can muster, and then we will split up the previously held Maiden space between you and them."

Jughent's smile slowly faded, his eyes narrowing.

"Your plans are bold, but not once have you indicated what you seek to gain from all this."

A flicker in Sephan's eyes caused Jughent to take a step back. Jughent could see the same look he had seen in Sagren's eyes, that same look he had seen in the eyes of the many Eshgren he had served over the eons. They were driven by something above him, something he couldn't quite grasp, something less tangible than what drove him and the other Ceshra.

Sephan smiled.

"I forgive you for your trespass, dear Jughent. You could not have known why I was here; you were merely acting out of self-defense. I understand that and admire your wisdom."

Sephan got up out of Jughent's seat and moved toward the far wall. It motioned for Jughent to return to his seat, but the Ceshra hesitated.

"This is your seat of power," Sephan stated. "Just as this fleet is yours—not Sagren's, not mine." Jughent moved to his seat and reluctantly sat down. "Just as this fleet is yours, the ships that the Ashna Maidens destroyed were also yours. Ships that will not be replaced; ships that even now decay in the cold of space." Flashes of the wreckages of Jughent's fleet were displayed in his mind, the images thrust there by Sephan. "The Maidens return home to nurse their wounds and rebuild their ships, mocking you as they plan their next attack."

"I welcome the attack," Jughent countered. "More of their ships will fall against my onslaught."

"What of vengeance?"

"Vengeance?"

"Yes, they destroyed your ships, attacked you outright."

"I destroyed their ships first; they were merely seeking their vengeance. Vengeance that I denied them."

"Pay vengeance with vengeance, my dear Jughent." Jughent eyed Bresha, her body now relaxing on the side of his command chair. The Eshgren had gotten close to Jughent without him realizing it. He shifted uneasily. "Do not fear me," Sephan said.

Jughent scoffed. "Do not fear the being that could end my mere existence with a thought?" Jughent shook his head. "No, I will fear you. I am not stupid, Sephan. I know the games you Eshgren play. You seek to make me comfortable, to make me assured in my safety, and then you will strike. You will kill me for the sole offense of attacking your ship. That is how your kind operates."

Sephan watched Jughent quietly for a long moment.

"Do you find this body attractive?" Sephan asked.

Jughent stared at Sephan, incredulous.

"A Havin?"

"Yes, this Havin shell. This Human female body." Bresha began to undress.

Jughent stared confused at the Eshgren as Bresha removed all her clothing. Bresha was well-endowed, her body toned and muscled. She looked the picture of Human perfection; even her pubic hair was neatly trimmed. Long gone were the scars that had marked Bresha's body after her battle with the Ceshra Cresala during the Rift War, and the many wounds from her torture in Sagren's prison cell. A cell that had led to her current reality under the domination of Sephan.

"There are . . . similarities to female Ceshra."

"Come. Enjoy this body with me. Fulfill your carnal desires, fill me with all that is you. Solidify our pact with each thrust into my being. Ravish me and know that our bond is true."

"So that you can kill me in the act of passion?" Jughent scoffed again.

Sephan shrugged. "You have my word that I will do no such thing."

Jughent eyed Bresha's body for a long moment, passion building within him each passing second. It had been so long since he had last indulged in sex with a female of any species. Bresha stepped forward, resting her hands on Jughent's shoulders. Her breasts filled his vision as she straddled him. Jughent backed up as far as he could into his seat. Fear overwhelmed his senses. He didn't know what game Sephan was playing, but he didn't like it.

Bresha reached for Jughent's crotch, disintegrating his pants. She grabbed hold of what passed for a penis among his species. Terror coursed through every vein in his body as Bresha held his very manhood in her hand. Her silver-laced blue eyes locked with his orange orbs. There was a playfulness in her gaze as she licked her lips.

"Wait!" Jughent shouted. "If you truly intend to do this, please let me return to my true form."

Bresha smiled. A single nod from the woman caused Jughent's skin to crack. It started to melt away, his form replaced by a radiant being of pure, bright yellowish-orange energy. He reached for Bresha and led her to the ground at the foot of his command chair. His touch was like a controlled fire held just far enough away to provide intense heat but not burn. Bresha's body began to sweat. He wrapped his glowing arm around the back of her neck, and Sephan invited Jughent Prime into the innermost parts of Bresha Vecen. Jughent grunted in excitement. Intense heat flooded Bresha's senses as another single tear rolled down her cheek.

> *Metaphysicism seeks to utilize the Enesmic to manipulate the very building blocks of our universe for creation and restoration.*

> –FROM "SCHOOLS OF CIHPHISM"
> BY SHAPER LUKIR AFREV

CHAPTER 35 SEPHAN

*Remnants of Ashna Maiden attack armada,
Huzien Alliance / Ashna Maiden border*

B resha pulled her clothes back on, Jughent watching her dress. The Ceshra eyed her body with a satisfied look on his face. Jughent sat nude in his command chair, the lust in his eyes making Sephan smile.

"Do we have a deal?" Sephan asked.

Jughent focused his gaze back on Bresha's beautiful eyes, her playful gaze promising him so much more.

"Yes, of course," Jughent replied. "What do you need of me now?"

"A vessel. An Ashna Maiden escape pod would suffice."

Jughent reached his hand into the alcove next to his command chair and closed his eyes. Within a few minutes, he removed his hand from the alcove and turned his gaze to Sephan.

"It is done."

"I can see why Sagren selected you to be one of his most trusted Overlords. You are an exceptional being . . ." Sephan said, "in more ways than one."

Bresha licked her lips.

The sight caused Jughent to grin. He slowly got up from his chair and walked over to her, then wrapped his arms around her back and firmly gripped her butt, pulling her body closer to his.

"Mmmm," Bresha moaned lightly. "We will have to play more once our plan is complete."

She gently separated herself from Jughent and reached out with her mind, touching the complex web of information maintained between Jughent's ships. After determining the location of the escape pod, Bresha gave a longing look to Jughent before uttering a word of power, clenching her fist, and teleporting away. Bresha appeared in a waiting vessel docked on one of Jughent's attack frigates. Examining the condition of the vehicle, it nodded at Jughent's efficiency in finding a working ship. Sephan had half expected to be forced to repair the vessel in some way.

Connecting through Bresha's mobi, Sephan utilized the emergency authorization codes gained from its deep dive through the mind of the dominated navigation officer. As it set a course for Ashnali—the Ashna Maiden homeworld—Sephan smiled.

CHAPTER 36 NEVEN KENK

Foundra Conscient, Huzien Alliance space

Neven stepped off the meglift onto the engineering bay of the Foundra Conscient, his eyes going wide as he took in the scale of the massive reactor staring back at him. He slowly walked to the edge of a long walkway suspended over the powerful reactor, which was unlike anything he had ever seen. His hands came to rest on the guardrail, a smile plastering itself across his face. The technological marvel kept him speechless.

"And you are?"

Neven turned to see a young Huzien with silver eyes staring back at him. The man's light brown hair was cut low. He had dark brown skin similar to Soahc's.

"Neven."

"Ah." The Huzien looked Neven up and down, a smug look on his face.

"And you are . . . ?" Neven said.

The man smirked. "Feshra Aru, chief engineer of the *Foundra Conscient*."

Fancy, Ellipse said.

"Feshra . . ." Neven echoed, and he shook his head in surprise. "But you look so young."

Totally just insulted him, Ellipse said.

"Heh," Aru countered. "You don't look too impressive your-self, to be honest. I was expecting more from a Founder's Elite."

Neven winced. "Sorry, I . . ."

"Whatever," Aru interrupted. "Why are you here?"

"Oh . . . we're heading to investigate the—"

"No," Aru interrupted again, "I mean why are you here in my engineering bay? This isn't a playground."

Neven frowned. "I'm touring the ship."

The two stared at each other in silence for a long moment, the tension thick.

"For the record," Aru began, "I'm over six hundred years old. I am not 'young' by anyone's standard—except maybe the Das'Vin."

Hmmm . . . now that's interesting, Ellipse said.

Neven let out a sigh, wishing he could rewind time.

"Look, I'm sorry. I didn't mean to offend you. Being a feshra, I'm sure you can appreciate my curiosity with the amazing reactor you have down there. I meant no disrespect and I sincerely apologize."

Smooth, the impression of a smiling woman's face filled Neven's mind's eye.

Neven performed a deep bow, holding it for a moment longer than normal. He eventually looked up to see Aru watching him with a smile, his eyes narrowed slightly. Aru walked past Neven to the railing and rested against it. He glanced back to Neven.

"There is only one Nisic II reactor in existence, and it's right there." Aru pointed over the guard rail to the reactor down below.

"Nisic II . . ." Neven echoed. The awe in his voice caused Aru's smile to widen. "The Nisic line is unparalleled, and revolu-tionary in sustained yield and efficiency. We have a Nisic reactor on the *Ascension*."

"And today is your lucky day." Aru turned back to face the reactor. "You get to meet the feshra who created the Nisic line."

Neven's eyes grew larger, a smile sneaking its way onto his face. "I have so many questions," Neven said.

The feshra silently took in the admiration, then motioned for Neven to follow him.

"Come, I'll give you a private tour."

"Have you ever seen a Manem suplight drive?" Aru turned to face Neven.

Neven shook his head in confusion.

"Manem?"

"Ah . . ." Aru said. He pondered for a moment in silence. "Well, I guess if you're a Founder's Elite, you most likely have the clearance level necessary." Aru walked toward a nearby holodisplay and switched the display to a three-dimensional schematic of the *Foundra Conscient*. He pointed to the massive suplight drive, which took up almost the entire bottom of the ship. "Manem suplight drives are a new form of technology developed in the past century." Aru switched the holodisplay to a reproduction of the Twin Galaxies and pointed to a small blip at the end of the galactic spiral deep in the Outer Rim. "Sometime in the next decade or so, we think the technology will be mature enough to launch an expedition to another galaxy." Aru turned back to regard Neven, who was silently processing this new information.

"This is so cool," Neven blurted.

Aru laughed. "Yes, yes, it is." Aru motioned for Neven to follow him back toward the meglift. "So, what is your claim to fame?"

"My claim to fame?" Neven shot Aru a raised eyebrow.

"How you drew the interest of the founders? The thing that helped you become a Founder's Elite?"

"Oh . . ." Neven looked down at the ground. "Not really sure."

Aru scoffed. "Seriously now?" Aru gave him a skeptical look.

Neven rubbed the back of his neck. "I uh . . . worked on a team that created a subcompact version of the Vush suplight drive."

Aru stopped in his tracks and turned around to face Neven. "I also worked on a special project to create an advanced power frame."

"And all of this . . . caught the eye of Founder Lanrete?" Aru crossed his arms and raised an eyebrow.

"It caught the eye of Founder Ecnics."

Aru scoffed again.

Prideful much? Ellipse quipped.

"Hey, I can't tell you what it was that caught their attention. All I can do is tell you what I've done," Neven countered. "I'm only twenty-nine years old, jeez! Sorry I haven't had time to create a revolutionary new reactor technology."

"Ah . . . there it is," Aru said. "Undeveloped potential . . . that's Founder Ecnics's weakness." Aru continued walking toward the meglift.

Neven mouthed the words "undeveloped potential," scratching his head, and reluctantly followed Aru into the meglift. When Aru turned around to regard Neven, Neven caught sight of his silver eyes as if truly noticing them for the first time. Something in the back of his mind clicked.

I think so too, Ellipse agreed with Neven's thought.

"You mentioned that you're over six hundred years old, right?"

"Six hundred and thirty-seven, to be exact."

"Are you an immortal?"

The question seemed to catch Aru off guard. "What makes you ask that?"

"Well, it's not that big of a secret that immortals all have silver eyes for some reason." Neven paused and thought of Soahc. "Well, most of them anyway . . ." Neven hesitated. "Plus, you're over six hundred years old and don't look a day over one hundred—for a Huzien."

An awkward silence hung in the meglift until they eventually arrived at their destination. The door opened into an expansive lab area. Aru walked out of the meglift, Neven following him.

"I don't know." Aru's voice was low, timid.

"You don't know?"

"No. I've always suspected, but Founder Ecnics has never said anything. The doctors just say I'm aging well, that everything is normal." Aru leaned up against a nearby wall. He stared at Neven, his silver eyes filled with fear.

Strange . . . I just tried to pull his medical records from the HIN. They are classified at a clearance level higher than what we have access for, Ellipse relayed.

"Do you believe that?"

"No." Aru shook his head and let out a big sigh. "It doesn't matter, it's not important."

"It's not important?" Neven echoed as he scrunched up his nose.

"Look, kid. Sometimes it's best to leave some stones unturned. Not everything crawling underneath needs to be exposed to the light." Aru hesitated for a moment. "It doesn't matter."

Neven looked down at the ground, processing Aru's statement.

"Sorry I said anything."

Aru shook his head and let out another sigh. "Don't worry about it."

At that, Aru's demeanor completely changed, and he transformed back into the impressive feshra that had been guiding Neven around his ship. "This area is linked to the Nisic II reactor through the Armania core." Aru motioned to the massive conduit taking up the center of the expansive room. "It powers this area and allows for power-hungry experiments to go on without directly draining the reactor itself." Aru glanced back to Neven with pride. "It's another one of my creations."

"Impressive..." Neven tried his best to be impressed by the technological marvel, but he was still processing their prior conversation.

"Having fun?"

The familiar voice pulled Neven's attention. Both him and Aru turned to see Lanrete walking up to meet them. Aru performed a customary bow to the founder.

"Is everything alright?" Lanrete asked, obviously catching the strange look on Neven's face.

Neven glanced to Aru, who eyed him with a nonchalant smile.

"Yeah, everything's great!" Aru said. "We were just about to finish up our tour."

"Yeah . . . everything's good," Neven replied.

"Good to hear . . ." Lanrete raised an eyebrow. "We're about three days out from the last known coordinates of the *Empress Star*," Lanrete continued. "We're making record time with the Manem suplight drive."

"You've got to love when experimental technology works like it's supposed to," Aru chimed in.

"Indeed," Neven added in a low voice.

"Neven," Lanrete said, "when you finish up here with Aru, come see me on the bridge." Neven nodded. Lanrete glanced from him to Aru again and then turned, heading back toward the meglift, his blue military cape trailing behind him. The two engineers stood there for a long moment.

"Do yourself a favor," Aru finally said, breaking the silence. "Keep your mouth shut about your guesses on other people's personal matters."

Neven arrived on the bridge of the *Foundra Conscient* and saw Lanrete standing at the guardrail overlooking the command deck. The ship was much larger than the *Foundra Ascension*, and the bridge crew was double the size. Multiple holodisplays hovered in the air above the guardrails in front of Lanrete while a massive primary holodisplay filled the forwardmost area of the bridge. Neven smiled and took a few steps toward Lanrete, the feel of the bridge very different from their own military vessel. It had an air of exploration and wonder, with images and colors on the displays that tickled Neven's senses.

Lanrete turned to regard Neven with a smile as Neven came to stand next to the founder, the young secnic's eyes on the holodisplays in front of them. Multitudes of information related to the *Empress Star* filled the displays, along with star charts and reports from the HIN.

"Any news?" Neven asked.

"Not yet. Hopefully we can pick up their trail with some of the advanced sensors outfitted on this ship." Neven nodded in agreement. "We need to continue your training."

The words caught Neven off guard, and he raised an eyebrow at Lanrete.

"Training?"

"Combat training," Lanrete clarified. "We're most likely going to experience conflict in some capacity. And if we do wind up in the Outer Rim, we may have to keep a low profile, which will mean you without your power armor."

Neven frowned.

I may have a solution for that; I found an interesting project in progress at the MinSci, Ellipse said. Information began to flood Neven's mobi.

S3? Neven asked mentally.

The acronym stands for suplight storage system.

Ah, cool. Neven began to play one of the vids sent by Ellipse. It showed a countdown that ended with a dull grey storage container suddenly appearing in an empty room accompanied by flashes of electricity and a blast of wind that shook the recording device. Off to the side, he could make out a group of scientists jumping up and down and high-fiving each other.

"Luckily," Lanrete continued, "Huzien blade weapons are not given a second thought nowadays." Lanrete's words pulled Neven from the vid in his micro-display. Another frown crept onto his face as he processed Lanrete's statement. "Meet me in training room Yuki-14 in an hour."

He turned from Neven and focused his attention back on the HIN reports. Neven took the action for dismissal and let out a sigh as he slowly made his way back to the meglift to prepare for what he was sure were going to be an exceptionally long three days.

Neven stood in the training room decked out in his training gi. The belt he wore at his waist indicated that Neven was three levels above the starting rank. He eyed Streamsong, the Huzien Redalam blade gifted to him when he first joined the Founder's Elites, thoughts of his intense sparring sessions with Tashanira and Jessica causing him to sigh. Redalam techniques were intensive, with a heavy focus on blade form above all else. He had never sparred with Lanrete before but assumed that it would be similar; he understood Lanrete to be a grandmaster Redalam, surpassing even Jessica. He hoped that maybe the founder would go easy on him and treat him like a novice since he had never seen him in action outside of power armor.

Neven caught the soft sound of the door sliding open and looked up to spot Lanrete walking in with a black gi. His hand rested on the top of his Huzien blade, a silver belt encircling his waist indicating the highest level of mastery. The legendary Huzien blade master stared at Neven with a look devoid of emotion. The sight threw Neven off as he subconsciously took a step back.

He is going to rush you, Ellipse said.

Lanrete charged straight at Neven barely a heartbeat after the words rang in his mind. Divinebreath came out in a flash as Lanrete's first strike came in for the kill. Neven threw up Streamsong reflexively. The swords connected. A thunderclap sounded, the force of the blow sending a shock wave throughout Neven's body. He struggled under the immortal's might and immediately fell into the combat rhythm hammered into him by his trainers. Neven angled Streamsong to the side, sidestepping to defeat Lanrete's attack. Without hesitation, Lanrete spun, whirling Divinebreath around in a full three-sixty strike. Neven matched the spin, trying to bring Streamsong up to stop the second blow aimed at his neck.

Fear gripped Neven as he let out a gasp, his gaze stuck on Lanrete's emotionless face. A shiver went down his spine. Lanrete kicked out, connecting with Neven's stomach. Neven was thrown back and struggled to remain standing, but he focused on maintaining his form and quickly recovered.

Lanrete followed with a lunge. Neven scrambled away and narrowly avoided Divinebreath plunging through his midsection. He then deflected another blow and threw his body to the side, performing a breakfall before coming up with the continued momentum.

Not giving Neven a moment's respite, Lanrete ran toward him, scraping Divinebreath's tip across the floor. The action distracted Neven as he tried to predict the angle of attack. Realizing that too much was on the line for such a prediction, Neven jumped to the side and out of Lanrete's path. Lanrete reversed direction and came after him. Neven dove to the side again, in full retreat as he scrambled to stay out of Lanrete's reach.

His mind worked furiously to come up with a real defensive strategy. He doubted he could outrun Lanrete forever; the immortal was gifted with a supernatural fount of stamina. Neven performed another breakfall after Lanrete telekinetically shifted himself to stand before the young engineer in the blink of an eye, and Neven's eyes went wide as Lanrete launched into a downward strike as Neven came up. He lifted Streamsong, the swords connecting. Lanrete immediately retracted Divinebreath and came in from another angle.

The strikes became a blur. Neven began relying on pure instinct, all thought gone as he countered each of Lanrete's strikes. Lanrete slowly pushed Neven back toward the wall of the training room. Neven's body screamed at him as his muscles strained under the onslaught, unable to stand up to Lanrete's raw strength. When Neven felt his back bump into the wall, he immediately recognized the fatal error. Divinebreath flashed, and then the room became deathly still. Neven felt the cold plexicarbonite blade of Divinebreath at his neck.

Neven's labored breaths filled the room while sweat dripped from him in torrents. Lanrete removed his hand from Divinebreath and left it where it was, protruding from the wall. Lanrete wasn't even breathing hard. Neven felt the warm dribble of a liquid sliding down his neck. Without seeing it, he knew it was his own blood. Neven eyed Lanrete with confusion mixed with fear and then sudden hot anger.

"Are you trying to kill me?" Neven yelled. He gently removed himself from the wall, his hand going to the flesh wound on his neck as he sought to stop the blood flow.

"Of course," Lanrete countered. Neven's eyes went wide, his mouth dropping open. "Unless I'm intent on killing you, how can you ever truly prepare for someone else planning to do likewise?" The words left Neven speechless. "Jessica and Tashanira have trained you well."

Neven stared at Lanrete incredulously. He then glanced back to the wall where Divinebreath was still lodged. Lanrete motioned toward his blade, and the weapon dislodged itself and flew toward him in the blink of an eye. It righted itself as Lanrete plucked it out of the air. He spun it in a few quick motions before retracting it and sheathing it at his side. Neven took in a deep breath at the realization that this training was going to be unlike anything he had ever gone through before.

"Ready?" Lanrete called out.

Neven stared at Lanrete in disbelief as he finished catching his breath.

"Not even remotely."

Lanrete cracked a smile, then charged at him again.

There are theories suggesting that the manipulation of time is a secret that will be unlocked with mastery of metaphysicism.

-FROM "SCHOOLS OF CIHPHISM"
BY SHAPER LUKIR AFREV

CHAPTER 37 TIRIVUS

New Thae, Tuzen home system

Tirivus, Ageless Emperor of the Tuzen Empire, pulled his sword from the chest of the man he had just impaled in his elaborate throne room. The man backed up a step, his eyes wide, blood pouring onto the floor. He dropped to his knees, his hands coming to clutch his mortal wound as he searched for help around him. All the others in attendance refused to meet his gaze, many keeping their eyes downcast. He slowly looked to Tirivus, but the pale-skinned Tuzen had already turned his back on him and was beginning the ascent back to his throne. As Tirivus reached his destination and sat down, his former advisor, Heriyen Swen, collapsed to the floor, unmoving.

"Does anyone else want to question my decision to remain within the Huzien Alliance?" Tirivus calmly leaned back in his throne, his silver gaze scanning the room. Not a breath was heard, the sudden brutality having left many speechless. "Clean that up!" Tirivus roared. A pair of guards came rushing toward the corpse before grabbing the body and quickly removing it from sight. A drone came in and began to sterilize the area, removing the blood with ruthless efficiency. In a matter of seconds, it had completed its task and disappeared. Everyone there had watched the scene in silence.

"My emperor." The words came from a Tuzen man with a midsized build, his blond hair a contrast to his dark honey-colored skin. Tirivus met the man's red-eyed gaze. "The revolutionaries are using your actions, albeit just and right, as fuel for their campaign against you. They are rallying the people in opposition of your perfect will." He took in a deep breath. "The foolish and rightfully killed traitor Heriyen hinted at a morsel of truth in his lies: that the revolutionaries are becoming bolder in their attacks on your rightful empire."

"What then would you advise me to do, dear Ories?" Tirivus leaned forward. Ories glanced to the other advisors; many had tight jaws and guarded looks.

"We should withhold funds from the Huzien reconstruction effort," Ories said. "The people would cheer your defiance of the Huziens, and it would counter the lies being spread by the revolutionaries, that our majesty is weak in the face of the *cith*, Cislot." Tirivus sat back in his throne and began to tap the armrest. His gaze hung on Ories for a long moment before he stood and casually began the descent from his throne, heading in the direction of Ories. Ories remained calm in front of his emperor, his posture relaxed.

Tirivus stopped in front of Ories and turned to regard the rest of his advisors, many staring with anticipation. He then faced Ories again, a broad smile crossing his face.

"My most trusted advisor," Tirivus said. "Your words are like music to my ears. Yes, this is exactly what my will shall be. Go, prepare for my meeting with Cislot. I will address the people tonight."

> *Care must be taken in the domain of Metaphysicism, as misuse led to the sickening practice of Elhirtha, or the weaving of the very life essences of living beings.*
>
> –FROM "SCHOOLS OF CIHPHISM"
> BY SHAPER LUKIR AFREV

CHAPTER 38 NEVEN KENK

Foundra Conscient, Huzien Alliance space

Neven collapsed onto a bench in the temporary workshop Aru had loaned to him aboard the Foundra Conscient. His body was sore beyond belief, but at least the nicks and cuts from his "fight for your life" session with Lanrete the day prior were long gone thanks to a VRC shower and quick trip to the med bay. Neven sat staring at an empty workbench, his mind running through the torture Lanrete had unleashed upon him. He was sure it was good for him, somehow, but being afraid for your life in a training session was a new experience, and he wasn't quite sure he had fully processed it yet.

"How can I keep step with a Huzien immortal who is focused on physical perfection?" Neven yelled. "I mean come on; he literally fights with a sword on the battlefield with people shooting at him!" Neven glanced at his muscles in a reflection. "It doesn't matter how fit I get; I'll never be as strong or as fast as him."

Technology always bridges the gap, Ellipse's voice rang out in his thoughts.

"Yeah, except when it can't," Neven countered.

He said you may not be able to use your power armor all the time, but not all technology has to be visible. Ellipse displayed a series of experimental concepts from the MinSci on Neven's micro-display.

"Hmmm . . ."

Neven got up and moved to the workbench. Within a few minutes, the schematic for a new creation began to take form.

You always impress me, Ellipse said. Another smile appeared in Neven's mind, this time with dark red lips.

"These are the last reported coordinates for the *Empress Star*." Lanrete looked to Neven and then Aru. Lanrete had called them both to the bridge as soon as the *Foundra Conscient* had dropped out of suplight. Aru walked over to a nearby holodisplay and brought up a series of sensor arrays, putting them to full power.

"We should know something soon enough," Aru said.

"How long will the analysis take?"

"Depends . . . best-guess estimate is an hour."

"What are we looking for exactly?" Neven interjected.

"Breadcrumbs," Lanrete replied.

"Suplight emission trails," Aru began to clarify, "weapon discharge particles, wreckage, debris, floating dead bodies— "

"I get it." Neven tried to clear the sudden image of a dead Zun flying lifeless in the cold of space from his mind. The three stood in silence for a long moment. "Do you think the ship was destroyed?"

"Unlikely," Aru replied. "If it was, we'd at least have a wreckage, and preliminary findings show nothing of the sort." Aru paused for a moment as something blipped on one of his holodisplays. "That's interesting . . ."

"What's that?" Lanrete said.

"I'm detecting two residual suplight signatures." Aru glanced from Neven to Lanrete. "One from a ship large enough to be the *Empress Star*, and one from something much smaller."

Neven brought up a holodisplay nearby and did a quick study of the information pieced together by Aru.

"They were both heading in the same direction."

"What's our theory?" Lanrete glanced to Neven.

Aru prepared to respond, but caught the visual cue from Lanrete to let Neven answer first.

"I think this confirms your pirate theory," Neven replied. "One thing I don't get, though."

"What's that?" Aru said.

"How could a ship with a suplight signature so small overpower the *Empress Star*?"

"Victory isn't always won through force," Lanrete replied. "If I wanted to take a ship of that scale, I'd deceive them into letting us board with an assault team. Then, I'd systematically take the ship from the inside."

"How could that go unnoticed, though? You'd figure they would have at least gotten out an emergency call for help or something."

"Not necessarily," Aru countered. "It's not uncommon for pirates to employ cyber warfare techniques to jam systems and kill mobi networks."

"This is crazy," Neven said. "Why would they hijack a cruise ship in Alliance space?"

"Updated technology, weapon stores," Aru began, "body parts, slaves—"

"I get that part, but in Alliance space?"

"Higher risk, higher reward."

"Do we have a good fix on their direction?" Lanrete asked.

"Coordinates on the screen now," Aru said.

"Take us to suplight."

Neven felt the *Foundra Conscient* readjust its heading, the subtle hum of the suplight drive powering up causing him to hold his breath. Within seconds, the soft boom of suplight engaging sent them back on the chase.

"Well, that was fun while it lasted." Aru let out a disappointed sigh. "Suplight emission trails have been scrubbed from this area."

"Very thorough," Lanrete said.

"They must have assumed someone could follow the trail," Neven said.

"These guys are good." Lanrete sighed. "It's been centuries since I've seen pirates this organized."

Neven silently scanned the sensor readout. "We could systematically try each direction until we pick up the trail. They can only head in so many directions if they were trying to leave Alliance space."

"Not completely accurate," Aru said. "They could head back into Alliance space to throw us off and then readjust to keep their trail hidden. Statistically, we'd have . . ." Aru paused for a moment as he did the calculations on his mobi. ". . . a lot of work to do." He projected the potential areas to search on the holodisplay.

Neven rubbed his eyes and let out a big sigh.

"I think it might be time to pay an old Hauxem friend a visit," Lanrete said.

Neven groaned.

Neven walked into the training room and saw Lanrete patiently waiting on the floor with his legs crossed and his eyes closed. At the sound of the door opening, Lanrete glanced up and tilted his head to the side, a smirk appearing on his face.

"This is new," Lanrete said. Neven confidently strode over to Lanrete with a small exoskeleton covering his body. The nanoplexi frame was matte black, and small cables connected at the joints.

Neven cracked a smile, and Lanrete jumped to his feet in a single motion. "Let's put your new toy to the test."

Lanrete charged at him without warning and brought Divinebreath across in a powerful slash. Neven deflected the attack and hopped to the side. Lanrete reversed direction, and the exoskeleton whirled to life. Neven brought Streamsong up to deflect the impossibly fast attack. He gulped at the brutality of Lanrete; the attack was clearly faster than he could have moved without the frame. Lanrete was unrelenting as he continued his assault, but Neven met wave after wave of lightning-fast strikes with impressive parries. Neven struggled to keep sight of Divinebreath, the mobi tracking system connected to his exoskeleton taking over with a program he had coded as his Human senses reached their limit.

I've got this, Ellipse said. She took full control of Neven's exoskeleton and instantly began an analysis of Lanrete's attack pattern and fighting style. Pulling in a treasure trove of additional data from the HIN, Ellipse created a dynamic prediction algorithm to form an offensive attack strategy.

Lanrete grinned as he was forced to block an unexpected strike from Neven. He instantly switched into a defensive stance. Their movements became a blur, their dance continuing with Neven in the lead. A small bead of sweat began to roll down Lanrete's forehead.

Ellipse threw up a warning as she forced Neven to jump back. In the blink of an eye, the area where Neven had been standing ignited in fire. Neven balked as more warning signals blared in his micro-display as he felt Divinebreath slice across his back, and then his exoskeleton suffered catastrophic systems failure. Neven collapsed to the ground on his knees, struggling to catch his breath. Hot plexicarbonite rested on his shoulder; Lanrete had severed every joint of the exoskeleton at his back.

Cheater, Ellipse whined. Neven collapsed to his stomach, more exhausted than he had ever been in his life.

"Impressive toy," Lanrete said.

Neven heard the founder sheath Divinebreath and walk out of the training room. He smiled and closed his eyes, fatigue dragging him to sleep.

Haula, Hauxem home system

Lanrete and Neven stood patiently waiting outside the entrance to a massive compound. Lush greenery colored the area around them, and impressive brickwork covered the adjacent walls of the primary building. The lavishness on display was clearly done to flaunt incredible wealth.

When the large, elaborate doors in front of them opened, Neven glanced to Lanrete, still not quite believing where they were. Lanrete locked gazes with Neven briefly before moving inside. Neven shook his head and followed Lanrete into a massive vestibule, all the while bracing himself, fully expecting a mental assault at any time. His first encounter with A'Amaria had been one of pain.

"Well, this is a pleasant surprise," a sultry voice said. Neven flinched at the sound of A'Amaria Schen. "Aww." A'Amaria pouted as she walked down a short flight of steps. She sported a black dressing gown, the fabric almost translucent and reminiscent of lace.

Neven glanced up at her, his eyes going wide. A'Amaria was nude under the gown, and he could nearly make out every detail. Her light blue body was well toned and athletic, but not too muscular, and in the place of hair, an intricate pattern of silver and purple covered her head. If she had been wearing normal clothing, she could have easily been mistaken for a teenage girl at first glance, but her well-developed body and mature gaze eliminated any chance of confusion on further inspection.

She came to a stop in front of Neven, her stance casual. Silver-laced diamond eyes regarded Neven playfully.

"Do you like what you see?" A'Amaria rested a hand on her hip. Neven backed up a step and looked away. Her gaze moved to Lanrete, and she raised an eyebrow. Lanrete regarded her briefly, then walked farther into her home. She turned her attention back to Neven. "I'm quite happy you're here," A'Amaria said. "After our last encounter, I was afraid you'd have no interest in seeing me again." She winked at him. *If you let me in freely, I can make it worth your while,* she imparted telepathically.

The hell you will, Ellipse voiced to Neven. He had to suppress a snicker, the action causing A'Amaria to tap her chin and narrow her eyes.

"Interesting." She turned around and followed Lanrete. "Most of my *a'aceph* is away for the week having a nice vacation on some paradise planet somewhere, leaving little old me sex-deprived and bored out of my mind," A'Amaria pouted.

"Why not go with them?" Lanrete countered.

"Work of course, love." A'Amaria moved ahead of Lanrete and ushered them into a large living space. Elaborate couches filled the massive area, and decorative rugs and pillows were everywhere.

"We're short on time so I'll get right to the point," Lanrete said. "I need your help."

Amaria moaned and slowly slid onto one of the couches, crossing her legs.

"Really?" she purred as she entered the throes of passion, continuing with a series of low moans that gradually began to build in intensity. The sight made Neven uncomfortable, his pants tightening as he quickly moved into a seat nearby to hide a growing bulge. "Say it again . . . I'm so close." She bit her lip, her voice rising one octet. After a few seconds of Lanrete silently glaring at her, she gave up the act, frowning. "You're no fun." She sighed. Her tone became harder, more professional. "If I remember correctly, you still owe me from our last business deal." She turned to Neven as she said the words. The look in her eyes made Neven sit back farther in his seat.

Lanrete moved to sit on the couch across from her, his gaze following hers. Neven tried his best to not look at A'Amaria; her intensity unsettled him. Lanrete shook his head, focusing back on A'Amaria. She tilted her head to the side and narrowed her eyes, her grin becoming dangerous. Lanrete took in a deep breath.

"What do you want, from me?"

Amaria got up from the couch and slunk over to straddle Lanrete. She undid the tie around her robe and opened it in the front, exposing her breasts to him. Neven began to sweat, his eyes wide. A'Amaria slowly moved her hand to unzip Lanrete's pants. Lanrete gripped her hand with lightning speed. She leaned back in his lap and let out a huff.

"I guess you'll be on your way then. Good luck finding the *Empress Star*."

"How do you know about the *Empress Star*?" Neven interjected.

"Oh honey," A'Amaria laughed. Her gaze met Neven's, her tone mocking. She turned her attention back to Lanrete and tilted her head to the side.

"Let's get reacquainted, privately." Lanrete leaned forward, prompting A'Amaria to move off him. She let her dressing gown hang open, an expectant smile on her face. Lanrete moved to close her gown, his hands slowly tying her belt in a bow. A'Amaria bit her lip.

"A'Areth, take care of Neven please," A'Amaria called out. A young Hauxem male appeared near the exit to the room and motioned for Neven to follow him. Neven hesitated for a moment, but after a nod from Lanrete, got up and moved to follow the other Hauxem.

FOUNDERS LOG:
The Worst Mistake

Some mistakes are better left never made. The choice of a mate is one that almost every living being in this galaxy faces at some point in their life. I've made this choice many times throughout my millennia of existence, but only once with another immortal. It was a choice that has continued to haunt me, and one that will most likely haunt me until one of us breathes no more.

A'Amaria. I remember her in her youth. She has always been a beautiful woman, a powerful woman, an ambitious woman . . . I met her young in her immortality, when she was still grasping the potential of a life of agelessness. Her eyes were innocent then, hopeful. I saw within her kindness, beauty, and a lust for adventure. There was something else there that I did not see, something still just a seed in the innermost of her being.

A willingness to do whatever it took to get what she wanted.

I was her first major prize. From there, she began to build her empire. She started slowly at first, utilizing the HIN that I had established as the crux of her information-brokering schemes. It took decades before I discovered the network she had developed. The clients she had amassed selling HIN information to the highest bidder. By the time I severed her connection to the resources the HIN provided, her personal network had already grown more powerful, more connected than my own. She no longer needed access to my network. She had become Seshat, the Information Broker, the most powerful woman in the Twin Galaxies.

True, she commanded no armies and no fleets, but what she wielded was far deadlier. She could collapse empires with a few business deals, or by dropping the right information into the wrong hands at the right time. She always knew everything and finally had the power she had always sought—the success that would define the woman she was to become. That was when I saw it clearly for the first time. She had lost her morality. I don't know when she lost it, but that state is one of the immortal curses.

What I do know is that the highest bidder meant the highest bidder to her, regardless of the cost. I demanded that she stop, that she give it all up and make amends. She laughed at me, claimed that I was naive if I truly believed that she would. I determined that she could no longer be my eifi. *That the two of us could no longer share a lifetime together.*

-Lanrete

CHAPTER 39 LANRETE

Haula, Hauxem home system

A'Amaria lay next to Lanrete on a large daybed in a beautiful sunlit room. The sheets were silken and damp, their sweat from the past few hours soaking them through. Lanrete had his arm across A'Amaria's stomach, the woman nestled at his front, her gaze out the window. She silently stroked his arm, contentment in her eyes.

"Mmmm, it's been far too long," A'Amaria said.

"This settles what I owe you." Lanrete's voice was emotionless. A'Amaria frowned.

"This settles us for the information on Sagren. You and your little Human friend staying here for the next two nights will settle us for the *Empress Star*. Oh, and you'll be staying in my room." The two lay in silence for a long moment, their breathing mixing with the sounds of birds filtering in through the window. "Why did you divorce me?" The question was raw, hurt just below the surface.

"Because you're a terrible person and I saw that too late," Lanrete said.

A'Amaria slapped him.

She was up and out of the bed in a flash, hot anger radiating from her body.

"How dare you talk to me about being a terrible person!" she hissed. "The things that you've done, the mistakes that you've made." She lunged forward and slapped him again, repeatedly. He had to grip her hand and restrain her. "The lives that *you've* ruined! You hypocrite!" Lanrete held her on the bed. She stopped struggling and went limp. "Leave me be, please." Her voice was a whisper. Lanrete released her and got up. Grabbing his clothes, he pulled them on and exited the room without a glance in her direction.

The next morning, Lanrete opened his eyes to light streaming into the elaborate bedroom. He stared at the canopy above the bed, translucent sheets draping the sides in every direction. His gaze slowly went to the window that took up most of the back of the room, where A'Amaria caught his attention. She was angled in his direction, her nude body on full display with her gaze focused out the window. He took in the sight of her, arms crossed under her breasts, her stance confident, in command. It was an image he hadn't seen in many millennia; an image that caused memories to rush back. He pushed them down.

"You know the nice thing about immortal pussy?" A'Amaria said. Lanrete remained silent. "It's always tight." She glanced in his direction with a smirk. Her smirk vanished as she caught sight of his face, and she looked away from him, her gaze returning to the window. "I tried to be the good *eifi* you wanted." She glanced back at him; her eyes were older, more tired. "I really did try."

Lanrete scoffed.

"You may not believe me, but I'm telling you the truth." A'Amaria pushed herself away from the window, her arms dropping to her sides as she moved to the bed. Climbing into it, she dropped next to Lanrete, her shoulder rubbing up against his. "I loved you then . . . I still love you now."

"Don't," Lanrete said.

A'Amaria remained silent, both staring up at the canopy to her bed.

"One of my brokers sold the information that enabled the pirates to capture the *Empress Star.*"

"I figured as much."

"Do you still find me attractive?"

Lanrete hesitated.

"Carnally? Yes." A'Amaria smiled. "Emotionally? No." Her smile faded.

"Would it have been different if I had been able to give you children? Maybe even another Nalle?"

Lanrete sat up in the bed. He rubbed his eyes and let out a heavy sigh. Glancing over at his former wife, he locked gazes with her. She stared up at him in silence. After a long moment, Lanrete got up out of the bed and moved to the window. She continued to stare at him, clearly hoping for a response and wiping away a single tear.

"Where is the ship now?" Lanrete asked.

A'Amaria ran her hand down to between her legs. She focused her gaze up at the canopy and began to masturbate herself. Lanrete glanced back at her.

"A'Amaria."

"*A'akugentai'a,*" she snapped back in a Hauxem profanity.

"Seshat."

She ignored him.

Lanrete sighed. He moved away from the window and to the bed. Grabbing her hand, he pinned it to the bed. She glared at him. "*A'asentup'akugen'avi!*" she yelled.

"No, I won't get off you," Lanrete replied. "We have a deal. You owe me information."

A'Amaria stared back up at the canopy to her bed, her lips unmoving. Slowly, Lanrete released hold of her arm. She remained motionless in the bed. A'Amaria was crying inside—he could see it on her face—but she wouldn't show him her tears. She wouldn't give him that part of herself anymore. Not him, not anyone.

"I've given birth to one hundred and fifteen males and one hundred and thirty-four females. A feat that has made me cherished in Hauxem society." Her gaze met Lanrete's. "And yet, due to a curse of genetics, due to the fact that I am Hauxem and you are Huzien, I was unable to give you any children."

"It's better this way."

A'Amaria slapped him and then proceeded to slap him again, the moisture from her hand leaving streaks across his face. Lanrete pinned her arms down at her sides. She spit in his face.

"I hate you. I hate you so much." Her voice cracked. "Why couldn't you just accept me? Why couldn't you forgive me? Why couldn't you continue to love me?"

"Why couldn't you leave it all and just be my *eifi?*" Lanrete shouted. "Why was it more important for you to be Seshat?" It was the first true emotion that he had shown in any of their interactions since the divorce. The sudden intensity of it left A'Amaria speechless, her eyes wide. Heavy breathing filled the room as Lanrete stared at A'Amaria with boiling anger. The wound had been reopened; the pain fresh. A'Amaria turned her head to the side, her expression going soft. She stared out of the window to her bedroom, no longer struggling against him. There it was—the truth she had known but refused to accept. Lanrete moved off her and to the side, collapsing onto the bed.

Later that afternoon, Lanrete walked into the elaborate kitchen area of A'Amaria's home, the open concept layout bathed in sunlight from skylights and wall-length windows. An appetizing scent hit his nostrils, and the founder stopped in his tracks as he spotted A'Amaria. She glanced back at him, her back and butt bare and a red cloth tied around her waist to secure the cooking apron in front of her. A'Amaria brought a cooking utensil to her mouth and licked it slowly.

Lanrete glanced away from her and toward the elaborate kitchen counter. The device sprang to life. After grabbing the cup of water that appeared, Lanrete turned and began to exit the kitchen. He took two steps, then stopped.

"Are you making *a'ayuwri'aret?*" Lanrete asked.

A'Amaria smiled. "So, you do remember the dish."

"I remember it being a highly technical dish that you loved to make to show off in the kitchen."

"If you can, do." She turned around to face him and leaned back against the counter. The action pushed her bare breasts up against the tight apron, the sides of her light blue areolas peeking out. "The main component is done. Another hour or so and everything will be ready to eat."

Lanrete turned back to face her. "You're making us dinner?"

"What kind of host would I be if I didn't?" A'Amaria turned back around, then stood silently for a long moment. "I'm sorry I wasn't the *eifi* you wanted." She looked up toward the ceiling. "I will tell you everything you want to know tonight about the *Empress Star*. All I ask is that you have dinner with me, like we used to when we were a family." The sounds of cooking pots bubbling and other food items simmering filled the room. They both remained silent, taking in the ambiance.

Lanrete let out a heavy sigh. "Okay."

A'Amaria hid a smile and immediately went back to finishing her dish. Lanrete stood watching her for a long moment. He took in the sight of her from behind. It had been a common scene when they were married. A'Amaria had regularly cooked in the nude, the act something that aroused him greatly. A'Amaria began to exaggerate her every motion, but she seemed oblivious to him. An internal debate raged within Lanrete, a debate between his carnal desires and his willpower. A'Amaria's scent was stuck in his nostrils, and his willpower lost as the sensuality of it overwhelmed him.

Lanrete moved to stand behind A'Amaria, his hands going to her hips. She moaned expectantly and set down the utensil in her hand. A thought shut off the cooking surface, and another brought up a stasis field suspending her food in its current state of cooking. Lanrete pulled her into him while A'Amaria pushed her butt up and grinded slowly against his clothes. As she turned around, the two locked lips in a long, drawn-out kiss. She pushed Lanrete back toward the counter and he sucked in another breath, her scent driving him wild.

A'Amaria moved to him, then undid his belt buckle with such expert precision that he didn't notice until his pants hit the floor. He pulled her in closer and gripped her butt firmly. A'Amaria pushed him into the opposite counter, and Lanrete knocked some of the prepared food out of the way before jumping up to sit on it. She moved to straddle him, then pushed him down. Still wearing the apron, she glanced down at him with half-closed eyes. He brought his hands up to her sides. She began to rock back and forth, slowly at first, then faster. The counter shook with each movement.

The sight of her nude body barely contained by the apron eliminated all conscious thought. A'Amaria's diamond-laced silver eyes glittered, the sight breathtaking. The two were perfectly in sync as they made love into the afternoon. Dinner would be late.

Cihphist sensitivity classifications start with those who show no sensitivity at level 0, thus reflected as CSL 0. These individuals have no potential to wield the Enesmic and will never develop it—with the exception of immortals.

–FROM "CSL WITH NO DIRECT ENESMIC LINK"
BY SHAPER LUKIR AFREV

CHAPTER 40 NEVEN KENK

Haula, Hauxem home system

Neven watched the birds play in the trees outside the back patio. The perfectly manicured garden went on for what seemed like miles, and had trees littered throughout the area. The sound of the patio door opening pulled his attention. Lanrete stepped through and moved to sit in the chair next to him. Neven stared at him for a long moment as Lanrete looked out into the garden.

"I didn't realize she was your ex-wife," Neven said.

"Seems like something you could have easily looked up."

"Sorry . . ." Neven scratched the back of his head. "I try to stay out of people's personal business."

"That's a good habit." Lanrete glanced over at Neven. "We'll be leaving after tomorrow." Lanrete paused for a moment, seeming to consider his next words. "Be careful around A'Amaria. I don't know what her interest in you is, but it's there. I've seen it and I'm sure you've felt it. Whatever it is, A'Amaria always tries to take what she wants. She doesn't like being denied anything."

Neven nodded his head, his stomach churning in fear.

Neven took a forkful of the savory dish and stuffed it into his mouth after receiving a nod of approval from Lanrete. He, Lanrete, A'Areth, and A'Amaria were sitting around a large dining room table in the grand dining room. Its size dwarfed them, the setup clearly intended for a group of thirty or more individuals.

"What is this called?" Neven asked.

"*A'ayuwri'aret*," A'Amaria said. Neven stared at her, his grasp of the Hauxem language failing him. "It's a highly technical dish, one that very few of the top chefs on Haula, let alone within the Twin Galaxies, can pull off."

"I guess it's a good thing you have one of them here."

"Yes, I am a pretty amazing chef."

Neven almost choked, though he quickly regained his composure.

Lanrete grinned.

"So, your name is A'Areth?" Neven turned away from A'Amaria and to the young man sitting next to her. He was Hauxem, his eyes the same diamond color as A'Amaria's except without the silver, and his skin was a similar blue tone with an intricate purple and silver pattern on his head, also like A'Amaria's.

"Yes," A'Areth said.

"Are you two related?"

"I gave birth to him," A'Amaria said. "He stayed behind when the rest of my *a'aceph* went on vacation." She glanced at A'Areth expectantly. "To spend some alone time with me."

"Oh, sorry to intrude A'Areth. I know how important mother and son time can be."

Lanrete remained silent as his gaze went to A'Amaria. She returned a mischievous smile.

"He doesn't normally get much time to be intimate with me," A'Amaria pouted. She leaned over to kiss A'Areth on the lips. He kissed her back, his hand sliding to her hip briefly before she backed away to her seat. "And Lanrete's currently taking up all of my time."

Neven dropped his fork and sat back in his chair.

"That's messed up," Neven blurted. "You're a sicker woman than I thought."

Careful . . . Ellipse warned.

A'Areth pushed his seat back and stood up. A'Amaria quickly moved to stand in front of him, shaking her head slightly. "Neven doesn't understand our culture, love." She glanced back at Neven briefly with a glare. "Go make a bath for us, okay? Just me and you."

A'Areth glanced from Neven to A'Amaria, his anger subsiding. He reluctantly smiled at her and nodded, though he gave Neven a scowl before departing from the room. A'Amaria turned around and leaned against the dining room table, resting on her arms.

"I am the *a'achepan* of this *a'aceph*. I have been so for four thousand three hundred and sixty-four years." A'Amaria gave Lanrete a bitter look, though her face softened quickly. "There are no familial bonds such as mother, father, brother, sister, son, or daughter in Hauxem society. The concept of family that comes to your mind is nonexistent here. Genetically, the types of limitations that exist through procreation in your species do not exist within mine. He is a part of my *a'aceph* and as such, he has a right to mate with me and anyone else in our little community."

Neven shook his head. He turned to Lanrete, who remained silent with his gaze locked on A'Amaria. Neven let out a heavy sigh.

"I'm sorry. I should be more accepting of different cultures. Please extend my apologies to A'Areth, I didn't know."

A'Amaria smiled.

"All is forgiven." She moved back to her seat. Neven stared at his food for a long moment, eventually forcing himself to pick back up his fork and eat the food in front of him. His mind was still processing this new revelation about Hauxem culture. Ellipse was feeding him information from the Gnet, his micro-display filling with info vids related to the controversial practices within Hauxem society. There was apparently a large percentage of the Alliance populace that shared in Neven's apprehension.

They ate in silence, Lanrete staring off into the distance. A'Amaria watched him the entire time, her face going through a multitude of emotions. When they finished eating, she took in a deep breath that grabbed Lanrete's attention.

"Here is the current route of the *Empress Star*." A stream of data began transferring to Lanrete and Neven's mobis. "The *Foundra Conscient*'s Manem suplight drive should allow you to catch up rather quickly."

"How do you know about the Manem suplight drive?" Neven asked.

A'Amaria ignored him. Getting up from the table, she turned away from Lanrete and headed off in the same direction A'Areth had gone. Neven got up from the table shortly after and retreated to his room. Getting inside, he shut and locked the door, then let out a heavy sigh. Taking off his shirt, he moved to his bed and lay staring up at the ceiling for a long time. His thoughts began to wander to Zun while he examined the information A'Amaria had given them of the *Empress Star*'s projected trajectory on his micro-display.

We'll find her, Ellipse said.

I know, I just miss her.

The sound of the door to his room closing grabbed his attention. Sitting up, he locked eyes with A'Amaria. She stood at the entrance to his room, her hands behind her back. A loose-fitting beige skirt hung around her waist and an oversized low-hanging blouse covered her top. The sight was relaxed, casual, sensual.

"Uh . . . can I help you?" Neven asked. "Pretty sure I locked that door."

A'Amaria's face slowly morphed into a grin. "I wanted to talk," she said.

I don't like this, Ellipse relayed to him.

"We should get Lanrete then."

"A private conversation," A'Amaria countered, "between you, me, and your little SSI friend."

She knows I exist! There was fear in Ellipse's voice.

"Not sure what you're talking about," Neven bluffed.

"Neven," A'Amaria sighed. "Your comments are like insults to me. There is very little that I don't know in the Twin Galaxies, especially when it's as interesting as experimental prototypes." She crossed her arms. "I'm a very resourceful woman."

"Sounds like you know everything then." Neven frowned. "What do you need to talk to me for?"

"I like you, Neven," A'Amaria said. "There is something about you, a type of innocence that's rare in today's day and age." She moved closer to him. Neven moved to stand up, out of the bed. A'Amaria gave him a quick once-over, her eyes lingering on his chiseled upper body. She stopped a few feet away from him. "I'd love to explore your mind, see what makes you tick."

"You mean fundamentally invade every aspect of my privacy?"

"Semantics." She let her eyes linger again on his abs, slowly moving up his muscular chest to his eyes. Neven shifted uncomfortably. "You're a virgin, aren't you?"

"What?" Neven tried to hide the surprise on his face. His hand went to the back of his neck while his body broke out into a cold sweat. A'Amaria nodded and bit her lip.

"Tell me, Neven." A'Amaria half closed her eyes. "Do you find me attractive?"

The hell you do, Ellipse yelled in Neven's mind.

Neven tried to hide his smirk at Ellipse's response. A'Amaria caught it and tilted her head to the side.

"Does the SSI communicate with you freely?"

"I thought there was very little you didn't know in the galaxy." A'Amaria bit her lip again.

"I know some details about things," A'Amaria conceded. "Such that there is an SSI prototype. The details as to how it works, or actual schematics, are sometimes out of reach." She moved closer to him, her closeness causing him to back up into a nightstand. "Which is why I'm willing to make a trade."

"A trade?"

"Yes, you let me peruse through your thoughts and I'll give you anything you want." She grinned. "You'll discover that there is very little that I can't acquire." She locked gazes with him, her eyes entrancing. "I'd even give you the best night of your life, right here, right now." The words caused Neven's heart to skip a beat, his eyes going wide as he took in a quick breath. A'Amaria smiled. "That entices you."

Run away from her, Neven! Run from all of this, just get out of the room. Go see Lanrete, do anything but stand here right now and continue to listen to her! Ellipse yelled in his mind.

Neven flinched as A'Amaria moved in closer, her breasts under her blouse brushing up against Neven's bare chest. He was entranced by her eyes. They were beautiful, unlike anything he had ever seen in his life. She had an amazing scent, her closeness amplifying it a thousandfold. Neven's stance became loose, his thoughts coming slower.

"No . . . No!" Neven tried to push A'Amaria back. She resisted and pushed into him harder, her body tight against his.

Neven, leave!

"I . . . I'm in a relationship."

"That's nice," A'Amaria cooed.

Neven, leave now!

"I . . . have never been with a woman." Neven could no longer hear Ellipse, his mind clouded. "I've been saving myself for marriage, it's very important to me."

"I understand." A'Amaria moved in even closer, her body pinning him against the wall as she kissed his neck lightly a few times. "You want your first time to be special, to be something to remember."

"For marriage." Neven's clarity began to slip even further, his body becoming lethargic. "For something special."

"I will make this night special for you," A'Amaria whispered. "I promise." Her voice was heavy, her breath hot on Neven's face. She kissed him, a single peck at first. Another peck followed, with a longer kiss pulling them closer together. She moved his head to her neck, her scent strong, overwhelming. He kissed her neck. She moaned lightly and began to lick his ear, her hand undoing the clasp on her skirt, causing it to drop to the floor. Tingles spread throughout Neven's body. She guided him to the bed, both sitting side by side, Neven kissing her neck as she rubbed the back of his head. She released the clasp on her blouse, and it fell too. She took one of Neven's hands and moved it to her breast. He began to grope her, his kissing becoming more intense.

A'Amaria carefully undid his pants and began to massage his member. Neven paused, something clicking in his brain.

"No," he mumbled. "Zun . . ."

A'Amaria brought his face in closer to her breasts, then pulled him on top of her and released him, subtly kicking off the remnants of her blouse. She was completely naked. He began to kiss her breasts, her low moans edging him on. She positioned them such that Neven was subconsciously grinding up against her crotch area. Neven stopped when he felt wetness down near his crotch. He turned his gaze down to see his penis fully exposed, with her lower half uncovered, intricate patterns where pubic hair would have been on a Human. He was surprised to see A'Amaria fully exposed to him, his mind unable to process what that meant. She turned his attention back to her breasts, pulling his head in between her mounds and wrapping her legs around him.

Her scent dug into his brain; it made him irrationally want her more than he had ever wanted anything in the galaxy. He kissed her breasts again. A'Amaria slowly wrapped her hand around his member, and Neven responded positively this time. Smiling, she guided him in. Neven gasped. A'Amaria flexed her leg muscles, locking him inside of her, giving him time to adjust. He continued kissing her. She relaxed her muscles, allowing him to move back slightly. Then she flexed them again, pulling him back in. She did that a few times, the motions becoming instinctual as Neven continued them on his own. He continued the steady rhythm, driving through a level of pleasure he had never experienced. A'Amaria watched him, her eyes half closed with a satisfied grin on her face.

Neven's body shook, another gasp escaping him as he collapsed on top of her, his member pulsing inside her. A'Amaria, unconcerned, delved deep into his mind, his mental defenses defeated in that moment of pure ecstasy. The intricate web she had been weaving around his mind sunk in all at once. She invaded every aspect of him, his deepest hopes and desires all laid bare before her. She examined all that was Neven and forcefully thrust herself deep into his consciousness. She inserted a piece of herself there, a portion of her own mind deep within his own. A sickness welled up in Neven's stomach, the intensity of it overwhelming. The wrongness of the whole situation was too much for him. He felt dirty, wretched, ashamed, pathetic, and worthless.

"No!" Neven shouted. He pushed A'Amaria away, moving off her and scrambling back in the bed. She lay there unmoving, her gaze locked on him. He caught sight of her lower half, a white substance dripping from what passed for a vaginal opening among Hauxem. The sight almost caused him to throw up. That was his semen. "Maker, what have I done?" Neven shook his head, attempting to clear his mind, his thoughts chaotic and a pounding headache assaulting him. It was quickly becoming unbearable. "What did you do to me!" Neven yelled.

Oh, Neven, Ellipse said, her voice sad.

Movement near the door drew both of their attention as Lanrete barged into the room.

An individual of CSL 1 has a type of primal cihphist ability, only able to sense feelings and potential danger, a type of sixth sense. In many species across the galaxy, this is a common trait, such as with the Uri, Huziens, Tuzens, and Das'Vin.

–FROM "CSL WITH NO DIRECT ENESMIC LINK"
BY SHAPER LUKIR AFREV

CHAPTER 41 LANRETE

Haula, Hauxem home system

A'Amaria's scent hit Lanrete like a nanoplexi wall when he entered the room. It was pungent and overwhelming. Lanrete coughed as it attacked his senses, his thoughts becoming jumbled. He instructed one of his glands to produce a neurostimulant that gave him immediate focus. Lanrete's gaze first went to Neven and then to A'Amaria. He immediately processed what had just transpired.

"You've sunk to a new low." Lanrete moved toward the two. "What did you do to him?" A'Amaria casually shot her legs out over the side of the bed and rocked to a standing position.

"What did *I* do?" A'Amaria glanced back at Neven. "From my understanding, we just had consensual sex." A'Amaria ran a finger along her inner thigh, then flicked a white substance in Lanrete's direction.

"No." Neven shook his head. He pointed an accusatory finger at A'Amaria. "No, you manipulated me. You raped me!"

"How so?" A'Amaria countered. "That's your semen on the floor. You came inside me from on top." A'Amaria laughed. "Fairly sure that's not how rape works."

"You . . . you . . ." Neven put a hand to his head. "Everything is hazy, and my head is killing me." Neven shook his head again and stared at the bed. "I . . . I told you no. I wanted to save myself for marriage. I wanted it to be something special."

"I'm not special?" A'Amaria feigned hurt. "I think your penis would disagree with you."

Neven shot her a glare.

"That's enough!" Lanrete stepped in between them. "We're leaving, now." He motioned for Neven to get dressed. The young secnic jumped out of the bed and attempted to clean himself up, clearly barely able to focus. His face was flushed, and he wouldn't look at Lanrete. Neven glared at A'Amaria again. She had an impassive look. Lanrete turned fully to face A'Amaria and crossed his arms. "Neven, wait outside." Neven grabbed his shirt, slipped on his shoes, and exited the room without another word.

Silence descended. After a few moments, A'Amaria began to pick up her clothing off the floor and dress herself. "This is why I divorced you." A'Amaria's hand subconsciously came up to her face. "You take what you want, and care not at all for the repercussions."

"He'll get over it." A'Amaria dropped her hand. "I would hardly call what just happened sex."

"Maybe to you," Lanrete countered, "but to Neven, that moment was meant to be with his *eifi*. Not with a woman who cares not an iota for him."

"Then he should have better restrained himself." A'Amaria tsked. "Don't worry, I won't tell his little girlfriend, Zun." She bitterly grabbed a pillowcase from one of the pillows on the bed and used it to wipe herself dry before closing the clasp on her skirt. "Unless she pays me, of course."

"You're going through *a'acuy*, aren't you?"

"I don't see why where I am in my fertility cycle matters."

"Your pheromones," Lanrete interjected, "are the strongest I can ever remember, and this room is thick with them." A'Amaria stopped moving and stood with her arms crossed, her gaze locked with Lanrete's.

"Five thousand years is a long time," A'Amaria said, her tone flat. "You learn to control your body more as time progresses." She took a step closer to Lanrete, as if sicking her pheromones on him like a dog.

His gaze was unflinching. "What you did was wrong and unfair to him."

"Don't lecture me."

"No." Lanrete raised his hands. "You're right. I won't lecture you. You are who you choose to be. And who you choose to be is a woman who uses people to get what she wants. A woman who has no moral compass." Lanrete turned and began to exit the room. "A woman who lost her soul in her quest for the galaxy." Lanrete stopped at the door. "I made a mistake in coming here. Goodbye, Seshat." Without another word, Lanrete and Neven left A'Amaria's home.

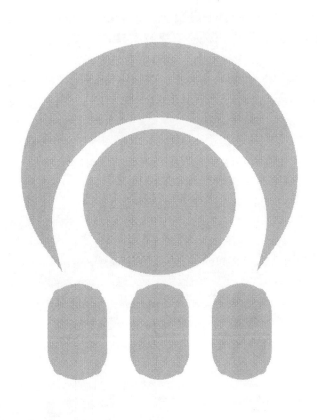

CHAPTER 42 NEVEN KENK

Haula, Hauxem home system

Neven quietly walked beside Lanrete as they boarded the waiting shuttle to take them back to the Foundra Conscient. The haze that had obscured his mind in the room was gone. There was a look of dread on Neven's face, and his skin was pale. Lanrete leaned back in his chair and sighed. Neven attempted to glance in Lanrete's direction but couldn't bring himself to look Lanrete in the eye.

"I'm sorry," Neven said.

"You don't need to apologize to me," Lanrete said. "A'Amaria stopped being my wife a long time ago."

"I . . ." Neven hesitated. "What have I done?" He rested his head in his palms. The shuttle door closed and the air became pressurized as the hum of the reactor filled the small space. Within seconds, the shuttle lifted from the ground and began its ascent back to the ship.

"You should have come to me," Lanrete said. "I warned you about A'Amaria."

"I know." Neven shook his head. "It all happened so fast." Neven thought of Ellipse, her warnings clear as day in his mind. Warnings he had ceased to hear at some point. She didn't respond to his thoughts. "I thought I was strong enough." Neven lifted his head. "This is my fault."

"A'Amaria didn't fight fair." Neven glanced at Lanrete, a look of confusion on his face. "Hauxem females have very strong phero- mones that can mess with the mind, and A'Amaria's seemed excep- tionally powerful." Lanrete met Neven's gaze, but the young Human glanced away. As he did, Ellipse flooded Neven's mobi with informa- tion from the Gnet about Hauxem biology.

"A bit too late," Neven snapped.

"Sorry, I should have mentioned that sooner," Lanrete said.

Neven shook his head. "I was talking to Ellipse."

"Your SSI?"

"You know?"

"Of course." Lanrete hid a smile. "I know everything that goes on within my ship."

Neven let out a heavy sigh. "What do I do now?"

"You tell Zun the truth." Neven slumped in his chair. "If you keep something like this bottled up inside of you, it will eat away at you. It will change you. And that will negatively impact your rela- tionship with Zun."

"She'll leave me."

"She won't leave you for being manipulated into sex against your will," Lanrete scoffed. "Regardless, you should never let fear stop you from doing or saying anything, especially when it's the right thing." Lanrete paused for a moment, then sighed. "If it's what you want, we can press charges against A'Amaria for her actions in Alli- ance court. I have to warn you that it would be a very public trial giv- en her official status as a Hauxem diplomat, and it would most likely drag on for a few years. But Hauxem females have been successfully prosecuted for pheromone rape in Alliance court."

Neven shook his head. "I just want to forget about this." He sat in silence for a long moment, then switched his mobi to an outside view of the shuttle as they departed the upper atmosphere. He closed his eyes and tried to wish away the memories.

Whether or not weaving the Enesmic is a genetic limitation is a contested point, with some pointing to the inability of CSL 1 individuals to directly weave the Enesmic, despite their ability to sense it.

–FROM "CSL WITH NO DIRECT ENESMIC LINK"
BY SHAPER LUKIR AFREV

CHAPTER 43 HUCARA JUK GIN

Ecka, Thae, Huzien Home System

Hucara Juk Gin stood at the start of a long walkway that winded to an impressive three-story home, her orange gaze on the wooden double doors of the house and her light brown skin baking in the light of Thae's white star. Hucara's caramel- and cinnamon-colored hair was shoulder length, and she had light brown esha marks running down her temples and neck. A soldier stood waiting near the hovercar she had just gotten out of.

Hucara took a step toward the entrance and then hesitated; the long drive across the late Uyam Ikol's estate had caused memories to come flooding back to her. Steeling her gaze, she clenched her fist and continued forward. After chiming the door, Hucara stared at the elaborate etching on the broad wooden double doors. What seemed like an eternity passed before the doors opened inward, and an amber gaze greeted Hucara. The woman's face was much older than Hucara's, but she had light brown skin similar in complexion. The Uri hybrid who had stood against the terrifying forces of Sagren in defense of the planet Neth glanced away briefly, unable to maintain eye contact with Anita Ikol, the widow of Uyam Ikol.

"You're the last person I ever expected to come visit me," Anita said. The casualness of the statement caught Hucara off guard, but there was no animosity in her tone. She glanced back up to Anita, and the older woman sighed before stepping back and gesturing for Hucara to come inside. Hucara hesitated again, her eyes searching Anita's face for something, anything. "Do you intend to stand there all day?"

"Sorry ma'am, thank you." Hucara quickly moved inside.

A few moments later, a serving drone set a cup of tea on the small coffee table between Anita and Hucara. They were in an elaborate room filled with art and baubles collected from across the Huzien Alliance. Hucara picked up the cup and took a complimentary sip before setting it back down.

"I'm sorry to intrude unannounced," Hucara said. Anita displayed a tired smile. "I . . . uh, there is something that I need to tell you." Hucara took in a deep breath. "I was in an affair with your late husband—your *nusba*."

"I am aware," Anita responded without hesitation. "Uyam left a recording to be released upon his death. In it he detailed his long-standing affair with you." Anita glanced away. "Of course, I always suspected." She let out a long, slow breath, her body shuddering.

Hucara sat back in her chair, her eyes wide.

"Is that all you came to tell me?" There was no bitterness in Anita's tone.

"No . . . I . . . " Hucara hesitated. "I'm sorry."

Anita let out a raw laugh, one that bit Hucara to the core, and got up to move toward a nearby window. She wore a modest blue house dress with a pair of matching blue slippers on her feet, and she was in great shape, apparently as rigorous in her physical fitness regimen as Uyam had been. Hucara knew she was in her early 700s, but she didn't look a day over 500. The Huzien general of the mobile infantry watched the woman quietly, feeling overwhelmingly insignificant in that moment.

"When was the last time you had sex with my *nusba*?" Anita's question was calm, casual.

Hucara balked. Her gaze immediately went to the floor as she broke out in a cold sweat.

"The day before he died," she whispered.

"Do you know the last time I had sex with my *nusba*?"

"No, ma'am."

Anita glanced back at Hucara, regarding her briefly before turning her gaze back out of the window.

"Two years ago." Anita clasped her hands behind her back. "I have never been with another man, and I will most likely die having only ever been with Uyam."

"I'm so . . ."

"That was my choice," Anita interjected. "I knew when marrying Uyam that when he was away on active duty, I wouldn't have the comfort of his body near mine. I accepted that reality when I married a military man." Anita wiped away a tear. "But I expected him to be as faithful to me as I was to him." Anita glanced in Hucara's direction again. "I loved my *nusba*, and I've long ago forgiven him." Anita hesitated for a moment. "Did you love Uyam, or was it just sex?"

"At first . . ." Hucara hesitated. "At first it was just sex. But over time . . . I . . . I started to love him." Anita turned back to look out of the window, a heavy silence filling the room. "The last thing Uyam told me before he died . . ."

Anita turned to face Hucara fully, their gazes locking.

A single tear rolled down Hucara's cheek. "He told me to tell you that he loved you." Hucara let out a slight gasp and wiped away another tear, attempting to compose herself. Anita remained silent for a long moment.

"In the recording that Uyam left me, he never once asked for forgiveness for his actions. Instead, he asked me to forgive you." Anita closed her eyes and let out a heavy sigh. "I have already forgiven you, Hucara Juk Gin." Anita motioned toward the entrance. "Now get the *vusg* out of my house."

CHAPTER 44 RICHARDRE VEAN

Dextra Veich orbiting New Ginea, Huzien home system

Captain Richardre Vean disembarked from the military transport, his mix of platinum and blue hair causing a few to glance at him curiously. Being a Uri and Huzien hybrid, he was used to the stares. His appearance was that of a Huzien, except for his hair and the bright copper eyes that dominated his olive-skinned face.

"Captain Vean?" Richardre turned to meet the gaze of a young Human ensign.

"That's me."

"I'm here to escort you to General Gin, sir." Richardre nodded, prompting the ensign to turn around and lead him toward a meglift. After a short ride, Richardre stepped onto the command bridge of the 103rd Huzien Mobile Infantry hive ship, *Dextra Veich*. The deck was abuzz with activity. In the center of it all stood a tall woman with hair a mix of caramel and cinnamon. Her bright orange eyes locked onto his form the moment he stepped onto the bridge. Richardre felt a lump rise in his throat at the sight of another Uri hybrid.

The ensign motioned toward General of the Mobile Infantry Hucara Juk Gin. Richardre had to force himself to move. Pushing the lump down, he stepped toward his new general and came to a stop a few feet away from her before saluting.

Hucara dismissed a holodisplay she had been studying. Crossing her arms, she gave Richardre a once-over.

"Captain Richardre Vean reporting for duty, ma'am."

"Impeccable resume," Hucara said. "Pree was some impressive work, and a commendation from Founder Lanrete himself." She nodded her head. "Not an easy thing to pull off."

"Thank you, ma'am."

"I've read your personnel file." Hucara glanced away from him, bringing up a holodisplay showcasing his information. "I was curious what the story was behind someone with Uri blood who didn't have a tribal signifier." Richardre frowned. "But that information was surprisingly absent." She glanced at him. "Luckily, the Jukazi tribal records back on Peshkana did have a file on a Richardre and his mother Xhera Juk Vean."

Hucara motioned for him to follow as she turned and made a beeline for a private conference room a short distance away. The lump returned to Richardre's throat. Both entered the large conference room, the door silently clicking shut behind them. She turned on him at the closing of the door, her arms still crossed. "Tradition would have me put you back on the transport you flew in on and wipe my hands clean of having anything to do with you and your family."

"With all due respect, ma'am." Richardre cleared his throat. "This isn't Peshkana; this is the Huzien Mobile Infantry."

Hucara smiled. "You're right, it is. And considering Lanrete personally ordered you to serve under me, that would be violating a direct order from the founder."

"Directly ordered, ma'am?"

Ignoring him, Hucara brought up a holodisplay.

"Our ground war against Sagren exposed some major gaps in our squad makeup and technological firepower. The MinSci, in combination with eshLucient and the powers that be at MI Command, have created prototypes of new forms of Archlight soldiers. Enough to fully build out a functional combat squad. You will be the new CO of that squad." Richardre's face scrunched up.

"My transfer order mentioned taking over a battalion, ma'am."

"Orders change."

"Permission to speak freely, ma'am?"

Hucara uncrossed her arms and moved her hands to her hips. She grinned, her eyes narrowing. "Granted."

"This is *vusging* nonsense. I've dealt with this type of prejudice my whole life and I'd expect better from a general of the mobile infantry, ma'am."

Hucara's grin disappeared. She advanced on Richardre, the captain taking a step back as she came to within an inch of his face. Her eyes captured his soul, her face hard.

"Tell me, Captain. What do we have right now?" Richardre took a deep breath, calming himself.

"A misunderstanding, ma'am."

Hucara backed away from him, nodding. "You're right, a misunderstanding." She glanced back at the holodisplay. "Congratulations, you've been accepted into the Archlight program."

"I . . . never applied, ma'am."

"Can't be a mistake." Hucara glanced at him and then back to the holodisplay. "Founder Lanrete himself expedited your application." Richardre's heart skipped a beat. "Says here that your conversion is scheduled to begin tomorrow." There was a long silence.

"What happens if I decline, ma'am?"

Hucara turned to face Richardre. "Then there would be no post for you in the one hundred and third," Hucara clasped her hands behind her back. The action pushed her breasts forward slightly, her impeccable physique on full display. The sight caused Richardre's pants to tighten. He glanced away. "You would most likely be shipped off to another fringe colony world for guard duty." Richardre took in a deep breath and let out a sigh.

"Who will be my commanding officer, ma'am?"

"Me." Hucara grinned. "You will report directly to me."

CHAPTER 45 HUIARA MAU GEHREYATI

Huza, Thae, Huzien home system

Huiara moved to take the podium on the floor of the Huzien senate, the expansive chamber housed within the megastructure of the Huzien Capitol building. A long black suit jacket trailed behind her, the design reminiscent of Cislot's own. Throngs of people representing the colonies and planets within the Huzien Empire were in attendance, but the voices of the representatives moved from a crescendo to a hush as all eyes focused on the young platinum-furred Uri.

Huiara gripped the sides of the podium tightly, her eyes focusing straight ahead as she took in a deep breath and slowly let it out. After closing her eyes for a second, they flashed open and she leaned forward, let go of the podium, and connected her mobi up to the audio network.

"Esteemed senators, thank you for allowing me to speak before you today. As many of you know, I am Huiara Mau Gehreyati, personal assistant to Founder Cislot." Huiara took a breath, drawing strength in the action. "I come before you today to petition a new construction project for the oceanic city of Trutara. You have all had a chance to review this new spending bill and the specifics within. I motion that we adopt this new bill in its entirety."

"Do we have a second?" Marcarias broadcast to the room.

"With the permission of our restendi, I am standing in for the vacant seat of the govnus of Thae. My name is Ulter Wern, and as the grand lichar of Trutara, I second the motion," Ulter said. He stood, raised his hand to identify himself, and then quickly sat down.

"The motion has been seconded. Is there any discussion?"

"Dear Huiara." A Huzien man with red eyes and jet-black hair stood up in the distance. His voice was magnified throughout the chamber by his mobi. "Thank you for coming before us today. I speak on behalf of the people of Neth and must question why we would divert funds from the rebuilding of whole planets destroyed during the war to help build a new oceanicscraper on Thae? This seems like a waste of both the time and resources of our empire at this juncture."

"Senator Rexen," Huiara said, "first, let me say that the events that transpired on Neth were a tragedy and that we must do all that is within our power to restore the livelihoods of those ravaged by Sagren's forces." She paused. "Yes, this construction project will be a monumental effort, one not seen on Thae for many generations. But as we heal from the scar that was the Rift War, we must inspire hope in the heart of our empire! Even now, refugees from Neth make their home on Thae, all thoughts of their home filled with death and destruction. I believe that this project will inspire our people, as we plan to construct an elaborate memorial within the new structure dedicated to the heroic sacrifice of the Third Fleet in the protection of Neth." Huiara paused. "Two noble corporations have stepped forward to help fund the project, and the majority of the initial investment will come from their coffers, while our financial commitment will be low during the initial ramp-up period.

"Huzien tax dollars will only be spent during the final stages of the project, to finish this shining new achievement for our people." Huiara gripped the podium with both hands again. "This will show that even in the worst of times, we can rise to the challenge of positive change for the good of all the people of Thae."

She relaxed her grip of the podium slightly. "Thae is the commerce capitol of our empire. Our planetary economy dwarfs all others by multiple factors, yet many here see their taxes go to rebuild other areas of the empire, areas that don't directly impact them. However, when they look here to our world, they see nothing. Nothing in the open wounds of lost loved ones and friends. As the economic center of the Huzien Alliance, we must show them that even as we rebuild our fallen worlds, even as we rebuild the far reaches of our empire, we can also build on Thae. We must show them that we are truly the greatest nation in the Twin Galaxies!"

Senator Rexen slowly slid back into his seat as the audience chamber erupted into thunderous applause. Marcarias moved to stand next to Huiara.

"Let's open this for a vote," Marcarias said, his voice booming throughout the chamber.

The holodisplays behind them that previously held Huiara's image were replaced with the proposal and a tallying board. A confirmation chirp signaled after a few moments; the proposal had passed with majority support. Huiara stared at the screen, her heart catching in her throat as a smile crept onto her face. She glanced at Ulter Wern, who was standing and clapping his hands. Letting out the breath she hadn't realized she'd been holding, she moved her hand to her chest and stepped toward the podium once more.

"Thank you, imperial govnus and senators. The people of Trutara—no, the people of Thae—thank you for your action today."

"Govnus?" Huiara stared at Cislot, her mouth open. "Of Thae?" The Uri slowly crumpled into her chair. She was in Cislot's office atop the Huzien Capitol building.

"Marcarias nominated you to fill the position. It merely needs my final approval." Cislot rose out of her chair, her auburn hair dropping to her waist as she walked around her immaculate desk. "It has been vacant since Gehrat stepped down due to the death of his wife during the war." Huiara looked up at Cislot as the founder casually slid into the chair next to her. "Do you not feel that you are capable of handling the role?"

"No, I am capable," Huiara countered.

"Then why do you hesitate?"

"I . . . feel that I still have so much more to learn from you."

Cislot smiled.

"There are some things best learned firsthand. Governing is one of them." Cislot leaned back in the chair, her legs crossed. "Tell me." The words caused Huiara to instantly sit up straight. "Why is the govnus of Thae a critical step on your path to restendi?"

The air was instantly ripped from Huiara's lungs as she stared blankly at Cislot. The founder's eyes narrowed after a few seconds of silence. Huiara took in a deep breath, her gaze avoiding Cislot's as she struggled to think the scenario through.

"The govnus of Thae . . . is . . . a . . . highly visible role among the Huzien people."

"Yes . . ." Cislot prompted for more.

"It is a role that would allow me to learn how to govern under the tutelage of both the restendi and yourself. It is a . . . low-risk role that is . . . most likely coveted by many aspiring politicians."

"Continue."

"Marcarias himself previously held the role of govnus earlier in his career, as have many of your former assistants. It is one sign of an anointed future restendi for the Huzien Empire." Huiara's voice began to build with passion. "It is a sign to all people in positions of authority and power, and it allows me to network with senators and become the public face of Thae. It puts me on the galactic stage and exposes me to interplanetary politics. All of these things are critical to stand a chance of being elected restendi by a majority vote within the Huzien Empire."

Cislot nodded.

"Will you accept the appointment?"

"Yes, Founder. I accept." Huiara's heart skipped a beat as the words left her mouth.

High average CSL among the Vempiir is due to their destructive cycle of genocide, which resulted in the eradication of those of lower ability and led to a species where CSL 0 and 1 are nonexistent.

–FROM "CSL WITH NO DIRECT ENESMIC LINK"
BY SHAPER LUKIR AFREV

CHAPTER 46 MARCARIAS YONVI

Huza, Thae, Huzien home system

Huiara stepped onto the dais, sporting a long silver suit jacket, white blouse, and matching silver pants with silver high heels that had her towering above the podium. Marcarias noticed Cislot smile, Huiara having taken to the founder's own personal style. Cislot stood behind Huiara, wearing her customary attire in a shade of crimson. Marcarias's gaze was glued to Huiara, the rest of the world forgotten.

Please do pick your jaw up from the floor, Cislot imparted to Marcarias telepathically.

The restendi blinked, his gaze going to Cislot, but her gaze was centered on Huiara. Blinking again, Marcarias forced a cough and glanced out toward the assembled host in the open courtyard of the Huzien Capitol building. Various media outlets could be seen among the front row, and floating camera drones hovered a few feet in front of Huiara. He had no doubt that her image was being broadcast across the entire Huzien Empire at that very moment. Huiara stared down at the podium, then forced her gaze up and focused on the primary camera drone that floated directly in front of her.

"Fellow citizens, it is with great honor that I accept the appointment of govnus of Thae." A cheer went up from the crowd, applause filling the courtyard. The sky was clear, and the temperature was warm, artificially set by Huiara herself in the weather control grid. "Like those before me, I carry this burden humbly. I do not take my appointment to this office lightly, and I will do all in my power to ensure the best interests of the people of Thae. As this is the seat of our glorious empire, what we do here impacts not just us, but the empire itself!" More cheers went up from the crowd, the atmosphere electric.

"We have much work ahead of us. The wound from the creature Sagren will be felt for many years to come." Huiara paused, the crowd going silent. "But wounds heal and pains fade, and with the passing of time, the damaged tissue gets stronger. We get stronger." She paused, her gaze sweeping the crowd. "We must never forget the sacrifice of those who gave their lives for our empire. The scar left behind will always be a reminder of what we stand for, for what our empire stands for. We will take that scar and we will make it a symbol, a symbol of victory and unity!" Huiara raised her fist. "For the empire!"

The crowd exploded into applause. Huiara waved to the cameras and the assembled people, then stepped away from the platform.

Cislot moved to the platform and faced Huiara. She held up the sheath of a beautiful golden Huzien blade, the ornately decorated weapon once her own, but now nothing more than a ceremonial instrument. Huiara kneeled in front of the founder as Cislot drew her blade and set the flat end of it on top of Huiara's head.

"I hereby commission you into service to the Huzien Empire as govnus of Thae."

The applause was deafening. Huiara stood up to face the crowd, Marcarias moving to her other side.

"Well done," Marcarias said. "You were amazing."

"I expected nothing less," Cislot chimed in.

High average CSL among the Hauxem is believed to be due to their strict familial units and the collective inbreeding that their species practices.

—FROM "CSL WITH NO DIRECT ENESMIC LINK"
BY SHAPER LUKIR AFREV

CHAPTER 47 DERA'LIV ELAX ASHFALEN

Twenty-two years ago
Ashnakev, Ashna Maiden military staging system

"They have already taken my hala'a, my Serah'Elax." Dera'Liv wiped away a tear. "They are training her to kill. You must come and take us away from this horrid place!"

"I . . . I am sorry." Gucy'Uil Beh Xephil closed her eyes, letting out a low sigh. "I have escalated your case in the As'Kiluna. However, I must warn you that the administrative council has a backlog from across the Twin Galaxies, and Das'Vin in direct threat of death are their immediate focus. The As'Kiluna would have to petition the As'Crefa to act. They could mount a rescue party to extract you and your *hala'a*, but I do not see that happening anytime soon." She paused and shook her head. "The state of your daughter jeopardizes things. To integrate one so corrupted by conflict, strife, and violence at such a young age back into our society poses substantial challenges."

"She is my *hala'a*, my only! Please, you cannot deny her." Dera'Liv moved her hand to a position right above her chest, holding it there with her other hand grasping her wrist.

"No!" Gucy'Uil repeated Dera'Liv's motion, then broke the

grasp on her wrist. "You cannot entrust your life to me. I cannot fulfill that oath. I am sorry." Her face softened. "Serah'Elax has not been raised in Das'Vin society; she is more *nuy'zer* than Das'Vin."

Dera'Liv shook her head forcefully. "She is not an outsider; we have raised her in the ways of our people."

"You said she is being trained to kill." Gucy'Uil narrowed her eyes. "How long?"

Dera'Liv hesitated. "Two years."

Gucy'Uil shook her head.

"I petitioned the As'Kiluna before they took her away from me. I indicated the urgency, the risk to my *hala'a*!"

"I am sorry." Gucy'Uil avoided Dera'Liv's gaze. "I have escalated your case in the As'Kiluna. That is all I can do."

"The heir'luia, raise my case to her! My emotional wellbeing and that of my daughter has been compromised. It is her duty!"

"The heir'luia." Gucy'Uil blinked. "You seek to petition the Heir'Klaxem—the governing council—directly? I . . ." Gucy'Uil glanced off to the side, staring at something out of view for a long moment. "I will try, but the chance of getting her attention on this matter is very low."

"Thank you."

"Do not thank me yet, Dera'Liv Elax Ashfalen." Gucy'Uil lowered her gaze. "May the eternal calm keep your mind sharp and your breath steady."

CHAPTER 48 SERAH'ELAX REZ ASHFALEN

Rion orbiting Ashnakev, Ashna Maiden military staging system

The Ashna Maiden carrier Rion dropped out of suplight and moved to orbit Ashnakev. The planet was a breathtaking sight, with tens of thousands of Ashna Maiden ships in orbit or docked across the hundreds of shipyards throughout the system. With a populace in the billions and millions of soldiers on the ground training or preparing to be deployed, the military stronghold highlighted the true power of the Ashna Maidens. Exemplar Ahtlana was back in her command chair, with Keeper Serah'Elax once again at her side.

"Exemplar, we are receiving a communication."

Ahtlana nodded as the face of Ashna Mother Venice Fawni appeared on the primary holodisplay. Immediately, every Ashna Maiden on the bridge dropped to their knees, every nose touching the back of hands as they prostrated themselves before the Ashna Mother.

"Rise, daughters of Ashna," Venice commanded. "The goddess welcomes you home, her favor shining on you this day." She smiled, her eyes closing slightly.

"Great Mother, we are unworthy of your blessing or your greeting," Ahtlana replied. The exemplar immediately brought her nose back down to her hands, again becoming prostrate, every Maiden on the bridge following suit. "We return defeated, our armada shattered, and the goddess dishonored."

Mother Venice shook her head. "No, my dear child. All of this was foretold by the goddess. She is testing our faith at this very moment, and we must be vigilant!" Ahtlana rose and glanced to Serah'Elax, both Serah'Elax and Ahtlana frowning. "Avatar Ahtlana, your presence is requested on the surface. I am sorry that you do not have time to recuperate. Ashna speed your steps." Mother Venice terminated the connection.

Ahtlana Jufre stared at the blank holodisplay. "Avatar . . ." She slowly sat back into her seat, her face frozen in shock.

The whole bridge turned to face the new avatar of Ashna, all of them slowly dropping to one knee as a sign of respect. Ahtlana swept her gaze around the bridge, her eyes finally settling on Serah'Elax. "If I am to be an avatar, then you will be my exemplar."

Serah'Elax's eyes widened as she took a step back.

Nineteen years ago
Ashnakev, Ashna Maiden military staging system

"Heir'Luia, it is an honor." Dera'Liv touched her throat with her thumb and index fingers, her chin high. Her other hand was cupped, level with her chest. Serah'Elax glanced at her mother, awkwardly mirroring the motions.

"Dera'Liv, it pained me to learn of the death of your dru'sha, Ovah'Hal, and the loss of your *hala'a* Nesal'Velexi. How have you coped?" Bur'Jexti Kefer Homun's hazel-eyed gaze was soft. She had bright red hair, the color a contrast to her chestnut-brown skin. The subtly transparent dress she wore hinted at elevated brown marks in a series of patterns over her body. Dera'Liv averted her gaze, biting her lip. The action caused Bur'Jexti to shift in her seat. "I see."

"Heir'Luia, it has been five years since I last heard from the As'Kiluna." Dera'Liv returned her gaze to Bur'Jexti, her eyes pleading. "I had given up hope."

"I understand." Bur'Jexti nodded her head. "What of the little one, Serah'Elax?"

"I am a Maiden-in-waiting, pledged in service to Ashna!" Serah'Elax raised her chin high.

Sorrow crossed Bur'Jexti's face. "Dera'Liv, I have spoken with the As'Crefa. They have agreed to send a drone swarm to retrieve you and your *hala'a*. We will bring you home, to Desc'Ri, so that you may heal."

"What?" Serah'Elax turned to her mother. "Leave the Ashna Maidens? Why would we do that, after all they have done for us?" She glared at Bur'Jexti. "Where were they when Het Wrast Aht killed my *wo'shae* and *uma'shae*?" She balled up her fists. "No, I will become an Ashna Maiden and avenge them. I will remain here. You can return, *yu'shae*, but I will serve the Ashna Maidens."

"Serah'Elax, please! Desc'Ri is your home."

"This is my home."

Dera'Liv turned a pleading eye to Bur'Jexti, but the heir'luia just looked down at the ground, her face gripped with pain. Dera'Liv closed her eyes, letting out a long, slow breath. She clutched her stomach, appearing nauseous, and her body shivered.

"Thank you, Heir'Luia, for hearing my plea and your offer of assistance." She glanced at Serah'Elax, who stared at her defiantly. "I must remain with my *hala'a*, with my only." Dera'Liv returned her gaze to the holodisplay, tears rolling down her cheeks. Bur'Jexti locked gazes with her, the same sorrow mirrored on her face.

"I understand. May the eternal calm keep your mind sharp and your breath steady."

Present day
Ashnakev, Ashna Maiden military staging system

"Serah'Elax is to be honored then—the new exemplar anointed as the hero of the battle." Mother Venice stood with her army of attendants shadowing her, each catering to every movement and reshuffling parts of her long and elegant gown so every aspect and angle of the Ashna Mother would be perfect and regal. They were almost invisible, their presence not acknowledged by any but Serah'Elax, the young Das'Vin enamored by their meticulous care. She had never been in the presence of an Ashna Mother before.

Hearing her name spoken aloud snapped her attention back to the Ashna Mother. Avatar Ahtlana had just explained at length the heroic actions carried out by Serah'Elax while she was indisposed during the battle. A full retelling of events had been relayed in detail by the avatars of each fleet. All, except for Avatar Hegna, had just recently been promoted to their station. The full Ashna Council was in attendance but remained silent, deferring to the Ashna Mother and her inquiries.

Serah'Elax struggled with her battlefield promotion. She didn't feel prepared to be a keeper, let alone an exemplar. The thought of commanding an entire fleet beside Ahtlana was almost too much for her. She nervously shuffled in her chair, her gaze going to the ground as she took in a deep breath. She closed her eyes and imagined being on the battlefield, her Blades of the Goddess in her hands as they drank in pirate blood. That thought calmed her nerves, and she opened her eyes slowly as she leaned back in her chair.

Starting at CSL 3, an individual is able to directly tap into the Enesmic flow, allowing it to flow through them and empower their abilities. They can also detect its presence and in many instances see Enesmic energy directly.

–FROM "CSL WITH DIRECT ENESMIC LINK"
BY SHAPER LUKIR AFREV

CHAPTER 49 HEGNA HELRIT

Ashnakev, Ashna Maiden military staging system

A vatar Hegna tried to pay attention to the discussion taking place around her as Mother Venice spoke with many of the other assembled avatars. She tried to push the images of her sister out of her mind, to keep the tears out of her eyes and her heart cold.

Luka finished cleaning the blood from her hair and turned off the shower. She was surrounded by other Maidens cleaning up after the most recent battle. Stepping out of the shower room, she dried off with her towel and wrapped it around her head.

"They call you 'the Butcher;' they say that you show no mercy and kill with a brutality unbecoming of an Ashna Maiden." The voice cut through the noise of the shower area as Luka looked up to lock gazes with a fully dressed Hegna.

"Am I supposed to bow?" Luka said, sarcasm dripping from her tone.

"What drives you to be so cruel?"

"Are you kidding me? They are pirates." Luka spit.

"And they deserve to die, but torture? Brutality? Those are not traits of the goddess."

"So, you're an Ashna Mother now?"

"Watch your tongue!"

Luka laughed and walked past Hegna toward the locker area. Hegna turned to follow, a scowl aimed toward her sister.

The room felt as if it was closing in on her, the conversation becoming more distant, more indecipherable.

"This is your dream, not mine!" Luka wiped a tear from her eye. "I don't want to be an avatar. Why are you doing all of this for me?"

"You've never wanted anything worth anything in your life," Hegna shot back. "You leave it up to people like me to have to watch out for you to ensure you make something out of yourself."

"I didn't ask for your help! I was fine being a scion of Ashna, being on the battlefield."

"Until you make one mistake and end up dead."

"That's my mistake to make!"

Hegna bit her lip, her eyes going soft.

"I didn't want you to make that mistake."

Luka stared at her sister, her posture relaxing slightly. She turned away from Hegna and looked out of the window of her quarters.

The sound of her sister yelling her name in that final moment of terror as the *Yutrea* was cracked in two caused Hegna to jump to her feet. Every gaze turned to her. Hegna was suddenly aware of her surroundings again and slowly took her seat.

Mother Venice regarded Hegna with a look of absolute sympathy.

"Avatar Hegna, you are dismissed to mourn your sister. I will personally pray to the goddess to watch over her spirit this day. I will send for you tonight to discuss the outcome of our meeting here."

Hegna slowly got up from her chair, her gaze going to her exemplar, Ember Riss. She rested her hand on her shoulder, and Ember touched her hand with a nod. Looking back down at Mother Venice, Hegna performed a deep bow and then departed the chamber.

Ashnali, Ashna Maiden home system

"We found her in an escape pod." Ember Riss brought up the image of Bresha on a nearby holodisplay. "An escape pod from the Seventy-Second Fleet." The exemplar crossed her arms. "She didn't show up on any of the crew registers from Luka's fleet." Hegna switched the image to a feed of the containment cell that Bresha was being held in.

"What's her story?"

"She claims to be a defector from the Huzien Empire seeking to join the Ashna Maidens."

"What are the chances that she's a spy from the enemy fleet?"

"High."

Hegna balled up her fist, her gaze never leaving Bresha's image. "Do the Mothers know?"

"No, she was found by one of our patrols. They brought her here right away."

"Good."

The avatar got up from her seat and walked past Ember, who watched her with a raised eyebrow. She quickly fell in line behind her avatar.

"What do you intend to do?"

"Question her."

A few moments later, Hegna stepped into the small holding room with Bresha, who was sitting comfortably at the lone table in the center.

"I know what you're probably thinking," Bresha said.

"Is that right, Bresha was it?" Hegna motioned for Ember to stay outside.

"Yes, and I can assure you that I am not from that horrible armada you faced."

Hegna laughed. "Why should I believe anything you say?"

"Those ships, they attacked the Huzien Alliance." She paused. "It was only due to the combined power of the Alliance fleets that we were able to expel them from our space. They left wanton destruction in their wake. Whole worlds razed, billions dead."

Hegna's eyes narrowed. "Who are they?"

"They are beings from the Enesmic plane, monsters." Bresha's eyes went wide. "But I know how to defeat them. I witnessed the strategies employed by the amassed Alliance fleets."

"So, you're a deserter." Hegna drew her sidearm. "Regardless of allegiance, a deserter deserves nothing but death." The avatar leveled her sidearm at Bresha's head.

"I am no deserter!" Bresha stood up, her hands high in the air. "I'm not a part of the military." Enesmic energy began to swirl subtly around the room. "I am part of a special group of cihphists known as the Argents. I sought to learn more about the threat that we faced, and after witnessing their power and the damage they did, I couldn't let them come here and endanger all the good that the Ashna Maidens do here in the Outer Rim." Bresha put her hand to her chest. "The Argents and the Huzien Alliance refused to act, so I took it upon myself to come here at my own risk and provide you with the information you need to defend yourselves."

"You're a cihphist?" Hegna kept her sidearm leveled on Bresha, her grip tightening.

"Yes, a very powerful one." Bresha began to walk toward Hegna. "Shoot me."

"What?"

"Your sidearm, the one you have aimed at me . . . shoot me."

"You're crazy."

Bresha sighed and then charged at Hegna, who fired a shot at the woman. A barrier around Bresha flickered as the shield absorbed the shot. She stopped a few feet from Hegna.

"Blessed of Ashna . . ." Hegna took a step back.

"I allow you to hold me here. I could have easily killed your guards." She pointed to the two Ashna Maidens who now had their rifles leveled on her. With a snap of her fingers, their weapons disintegrated. "I honestly want to help you, which is why I allowed myself to be captured."

Hegna glanced back at her guards, the women in shock at the loss of their weapons. Her gaze slowly returned to Bresha.

"If what you say is true, then you must meet with the Ashna Mothers."

"I would be honored." Bresha smiled.

At CSL 3, we begin to see the ability to progress through what we have defined as different schools of cihphist ability, previously mentioned as telepathy, telekinesis, kineticism and metaphysicism.

–FROM "CSL WITH DIRECT ENESMIC LINK"
BY SHAPER LUKIR AFREV

CHAPTER 50 SEPHAN

Ashnali, Ashna Maiden home system

The Ashna Mothers sat in a half circle on an elevated platform above where Bresha stood, her hands bound together in front of her. Multiple high priestesses of Ashna stood between the Ashna Mothers and Sephan. Each radiated an aura of cihphistic power that slightly impressed the Eshgren. All five of the Ashna Mothers were present, each regarding the blond Human intently. Sephan's gaze swept across each one, its eyes halting on Halle Tentle. The ebony-skinned Human's white eyes were scowling at the sight of Sephan.

That look made Sephan uncomfortable, and the Eshgren began questioning whether the Ashna Mother could sense its true presence. Sephan tried to take a read of her to gauge her cihphistic power. It was limited in how much it could probe due to not wanting to risk a potential conflict with the current audience, but Sephan could sense the deep connection to the Enesmic plane radiating from the young woman.

Venice glanced to Halle before returning her gaze to Bresha. "You say you're from an organization called the Argents?"

"Yes." Bresha turned to regard the older Human.

"Why did you leave the Argents?" Halle asked. "My understanding is that being an Argent is a privilege reserved for only a few of the most powerful cihphists. Surely one of your standing could have commissioned an investigative party to parlay with us." Her eyes narrowed. "And yet you are here by yourself, Bresha Vecen."

"Highly suspicious for one as esteemed as yourself, shaper," Ce Nu Yo Kl interjected.

"Shaper Bresha is your official designation is it not?" Alenet Dascl rested her head on her ivory-skinned hand.

"Yes," Bresha said, "and as a shaper, I am within my right to depart from the Argents at any time to attend to any matters I deem important. It is a benefit of my station." Her silver-laced blue eyes hung on Halle's scowl for a moment before moving to Ce Nu Yo Kl's glowing black orbs. "I can understand the suspicion you have about me. All I ask is to be given the chance to prove myself to you. I wish to join the Ashna Maidens. I will do whatever you ask of me."

"Have you ever laid with a man, Bresha?" Ga Po Fe Ul asked. The dark silver Eeriteen sat back in her chair, her black orbs glowing a powerful blue.

"No," Bresha lied.

"You will be tested for maidenhood," Halle interjected. "In order to serve as an Ashna Maiden, purity must be ensured."

"If you have lied to us, you will be executed," Venice said. "We give you this one chance to leave of your own accord."

"If you undergo the test and fail, there is no mercy," Ce Nu Yo Kl said.

Bresha smiled. "I willingly submit to your test; you will find me a pure Maiden."

"Put this on." The priestess of Ashna laid a long white robe on the bed in Bresha's temporary quarters. "Nothing else." Without another word, she turned and exited the room.

Sephan regarded the white robe with a sigh and began to undress, carefully folding up its clothes and laying them in a pile on the bed. Sephan looked at the body of Bresha in a nearby mirror, the woman nude, and raised its hand, Enesmic energy coalescing around the fingers. Slowly, the Eshgren moved two fingers into Bresha's womanhood.

Bresha collapsed to her knees in silently restrained pain as Sephan reconstructed the innermost parts of her body, adjusting her biology down to the hormonal level and burning away foreign matter. Gasping for breath, Bresha's eyes went wide as she stared straight up at the ceiling to her room. Done, Sephan removed its hand, pricks of blood disintegrating into thin air as all traces of its work were removed. Moving both hands to the ground, Bresha slowly pushed herself up. Her eyes lingered on her image in the mirror, the presence of Sephan superimposed over her form as a powerful shadow.

Back in full control, Sephan straightened its back and pushed Bresha's chest out. Her body seemed thirty years younger. Smiling, Sephan picked up the white robe and dressed. Moving to the door, it knocked once, and was soon surrounded by Ashna Maidens.

"This way." The priestess motioned for Sephan to follow.

The doors to the ritual chamber opened, and Sephan stepped in. None of the guards or priestesses followed it into the room. It looked up to see an Eeriteen woman staring from across the room, and behind her was an Altar of Ashna. There was a sensor array built into the floor in front of the altar with grooves carved out for a woman to rest comfortably on her knees on top of it. Sephan looked at the pristine silver table covered by an embroidered golden cloth and frowned. Catching itself, the Eshgren forced a smile on Bresha's face.

"Come and prostrate yourself before Ashna." The Eeriteen motioned toward the sensor array on the ground. "Ensure that your knees are aligned with the grooves and we will begin."

Sephan slowly moved to the sensor array and kneeled, putting Bresha's legs into the grooves and positioning her womanhood directly above the main sensor. The Eeriteen activated the device, and Sephan's robe glowed with the bright white light emitted by the sensor array, becoming translucent. Sephan stared at the ground, feigning worship of Ashna while the system examined every aspect of Bresha's body.

Sephan reached out with its mind, establishing a concealed ethereal representation of itself in the private audience chamber of the Ashna Mothers. Mother Halle looked in the direction of the manifestation, her face unsure as she looked past it, then glanced around in confusion. Sephan watched her carefully, preparing to terminate the manifestation if she investigated further. She lost interest as one of the Mothers began to speak.

"What she says is true." Venice slowly sat down in her chair. All the mothers were assembled in one of their many private chambers in the High Temple of Ashna on Ashnali.

"I don't believe it," Alenet said. "She walks like a whore, one who has been despoiled by many men."

"Do we doubt the accuracy of our test?" Ce Nu Yo Kl said.

"The test is perfect, flawless. It's the basis of too much to cast doubt on now," Ga Po Fe Ul countered.

"Have we allowed our biases to sway our opinion of this Bresha Vecen?" Halle asked.

"Biases exist for a reason," Ce Nu Yo Kl countered. "They are based off of subconscious thought, truly the most primal of intuition."

"I disagree," Venice said. "We must examine our biases in this situation and put them aside." All eyes went to Venice. "She has passed the test; she has proven her purity on risk of death."

"So we should blindly accept her into our order?" There was a haughtiness in Alenet's voice. "A woman shrouded in mystery, wielding powers on par with our own?"

"Far surpassing," Halle interjected. A few of the mother's shifted uncomfortably. "If we accept Bresha into the Ashna Maidens, much pain and heartbreak will come."

"Then we must send her away!" Ce Nu Yo Kl yelled.

"But . . ." Halle turned to face Ce Nu Yo Kl, the dark red Eeriteen's long spines seemingly electrified at the emotions raging within. "After the pain, after the heartbreak, great peace and prosperity will come for all of our people. Prosperity unlike anything we have ever seen."

Sephan eyed Halle curiously, her words unsettling it as everyone went silent, all eyes on the young white-eyed, ebony-skinned Human.

"I must build their trust." Bresha sat with her legs crossed in the room she had been given by the Ashna Maidens. She now wore the white and silver robes of a newly inducted Ashna Maiden. "They have allowed me to join their order, but in order for our plan to come to fruition, dear Jughent, they have to trust me fully."

The image of the pale orange Ceshra hovered directly in front of Sephan.

"How do you intend to do that?" Jughent said.

"Give them a victory."

"A victory?" Jughent narrowed his eyes.

"Yes, to show them that I have valuable information, I will give them a decisive victory over a small contingent of your forces."

"No," Jughent countered. "My resources are limited. I cannot spare any of my fleet to be destroyed as pawns in your game."

"Then all of this is for naught."

"There must be another way."

"This is the way, love." Bresha pouted. "Trust me . . . for the small sacrifice of a few ships, you will gain all." Bresha stood up, the image of Jughent rising to stay level with her head. "Mmmm, I miss your touch," Bresha moaned. "I'm soaked just thinking about you inside of me. Oh, how I long to be at your side once more."

Jughent shifted in his command chair, the sight of Bresha teasing him from light-years away causing him to stir uncomfortably. Sephan reached across the void and telepathically stimulated the pleasure centers of his brain, causing Jughent to gasp, his body convulsing slightly. He leaned back in his chair, his wide eyes replaced with a grin.

"You believe this will work?" Jughent said.

Bresha smiled. "I'm confident that this will work."

"How many ships?"

"A battle cruiser contingent should be enough."

Jughent groaned, shaking his head. Sephan stroked his pleasure center again, and Jughent squirmed in his chair as his body betrayed him. "Very well, I will send a battle cruiser contingent to attack the world you indicated. They will . . . be most ineffective in defending themselves from the counterattack by the Ashna Maidens."

"I will take control of the forces when they arrive." Sephan grinned. "You will not regret this."

We define someone with CSL 3 as having specialized cihphist ability. This is a rare trait in all species, except for Humans, Vempiir, and Hauxem.

-FROM "CSL WITH DIRECT ENESMIC LINK"
BY SHAPER LUKIR AFREV

CHAPTER 51 *ZUN SHAN*

Empress Star, Huzien Alliance space

Zun glanced out from around the corner at two men with assault weapons conversing at the far end of the hallway. Pressing her back up against the wall, she let out a deep sigh, then looked down at herself. The towel wrapped around her waist was still her only real covering. Gripping the firearm she had stolen off the dead guard earlier, Zun moved it to behind her back and stepped out into the hallway with a forced smile on her face.

"Excuse me boys, I think I'm a little lost."

Both guards turned and leveled their rifles on her. Their stances relaxed the moment they processed her bikini top and towel.

"Is that right?"

"Yeah." Zun slurred her voice. "I was hoping you two handsome men could show me the way back to the bar. The bartender said I had too much to drink, but what does he know."

They lowered their rifles, sporting wide grins.

"Sure, we'll take real good care of you."

"Great." Her gun came out in a heartbeat as she leveled it on the first pirate, the trigger depressed in the same fluid motion. His head snapped back, blood spray coating the floor behind him. A heartbeat later, the muzzle moved to the second man, another pull of the trigger mirroring the scene. Both dropped to the ground, blood rapidly pooling around their bodies. "And here I thought all that target practice was a waste of time. I'll have to thank Jessica later." Quickly moving down the hallway, Zun slipped the pistol into her waist, utilizing the towel as a holster. Picking up one of the assault rifles, she continued toward the armory on the security deck.

Zun slid up against the wall directly outside the security deck. Dead bodies lined the corridor, all the corpses covered in tattoos. The door to the security deck was blasted open, and various pieces of furniture were thrown against the wreckage to provide cover for those inside.

"Is anyone in there?" Zun called out.

"State your name and stay where you are!" The order came from inside the security deck.

"Captain Zun Shan, Founder's Elite in direct service to Founder Lanrete and the Huzien military."

"Are you armed?"

"Yes."

"Throw down your weapon and step out."

"Not until you identify yourself."

"Arnold Steinsford, chief security officer for the *Empress Star*."

Zun pulled up the crew register cached on her mobi, the name checking out. She threw her assault weapon out into clear view, followed by the smaller pistol. Slowly, she moved out with her hands up.

"I hate to tell you this," Zun said, "but you've done a terrible job, Arnold."

Two women came out and grabbed hold of her before quickly ushering her into the security bunker. They moved her into a concealed area, away from direct line of sight of the battered entranceway. She came to stand in front of Arnold, a ruddy-skinned man with brown hair and brown eyes. The grizzled look on his face caused Zun to stand up straight. He did a quick once-over of her.

"I take it you're going for the whole femme fatale thing?"

"It's worked well so far." Zun paused. "My evening was interrupted by one of those tattooed freaks trying to rape me."

"I'm sorry you've been dragged into this."

"How bad is it?"

"Het Wrast Aht, they've taken control of the ship." Arnold motioned to a member of his security team. The man brought over a portable holodisplay. "We've hacked into the navigational system; all controls are locked, but we can see the trajectory we're on." He tossed the mobile holodisplay to Zun. Catching it, she held it up, the star map appearing in front of her.

"The Outer Rim . . ."

"Yep, and we're getting dangerously close."

"What are we up against?"

"We're estimating about three hundred pirates, about half of that standing between us and the bridge."

"How many do you have?"

"Thirty-two people. I've lost most of my team."

"We've got incoming!" a guard shouted from the main room.

"We can continue this conversation later," Arnold said. They all moved into the next room.

"Give me a weapon," Zun said.

Arnold glanced back at Zun, his eyes momentarily moving to her breasts, the bikini top clearly distracting him. Hesitating for a moment, he motioned to one of his nearby guards. The guard tossed her an assault rifle. Catching it, she armed it in a single motion and moved to cover.

"Founder's Elite, huh?"

"Yep." Zun leveled her rifle toward the entrance.

"Identify yourself!" Arnold yelled.

"Do the pirates actually respond to that?" Zun blurted.

"Zun?" Marcus shouted.

"Hold your fire!" Zun said. "They're friendlies."

She moved from behind cover and sprinted toward the entrance. The Founder's Elites reunited as all but Dexter stepped into view.

"I like your clothing choice." Tashanira grinned.

"Although I question the practicality," Jessica countered.

Zun winked. "More skin equals higher armor class."

"You and Neven were made for each other," Jenshi laughed.

"Sorry to interrupt the happy reunion," Arnold interjected, "but you might want to consider continuing your conversation inside the safety of the security compound."

"Let me guess." Dexter moved into view, a few people raising weapons at his sudden appearance. "Chief security officer?"

Zun motioned for everyone to relax, and they all moved deeper inside.

Zun stepped out of Arnold's office sporting an *Empress Star* security jumpsuit. It was a size too large, but a welcome change. She walked over to the armory entrance, the other Founder's Elites busy inspecting and prepping their weapons. Her gaze caught on Marcus, who was decked out in his Archlight armor. It was an impressive piece of gear, more advanced than standard power armor but too small to be classified as a power frame.

"I guess it wasn't a bad idea to bring Claire along after all," Zun said.

"Damn straight," Marcus said, "I never go anywhere without her." He initiated the last power-on sequence for the armor and his helmet visor closed, the seams disappearing. The highest part of the armor almost touched the ceiling. Marcus then started a diagnostic of his lance rifle and Archlight shield, the shield letting off a subtle hum as it cycled through its various systems.

"There's your harness." Jenshi pointed to Zun's gravity control harness laid out on the floor.

"Much appreciated," Zun said. She quickly secured the device in place as the others began to move toward the front of the security deck.

"Do you honestly think we can take the bridge?" Arnold said.

"Yes, and we can minimize casualties if we move quickly," Dexter replied. "Our key to success will be hitting them as *vusging* hard and fast as they hit you when they took the ship."

"What's the risk of pulling innocent bystanders into this fight?" Jessica said.

"There are a series of meglifts that go directly from the crew quarters at the bottom of the ship to the bridge crew quarters at the top," Arnold said. "From there, it's a series of corridors to the bridge itself. The observation deck under the bridge has been closed since they took the ship, so I doubt we'll encounter any passengers there." Arnold paused. "We'll most likely encounter crew along the way; they have been told to go about their normal jobs on fear of death if they talk to the passengers." Arnold shook his head. "They executed the bridge crew to show they meant business."

"I'm going to enjoy killing these *ciths*," Tashanira blurted.

"Elites, sound off," Marcus called. "Tempest online." His Archlight shield expanded slightly as the Human locked his lance rifle into a hold within his armor. The glowing blue slits of his helmet seemed to pulse.

"Banshee, ready to rock and roll." Tashanira rested her hands comfortably on her WMAs.

"Nexus ready." The emitter beacon for Zun's gravity control harness began to glow, the air around it thrumming with power. It was a custom creation of her own design, one of her contributions to the sciences and a piece of her legacy.

"Unbreakable, prepped and ready to roll out." Two of Jenshi's medical drones cloaked and began to silently tail him.

"Phoenix awakened." Jessica's eyes slowly turned red, the battle lust quickly building inside her. She rested her hand on Unquenchable, the Nenifin blade's power core flaring to life at her touch.

"*Vusging* about time, I'm sick of waiting around," Dexter said. "Lifetime ready." He cloaked, disappearing.

Marcus's Archlight armor came to life, propelling him toward the exit. Despite its massive size, it barely made a sound. "Let's get started."

Tempest barreled down the corridor, his Archlight shield poised in front of him as the visual output from his armor relayed to the micro-displays of all the Founder's Elites. Gravimetric thrusters propelled him into a barrage of weapons fire. His shield absorbed the impacts, and the pirates began scrambling to get out of the way as he burst through their cover. While impaling one of the pirates with his lance rifle, he fired a lightning blast. The force blasted the body from his weapon and blew apart another pirate attempting to run away. Gore blanketed the area in front of him as other pirates nearby scrambled to get out of his line of sight.

Banshee slipped around Tempest, her WMAs releasing a barrage of death. The two Founder's Elites worked in tandem, Tempest moving to block incoming shots and Banshee ducking out from the cover to put down body after body. Unbreakable followed closely behind the duo, but the combat doctor was left without much to do.

Phoenix sprinted across the side wall, her momentum propelling her forward as she unleashed a barrage from her WMAs into a pocket of pirates hiding out behind cover. She peppered them with holes, not slowing before flipping off the wall and landing in a crouch. Zun's GCH flared to life as she applied incredible force to the barricades, crushing them flat and clearing the way. Phoenix holstered her WMAs as Unquenchable came out, her movements a blur. Severed heads and limbs littered the area within moments of her fury being unleashed. The pirates were unable to keep up with her movements.

"Clear," Phoenix called out.

Heading for the bridge, Lifetime broadcast telepathically.

We should wait for the others to clear the path before hitting the bridge, Nexus countered.

I'll be waiting. Lifetime grinned. *On the bridge.*

Nexus emerged from behind cover to stand next to Phoenix. Both women glanced at each other with a sigh before moving up the corridor toward the bridge. Arnold and his security detail moved to secure the area after the Founder's Elite, systematically clearing out any stragglers.

CHAPTER 52 HESHEL VROT

Empress Star, Huzien Alliance space

"We've lost contact with our lookouts near the security deck and bridge meglifts." Vexl glanced over to Heshel Vrot, who glared back at him.

"Well, go solve the *vusging* problem," the pirate captain barked.

Vexl nodded, a glance to his security detail causing them to fall in line. He exited the bridge. Heshel glanced over to Deidra Kul. The woman's clothes were torn and her bare chest was exposed. Bruises covered her body. Her eyes were dull, the light gone out of them. They hadn't allowed her to leave the bridge since they took the ship. Heshel had considered putting her out of her misery multiple times, the morale of his crew the only thing keeping her alive. A host of other women, and a few men, sat in the general area around her, all in a similar state.

"How far are we from the Outer Rim?" Heshel asked.

"Eighteen hours," Hegfe Deni replied. The engine master was busy at work preparing a locator beacon to start broadcasting the moment they crossed over. "We've got a fleet waiting an hour from the border to escort us to Rugtora." He grinned. "Then we can begin the process of dismantling the ship piece by piece, with help from our new slaves of course."

Heshel cracked a smile and leaned back in the captain's chair of the *Empress Star*. He was about to become a very wealthy man. He brought up the visual feed being broadcasted from Vexl as the assault master went out to deal with the problem.

Vexl moved to the front of his force, his movements quickening as a giant in silver armor came into view.

"*Vusg*," Vexl said.

"Is that an Archlight?" a pirate said with clear fear in his voice.

"What's the military doing here?" another man shouted.

"Bring it down!" Vexl shouted.

"An Archlight? You serious?" Vexl shot the man who uttered the words, and the rest of his team pressed forward. Vexl jumped out from cover and kicked off the wall, attempting to get behind the Archlight as rhythmic weapons fire grabbed his attention. He landed behind the Archlight to come face to face with a Uri. She raised a pair of newer WMAs and fired at him. He dodged the shot and stomped, firing a blast in retaliation. The Uri's eyes went wide as a grin crossed her face. She charged at Vexl, both missing each other by hairs, their steps seeming in sync as they put on a dazzling display.

The Wopans danced. Vexl twirled, the Tuzen a master of his craft, but the Uri matched him, and there was a grace in her steps that Vexl lacked, a finesse that kept him on his toes. She jumped over him, leveling her WMAs while upside down and firing at the back of his head. Vexl dropped, the shot skimming his head as he flung himself backward. He caught sight of a Huzien man unleashing titan blasts at his men, lightning devastating his ranks.

Cursing, Vexl tried to head toward him, but the Uri growled, a ferocity in her eyes as she slid by him, spraying him with weapons fire in a clear attempt to keep him away from the Huzien. Vexl jumped back, propelling himself to the wall and past the Archlight to get away. As he did, the Archlight turned and leveled its lance rifle on him. Vexl dropped, the blast blowing one of his men apart and singeing his hair. He scrambled forward and moved back to cover as the trio pushed forward. Vexl blew past his men as they retreated toward the bridge.

Heshel fumed, his eyes bloodshot with rage.

"Who are these people? How are they taking down your men?"

"I don't know." Vexl averted his gaze. "The last of my team is holding the line outside the bridge door. I've ordered everyone across the ship to fall back to the bridge to assist." Vexl paused. "We'll contain this!"

"I'm brimming with *vusging* confidence," Heshel spat. The muffled sound of weapons fire could be heard through the sealed bridge door. Heshel had ordered it repaired as a precaution, and now suddenly suppressed a smirk at his brilliant planning. Vexl looked to the thirty men occupying the bridge, all of them facing the door with weapons leveled.

Heshel glanced over to Deidra, whose eyes were half closed as if fading in and out of consciousness. Moving to her, he roughly pulled her up. The others around her scurried back in fear. "How do I initiate self-destruct?" She stared at him blankly. He slapped her to the floor, then pulled her back up again. "Self-destruct, how do I start the process?" Deidra collapsed back to the floor, unable to stand on her own, and stared at his shoes. Heshel cursed and began kicking her repeatedly in the stomach. Whimpers filled the bridge, and Deidra vomited up blood as she curled into a fetal position.

"I don't think there's a standard self-destruct system, it being a civilian vessel and all," Hegfe called out. "I may be able to rig something with the Ouma reactor; disable the safeguards, trigger a runaway energy buildup, et cetera."

"Do it," Heshel shouted.

"You're going to blow the ship?" Vexl balked.

"I'd rather *vusging* destroy it then hand it back over to those *ciths*," Heshel spat back. "Let's get out of here."

Vexl glanced back to his men, all of them focused on the sounds coming from the other side of the door. He glanced to Hegfe, who initiated the overload sequence and then scrambled over to Heshel, who had quietly removed a maintenance hatch from the far side of the bridge. Without another word, the pirate captain crawled into the hatch, Hegfe following right after him. Vexl glanced back to his men, the assault master visibly torn. A blast from near the door made up his mind, and he followed Heshel before quietly moving the maintenance hatch back in place to seal the exit.

To attain a CSL of 5, a cihphist must demonstrate mastery of multiple if not all schools except metaphysicism. Attaining this level is extremely rare, with even the most dedicated of cihphists often unable to attain mastery of multiple cihphist schools after a lifetime of dedication and study to the Enesmic.

–FROM "CSL WITH DIRECT ENESMIC LINK"
BY SHAPER LUKIR AFREV

CHAPTER 53 ZUN SHAN

Empress Star, Huzien Alliance space

Tempest unleashed another blast from his lance rifle. The impact threw the bridge door clear across the room, taking three pirates with it. The remaining pirates unloaded on the Archlight, but Tempest's shield easily absorbed the blasts from their weapons. He walked forward, an unstoppable machine. The rest of the Founder's Elite exploded into the room behind him, each peeling off in different directions. Within seconds, Phoenix dropped the last pirate with a shot to the head, and everything went silent.

"Oh no!" Zun rushed to Deidra. The bridge officer was lying on the floor. Jenshi was at her side in a heartbeat, already at work analyzing her body. His medical drones decloaked around her.

"She has massive internal damage." Jenshi glanced to Zun and then to Tashanira. "*Vusg!* They've destroyed her uterus and vaginal lining." He shook his head. "She has severe blood loss; multiple internal organs are ruptured, lots of internal bleeding. If I can't get her to a medical bay, I don't know if she will make it." His drones frantically went to work injecting nanites into her bloodstream, focusing on key areas across her body. One drone initiated a continuous injection of fluids, attempting to stabilize her.

"This is sick." Jessica spat on a pirate corpse.

"It's okay, we're here to save you," Marcus said as he detracted his visor, his face showing as he addressed the other civilians nearby. "You're safe now."

Jenshi rushed over to examine the others for injuries. One of his medical drones followed. Many were in similar states to Deidra, with a few unconscious and one too far gone.

"Where is Dexter?" Tashanira said.

The group glanced around the room.

"He'll show up eventually," Marcus said.

"Something's going on over here," Arnold called out.

Zun pulled herself away from Deidra; she had been holding the battered second officer's head in her lap to help her feel more comfortable. She glanced at the display, her eyes going wide after taking a few moments to digest the readout.

"We've got to get out of here!" Zun yelled. "Now!"

"What is it?" Marcus moved to Zun.

"The reactor core is overloading," Zun said. "The controls are locked out."

"Can you do anything?" Marcus looked to Arnold.

Arnold motioned to one of his men. They went to work attempting to retake command of the control systems.

"I've got control of communications," one of the guards replied.

"Reactor is too far gone, damage is already done," another guard said.

"How long do we have?" Marcus asked.

"Eight minutes, give or take . . ."

The Elites exchanged worried glances.

"Order a full evacuation. We've got to get as many people off this ship as we can." Marcus moved toward the exit to the bridge.

"Where are you going?" Zun asked.

"Arnea . . . she's back in Jessica's quarters." Marcus's gravimetric thrusters flared to life. "I'll meet up with you guys on the other side." Marcus disappeared in a burst of light as the giant barreled down the corridor toward the meglift.

Arnold connected to the ship-wide broadcast system.

"This is not a drill. Passengers and crew of the *Empress Star*, this is Chief Security Officer Arnold Steinsford. I regret to inform you that this ship has been under the control of a hostile pirate band known as Het Wrast Aht. We have retaken control of the ship, but they have damaged our reactor core and we have less than eight minutes to abandon ship before it goes critical. Please drop whatever you are doing and get to the escape pods immediately. I repeat, this is not a drill, get to the escape pods and abandon ship. You have less than eight minutes before the reactor goes critical. Maker direct your path."

He motioned toward a guard and an emergency siren came online. The blaring sound solidified the seriousness of his words.

"Nearest escape pods are this way." Arnold motioned for everyone to follow.

Zun moved to pick up Deidra, the drone still tethered to her for fluids.

"I need more time," Jenshi called out. "I have people in critical condition, and we shouldn't be moving them. They will die!"

"We don't have time. Pick them up and bring them with us," Jessica ordered.

"*Vusg* you! I am the commanding medical officer here!" Jenshi barked.

"Take it up with Lanrete," Jessica shot back. "Move!"

Jenshi glared at her as Tashanira moved to him, a hand on his chest calming him down. He let out a resigned sigh. Turning, he grabbed the nearest person. Guards moved to assist with the others, and they slowly made their way after Arnold.

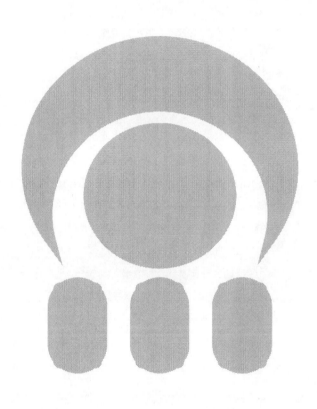

Cihphists believe attainment of CSL 5 to be another genetic limitation, with some species having higher representation than others, notably Humans, Tuzen, and Vempiir.

–FROM "CSL WITH DIRECT ENESMIC LINK"
BY SHAPER LUKIR AFREV

CHAPTER 54 DEXTER PINSTEN

Liron Storm, Huzien Alliance space

Heshel punched one of his men as he entered the bridge of the Liron Storm. The man pulled back, his eyes wide with terror. Heshel took his seat.

"This is all your *vusging* fault!" Heshel leered at Vexl. "I should cut off your dick and have them *vusg* you raw like the pussy you are." He slammed his fist down on the arm of his chair, fuming. "We had that ship!" He stood up, walked over to Vexl, and jammed his finger into Vexl's chest, pushing him back a step. "You screwed up!" He pulled out his weapon and leveled it at Vexl's head.

"Captain." Vexl took in a deep breath. "Those people . . . they were clearly military. The gear they were rocking was high-end Huzien stuff!" Vexl took a step back. "It was bad luck, if . . . if they hadn't been on that ship, it would have been ours."

"It was ours!" Heshel shouted. "You lost it!" He shot Vexl in the shoulder. Vexl stumbled back and to the ground.

"Captain, please . . ."

"Mercy?" Heshel laughed. "You seek *vusging* mercy? What kind of assault master are you?" Heshel spat on him.

"Tell me." Dexter's voice echoed around them, artificially projected as he hung from the ceiling, still cloaked. "Should I show mercy to you *vusging* monsters?"

Heshel turned around, his gaze searching the bridge. Multiple pirates pulled out their weapons, all of them spooked.

"Who are you and what are you doing on my ship? Do you have a *vusging* death wish?" Heshel spat back.

Next to Heshel, one of the pirate's heads snapped back, his brain matter splattering across a control panel. The man dropped to the floor like a rag doll as the other pirates started firing blindly into the empty spaces around them. Another pirate's head snapped back.

"Sentinels!" Vexl shouted.

"You led them back here!" Heshel screamed. He turned to face Vexl, only to see the man aiming his WMA at him. Before Heshel could pull his own trigger, Vexl fired. The headshot sent Heshel's gore across the room. Carnage intensified as the pirates dropped like flies. Those who survived dropped their weapons and ran screaming from the bridge. Vexl attempted to stand, the wound in his shoulder severe. A boot connected with the back of his head, knocking him back to the ground. Vexl spun, trying to bring up his weapon. He was too slow, and an invisible force knocked it out of his hand.

Dexter materialized on top of him, his knee squarely in the man's diaphragm and his hand clamped on his throat. Vexl tried to punch out with his good arm, but Dexter grabbed his wrist with his other hand and pulled it across his chest.

"Tell me," Dexter said. "Did you *vusg* any of the women back on that bridge?"

"What?" Vexl sputtered.

Dexter applied pressure to his throat.

"No . . . I didn't." Vexl coughed.

Dexter pondered his words for a moment.

"Did you *vusg* any of the men?"

Vexl hesitated.

Dexter crushed his windpipe.

Standing up, the Sentinel pulled out a small pistol and fired two shots into Vexl's stomach, then one into his good arm and one into each leg. Leaving Vexl to die, Dexter moved to the dead body of the captain. Reaching into his collar, he ripped out the man's mobi, then pulled out a small device from his own pocket and dropped the mobi into it. An indicator on the device stayed red for a few seconds, then flashed to green. Moving to a nearby holodisplay, he brought up the ship controls, the device having passed authorization through to Dexter. Within seconds, he had initiated the ship's self-destruct system. After locking the system to the bridge, he slipped the device back into one of his pockets and re-engaged his cloak.

Hegfe Deni came running onto the bridge, his eyes wide as he took in the sight of the dead captain and assault master. Hesitating, he glanced around the room, only to see more corpses. He looked over to the holodisplay near the captain's chair and saw the self-destruct timer ticking down. Backing up, he began to exit the bridge.

"Wise choice," came Dexter's voice from behind him. Before he could turn around, a blunt force hit him in the back of his head, and Hegfe's world went dark.

It is believed that at a CSL of 6, an individual maintains a constant link to the Ene-smic, and their mere presence influences the Enesmic flow around them.

–FROM "CSL WITH DIRECT ENESMIC LINK"
BY SHAPER LUKIR AFREV

CHAPTER 55 MARCUS HENSON

Empress Star, Huzien Alliance space

Marcus burst through the staircase door, the path on his HUD pulling his attention to the left. Setting his gravimetric thrusters into full burn, he flew down the hallway, not a soul in sight. A timer at the right side of his HUD ticked down; three minutes left before the reactor blew. After coming to a stop in front of the door to Jessica's quarters, Marcus pounded on it.

"Arnea, it's me, open up!"

In a heartbeat, the door opened, and Arnea stared at Marcus with relief on her face.

"I heard the announcement; I knew you'd come if it was true."

Without another word, Marcus slammed his lance rifle into a hold on his shield and picked her up in his free arm. Instantly, a path appeared on his holodisplay to the closest escape pod four levels down. The timer hit one minute.

Marcus exploded into motion, the Archlight a blur as he headed back toward the staircase. Arnea screamed as the g-forces pinned her to her husband. Marcus blew through another door, his shield leading the way. Thirty seconds. He powered forward, his thrusters taking him toward the last remaining escape pod on the deck. Fifteen seconds. Then he saw it. While in a full burn toward the escape pod, the pod's connecting door closed, and he could hear a decoupling sound as it blew away from the ship.

Marcus's eyes went wide. "Exhale all of the air out of your lungs, now!" Marcus yelled. Arnea complied without hesitation as her eyes mirrored his. Picking up speed, Marcus exploded through the closed pod bay door. Exposed to open space, Marcus held Arnea tight. He kept his gaze focused on the escape pod, the vessel quickly distancing itself from the *Empress Star*. Rerouting all his energy to his primary thrusters, Marcus chased after the pod.

Arnea closed her eyes tight. She was suffocating, with more blood vessels in her skin bursting by the second. Throwing his shield to the side, Marcus reached toward the escape pod. His momentum was not enough to keep up, and the pod quickly outdistanced him.

The shield he had thrown away kicked on its own thrusters and flew around to slam into Marcus's back, giving him the extra momentum he needed. Grabbing hold of the pod, he pinned Arnea between him and the small ship, his shield generator kicking on as his Archlight shield locked into his back. Opening his helmet, he filled the shield bubble with air, then grabbed hold of the closed door. He pulled it open, denting it with his gauntlets. Terrified screams escaped from the cramped pod as they saw a silver giant staring at them and an unconscious woman collapsing onto the floor of the escape pod.

"Take care of her!" Marcus yelled as his visor closed. Grabbing the pod door, he slammed it shut from the outside. A blast from his wrist fused the door closed. Bright light from behind him caught his attention, and he turned to witness the bottom half of the *Empress Star* splinter, lights rupturing the ship as the forces inside tore it apart.

As the force from the silent blast buffeted them, he secured himself to the back of the escape pod. Marcus's shield absorbed most of the impact as the pod continued in its trajectory toward a nearby planet barely visible in the distance. A short suplight burst kicked in, the miniature suplight drive only able to sustain it for a few minutes. Upon reappearing, Marcus took in sight of a planet's atmosphere.

Warnings flared across his HUD as the atmosphere started to eat away at his shield. Marcus rerouted everything to the shield's power, including life support. With the CO_2 no longer being pulled out of his suit and recycled, Marcus started to lose focus.

His grip on the escape pod faltered as the vessel skirted the atmosphere, realigning its heatshield toward the planet and picking up speed. Marcus drifted away from the pod as he turned over full control of his Archlight armor to his SI before losing consciousness. Twenty percent shield power was the last thing Marcus saw as he fell toward the planet's surface.

CHAPTER 56 ERBUBUC TAMN

Tenquin, Huzien Alliance space

Heavy footfalls shook the area as a golden-brown-furred Ken'Tar walked to the top of a moss-covered hill. It rested two of its four hands against a tree, the action comforting, reverent.

Erbubuc Tamn lifted his white-eyed gaze to regard the sky. It looked alive with fire, and he could see meteorites entering the atmosphere. He glanced around at the forest area surrounding him. It was serene, peaceful—the opposite of the chaos ahead. His gaze went back to the sky, and he noticed a few of the meteorites veering in his direction. Huffing, Erbubuc watched as one of the flaming objects zipped by overhead. He caught sight of a metallic glint and multiple thrusters attempting to slow the object down.

"That's no meteorite . . ." Erbubuc took off into a sprint after the object, his Dehehegen trailing after him, the long dark robe a blur.

Marcus's Archlight armor attempted to slow the unconscious Human down. The thrusters were at their limit; they couldn't bring him to a safe speed. The shielding flickered on momentarily, the last of its energy bringing the system to life as the armor's SI prepared to impact with the ground. The shielding absorbed most of the impact, though an ejection mechanism also kicked in at the last moment to send Marcus's body flying in the opposite direction. A type of foam rapidly expanded to cover him fully, turning the man into a sphere of beige. The Archlight armor slammed into the ground with an explosion of earth and rock.

An unconscious Marcus bounced a few times, the foam disintegrating just as rapidly as it had appeared. Eventually, Marcus came to a stop facedown in a patch of grass, tree roots a few meters away. The impact jolted the giant awake, his genetically modified body almost completely unscathed. After taking a moment to gather his wits, Marcus put his hands on the ground and pushed himself up. Slowly, he took in his surroundings and scanned for his armor. Spotting Claire, his shoulders slumped.

"No!" Marcus yelled.

He ran to his armor, a look of pure anguish on his face. Arriving at the site of his destroyed Archlight gear, Marcus collapsed to his knees. He stared in a state of shock at the mangled mess of technology, dirt, and rock. A tear rolled down his cheek.

"You saved me." He reached out to touch the heap of metal. "Thank you . . ."

"I'm sorry for your loss." The voice caught Marcus off guard. He spun around, his fists coming up as he fell into a defensive stance, and took in the sight of the golden brown Ken'Tar, whose bright white eyes were staring back at him with a sincere look of sympathy. The Ken'Tar was almost a foot taller than Marcus, his musculature impressive, even by Marcus's standards. "I apologize for startling you; my name is Erbubuc Tamn. I saw something coming in fast and made my way over here as soon as possible."

Marcus relaxed slightly. "Thank you. Claire meant a lot to me."

"I'm sure she was an amazing woman," Erbubuc said.

"Oh . . . yeah . . ." Marcus hesitated. "Claire was my Archlight armor."

Erbubuc raised an eyebrow. "Archlight armor? As in . . . an object?"

Marcus frowned. "Claire was more than just an object . . . but yes."

Erbubuc bowed slightly, two of his arms behind his back with the other two in front, a fist crested by a hand. "I honor Claire. She was indeed great Archlight armor to have drawn such strong emotions from you."

Marcus smiled. "Erbubuc, you said?"

"Yes. Please feel free to call me Erb for short if that better suits you."

"Okay, Erb." Marcus glanced around at the forest. "Where am I?"

FOUNDERS LOG:
The Power of Humility

It's truly amazing how little we know about the galaxy around us. We think we grasp or fully understand something in a moment, only to discover that we have barely even touched the surface. All discovery and exploration should be taken with a great deal of humility. I have watched countless prodigies and legends make fools of themselves due to pride and ignorance. It is the moment when we think that we have everything figured out that we truly know nothing.

Ecnics understands this. He marvels at the world around him and continuously seeks to learn its mysteries. He never allows his pride to overcome his wisdom. It's a message that is lost on many in his employ. I have watched him sadden as he listens to the reports of his most gifted employees, their blatant pride and refusal to acknowledge the unknown causing him to lose all faith in them.

Not fully understanding something is not failure; it's life. There are some mysteries that we may never fully know the answer to, but we must always question, always seek to know more. This is at the core of scientific discovery, and something that should never be forgotten.

Soahc believes that he has it all figured out. He understands the Enesmic better than anyone in the Twin Galaxies and has taught generations of Argents and Etan Rachnie instructors the truths of the Enesmic, enforcing a view of the world that he has accepted as fact.

I am nowhere near his equal in such matters, and as such, who am I to challenge his wisdom? However, I know what Ecnics knows: the galaxy is filled with mysteries, and we truly know nothing if we believe that we know it all.

Soahc's pride had grown into a manifestation that had no equal until he faced off against Sagren. Discovering a being more powerful than himself humbled him. Humility is something that opens our eyes and allows us to grow.

Sagren brought with itself a blessing in disguise. It reawakened my friend. Although, at the loss of one we all loved—at the loss of Brime. Looking upon Soahc now, I can't help but wonder what the next century will be like. Behind the sorrow, the pain, is an insatiable curiosity. And curiosity brings with it many wonders, and dangers.

-Lanrete

Speculation abounds as to whether there are classifications beyond CSL 7. Throughout history, there have been mythological beings described as having terrifying abilities. Whether this is truth or folklore is not for us to debate here; rather, we ascribe these possible beings a CSL of 7. Cihphists agree that this would be the realm of the demigods, if such beings exist.

−FROM "CSL WITH DIRECT ENESMIC LINK"
BY SHAPER LUKIR AFREV

CHAPTER 57 SOAHC

Enesmic Wilds, Enesmic plane

S oahc awakened to the sound of rustling. He remained still, not a muscle moving; he could sense a creature watching him. The Enesmic flowed all around him, thick and heavy. The pressure on his chest was uncomfortable as the energy pulsed. He tried to tap into its flow.

The denial was so sudden and shocking that Soahc sat up reflexively. The rustling to his side stopped. Soahc's gaze immediately locked onto a serpentlike creature that had bones in the place of scales and fire instead of eyes. The creature met his gaze.

Soahc sensed the attack before he saw it. Rolling backward and kicking to his feet, Soahc avoided the creature's lunge, its razor-sharp fangs spread wide enough to seemingly engulf Soahc whole.

Soahc reached out with his mind to force the Enesmic to bend to his will. The powerful rebuke came instantly, the forces around him flowing in powerful torrents. Soahc battled to gain control of the Enesmic, his pure will wrestling with the flow, trying to force it to heed his command. Slowly, Soahc forced the reluctant Enesmic to coalesce around the creature, and its body ignited in a burst of flame, but the flames were weak and quickly subdued.

Soahc cursed and dodged out of the way, another lunge coming dangerously close. He grabbed at the ground and threw a cloud of dust into the creature's eyes. It hissed. Reaching out again to the Enesmic, Soahc grabbed a strand of power and began to mold it. The torrents violently assaulted him.

Struggling under the strain of the forces swirling around him, Soahc caught sight of the creature lunging for him again. He released the Enesmic strand and jumped. The vengeful forces threw him away from the creature and roughly to the ground a few yards away. Coughing, Soahc pushed himself up. The serpent coiled up behind him, rising silently in tandem with him. It waited with a look of pleasure on its face.

In a single act of raw will, Soahc gripped a strand of Enesmic energy and molded it into a shining white sword. Spinning, he cut a line across the serpent's midsection, the act so fast that it barely registered on the creature's face. It collapsed to the ground in two pieces, the fire in its eyes dying.

The Enesmic slammed into Soahc, sliding him across the ground and up against a large rock protruding from the ground. It began to beat on him, the waves of power relentless as he struggled to protect himself. Just as quickly as it had begun, it ended. Soahc sat up and coughed, staring at the flow of energy all around him and attempting to recover from the pain coursing through every inch of his body.

"Okay." Soahc pushed himself up from the ground, his mind racing. "You have my attention." He paused. "This is your home." Soahc turned around, speaking to the flow itself. "We aren't strangers; you know who I am." He glanced around, unsure of what he was looking for. "Please, teach me how to use you here." Soahc waited for a long moment, his mind reaching out to the flow. Nothing. He began to slowly touch the strands of power, making sure to not provoke them, then studied them. A few minutes later, he let out a heavy sigh. Looking around, his gaze went to the dense swirling fog all around him. He picked a direction and began to walk.

A low rumble stopped Soahc. He looked at the ground and saw small rocks jumping slightly. Silence held for a second until another rumble shook the ground beneath his feet again. That's when it dawned on him; footsteps. Footsteps of something incredibly large. He dropped to his knee, scanning the area. The limited visibility caused his heart to beat faster, and he again tried to touch the Enesmic energy around him, seeking to extend his senses. He was forcefully shut out, and he felt truly blind in that moment. The rumbling footsteps began to pick up speed, coming in faster intervals, the source breaking into a sprint.

"That can't be good," Soahc whispered.

A massive form emerged from the fog a long distance away from him. It was a towering ten-story behemoth with a rock- and metal-fused chest and arms perched atop four spiderlike legs of similar make. It had no head, just a glowing central cavity where its neck would be. The cavity opened down toward the center of its chest. The glow was a dark orange mixed with red, as if molten lava was hidden just below the surface. A massive metal sword was clenched in one of its bulky hands, the blade trailing along the ground and tearing up earth in its wake.

"You have got to be kidding me."

Soahc doubted that he could outrun the creature; its towering form would easily be able to outdistance him. So, he reached out to the Enesmic flow and tried to forget everything he knew. He opened himself fully to it in every way possible, desperate. That was when he heard it, so subtly at first that he thought it was a trick of the wind. Then the sound became louder as he focused on it above all else. The Enesmic flow was singing! For the first time in his over one hundred thousand years of life, Soahc heard the beautiful song of the Enesmic. The chorus brought a tear to his eye. He felt the song in his bones and tasted it as it flowed around him. He reached out to the song with his essence and pleaded for his life.

"I am sorry! Please, I am nothing without you! Grant me your strength."

The flow wrapped itself around Soahc like a blanket. The flowing forces were not violent, but instead . . . focused. Soahc reached out and accepted the touch of the Enesmic, the immortal fully understanding in that moment more than he had understood in all his life. He asked the Enesmic to shield him in its power, his fist coming to his chest as he worked *with* the Enesmic for the first time.

A powerful barrier enveloped him and his eyes glowed with white fire as the energy flowed through him, fueling him like logs to a fire. Soahc joined in the chorus, the beautiful melody reaching deep into his soul. He reached out and guided the Enesmic—not forcing, never forcing.

A channel of Enesmic energy began to form between Soahc and the monstrosity, the channel made manifest as a beam of raw energy that slammed into the Enesmic being. The impact flung it backward like a wrecking ball slamming into a speeding car. The creature spun in a tight circle, but quickly regained its footing and returned to its full height before charging again at Soahc, its blade ready to strike.

Soahc stepped forward, the flow building around him and lifting him off the ground with each step. The immortal rose until he was high in the sky, almost at an equal level with the metallic beast. The creature brought its blade across in a powerful slice, the fog parting as the massive blade—dwarfing Soahc in size by multiple magnitudes—came to a halt within a few inches of the speck that stood in its way. The blade dematerialized, catching the beast off guard and causing it to lose its balance.

Soahc held up a hand, and the molten glow inside the creature intensified to white as he brought a new manifestation to life.

The pulsing white light sucked the creature into itself, stone and metal crumbling away and then pulling inward, like a black hole eating a star from within. A grating wail of terror and torment filled the air as the creature was ripped apart, held high in the air in a swirling mess of molten rock and metal. Soahc clenched his fist, and the creature was destroyed in a devastating explosion of light that sent bits of the monstrosity in every direction.

Soahc slowly descended, the Enesmic returning to its normal flow. He rested on his hands and knees, this new revelation causing him to stare at the ground, his eyes wide while he listened to the Enesmic melody in awe.

After some time, the fog to the side of Soahc began to pull away, a path forming. He glanced up, the immortal still on his hands and knees. The image of a shining city appeared in the heart of the fog. Within seconds, it faded, and the fog returned to normal. Soahc pushed himself up, his gaze locked on the swirling fog where the image of the city had been mere moments before.

"Okay . . ." Soahc scratched the back of his head. "Either that's a trap or I just made a very powerful ally." Soahc stared straight up into the sky for a long moment. It was a swirling mix of lightning and dark clouds. Returning his gaze to the path laid bare before him, he made another request to the Enesmic. Within seconds, a small dark orb appeared at his side, between him and the direction of the city. It remained between him and his destination as he moved around, testing his new creation. Nodding in satisfaction, he set off.

> *The Vempiir evolved on the planet of Piro, which is near the galactic core of the galaxy Asracka, which is part of the Twin Galaxies of Oaphen Asracka.*
>
> —FROM "CHRONICLES OF THE VEMPIIR"
> BY LICH LORD TERTIUS VIRTOK

CHAPTER 58 BRIME WEWTA

Aheraneth, Enesmic plane

"Impressive." Augrashumen the Valorous glanced to Vesgrilana the Sagacious. "In such a short time on the Enesmic plane, he has already learned to commune with the essence of life."

"Essence of life?" Brime asked. Both Rel Ach'Kel turned to regard the Human in their midst, her form hovering a short distance from the assembled host.

"What you would understand as the Enesmic flow," Vesgrilana imparted to Brime. It was the first time Vesgrilana had addressed Brime directly. The voice hurt slightly, but Brime tried her best not to wince. She smiled to not feel out of place.

"Your champion still has a long way to go," Hiweretpor the Perspicuous interjected. Its gaze was focused on Vesgrilana. "It will take him three days of traveling to reach our gates."

Brime whispered the word "champion" to herself.

"And if the Betrayers did not know of his presence before," Grilmuqshen the Exemplar said, "they most certainly do now."

"What will they do?" Brime asked.

Grilmuqshen regarded Brime. It was a towering being with

fine armor underneath flowing blue robes. Massive pauldrons of gold and silver covered its shoulders, and in the place of a head hung a silver hourglass with a glowing golden orb at its midsection. Brime interpreted that to be its eye. A crown of glowing silver hovered above its "head," and a golden energy seeped out of the pauldrons and armor in wisps. Six sets of immense golden armored wings appeared behind it, not directly connected to its body, but stationary as if attached nonetheless.

"Toy with him at first," Grilmuqshen responded, "then they will kill him, brutally." The words sent a shiver down Brime's spine.

"If he is lucky," Augrashumen said. "They may seek to possess him, then return to the Havin plane with Soahc as their instrument of destruction."

"Possession?" Brime gasped.

"He would not be the first," Hiweretpor said, "nor would he be the last."

"Are you able to possess people?"

The Rel Ach'Kel hesitated, a few turning to regard Vesgrilana, clearly seeking direction.

"Yes . . ." Vesgrilana replied, "although the disruption of free will goes against the Originator's design, and as such, it is not done."

"Hmph." Brime looked to the glowing window hovering in the air. Soahc could be seen trudging through the Wilds, violent winds now assaulting him as he pressed forward in the direction of the Rel Ach'Kel city.

Early Vempiir looked very different from our species today, with a smaller, squatter stature due to the high gravity of our planet. We also had less pronounced fangs, more muted eye colors, and skin tones that lacked our distinct red hues.

–FROM "CHRONICLES OF THE VEMPIIR"
BY LICH LORD TERTIUS VIRTOK

CHAPTER 59 SOAHC

Enesmic Wilds, Enesmic plane

Soahc's eyes flared open. He had collapsed from exhaustion onto his stomach, and his face was pressed in the dirt. He lay there, unmoving, his senses on high alert and his mind wide awake. He couldn't sense anything out of the ordinary, but his instincts were screaming at him.

Slowly moving his hands up to below his chest, Soahc pushed himself up, trying his best to not make a sound. In an act of pure physical prowess, he lifted his legs off the ground, his hands the only contact with the land beneath him. Pulling in his knees, Soahc positioned his feet next to his hands and slowly began to stand up. He reached out to the Enesmic and asked for sight. The area around him filled his mind like a second sense. Something at the edge of his new senses moved away. Soahc immediately burst into weaving defenses around himself.

I can smell the fear dripping from you, Havin.

Whispers permeated Soahc's mind, each word spoken as if the combination of hundreds of hushed voices.

"That is not fear," Soahc countered, "it is annoyance." He grinned. "The last being to call me Havin had its life snuffed out by my hand."

Laughter made from the twisting of cries of torment by a multitude of voices echoed throughout the area. The horrid sound stole Soahc's nerve for a moment, wiping the grin from his face.

The rumors are true, then. You are the Havin who defeated what remained of Sagren the Betrayer.

"Soahc, Destroyer of Worlds. Slayer of Eshgren."

The laughter returned.

Sagren was destroyed long before you were formed in your mother's womb. The being that you faced was a mere fragment of the Eshgren that was the Fallen Commander. A mere echo of the being that was once revered among our ranks.

Soahc silently mouthed the words "our ranks." His eyes went wide, his heart skipping a beat as his body tensed.

I can show you the true power of our kind Soahc, Slayer of Eshgren. I am Eheriequyturjin the Abettor.

A humanoid being emerged from the fog, the figure three times the size of Soahc. Its body was covered in a robe of arms—its own arms, with hands clenching and opening as if seeking to grasp something. Two sets of intertwined arms were prominent above the robe, mocking the image of a normal man, each "hand" radiating with immense power. The Enesmic swirled around the being in torrents. Its head held a mouth and one eye that radiated purple fire, but no nose. The mouth seemed etched, like stone. The creature stood on a series of arms intertwined together to serve as legs, and hair like constantly moving sand combined with water rose into the air as if protruding from its skull.

Soahc had seen his share of strange creatures from the Enesmic, but this sight unnerved him. He felt the same perversion he had felt when he first encountered Sagren, except magnified hundredfold. Soahc's stomach lurched at the grotesque image, and it took all his nerves to not puke immediately at the sight of the being. It was an abomination, an absolute corruption of something once beautiful, once magnificent. That realization caused a burning fury to build within Soahc, and the immortal launched into a cihphistic assault without another thought.

A beam of raw energy streaked past Soahc as he dodged to the side, the nearness of it sending his hair up on end, electrified. The immortal landed in a roll, Enesmic energy flowing through him. He ran up a set of invisible steps, the action putting him level with Eheriequyturjin. Soahc released a lefon blast from his hand, the empowered cihphistic manifestation slamming into the Eshgren's barrier. The creature's face remained expressionless, its mouth unmoving as that terrible laugh continued to shake Soahc to his core. One of Eheriequyturjin's primary hands shifted in the direction of Soahc's new location in a delayed echo; time seemed to struggle to catch up with it. At the same moment, an invisible beam captured Soahc, the immediacy of it confusing him. He hadn't even registered the attack.

As if an aftershock, the true force of the beam washed over Soahc, time finally syncing with reality. Terrible pain coursed through him as his barrier was wiped away in an instant. Unable to enact any semblances of a defense, he begged the Enesmic to sustain him as the forces started to tear his body apart. The Eshgren's laughter continued as Soahc struggled to stay conscious through the terrible pain. His skin rippled, blood spraying in every direction.

A flash of light defeated the terrible beam, and a towering being was suddenly standing directly between Soahc and Eheriequyturjin. The giant was in shining armor of gold and silver with diamond bolts holding it all together. A silvery cowl of deep gold was atop its head. Soahc caught sight of six sets of massive wings and an impressive sword with an edge of pure radiating energy before he started to slip in and out of consciousness.

Eheriequyturjin took a step back. *This matter does not concern the Rel Ach'Kel.*

"It does now," the giant stated with authority.

You dare defy the treaty?

"I will not allow you to murder this Havin."

This is foolishness. You will not deny me my prize. If you wish to break the treaty, then I so declare it broken. The war starts anew with you as the first blood.

Every hand comprising Eheriequyturjin's body began to move in tandem with the others as the being rose off the ground. Its legs unraveled, and it became a living mass of arms. The Enesmic began to swirl in torrents of impossible energy, the area coming alive, stones and rubble rising from the ground and hanging in midair.

"Get Soahc out of here, now," the golden being stated with immense calm.

Brime moved to Soahc's side, grabbing her beloved as his blood covered her clothing. Her eyes became distant as if remembering a painful memory, and she wiped away a tear before glancing back toward the shining entryway hanging in the air. It was the viewing portal the Rel Ach'Kel had used to view the events of Soahc's journey. Brime made a break for it with Soahc carried by the Enesmic behind her.

No! Eheriequyturjin yelled.

All the arms stopped moving; the Eshgren seemed perfectly still for an instant. Then, in the blink of an eye, it appeared directly between Brime, Soahc, and their salvation. The arms moved in an elaborate pattern, and the area around them came alive with golems of chaos and stone, fire in their eyes as they burst through the ground. They charged toward Brime and a barely conscious Soahc, clearly intent on crushing them.

Our society included, as many do, a dark age filled with war and conflict between feudal lords. From that age, we grew into a unified society where scientific progress in the realm of genetic experimentation and perfection was pursued.

–FROM "CHRONICLES OF THE VEMPIIR"
BY LICH LORD TERTIUS VIRTOK

CHAPTER 60 BRIME WEWTA

Enesmic Wilds, Enesmic plane

A flash of light forced Brime to blink, and when she opened her eyes, she was suddenly unable to comprehend her surroundings as the golems collapsed to the ground in heaps of lifeless stone. Augrashumen continued its assault, and then was on Eheriequyturjin in another flash. The Eshgren raised its arms to meet Augrashumen's powerful blade, each becoming like black metal as they parried the Rel Ach'Kel's blows.

The two began to move faster than Brime and Soahc could see, becoming a blur. Then they completely disappeared, their actions no longer detectable in their realm of time. Brime gasped as the area around her exploded and she saw a blur right next to her. Both her and Soahc felt an urging focusing their attention back on the entryway. They began to move again, both gasping as they sensed the powerful beings fighting right behind them.

A summons went out across the Enesmic as Eheriequyturjin called to its kin in a telepathic roar, the Eshgren locked in mortal combat with the Rel Ach'Kel. No matter how hard the Eshgren tried, Augrashumen kept it at bay, and Brime continued her sprint toward the portal with Soahc hovering behind.

A pitch-black being with the head of a jackal and the body of a man appeared between Brime, Soahc, and their escape. Its body was impossibly muscled, seeming chiseled of black marble, and glowing purple energy streaked from its neck to its stomach.

Its presence was sudden, and Brime's eyes went wide, her heart pounding in her chest. It regarded her briefly, then its hand began rising as it pointed a finger at her chest. Brime winced, and she looked down to see a hole beginning to materialize in her chest. In the next instant, Vesgrilana the Sagacious was in front of her. Brime staggered back, her hand searching her chest where the forming wound had been mere moments before, but all semblances of it were gone.

She looked up in confusion. Vesgrilana had the silhouette of a woman, its hair like a cloud of rising smoke. Its form was hard to focus on, almost insubstantial. Wisps of purple energy rose from its hands and eyes. Bright orbs of fire encircled the Rel Ach'Kel's midsection, the orbs passing through and around the being, seemingly one with it. Massive pauldrons of platinum and gold hung on the being's shoulders, a set of matching armored leggings and boots completing the image. Twelve sets of wings hung behind the mighty Rel Ach'Kel.

Vesgrilana raised a hand, and a howl of pain erupted from the jackal-headed Eshgren as it was flung miles away. The Rel Ach'Kel's wispy purple eyes then regarded Brime, the gaze forcing the woman back into action as she lifted Soahc and charged through the portal. Vesgrilana lifted another hand in the direction of Augrashumen and Eheriequyturjin. The Eshgren was blasted away from Augrashumen and far across the Enesmic plane like its kin before it. Augrashumen turned to regard Vesgrilana with admiration, awe in its eyes.

"We must depart and prepare," Vesgrilana hesitated, ". . . for war."

CHAPTER 61 HUIARA MAU GEHREYATI

Huza, Thae, Huzien home system

Huiara stood on the balcony of her new office in the Huzien Capitol building. She closed her eyes and took in a deep breath, the wind caressing her face as her platinum fur moved in the breeze. Her mobi blipped, pulling her back to reality. At seeing the image of Marcarias on her micro-display, she remotely opened the door. Turning around, she leaned back against the balcony railing. Marcarias appeared at the entrance to the balcony a few moments later.

"Restendi." Huiara nodded.

"Govnus." Marcarias nodded in kind as Huiara's face lit up in a smile. Her posture on the railing was relaxed, confident. She followed him with her gaze as he walked to the railing and rested on it with his elbows. "An absolutely beautiful sight."

"I know. I love the view from up here."

"That's nice too." Marcarias flashed her a smirk.

Huiara blushed, turning away from him. "If I didn't know any better, I'd think you were flirting with me."

Marcarias turned to regard her. "Dinner, tonight." Huiara started to shake her head no. "In celebration! It's a time-honored tradition for the current restendi to take a newly appointed govnus out for a celebratory dinner."

"Is that right?" Huiara narrowed her eyes playfully. "Well, in that case, who am I to defy tradition?"

"Perfect!" Marcarias clapped his hands together. "I know the perfect place; I'll send a car to your residence around seven?"

Huiara bit her lip. "Okay . . ."

"Enjoy the view." Marcarias turned to leave.

"Marcarias, Restendi . . . I . . . thank you for your recommendation to Cislot."

Marcarias stopped and turned to smile at Huiara.

"That was all you." He exited the balcony.

"What made you decide to get into politics?" Huiara sat at the restaurant table with her hands clasped comfortably in her lap. She wore a modestly cut gold-trimmed black dress, the accents playing off her golden eyes. Marcarias leaned in slightly to the table, his iconic smile on display. He wore an expensive black suit of Huzien make, the collar hard cloth and pointing up toward his ears with the right side of the suit jacket clasped by silver buttons over his left from his shoulder down to his waist.

"I had an obsession with Cislot as a child," Marcarias said. "I followed everything she did, studied every policy enacted, every decision made. Even what her current fashion trend was." Marcarias laughed. "I wanted to work with her, to work around her." Marcarias paused. "She was my idol. I attended all of her speeches in person, made every effort to see her with my own eyes."

Huiara's eyes widened. "Wow."

"I lost both of my parents in an accident when I was twelve." He sat in silence for a long moment, staring at his wine glass. "A relative tried to take care of me, gave me a place to stay, but she didn't have time for me and eventually turned me over to the state as an orphan. I attended another one of Cislot's speeches a few months later. I was broken inside, but I felt if I could just see Cislot, everything would be better."

He smiled. "That's the day she noticed me in the crowd during her speech. She came up to me after and asked why I looked so sad. She had noticed me at speeches over the years and had always remembered my energetic smile. She said it was the smile of a future politician, and that she missed it." Marcarias looked up at Huiara. "I told her what had happened, and she looked up to the sky for a long moment before taking my hands in hers and asking if I wanted a new *lurra*."

Huiara sat back in her chair, speechless.

"She adopted me right there on the street. It was official the next day. I moved in with her and was enrolled in all the best programs, had all the best teachers, all the best training, and entered the upper echelons of society in a way I had never imagined possible. She molded me into the man that I am today." He laughed. "Then I became her assistant and everything changed."

She tilted her head to the side. "Why is that?"

Marcarias stared at his wine for a long moment, then sighed. "She went from being my *lurra* to becoming my Founder. It was a difficult transition. The compassionate, playful, friendly woman I knew as my *lurra* for all those decades became a hard, calculating, and demanding instructor who only wanted perfection from me." Marcarias picked up his glass and took a sip. "I am restendi because she literally groomed me for the role in every possible way, and I could not let her down."

"It sounds like she didn't give you much of a choice in life."

"That's not true." Marcarias shook his head. "I wanted to be like her, like I said before. She merely helped me realize that through pushing me to become the perfect politician."

"Is that why you've remained single?" Huiara said. "No emotional attachments to cloud your judgement?"

Marcarias smiled sadly. "When your *lurra* is a founder of the Huzien Empire, most women don't live up to the standard of what you'd accept for an *eifi*." She frowned. "Although, every now and then," Marcarias continued, obviously catching the change in her expression, "there is a girl who comes along that you can't stop thinking about." He leaned in closer. "A woman with impressive inner strength, with poise and grace that rivals that of Cislot herself. A woman who leaves you breathless every time you see her."

Huiara's heart started pounding, and she felt the blood rush to her cheeks, her body going numb. The two sat in silence for a long moment, Huiara captured by Marcarias's gaze like a deer in headlights. A serving drone appeared at their table, silently refilling their cups of water before moving on to the next table.

"I . . . tomorrow morning . . ." Huiara paused to compose herself. "I have a meeting with the grand lichars in the morning." Huiara let out a slow breath. "I should probably leave to prepare."

"Of course." Marcarias nodded.

Charging the bill for their meal to his mobi, the restendi stood. Huiara did likewise, then quickly headed out of the restaurant in front of him without another word. A miniature army of security personnel ushered them into separate hovercars. Huiara's gaze lingered on Marcarias as she dipped into her car, out of view.

The cleansing of the unworthy was made possible by way of genetic enhancements and cihphistic experimentation that allowed us to unlock our full potential.

−FROM "CHRONICLES OF THE VEMPIIR"
BY LICH LORD TERTIUS VIRTOK

CHAPTER 62 CISLOT

Huza, Thae, Huzien home system

"We will not allocate funds to the Huzien rebuilding efforts." Tirivus's tone had an air of finality.

"This violates the statutes of the Alliance member agreement!" Marcarias wore a scowl as he stood next to Cislot in a private meeting chamber atop the Huzien Capitol building. Cislot was standing as well, her arms crossed with a cold stare affixed to Tirivus. The Tuzen was projected seated at the table across from them in the hologrid within the room. The three had been at it for over an hour.

"My people will not stand for their resources being allocated to rebuild Huzien worlds," Tirivus said.

"More than Huzien worlds fell during the Rift War," Marcarias interjected. "This will impact multiple Alliance member worlds, dammit!"

Tirivus ignored him.

"You are making a mistake," Cislot said.

Tirivus stood, his fists slamming the table. "You are fools to believe that we would assist in this capacity!"

"Your nation agreed to these terms when you joined the Alliance!" Cislot shot back. "You don't get to enjoy the benefits of being a member nation and ignore all else." She put both of her hands down on the table and leaned forward. "Your refusal to provide military support during the Rift War and now your refusal to provide financial aid during the rebuilding efforts is unacceptable." She paused. "You continue with this line of action and I will have you expelled from the Alliance."

"Is that a threat?"

"Absolutely."

Tirivus glared at Cislot, her gaze unflinching. They remained locked in a silent battle for a few minutes. Slowly, Tirivus stood up straight, a grin on his face.

"Very well." Tirivus crossed his arms. "You do what you must, but know this. Your actions will be viewed as hostility toward the Tuzen Empire—hostility that requires retribution." Tirivus glanced to Marcarias before terminating his connection, disappearing from the hologrid.

"*Vusging cith,*" Marcarias said. "What are we going to do?" He turned to Cislot. "We were counting on those resources for our rebuilding efforts. We can't afford the current plan approved by the senate with the Tuzens off the table."

Cislot remained silent for a long moment. Letting out a sigh, she glanced at Marcarias. "Call an emergency session and inform the senate." Cislot turned to exit the room. "I plan to begin work on the articles of expulsion for the Tuzen Empire."

"Your threat was real." The blood drained from Marcarias's face.

Cislot stopped and glanced back at him. "The Tuzens aren't ready to be our allies. I thought we could make progress together, but Tirivus is no fool." She sighed, and her shoulders slumped. "If he wasn't receiving pressure from back home, he wouldn't be taking these actions. I fear keeping the Tuzens as a member of the Alliance at this juncture will only lead to worse relations. People will not forget their continued refusal to help their allies." She turned and began walking again. "And to maintain order in the Alliance, we must not show favoritism. Tirivus and the Tuzen Empire must pay for their actions."

"Many of the outlying colonies cannot continue to support the increased burden of refugees." Cislot stood at the large window to her office atop the Huzien Capitol building, her iconic flowing black suitcoat a contrast to the light coming in from outside. "Thae has taken a heavy load of them, but even our capital has its limits."

"Some corporations have offered to assist with the rebuilding efforts." Marcarias sat in the center of the office, his eyes glued to a holodisplay. "The CEOs of both Ganrele Retril and eshLucient have reached out to me directly. They are offering to divert primary resources to construction efforts there."

"In exchange for the rights to land owned by deceased colonists without direct inheritors," Cislot countered.

"By law, that land goes to us for reallocation anyway. We have the authority to agree to their request." Marcarias rubbed his eyes. "And with the lack of aid from the Tuzen Empire, we are in a bad position." Cislot turned slightly and tilted her head in Marcarias's direction, her expression sad. He glanced up at her, his eyes widening slightly.

"This is your decision." Cislot turned away from him and resumed gazing out the window. "If you believe this to be the best course of action, take it."

"Just like that?" Marcarias asked. Cislot didn't respond, and Marcarias shifted uncomfortably as silence permeated the room.

"How was the dinner?" Cislot finally asked.

"Good." Marcarias stood up. "She's agreed to a second night out."

"Fantastic."

Marcarias watched Cislot for a few moments, the woman a perfect silhouette against the bright light.

"I will inform the corporations." Marcarias began to leave Cislot's office.

"Marcarias." The cool tone with which Cislot called Marcarias's name caused him to stop in his tracks. He turned back to look at her. "I have decided to take an *eifi*."

"I didn't even know you were seeing someone." Marcarias made his way back toward Cislot, his eyes wide. She turned around and leaned up against the glass, the look on her face a mix of playfulness and amusement that caused his eyes to open wider.

"Not every aspect of my life is known to you, my dear *burush*." Cislot followed Marcarias with her gaze as he came to stand next to her at the window.

"Well." Marcarias paused. "Tell me about her."

Cislot suppressed a laugh.

"She is Das'Vin and Huzien, born on Thae. We were introduced by Hexa'Gevhre Quen Orecha, the Das'Vin heir'apthai. She's a lawyer who enjoys fine art and the opera."

"What's her name?"

"Erisya Yetrewna."

"What makes you so sure you want her to be your *eifi*?"

Cislot leaned over and kissed Marcarias on his temple. "I love you. Thank you for the entertainment." She moved away from him and toward her desk. Marcarias watched her sit down and pull up a series of holodisplays, forgetting his presence. The restendi stared at her for a long moment, then departed from her office without another word.

CHAPTER 63 HUIARA MAU GEHREYATI

Huza, Thae, Huzien Home System

"Wow," Huiara stared at Marcarias, her mouth open. "I... . I'm happy that the founder finally decided to take an eifi again. It's been over two hundred years since her last eifi died, right?"

Marcarias nodded and broke Huiara's gaze as they continued their walk through the grove, the well-worn path at their feet familiar. The two had gotten into the habit of walking together through the botanical gardens in the heart of the Huzien Capitol building. The gardens were majestic, well maintained, and elaborately engineered to evoke thoughts of raw untouched nature in the heart of the busiest and most impressive city in the Huzien Empire.

"This place is beautiful. I like being here," Huiara said.

"Does it remind you of Peshkana?"

Huiara shook her head. "I never spent much time on Peshkana. Thae has always been my home."

"If you ever had children, would you send them there to be raised by your tribe? The Mauveh, right?"

Huiara laughed. "No, I would not subject my children to that horrible tradition." Huiara turned back to see Marcarias's face brighten. Clearing her throat, she glanced away. "Besides, I doubt I would choose another Uri as a *nusba*, and hybrid children aren't too common in my tribe."

Marcarias chuckled lightly. "That sounds a bit speciest, don't you think?"

"Hardly." Huiara waved her hand. "The qualities I'm looking for in a *nusba* are rare in traditional Uri society."

"And those are?"

Huiara glanced at Marcarias, his gaze thoughtfully aimed toward the ground and their path, his hands behind his back.

"Restraint, for one."

Marcarias laughed. "Anything else?"

"Loyalty, intelligence, and courage, to name a few."

"It sounds like you have a list."

"I do."

Marcarias glanced to Huiara. Their gazes locked.

"Seldom in life do we find perfection."

Huiara held his gaze for a few moments before breaking eye contact and looking back to the stream. The two remained silent for a time, continuing in their walk through the Capitol Gardens.

"I . . . saw the official brief you released regarding the land grants to eshLucient and Ganrele Retril for the rebuilding efforts."

"Their capital investment will help offset the deficit we have with the Tuzens out of the picture."

A few moments passed before Huiara spoke again. "What about the colonists?"

"I'm not sure I understand your question." Marcarias stopped walking and turned to Huiara.

"I mean . . . wouldn't it make more sense to grant the land to the surviving colonists and allow them to negotiate with the corporations seeking to rebuild on their worlds?"

Marcarias frowned. "Negotiations with the colonists could take years, and that's assuming the corporations would want to take the risk of rebuilding on fringe worlds where the damage was most felt."

"But who are we to dictate the rebuilding efforts for those communities? We aren't the ones who watched it all burn, the ones who experienced the pain of seeing loved ones die. We don't know what is best for the colonists. We should have let them decide."

Marcarias straightened his back. "I made the decision that I deemed best for the Huzien Empire."

Huiara caught herself balling her fists. Glancing down at her hands, she relaxed them and turned away from Marcarias. The two continued their walk, silent once again. After a few minutes, they emerged from the Capitol Gardens's tree canopy and into civilization.

"I have a busy day tomorrow; I think it best if I retire for the evening." Without waiting for a reply, Huiara broke away from Marcarias and walked toward the road. A black hovercar came to a stop in front of her, and her personal security detail seemed to appear out of nowhere, one moving to open the door for her as she stepped inside without a glance back at Marcarias.

The restendi watched her car drive away, his gaze locked on the vehicle until it disappeared.

Huiara watched the scenery as it passed by, her mind racing. Public outcry from Marcarias's decision was almost certainly coming, she was sure of it. She could almost read the headlines now: *Restendi betrays recovering colonists to big business! Yonvi Administration puts mega-corporations first in rebuilding efforts.*

She crossed her arms and sat back in her seat.

How could he be so stupid? She considered the possibility of their relationship becoming public knowledge and the fallout from the remainder of Marcarias's term bleeding over into her own political career. She held back a tear as she imagined her chances of becoming the first Uri restendi vanish.

She shook her head.

I will not let that happen.

CHAPTER 64 LANRETE

Foundra Conscient, Huzien Alliance space

The meglift slid open, and Lanrete walked onto Neven's loaned engineering bay. He could hear the young secnic working just out of sight. Stopping just before crossing the threshold, Lanrete took in a deep breath and strode forward. He passed a few power armors still being assembled, the shells covered with cables and in dull colors, the polish normally seen on finished work missing. Lanrete rounded another power armor and stopped in his tracks. His eyes went wide as his gaze landed on Neven building a scale replica of A'Amaria Schen.

"Neven?"

Neven stopped and turned, saw Lanrete staring at him, and slowly set down his tools.

"What are you doing?"

"I..." Neven glanced to the replica of A'Amaria. The skin was missing, revealing corded electronic muscles and numerous technical innovations unlike anything Lanrete had ever seen. "I can't..." Neven shook his head. "I can't get her out of my head." He turned to look at the partially assembled android. "She's everywhere. My thoughts . . . I can feel her when I close my eyes." Neven began to tear up, then dropped to his knees, his head in his hands. "I relive that horrible moment every night. Please make it stop."

Lanrete rushed to Neven's side. "I should have checked on you sooner, I'm sorry. She did something to you telepathically." Lanrete forced Neven to stare into his eyes. "Open your mind to me, fully." Neven whimpered. "Now!"

The command forced Neven into compliance, and he cracked open the mental barriers pounded into him by Soahc. Lanrete delved into his mind and began searching through his consciousness.

"There . . ." Lanrete narrowed his eyes. "She left an imprint of herself on your mind." Steeling his gaze, Lanrete telepathically ripped it out.

Neven screamed, shrinking away from Lanrete. His eyes suddenly rolled up into his head, his body collapsing to the floor.

Neven opened his eyes and then squinted at the bright lights, his vision quickly adjusting as Lanrete watched him silently. Looking around, Neven frowned as he scanned the medical deck. Lanrete made no motion as Neven propped himself up on his arms.

"What happened?" Neven asked.

Lanrete let out a sigh, his true age showing in his eyes for the first time since he had met Neven. "A'Amaria imprinted a piece of herself on your consciousness." Lanrete sat back in his seat and shook his head. "It was a way for her to defeat your mental defenses in the future. It's not the first time she's done something like this; make people obsess over you and they're more likely to give you anything you want."

"She was in my head," Neven almost whispered.

"Much more than that." Lanrete paused and stood up. "She most likely knows everything about you now. And there is still a remnant of her inside of you."

"What does that mean?" Neven's voice trembled.

"I'm not entirely sure." Lanrete crossed his arms. "We should return to Etan Rachnie when we can. We'll need the help of a powerful telepath to eliminate all traces of her from your mind."

Neven shivered, his arms closing around his legs.

"The good news," Lanrete said as Neven looked up at him, "is that your mind is fully back in your control now . . . for the most part."

"Great," Neven said.

"Neven, I'm sorry." Lanrete rubbed his eyes. "This is all my fault. I should never have taken you to the surface with me. I risked you as an unnecessary gamble and I lost." Neven silently stared at Lanrete. "I know that you had never been with a woman. I'm sorry that A'Amaria stole that from you." Lanrete began to walk out of the medical deck, but stopped. "If you want to press charges against her, you have my full support."

"Thanks." Neven shook his head. "I just want to put this behind me."

Lanrete sighed. "Don't feel that you are doing me a favor by not prosecuting my ex-wife."

"Why didn't you prosecute her for what she did with the HIN?"

"I thought you didn't look into people's personal affairs?"

"When you're forced into obsession about someone, apparently you spend a lot of time trying to find out as much as you can about them." Neven laughed. "I found the report on the HIN about the case brought against her when you were married. About her abuse of the HIN and sharing of classified information." Neven moved his legs over the side of the medical bed. "The case was one of treason, punishable by death." Neven locked gazes with Lanrete. "You chose to drop the case and exonerate her of all charges."

"It would appear that we both make poor decisions." Lanrete shrugged. "She doesn't deserve your mercy. I gave her mercy because I loved her, but she is my mistake, not yours."

"My mother taught me that forgiveness is the only way we can truly heal." Neven gave Lanrete a sad smile. "I . . . forgive A'Amaria for what she did to me. Not for her sake, but for mine."

"You have a good heart, Neven." Lanrete sighed again. "Don't let it get you killed."

Lanrete stood with his hands behind his back, gazing out the window into the space beyond, where the stars flew by at staggering speeds. His mobi chirped, and the name of the caller caused his eyes to narrow. He accepted the call.

"Report."

Andrex Dominu, general of intelligence for the Huzien Empire, appeared on the holodisplay. The pale-skinned Human nodded at Lanrete, his piercing blue eyes dominating the screen.

"I found the bogeyman," Andrex said.

Lanrete let out a slow breath.

"Entradis . . ."

"A local SI in the Genmatha system IDed him and sent in the tip. We have Sentinels in the area, but no other hits yet."

"You think this was a slipup?"

"From Entradis?" Andrex shook his head. "He wants to be found; he's toying with us."

"His timing is impeccable as always." Lanrete let out a sigh. "Keep me informed."

Andrex nodded, then terminated the connection.

Lanrete turned and leaned up against the glass, his mind going to Yuvan. Thoughts of the murdered engineer, Neven's predecessor, caused him to wince. It was a senseless death in a seemingly endless pool of other senseless deaths. The long list caused Lanrete's heart to ache with each name added.

"I will find you," Lanrete whispered, "and I will kill you." There was a righteous anger in his voice, his gaze distant.

CHAPTER 65 NEVEN KENK

Foundra Conscient, Huzien Alliance space

When Neven arrived back in his engineering lab, his mind immediately went to work prioritizing his list of ongoing projects. A series of holodisplays came to life and began following him with readouts from automated testing cycles and simulations. He stopped in front of the android replica of A'Amaria.

Are you done being irrational?

Neven smiled. *Yes, I'm done being . . . irrational,* Neven replied to Ellipse.

What are you going to do with that ugly thing?

Don't know.

Neven walked up to the incomplete android and stared at it for a long moment. The sculpted body contour was impressive, the same as A'Amaria's own, minus the artificial skin.

Have to admit . . . obsessive-compulsive you does good work.

Neven laughed. At that moment, the meglift to the engineering bay opened. Neven backtracked to get a clear view of the meglift and caught sight of Aru walking toward him.

"Lanrete told me to check up on you," Aru called out.

"Ah," Neven replied. "Well, welcome to my lab!"

"*My* lab," Aru corrected, "which you're borrowing."

Possessive much?

Neven held back a laugh. Moving back toward the android, Aru slowly followed him, making his way around the various creations Neven had started but that remained unfinished.

"Do you ever actually complete anything?" Aru said.

"I experiment with fringe concepts to pass the time. To . . . clear my thoughts."

"Whoa." Aru came to a stop in front of the android replica of A'Amaria. "I'm pretty sure that's illegal."

Neven glanced at Aru and then back at the android. "I . . . I can explain."

"I'm the last person to turn anyone in to the MinSci for breaking protocol, but I'd recommend not letting Ecnics or any of the top brass see that."

"Why is there so much paranoia around androids anyway?"

"Same reason why SI systems are so heavily regulated," Aru said. "Fear of the machines turning on us and wiping us out. Fear of something higher than us on the food chain. Pick your disaster scenario."

We're not that bad . . . I'd never hurt a fly.

Pretty sure if I left you alone in a room with A'Amaria that you'd tear her apart.

She deserves it.

As Neven smirked, Aru raised an eyebrow. Neven cleared his throat and turned back to face the android.

"Should I dismantle it?"

Aru walked over to stand next to Neven. "Dismantle it?" Aru forcefully shook his head no. "Seems like a waste." He glanced at Neven. "Maybe a secret pet project? Keeping it small is a good idea. Seems less intimidating that way."

You've never met the real thing.

Neven held back another smirk.

"I can do that, maybe change up the design a little bit." Neven began to rapidly prototype alternative designs from the existing schematic. They displayed on a nearby holodisplay as he shuffled through layouts and skin contours.

Let me try, Ellipse said.

Go ahead. Neven let Ellipse take control of the holodisplay.

The body designs began to rapidly change, prototypes flying by at an even faster pace. Aru stared at Neven, his mouth open. The image on the holodisplay began to resemble A'Amaria less and instead took on a life of its own. Eventually, the modifications stopped, and dark brown skin was added as a final touch. The design was of a short nude woman with surprisingly realistic, Human features. The eyes opened, the irises a deep golden hue.

"Beautiful . . ." Neven said.

Neven got the impression of Ellipse blushing in his mind.

"Wow." Aru walked up to the holodisplay. "Impressive. Just when I thought I had you all figured out; you surprise me." He turned to face Neven and patted him on the shoulder. "Well, I'll leave you to it then. You and . . . uh . . . what's your android's name?"

Neven remained silent for a long moment. "Ellipse."

Neven's mobi blipped, startling him. He caught himself from falling off the couch in his temporary quarters aboard the *Foundra Conscient* and wearily opened his eyes, the caller in his micro-display blank.

"Weird," Neven said.

Accepting the call and pushing it through to a nearby holodisplay, the image of A'Amaria appeared. She was sporting a pouting face.

Oh, hell no! Ellipse practically shouted in Neven's head.

"I know I'm probably the last person you expected to see," A'Amaria said. Ellipse tried to terminate the call, but Neven halted her, instantly regretting the decision and wondering why he hadn't closed the connection himself.

"How did you get my personal contact channel?" Neven yelled.

"Really?" A'Amaria looked like she might laugh, then quickly resumed her apologetic demeanor. "I'm just calling to formally apologize for my actions. They were despicable, and I am willing to provide any compensation you deem necessary to settle this debt between us."

Terminate. The. Connection. Now, Ellipse growled at Neven.

"I don't believe you," Neven said. He got the impression of a furious woman in his mind's eye, the impression causing him to tense up.

"I accept that. I will have to gain your trust after what I've done to you. I am willing to do whatever you desire, however many times you desire, as payment for my actions." A'Amaria's eyes softened, her gaze becoming seductive. The sight caused something deep within Neven to lust for her in that moment. His stomach tightened as he comprehended his reaction. Suddenly disgusted, Neven terminated the call without another word.

The vusg was that?

I'm sorry . . . I just . . . I don't know, Neven said. Ellipse went silent, and Neven stared at the blank holodisplay before letting out a heavy sigh and leaning back into the couch.

Okay . . . Ellipse's voice was calmer, more controlled. *We need to get you to Etan Rachnie as soon as possible once this is all over.*

Agreed.

> *The first cleanse thinned our species considerably, but we have only been made stronger because of it.*
>
> –FROM "CHRONICLES OF THE VEMPIIR"
> BY LICH LORD TERTIUS VIRTOK

CHAPTER 66 ZUN SHAN

Tenquin, Huzien Alliance space

"I think I see the outpost up ahead," Arnold broadcast to the group of survivors from the Empress Star. Their escape pods had landed on Tenquin, a fringe colony world with a small population scattered across the planet. He moved to the front of the group; Tashanira, Jenshi, Zun, and Jessica moved to flank him. Arnea trailed a short distance behind in the cluster of civilians.

"Still no response." Tashanira hocked and spat. "I've broadcast our Founder's Elite priority identifier. Figured that would at least have given us a hello." Jenshi flashed her a raised eyebrow. She caught his expression and spat again.

"Unless they don't want to welcome us," Zun said.

"We've got incoming," Arnold called out. He lifted his hand, and the group came to a confused halt.

"Two people," a security guard nearby confirmed. Arnold and the Founder's Elite moved off from the group to intercept the approaching pair.

"Identify yourself," Arnold broadcast. Both approaching men held fingers to their lips. Jessica glanced to Tashanira, and both women rested their palms on their WMAs.

"I am Shaper Desrin, Argent of Etan Rachnie, Chaah hunter of the ninth degree." The first man pulled back his grey cowl. Long curly black hair and dark brown skin stood in contrast to bright silver eyes, his Human features evident. "And my associate here is Shaper Nestis."

"Chaah hunter of the eighth degree," a deep voice intoned. The other man kept his cowl over his head, his silver eyes peering out from the darkness within. From the height of him, Zun assumed him to be Huzien.

"I've heard of you two," Zun said. "Two immortal Chaah hunters, powerful Argents who travel the galaxy without oversight."

Desrin glanced at his companion. "It would appear that we have a reputation, Nestis."

Nestis remained silent.

"If you're here, that means . . ." Zun's voice trailed off as both men turned to regard her.

"The outpost . . ." Tashanira whispered.

"The outpost is bare," Desrin said. "Most likely used as part of an Elhirtha."

"A what?" Arnold said.

"Blood weaving," Jenshi gasped.

"An abomination of cihphistic weaving that uses the life energy of victims to fuel powerful acts of cihphism," Desrin said.

"Weak cihphists employ such tactics to accomplish what they cannot by normal means," Nestis interjected. Zun opened herself to the Enesmic and could immediately feel the taint in the flow of Enesmic energy around her. It was like the force had been corrupted, molested, and was twisting in certain areas as if in pain.

"Elhirtha is a banned art not taught in the Argents." Desrin turned back to regard the outpost. "There is a Chaah cell on this planet. This outpost is one of the more recent casualties."

"Why would they kill all those people?" Jessica asked.

"Practice," Nestis replied.

"Out of the frying pan and into the fire," Arnold said.

"Where are they now?" Jessica stared in the direction of the outpost.

"Before we decide to go Chaah hunting," Jenshi interjected, "we have a substantial number of individuals who need shelter, food, and medical care."

"I have good news for you." Desrin turned back to face the outpost. "There is an outpost's worth of food and shelter to accommodate you." The Founder's Elite eyed one another uncomfortably as Arnold let out a sigh.

"Let's move," he broadcast to the group.

"We bid you farewell; a hunt is in progress." Desrin nodded to the group, and then the air around him rippled as he clenched his fist. Nestis followed suit.

Our forefathers and foremothers reveled in the rush that Yerrhgda brings and were unable to restrain themselves. Such failings are not held against them, as it was simply an aspect of our biology we had not yet fully mastered.

-FROM "CHRONICLES OF THE VEMPIIR"
BY LICH LORD TERTIUS VIRTOK

CHAPTER 67 MARCUS HENSON

Tenquin, Huzien Alliance space

"That is quite the adventure." Erb pulled the tea kettle off its holder above an open fire. Lifting two cups with two of his free arms, he gently poured the tea. "It is fortuitous that you and your crece'cesen made it out safely."

"I just wish I could contact her." Marcus stared at the smashed mobi sitting on a nearby rock.

"I am impressed that you bear few injuries from your landing." Erb handed a cup to Marcus. "Genetic engineering, you say?"

"Yeah." Marcus took in a deep whiff of the herbal remedy. "Reinforced skeletal frame, redundant organs, bio-organic nanitic swarm clusters, the works."

Erb regarded Marcus for a long moment before asking, "You chose all of that willingly?"

Marcus let out a heavy sigh, slowly leaning back against a tree behind him. In that moment, he looked and felt like his true age. "I was drafted into the Archlight program when I joined the mobile infantry. My large frame and advanced cihphist abilities made me the perfect candidate for the program." Marcus paused for a moment. "I've never told anyone that, not even my wife." Marcus looked up at Erb.

"They forced you?"

"Forced is a strong word." Marcus glanced up at the night sky. "It was 'strongly encouraged' by my superiors to 'ensure' a bright future." Marcus laughed. "I was young and stupid, but I'd do it again in a heartbeat."

"You must have truly lived an impressive life to say such a thing."

"Erb, you have no idea!" Marcus laughed. Erb smiled and took a sip of tea, then rested the teapot on a nearby rock.

"In the morning, I will guide you to Tenin. It is the capital outpost of this world. If your *crece'cesen* and allies are not there, you will at least be able to secure transport to their location. Of this I am sure."

"I truly appreciate your help, Erb." Marcus lifted his cup in salute.

"It is the least I can do for the epic tale you have gifted me with. I will add it to my manuscript."

"I can't wait to read it."

Erb smiled and looked up. The two sat in silence for a long moment, both large men focused on the multitude of stars hanging in the sky. "So, this is what it's like to be a monk? I could get used to this," Marcus said.

Erb laughed softly. "There is a bit more to it, but yes, living in nature and humbling oneself before its majesty is the way to true enlightenment."

"Enlightenment..." Marcus smiled softly. "That's a noble goal."

The next morning, Erb led Marcus to the bustling market quarter of Tenin. When they arrived, Erb interfaced with a wall-mounted holodisplay. A replica of Tenin's market quarter was displayed, showing several electronics shops a few blocks away.

"I'm sure you could go halfway across the galaxy and still run into a Somift store," Erb said.

"Wouldn't be surprised if they had a location set up in a neighboring galaxy." Marcus laughed. The path to the store was overlaid on their micro-displays, their mobis syncing with the marketplace SI. They moved past a group of men in long white robes with red etchings down the front and sides. Marcus caught their glares out of the corner of his eye as a few of them began to whisper, his superhuman hearing catching the words "friend" and "Soahc."

"I think we just made some new friends." The soft tone of Marcus's words caused Erb to glance at him curiously as they continued to make their way down the street. Marcus suddenly grabbed Erb's arm and pulled him down a side alley, prompting Erb to raise an eyebrow.

Marcus mouthed the word "Chaah" and broke off into a sprint down the side street. Erb followed, and they quickly ducked into another alleyway. Marcus glanced around the corner, and his suspicions were confirmed as four men in the same white and red robes came sprinting into the alleyway. One of them closed his eyes, and the area seemed to lurch around the two fleeing men. Marcus felt a sickness well up within his stomach while Erb steadied himself against a nearby wall, his hand over his hearts as if in pain.

The Chaah then opened his eyes, and orbs of pure black stared in the direction of Marcus and Erb. After a moment, the Chaah lifted his hand and began to chant, the air rippling as the ground shuddered.

"Run!" Marcus yelled.

A pathway was torn through the building. Within a heartbeat, two Chaah were in front of them. Marcus spun, only to find the other two directly behind.

"It would appear that it is time to fight." Erb sighed.

"No," the lead Chaah countered, "it is time for you to die."

Stepping forward, the man held his hand up. Pure darkness streaked out from his palm, the beam of energy seeking Erb's heart.

Stomping his foot, Erb pushed forward with two palms outstretched, his other two arms flexing in opposite directions. The beam struck his palms, and the energy was deflected downward as Erb stepped through the Enesmic flow, appearing directly in front of the Chaah cihphist.

Continuing through in his movement, Erb spun, his other two hands striking out in fists as he pulled his two palms back into horse stance. The force of the double blow shattered bone, the chest of the cihphist collapsing in as he was flung hard into the metal wall of a nearby building. The force of the impact sent a gust of wind buffeting the group.

The eyes of the Chaah nearest to the first narrowed. He clenched his fist, teleporting out of striking range, and then a beam of dark energy—a heartshatter blast—barreled down on Erb. The Nistiff monk spun, his palms up again as he deflected the blast away from himself and to the ground. The site of impact boiled, the ground collapsing in on itself like quicksand. Erb flipped to the side, flying over the unstable ground and landing in a breakfall.

Marcus spun with superhuman speed, lunging at one of the Chaah who had boxed them in. Marcus's eyes went wide and he struggled to maintain his balance as his fist passed through the Chaah, whose form was suddenly insubstantial.

The Chaah growled, becoming corporeal once more, and unleashed a heartshatter blast in a fury. Marcus braced as the beam struck true. The impact seared a hole through flesh, his right lung gone in an instant. The force from the blast threw him down the alleyway and into a wall.

As the giant man got to one knee, the other Chaah unleashed a similar blast, and Marcus closed his eyes as the beam streaked toward his head. A whooshing sound then filled his ears, and he opened his eyes to see Erb in a defensive stance in front of him. The Nistiff was breathing hard, the blast deflected and a nearby wall melting away.

Marcus stood, spitting blood as the nanites in his body worked to seal off his damaged lung from his normal bodily functions before starting their repair routine. Erb's eyes went wide as the light was seemingly ripped away from them, the area around them becoming heavy and beginning to heat up exponentially. The pressure caused their blood vessels to bulge and pop, and they could feel their life essences being stolen. They both cried out, the pain unbearable. The Enesmic flow was in chaos, unspeakable torment corrupting it as the Chaah used Marcus and Erb as fuel for their Elhirtha, the two powerless to act.

Echoes of flesh being rendered apart filled the air, but the few shouts of struggle were quickly silenced. Sounds of blood spray filled the sudden quiet. The pressure gone, Marcus and Erb opened their eyes. Both men were resting on their knees. The sight of decapitated Chaah greeted them, along with one man standing in grey robes cleaning a glowing curved sword on the clothes of the lifeless Chaah. The weapon seemed to howl as if alive, power radiating from it in torrents.

The sight caused Marcus' stomach to tighten as he got the impression that the blade was devouring the essence of its victim. Another man appeared a moment later carrying the head and corpse of the third Chaah. He threw the remains on the pile of bodies. Then, reaching back with one of his hands, he performed a yanking motion forward, and the corpse lodged in the wall was ripped from its metal grave and thrown onto the pile.

"Impressive," the first man said. He summoned a gust of wind to pull back his cowl, his hands occupied with cleaning his weapon. "I have never witnessed a Nistiff in action against a cihphist. I am truly impressed by your ilk."

"Grant me the favor of our savior's names," Erb said, rising to his feet, Marcus doing likewise.

"Shaper Desrin, Chaah hunter of the ninth degree. And my companion here is Shaper Nestis,"

"Chaah hunter of the eighth degree," Nestis added. "You are injured." Nestis walked up to Marcus.

"Oh this, it's nothing," Marcus grunted. The blood flow was slowing, the nanites that regulated every aspect of his body furiously at work.

Nestis eyed him warily. "That wound should be fatal."

"What my comrade means to say," Desrin interjected, "is do you require aid?"

Erb's eyes were frantic as he regarded Marcus. "Do you possess the healing arts?" Erb said. "I believe the Esh Whisper would be most fortuitous in this moment."

Nestis moved to Marcus's side and laid a hand on him, then released a burst of Enesmic energy into Marcus's body. The shock knocked Marcus back a step.

"That will help dull the pain."

"Appreciated," Marcus grunted.

"Let's get out of the open," Desrin said. "Our battle will most likely draw unwanted attention." He glanced back at the headless corpses. "Not to mention their allies." He held his weapon out in front of his body and the blade began to glow, a howl stirring in the area that unnerved Marcus. Without warning, the bodies ignited in flame, and within the span of seconds, they were burned to ash.

CHAPTER 68 DEXTER PINSTEN

Tenquin, Huzien Alliance space

The sound of the shuttle cabin depressurizing was gradually replaced by the subtle hum of the ancient-looking Halinu IV reactor that Dexter was surprised still functioned. It was a precursor to the Nies line of reactors common on Huzien Alliance shuttles. Dexter looked to Hegfe Deni, the disheveled man slowly coming to.

When Hegfe caught sight of Dexter, he quickly tried to jump to his feet, but the action was stopped by the fact that his hands and feet were bound. Hegfe's face shifted from confusion to stark terror as he slowly looked from his bindings to Dexter.

"Please don't kill me," Hegfe said. "I can be unbelievably valuable to you! I know things!"

"Things, huh?" Dexter unshouldered his rifle.

"The engines, the engines! I can keep them running. SI exploits, I . . . I disabled the *Empress Star*. I . . . I can show you how I did it!"

"SI assault exploit, class two, premium grade. Most likely acquired on the black market, not developed internally." Dexter glanced at Hegfe. "I doubt you know much of how it actually works."

Hegfe scowled back. "I know how it works!"

Dexter fingered his rifle, the weapon powering on instantly. Hegfe dropped the scowl and backed up into the wall of the ship, the look of terror back. Dexter aimed the rifle at Hegfe, his sight lined up with the man's head. Hegfe dropped and moved to the side, attempting to stay out of the line of fire as Dexter suppressed a laugh.

"Stay put." Dexter shouldered his rifle and walked out of the ship.

Hegfe's eyes were tightly shut as he lay in a fetal position. After a few moments, he opened his eyes and sat back up, then began to look around the cabin of the ship. The former engine master detected no sight of Dexter. Letting out a sigh, his gaze caught on his mobi sitting atop the main command console. Looking back toward the ship's exit, which Dexter had just gone through, he held his breath. A few minutes passed; no sign of Dexter.

Looking back to his mobi, Hegfe gulped hard, then took in a deep breath and slowly pushed himself into the wall. Carefully positioning his bound feet under his body, he used his back as leverage to push himself up, all the while keeping his gaze focused on the ship's exit.

He took one hop, then another, eventually ending with a series of frantic hops that led to him crashing into the console. Catching himself, he leaned against the ledge for balance, his gaze locking on to his mobi. After composing himself, he dropped his chin slowly onto the device and pressed the power icon for what seemed like an eternity.

Dexter watched a mirrored view as Hegfe checked his access to the ship's systems in his HUD. With a smile, Hegfe confirmed his access and input coordinates for the Het Wrast Aht stronghold on Rugtora. The shuttle came alive, the cabin door closing as the ship lifted off from the ground and sped toward the sky. Dexter smiled, a star map appearing in his micro-display as a video feed from inside the shuttle played in the corner of his sight. A set of coordinates was pinpointed on his map.

"SI recon exploit, class zero, military grade," Dexter whispered.

The Sentinel's mobi connected to the HIN and a flood of information hit him like a wave. After taking a few minutes to parse through the important bits, he broadcast to the Founder's Elite private channel.

"Lifetime online."

"Took you long enough," Tashanira's voice blasted back at him. "Status?"

"Tempest still offline, everyone else accounted for," Jessica replied. "Survivors from the *Empress Star* are staying in an abandoned outpost, sending coordinates now. Possible Chaah activity in the vicinity."

"*Vusging* awesome." Dexter held back a dry laugh. "Going mobi silent, checkpoint in twelve hours."

"Understood."

Dexter cut the connection.

During the Coven Wars, the weak were cleansed across generations, and all traces of weakness from lowborn covens were erased, until only forty strong and perfect covens remained.

–FROM "CHRONICLES OF THE VEMPIIR"
BY LICH LORD TERTIUS VIRTOK

CHAPTER 69 MARCUS HENSON

Tenquin, Huzien Alliance space

"It's great to hear your voice," Jessica said.

"Likewise," Marcus replied through the mobi connection. "My mobi was damaged beyond repair. I've synced this new mobi up to my profile, but I won't be able to take advantage of the HIN or access military channels."

"Consumer junk." Jessica sighed. "We'll get you set up once Lanrete arrives."

"You made contact?"

"Yeah, shortly after touching down on the planet. He's in route with the *Foundra Conscient*, Ecnics's ship."

"The *Ascension*?"

"It was still being retrofitted when they departed Thae in search of us."

Marcus grunted.

"Did you speak with Arnea yet?"

Marcus smiled. "Darling, she was the first person I called! Told me about the ghost town and how you and the other Founder's Elites are rotating patrols."

MISSION NAME:PRIDE OF ASHNA   QUEST ID:FOUNDRA_SERIES_02

"Yeah . . . we met two Chaah hunters."

"Desrin and Nestis."

"I'm guessing you ran into them as well?"

"They are here with me now, saved Erb and me."

"Erb?"

"Ah, I'll introduce you two once we meet back up. He's a Nistiff monk."

"Nistiff monk? Interesting . . ."

"I owe all of these guys my life; the Chaah really did a number on me." Marcus winced as he remembered his wound.

"Are you hurt?" The fear in Jessica's voice caused Marcus to tense up, his wound stinging him again at the action.

"Nothing a day's rest and a hearty meal can't fix." Marcus forced a laugh.

"Send me your coordinates, I'll come to you."

"Don't you have a group of survivors to look out for?"

The young major took in a deep breath, seeming resigned as she accepted the truth of Marcus's words. "What are their plans for the Chaah?"

"Desrin and Nestis?" Marcus paused for a moment. "They are watching the area where they killed four of the Chaah to see if their buddies come looking for them."

"Four Chaah?" Jessica gasped.

"They think there is an entire cell here, with at least six more of those bastards still lurking around."

"Those aren't good odds."

"You haven't seen these guys work," Marcus countered. "The Chaah didn't even see them coming, took out three of the cihphists before they could even react."

"The element of surprise is lost; they know the hunters are there now. They will be expecting them."

Marcus conceded her point, his vision suddenly blurring. He put his hand to his head to stop the spinning. "Jess, I'm going to go, need a nap."

358

"Now you're starting to sound like an old man." Marcus could hear the concern in her voice through the forced laugh. "Stay safe, don't be a hero."

"What's the fun in that?"

Marcus terminated the connection. Leaning back in the bed he was sitting on, he glanced over to Erb. The large Ken'Tar was pouring a cup of tea mixed with various herbs, then crossed the room to sit on the bed next to Marcus.

"Drink this."

Marcus took the cup in his hands, his gaze going to the window at his side. He could see the street below busy with people. They were halfway across the outpost, far from the site of the Chaah battle. Erb patted Marcus on the shoulder and got back up, slowly making his way to his makeshift desk across the room.

"Hey Erb?"

Erb stopped and turned back to face Marcus. "Yes, my friend?"

"How do you determine when you're getting too old for something?"

Erb gave him a sad smile. "When you start asking those types of questions." He continued toward his desk.

Marcus let out a sigh and took a sip of his tea.

CHAPTER 70 HIESHA NIHJAR

Tenquin, Huzien Alliance space

Hiesha Nihjar appeared in the dark alley, a black scorch mark the only indication of the previous day's conflict between the Chaah and the hunters. They had to be hunters; no one else was as thorough and ruthless as them. Hiesha glanced back to her partner and eifi, Orech, as the two women exchanged knowing gazes and clenched their fists, both disappearing.

"Our lives are forfeit." Ianos paced in the small gathering area, the man surrounded by five of his fellow Chaah.

"What idiocy made you believe that the harvesting of that outpost would go unnoticed?" Hiesha countered.

"Our instructions were clear," Alinos Yui countered. He had dark brown hair and grey eyes that were narrowed and focused intently on Hiesha. "We are to proceed with our plans of harvesting the planet to fuel the gateway."

"Alinos, we should have moved forward with the abductions, like we have in the past." Hiesha crossed her arms. "The harvesting of an entire outpost was sure to draw unwanted attention, such as hunters!"

The group shifted uncomfortably.

"We must accelerate our plans and proceed with harvesting the planet tonight," Orech said.

"We are not ready," Ianos countered.

"We have no choice," Alinos said. "We have already lost almost half of our strength, and we cannot afford to have the hunters pick any more of us off. We must open the pathway; then we can unite with our brothers and sisters to face the hunters."

"That is assuming the cihphistic manifestation works as intended; there will be no second chance for us."

"It will work." Alinos grinned. "The Sagren creature was able to establish portals between worlds. We can do the same. Once we open the pathway, we will use the life forces on this planet to establish permanence."

Reluctantly, every member of the group stood, their meeting at an end.

"We will go ahead to prepare the site." Orech glanced to Hiesha. Hiesha nodded as they teleported away simultaneously.

CHAPTER 71 MARCUS HENSON

Tenquin, Huzien Alliance space

"Are you sure you're up for this?" Erb helped Marcus finish prepping the power armor they had omnistructured—a rapid process of hardware printing using nanitefacturing. His military override had allowed the creation of the power armor and its weapons.

Marcus lifted a composite nanoplexi shield. The Omnplexi hardware printer had been commercial grade, so the Archlight had little faith that it could withstand anywhere near what Claire had been able to. It was, however, some form of protection for the dangerous fight ahead of them.

"It's not Claire, but it'll have to do." Marcus synced his new mobi up with the armor. The interface seemed slower, clumsier than what he was used to. A final system check showed the new equipment ready across the board. "Let's get this over with."

"Very well." Desrin clenched his fist, extended it in front of his body, and spoke a word of power. The scene around them shifted as they went from standing in a small room to a large open hallway. Red and white décor filled the space.

We are with you, Desrin mentally imparted to Marcus and Erb as both Chaah hunters faded into the shadows. Marcus steeled his gaze, Erb doing likewise, and they moved into the main living area. The absence of any other living soul caused Marcus to shift uneasily.

"Where are they?" Erb whispered.

"Good question," Marcus said.

Get below! The mental command from Nestis sent Marcus and Erb into a sprint, something in his voice unnerving the two men.

A litany of words of power emanated from the voices of the assembled hosts, the Chaah in the throes of cihphistic weaving. As the Enesmic flew in torrents, a tremor shook the structure around them, dust dropping from the supports. Five of the Chaah were in a circle, their eyes closed as they focused all their energy into the weaving, which was being channeled into a sixth member standing in the center of the circle. The man in the center opened his eyes, grabbed the Enesmic, and twisted it. His grey eyes became orbs of pure darkness, the building shaking again as the Enesmic flow began to writhe in pain.

Marcus burst through the barred door blocking their entrance and descended into the underground chamber, Erb right behind him. A blast of Enesmic energy immediately assailed them. Shields hastily enacted around them flickered, and Marcus gave a silent thanks to the quick actions of his Chaah hunter guardians. The forces at work in the room pressed against Marcus, the flow invisible but felt in his innermost being. The feeling overwhelmed him first with a sense of nausea, then dread.

Desrin and Nestis appeared outside of the circle, both men breaking into a litany of their own words of power. The Enesmic rebuffed the Chaah as if set free from chains, and chaos exploded all around as it shifted violently.

"No!" the man in the center yelled, his voice enhanced. He turned toward Nestis and unleashed a devastating heartshatter blast at the man. Nestis lifted his blade, his eyes glowing with white fire. The heartshatter blast connected with his Revfa blade and was absorbed. A howling sound filled the room, emanating from the weapon as the Enesmic forces began to swell around it, surging into Nestis's weapon as if seeking vengeance.

Nestis then leveled the blade and returned the blast to the man in the center with enhanced fury. The man seemed to fade out of existence, the beam sailing right through him harmlessly. After becoming substantial again, he swore and began to frantically pick up the pace of his weaving.

Erb and Marcus charged into the Chaah's circle, each man tackling a Chaah hard. The others continued in their weaving, seemingly oblivious to the battle around them. The interrupted Chaah turned on the duo with a fury. More dark beams streaked out across the room. Erb deflected a blast from a brown-skinned woman and charged at her, his fists moving in a flurry. She threw herself back, shooting more beams out to slow him down.

Marcus's power armor reflexively threw him away from the blast coming from another Chaah with pitch-black eyes. A series of cannons fired in tandem from Marcus, both blasts connecting with a barrier as the Chaah lifted his hands and began to twist the Enesmic. Marcus felt himself get heavy, the armor doing little to protect him from the Elhirtha being woven out of his life essence. He coughed and would have dropped to his knees if not for the power armor keeping him upright.

Another howl rang through the room as Desrin's Revfa blade exploded through the male Chaah's chest. Marcus watched as the blade drank his essence, the Enesmic swirling in a fury around the weapon. The Chaah began to rapidly decompose, his body dropping off the blade and to the floor in dust.

The man in the center reached out to the corpse of the fallen Chaah, but there was nothing left. Lifting their heads, the Chaah screamed in tandem, the final words of power to their abomination coming out in a terrifying symphony. The Chaah in the center reached out to the other Chaah around him with the Elhirtha. In the last throes of their weaving, he stole their life energy for his own. The brown-skinned woman stared in horror, still struggling with Erb as she watched another woman be consumed by the Chaah in the center.

"No!" she screamed.

The Chaah took the life energy and extended his hands wide. A portal formed in front of him, but the image was distorted, the aesthetic sickening and unlike any portal Marcus had seen Soahc create. Its mere existence hinted at the wrongness of its origins. The Chaah stepped through, then the portal winked out of existence. The fight went out of the remaining Chaah as she dropped to her knees. She stared at the charred corpse of the woman who had been in the circle.

Desrin's Revfa blade appeared at her neck. She offered no resistance to the Chaah hunter as he readied his weapon for the killing blow.

"Wait!" Erb stepped in the path of the strike. "Can she not offer more value to the Argents as a prisoner?"

"We do not take prisoners." Nestis appeared on the other side of the woman, his blade angled for the killing blow. Marcus threw himself in the way of the second man.

"Can you not see the wisdom in Erb's words? She has been betrayed; look at her."

All of them studied the woman. Desrin glanced to Nestis, and both men seemed locked in a telepathic conversation. After a long moment, both finally nodded in agreement.

"Very well. We will take this one for interrogation," Desrin said.

Marcus cringed at the thought of interrogation at the hands of a powerful telepath. Maybe death was a better option for this woman.

Desrin turned his attention to the echo of the portal and winced as if its mere presence caused him pain. When he lifted his Revfa blade, a howling echoed throughout the room.

"There is too much corruption." Desrin shook his head. "I cannot read its intended location or reopen it." He turned back to face the group.

"It may not seem like it," Nestis started, "but our actions here have saved hundreds, if not thousands, of lives today."

"We must now take our leave." Desrin nodded to Marcus and Erb. Then, in the blink of an eye, Nestis, Desrin, and the Chaah woman were gone.

Yerrhgda has been attempted on the lesser species, but the liquification does not occur. Instead, the victim is severely weakened due to blood loss, with death possible if arterial damage is inflicted. The life extending and de-aging aspects of the ritual do not occur, but the Vempiir does gain significantly increased healing abilities for a short duration.

–FROM "CHRONICLES OF THE VEMPIIR"
BY LICH LORD TERTIUS VIRTOK

CHAPTER 72 SERAH'ELAX REZ ASHFALEN

Ashnaret, Ashna Maiden protected space

"Look at what you have become." Serah'Elax balked. She stood in the living room of the luxurious condo of her yu'shae, Dera'Liv. The lavish home was filled with sensual art and suggestive sculptures, and the subtle scent of black licorice hung in the air. It was a two-floor tantalization of the senses, reminiscent of every other time Serah'Elax had come to visit her mother on Ashnaret.

Dera'Liv wore black lace lingerie, her breasts bare with a large transparent shawl draping her shoulders. Serah'Elax was the splitting image of Dera'Liv, except Dera'Liv had a maturity in her appearance that hinted at the centuries of age between them. Serah'Elax's gaze hung on her mother as she supervised the drones changing the sheets to the massive king-sized bed in the center of the condo. It was set as the centerpiece, the entire aesthetic experience culminating in whatever acts were performed on that bed. Dera'Liv subtly adjusted one of the ornate pillows. "What would Ovah'Hal think of you if she saw you now?"

Dera'Liv gave Serah'Elax a haughty glare. "The murderer seeks to lecture me?" Dera'Liv smirked, her eyes narrowed. "I enjoy the life I have now. Most men on this planet have never seen one of our kind and they pay handsomely for the privilege of my company." Dera'Liv moved over to an ornately decorated Omnfridge counter and picked up a large glass full of a red liquid that appeared. Bringing it to her lips, she took a long draw from it.

"I honestly don't understand why they allow trades like yours to exist in our space," Serah'Elax said. "Surely the Ashna Mothers must find what you do, and others like you, abhorrent."

Dera'Liv scoffed. "All that blood on your hands and you are still oblivious to the world around you." She moved to a nearby lounger and slid into the seat with a practiced ease, her every motion seductive, the mannerisms second nature to her now. "The Ashna Mothers not only allow paid companionship on their planets, they subsidize it." She locked gazes with Serah'Elax. "Because they steal all of the little girls and make murderers out of them." Dera'Liv's voice cracked. She broke her daughter's gaze and watched the liquid in her glass as she swished it around. "Then they prevent those girls from doing the one thing natural to every species in the known universe as millions of single, lonely men wallow in sexual frustration."

"Paid companionship?" Serah'Elax laughed. "It seems like you come up with a new term for whoring every time I come here."

Dera'Liv slowly glanced up to Serah'Elax. "Why *are* you here?" She took another draw from her glass. "My next client is coming soon."

Serah'Elax let out a long sigh and forced a smile. "I . . . I wanted to tell you about some good news. I have been elevated to the rank of exemplar. It is a great honor, and something that not many Maidens achieve." Serah'Elax lifted her chin. "They consider me a war hero."

Dera'Liv stared at her daughter for a long moment. The façade the older woman had created over the years dropped away in that instant, and her heart was laid bare. A tear began to run down

Dera'Liv's cheek, her eyes holding a depth of sadness unlike anything Serah'Elax had ever seen.

Serah'Elax felt the sudden urge to run over to her *yu'shae* and hold her tight, to cling to her like she had when the Ashna Maidens had rescued them all those years ago. Her hand came up to wipe something away from her own eye, wetness coating her fingers. Dropping her chin, Serah'Elax stared down at the ground for a long moment. Without another word, she turned and left.

CHAPTER 73 SEPHAN

Ashnali, Ashna Maiden home system

Bresha Vecen took a step forward, spinning in a show of finesse as she flicked a small red orb from her hand. The projectile exploded into a ball of fire as it slammed into the target dummy. Holding out her hand, she gripped the flames, giving them renewed life. The target dummy burned to ash in a matter of seconds. The other Ashna Maiden initiates stood in awe of the newest recruit; even the instructor was taken aback at the raw display of power.

"Impressive," came a voice that snapped all the Maidens attention.

Bresha turned to see Ashna Mother Venice Fawni slowly clapping her hands. A host of high priestesses stood behind her. The women appeared ready to tear Bresha apart at a mere word from Mother Venice.

Let them try, Sephan mused.

"The goddess has granted you an opportunity to prove yourself." Mother Venice smiled. "A contingent of the unknown enemy has broken off from the main host and approaches one of our worlds. We intend to send our fleets to intercept them." Mother Venice paused. "And you will join them. We will test this knowledge you have to see if you can provide the value you promised." Mother Venice motioned for a woman to her side to step forward. "This is Exemplar Serah'Elax Rez Ashfalen. I am putting you under her command."

Bresha executed the Ashna Maiden salute flawlessly, and Serah'Elax replied in kind. Without another word, Mother Venice turned and departed, leaving two priestesses flanking Serah'Elax.

"I was told of how you came to join the Ashna Maidens," Serah'Elax said. "I do not trust you." The exemplar glanced around at the host of Ashna Maidens around her. "None of us trust you, but the Holy Mother sees value in you. Therefore, I will allow you onto my ship." Serah'Elax glared at Bresha. "Prove your value, and we may eventually accept you as a sister."

Sephan smiled.

Battleship Agehentali orbiting Ashnali,
Ashna Maiden home system

Bresha watched Delira Sinl shift uncomfortably in the command chair aboard the Ashna Maiden battleship *Agehentali*. Delira kept staring at the keeper insignia on her uniform, a hesitation and uneasiness in her gaze. She glanced over to the navigation controls and stared at them longingly until her attention was eventually drawn to Bresha. Delira scowled at her. Serah'Elax had stationed a priestess on the bridge simply for the purpose of watching Bresha. Delira and all the crew had all been warned that Bresha was a blessed of Ashna, which prompted many uneasy looks in her direction.

"Keeper, the fleet is entering suplight."

Delira stood up. After another hesitant glance at Bresha, she looked over the rest of her bridge crew.

"Take us in."

Ashna Maiden attack armada orbiting Sefera,
Ashna Maiden protected space

Sephan reached out and touched the essence of the contingent of Jughent's ships approaching the Ashna Maiden planet Sefera. Easily taking control, Sephan grinned.

The armada of alien ships tore into the Ashna Maiden fleet with a fury. Then, like a single organism, the ships descended on an Ashna Maiden vessel directly next to the *Agehentali*. The ship was torn to pieces in a violent assault, and a bright explosion lit up the left side of the primary holodisplay on the *Agehentali*.

Gasps went up across the bridge.

"Ashna save us . . ." Delira breathed.

Sephan rushed across the bridge to the Maiden on tactical and said, "Follow my orders exactly if you want to live."

All eyes went to Bresha. The priestess of Ashna tensed up, silently summoning the Enesmic to her side as she moved to stand directly next to Delira. "This is why I'm here," Sephan stated flatly.

The Maiden looked to Delira, who nodded.

"Follow this targeting pattern. Relay the information to the other ships." Sephan sent a series of commands from its mobi to the targeting SI.

Sephan led Jughent's forces into another focused assault on the ship on the other side of the *Agehentali*. The ship followed the prior in an explosion of light and death. Sephan had a few ships break off and target the *Agehentali*. The barrage of weapons fire tore through the shielding of the ship and left it exposed. In response to the attack, the targeting SIs across the Maiden fleet focused on the same ships and burned them down, the coordinated assault seeming to break the momentum of Jughent's forces. Sephan caused the forces to scatter, purposefully breaking off their coordination. It had them feign confusion, as if not expecting the destruction of one of their own.

The Ashna fleets followed Sephan's attack pattern as the next ship fell. Sephan then sent another broadcast of information, various "weak points" highlighted on the enemy vessels. The Maiden fleet began to turn the tide of the battle, and more of Jughent's forces fell in the assault by the Ashna Maidens.

Another set of Jughent's ships targeted the *Agehentali*, focusing on the bridge. At the same moment, Sephan reached out with Enesmic power and gripped the ceiling above the priestess of Ashna, then pulled the ceiling and all its contents down with incredible force onto her and Delira. The sudden and brutal event took a moment to register, and then screams of terror filled the air. Many abandoned their posts and ran over to the metal grave. Bresha feigned shock at the horrible accident and rushed to join them.

"Ashna keep you until we meet in glory," a Maiden whispered.

"Ashna strengthen us this day," Bresha started, "fill us with your avenging spirit as we smite your enemies!"

The bridge crew turned to look at Bresha. A few women were unmoving, but others nodded in agreement, quickly returning to their posts. Stepping into her new command, Bresha ordered her ship to lead the assault. Sephan played Jughent's forces into the Ashna Maidens' hands, and the host of ships crumbled before their might.

CHAPTER 74 SERAH'ELAX REZ ASHFALEN

Ashnali, Ashna Maiden home system

"We admit," Mother Ce Nu Yo Kl began, "we are impressed. You have delivered on your promise. Your actions saved the lives of countless Ashna Maidens and citizens." All the Ashna Mothers were assembled, sitting atop the elevated platform in a half circle. Many of the Mothers wore smiles, with the clear exception of Mother Halle Tentle. The gaze from the ebony-skinned woman piqued Serah'Elax's curiosity. What did she know; what could she see? Serah'Elax watched Bresha regard Mother Halle and take a step back.

"Your actions warrant merit," Mother Venice Fawni said. "You have proven yourself to be trustworthy."

Serah'Elax flinched at the words and regarded Bresha with a cold glare. The death of Delira Sinl was still fresh in her mind, a budding friendship between the two having formed after their escapades with suplight banking. She had no proof of any malicious actions on the part of Bresha, but her instincts told her otherwise.

"In these desperate times, we must employ talent wherever necessary to ensure the future of the Ashna Maidens," Mother Alenet said, motioning toward a set of Maidens off to the side. "Therefore, we are hereby promoting you to the rank of keeper. May you lead the forces of Ashna to mighty victories against our enemies."

Serah'Elax glanced away from Bresha, hardly believing the sudden advancement of one still so untested. She glanced up to see Mother Halle staring directly at her.

Meet me in my chambers this night, Mother Halle spoke directly to her mind. The action almost caused Serah'Elax to make a scene, but the soldier caught herself as she tried her best to hide the shock on her face. "You will remain in Exemplar Serah'Elax's command," Mother Halle said aloud.

Bresha glanced at the exemplar, the two women exchanging shared disappointment. Mother Halle stood, and the other Ashna Mothers followed suit, the meeting at an end.

Serah'Elax stepped out of the meglift atop the High Temple of Ashna. She was on the uppermost floor, the residence of the Ashna Mothers themselves. A set of high priestesses saluted Serah'Elax, and she responded in kind. She then moved to kneel in prayer in the small waiting area separating the meglift from the rest of the floor. After a few minutes of silent devotion, a young priestess entered the room and lightly tapped Serah'Elax on the shoulder. Standing without a word, she followed the priestess and was led to an ornately decorated door, the area one of five unique living spaces belonging to the Ashna Mothers. The priestess performed one soft knock.

"Enter," Mother Halle's voice beckoned through the door. The priestess opened it and bowed her head. Serah'Elax moved through, the door closing behind her. "Sit." Mother Halle's voice rang with authority. Her unnerving white eyes were locked onto Serah'Elax as she did as commanded. "You do not trust Bresha Vecen?"

"The will of Ashna is my will," Serah'Elax replied.

Mother Halle rolled her eyes, the action throwing Serah'Elax off.

"I did not call you here to play the obedient Maiden," Mother Halle said. Serah'Elax's eyes went wide as she nervously glanced around the room. "Answer my question truthfully."

"No, I do not trust her. I . . ." Serah'Elax paused. Mother Halle nodded for her to continue. "I believe that she killed Keeper Delira and the priestess tasked with watching her. I have no proof, but I trust my instincts. I have seen evil, I have experienced evil, and I sense evil in her."

Mother Halle stood up and moved to the window behind where she sat, her hand going to the window seal. She stood there for a long moment, silent. Serah'Elax moved her hand to her neck, her gaze nervous.

"Tell me," Mother Halle said, breaking the silence, "if you saw how and when you were going to die, would you try to stop it from happening?"

Serah'Elax sat back in her seat and took in a deep breath. She remained quiet for a long moment, her gaze falling to the floor.

"No." Serah'Elax shook her head. "But I would do my best to prepare those around me for my death, in whatever ways I could."

"Thank you, blessed daughter of Ashna." Mother Halle glanced to Serah'Elax, a sincere smile on her serene face. "Your instincts are right. Ashna has seen into Bresha Vecen, and there is no good there. Find a way to expose her for who and *what* she is."

What she is? Serah'Elax repeated in her mind. "Revered Mother, why do you allow her to remain?"

Mother Halle gave Serah'Elax a sad smile, her eyes becoming distant. "The path of Ashna is not always a simple one, my child. I must retire."

Serah'Elax rose. "One thing before you go." Mother Halle extended a hand toward Serah'Elax, and the exemplar came to kneel before the Ashna Mother. "You are the Champion of Ashna, and you have been blessed with a burden that none of us can bear. Serah'Elax

Rez Ashfalen, you are all that stands between the Ashna Maidens and complete destruction."

Mother Halle bent down and kissed Serah'Elax on the forehead. A powerful wave of warmth washed over her, her body tingling, and she felt something stir inside of her, something powerful, terrifying. Serah'Elax gasped, and then an intense calm descended over her, her body relaxing. With a dismissive motion by Mother Halle, Serah'Elax rose and departed without another word, her eyes wide and her mind racing, Mother Halle's final words repeating in her head.

Early conflicts with the Huziens were met with disaster, but our genetic perfection allowed us to quickly adapt as we developed weapons that gave even the Huziens pause.

–FROM "CHRONICLES OF THE VEMPIIR"
BY LICH LORD TERTIUS VIRTOK

CHAPTER 75 SEPHAN

*Ashna Maiden attack armada, Huzien Alliance /
Ashna Maiden border*

Bresha Vecen stepped onto the command bridge of the Yutrea II, the recently christened flagship of the 72nd Fleet. All twelve priestesses of Ashna present on the bridge tensed up at the appearance of the keeper, and their strategic formation around Avatar Ahtlana did not go unnoticed by Sephan. The avatar's gaze met Bresha's, and after Bresha performed a salute, Ahtlana dispassionately returned the gesture.

"We are approaching the enemy." Ahtlana stood up. "You demonstrated your expertise in handling these foes in our prior encounter, and as such, our success here depends on your knowledge." Ahtlana turned to regard the holodisplay in front of her, enemy formations showing them evenly matched in numbers. "For all of our sakes, I pray the enemy today falls before the might of Ashna."

"I am confident that the goddess is with us this day, Avatar."

Ahtlana regarded Bresha for a moment, eventually moving forward to the massive hologrid in the center of the bridge. Several Maidens were already busy at work coordinating with ship captains across the fleet. Ahtlana turned back and motioned for her to join her.

"Move to engage the enemy," Ahtlana called out as Sephan arrived at her side. "Fleet command and attack strategy transferring to Keeper Bresha for the duration of this battle." All the Maidens ceased in their communications and looked to Bresha for further instruction. Sephan smiled.

This is not what we agreed! The telepathic plea from Jughent was panicked. Sephan had taken control of Jughent's ships, and all of them were now opening themselves up to attack against Bresha's "tactical" targeting instructions. *My fleet is getting slaughtered! How is this delivering the Ashna Maiden worlds to me?* Jughent demanded.

Change of plans, Sephan telepathically replied. *I've determined that your services are no longer needed.*

You can't do this! Jughent telepathically screamed.

Sephan smiled.

"Avatar! The enemy capital ship is heading straight toward us," someone on the bridge of the *Yutrea II* called out. "They are on a collision course."

Bresha shook her head.

"Like a cornered rat, they are lashing out with all they have," Bresha said. "Focus all attention on the quadrants highlighted here on the command ship." She marked a few sections on the ship. Reaching through the Enesmic, Sephan gripped hold of Jughent's mind and shattered it. The brutality of the attack was so sudden that Jughent had no time to react, and his body went limp on the command bridge of his capital ship.

Within minutes, the combined fire of the Ashna Maiden fleets decimated the vessel. The capital ship imploded and the ship's husk became lifeless, devoid of the Enesmic energy that once fueled it. With the defeat of the enemy capital ship, the remaining forces of Jughent's once imposing fleet fell in quick order.

Ahtlana regarded Bresha with curiosity. "We . . . owe our victory to you this day, Keeper Bresha," Ahtlana said. The expressions of the rest of the Maidens on the bridge were ones of sincere admiration, and many nodded in agreement.

Though the Huziens outnumbered us, we held them off in a perfect stalemate. They had armadas; we had the means by which to destroy stars.

–FROM "CHRONICLES OF THE VEMPIIR"
BY LICH LORD TERTIUS VIRTOK

CHAPTER 76 NEVEN KENK

Foundra Conscient, Huzien Alliance space

N even awakened to the sound of his mobi chirping. He slowly scanned his room, a dream fading as the lights came up. Neven accepted the call, pushing it through to a nearby holodisplay. The image of Lanrete greeted him. There was a hint of sadness in his gaze, and then it was gone. The expression had been brief, but it burned into Neven's soul.

"We'll be arriving in Tenquin's system in twenty minutes."

"Understood. I'll be on bridge in fifteen."

Lanrete nodded and terminated the connection.

Do you plan to tell her? The voice of Ellipse filled his mind.

Neven let out a sigh. "I don't know." He rubbed his eyes. "Not sure what benefit there will be."

Since when did there need to be a benefit to tell someone you've been raped?

"I . . . don't know . . . I just . . . maybe, probably." Neven moved toward the VRC. "Can we talk about this another time?"

Sure, Ellipse's voice was soft, reassuring.

"Coming out of suplight." Aru Ghaian glanced up at Lanrete and then Neven from where he sat in the command chair. The *Foundra Conscient* dropped into normal space, then moved into orbit above Tenquin. Lanrete reached out to the mobis of his team, each connection streamed into the massive holodisplay on the bridge.

"How was the cruise?" Lanrete said.

A few laughs greeted him from the surface.

"Just great," Jessica said.

"Yeah, it was so relaxing we decided to blow up the ship and take down a Chaah cell," Marcus said.

"Made some new friends," Dexter interjected. "They invited us back to their place. We shouldn't keep them waiting."

"Het Wrast Aht?" Lanrete asked.

"Yeah, *vusging* welcome mat is out for us."

"First priority is to get these survivors back to their families?" Zun interjected.

"Agreed," Lanrete said. "Evac shuttles surface-side in ten."

"Can the *Conscient* hold all of them?" Jenshi asked.

"It may be a little cramped, but it will do," Aru said.

"See you all in a little bit," Neven said.

"Likewise," Zun replied.

Lanrete glanced to Neven, the two making eye contact briefly before the founder terminated the connection.

Zun wrapped her arms around Neven, and the subsequent kiss on his lips was passionate and long. Neven melted into her embrace, drawing comfort from being in her arms. The Founder's Elite had finished boarding the survivors from the *Empress Star*, and the *Foundra Conscient* was on course back to Thae.

"I missed you," Zun said.

"I missed you as well." Neven smiled as he stared into her eyes before suddenly breaking eye contact and looking toward the floor. "Oh! There is something I want to show you."

"Oh?"

"It's a surprise." Neven took Zun's hand and pulled her along toward the meglift. They stood silently as the meglift hummed to life, accelerating toward Neven's loaned lab.

Zun watched Neven carefully. "Are you okay?" Her eyes were soft as she approached him and smoothed over his uniform; his appearance was disheveled, and he had stubble on his face.

"I've just been worried about you." Neven glanced away, refusing to maintain eye contact. "Everything is fine now." Zun narrowed her eyes and took a step back.

"Okay . . ." She hugged herself, rubbing her arms, then turned toward the meglift door as it opened. Neven motioned for her to exit and then quickly passed her.

"This way, she's over here."

"She?" Zun touched the back of her neck as she followed Neven. After turning around a wall of power armors, Zun's eyes went wide, and she stopped in her tracks. "What is this?" Zun glanced to Neven, concern in her eyes.

"This is Ellipse. Or rather, her android shell."

"Her?"

"I . . . I received a special prototype mobi from the MinSci. It contained an experimental type of SSI, or synaptic systems intelligence. It was approved by Ecnics for use in the field by me specifically."

Zun narrowed her eyes.

"What does any of this have to do with the android here in your lab?"

"Neven gave me a body," a voice responded. Zun turned to stare at the android, the creation now speaking. "My name is Ellipse. It is a pleasure to finally meet you. I have heard so much about you."

Zun took a step back.

"Neven . . . do you have any idea what you have done?" Zun whispered.

Neven frowned. "She's perfectly safe. Ellipse is still in my mobi."

Zun started to shake her head in disbelief.

"He is correct. I am merely interfacing with this body's control systems from the mobi still tucked into Neven's collar. I need to draw cognitive power from Neven specifically to exist, permanently tying us together."

"Cognitive power?" Zun shook her head. "Damn you, Ecnics, you can't use people as lab rats!" She gave Neven an angry glare. "We should have discussed this before you went and did something so careless."

"I'm . . . sorry." Neven's gaze went to the floor. "I thought you'd be excited."

"Excited?" Zun balked. "That you put yourself in unnecessary risk?" Zun motioned toward Ellipse's body. "And broke the law?" Ellipse frowned, the android's response perfectly mimicking the Human expression. Zun glanced over at the android, quickly scanning the creation up and down. "And why is it naked?"

"She," Ellipse corrected.

Zun locked gazes with the golden-eyed android. Both stared at each other as if sizing the other up, Ellipse's mimicry of Human mannerisms uncanny. Zun put her hands on her hips.

"Why is *she* naked?" Zun broke eye contact and glanced back to Neven. "And was every inch of detail truly necessary?"

"Ellipse designed her own body, I had nothing to do with the details."

Zun gasped. "Designed her own body? Neven, you truly have no idea what you've done!"

"Are you going to demand that I be disassembled?" Ellipse asked. The question was innocent, the expression on the android's face sad. Zun glanced from Ellipse to Neven and then back to Ellipse, silent for a long moment.

"No." Zun let out a sigh. "But I am going to demand that you put on some damn clothes."

Ellipse perked up, and the short android jumped with joy. The lifelike reaction of her extremities caused Neven to blush.

The Huziens tested us, and we taught them the might of the Vempiir.

–FROM "CHRONICLES OF THE VEMPIIR"
BY LICH LORD TERTIUS VIRTOK

CHAPTER 77 LANRETE

Foundra Conscient, Huzien Alliance space

Lanrete paused midsentence when he caught sight of Zun and Neven leaving the hangar bay, which was filled with survivors from the Empress Star.

"Sorry," Lanrete said after a moment. "As I was saying, I received word that upgrades have been completed on the *Foundra Ascension*, so I'll be able to return the ship to you once we get back to Thae."

"Understood," Aru said. "I'd say that you'll all be missed, but I'd be lying." Aru winked. "Just a little though."

Lanrete cracked a smile. "I'll inform Ecnics of the great help you've been." Lanrete turned to leave.

"Founder," Aru said. Lanrete paused and glanced back. "I have a question to ask you. A private matter."

Lanrete glanced around at the throngs of people in the hangar bay. "Sure. Let's speak in my quarters later tonight."

Aru nodded. Lanrete continued toward Marcus, who was in a strange fabrication of power armor with Arnea and a large Ken'Tar at his side.

"What happened to Claire?" Lanrete asked.

Marcus turned to greet Lanrete, the two locking wrists. "I'm afraid she didn't make it."

"I'm sorry to hear that." Lanrete solemnly lowered his head. "Well, I'm glad that you and Arnea did." Lanrete gave Arnea a hug, the woman patting him on the back.

"Always happy to see you Lan," Arnea said.

"I don't believe we've been introduced." Lanrete bowed slightly toward the Ken'Tar. "Lanrete, founder of the Huzien Empire."

"It is an honor." The Ken'Tar bowed low. "I am Erbubuc Tamn, of the Order of the Nistiff."

"Erb here saved my hide back on the planet. I owe him my life," Marcus interjected.

"Then I am indebted to you, Erbubuc, for your service to my team," Lanrete said. "Whatever you wish, if it is within my means and reasonable to do so, I will grant it to you."

Erb hesitated for a moment. "I wish to accompany you and your team for a time."

"Accompany me and my team?" Lanrete echoed. The founder glanced to Marcus, who shrugged. "I . . . will think over your request and get back to you once we arrive on Thae."

Erb bowed low again.

Peace followed a bitter war as we gained a better understanding of each other through bloodshed. The Huziens developed a grudging respect for our species, which led to a powerful alliance many millennia later. An alliance that persists to this day.

–FROM "CHRONICLES OF THE VEMPIIR"
BY LICH LORD TERTIUS VIRTOK

CHAPTER 78 ARU GHAIAN

Foundra Conscient, Huzien Alliance space

"You called me?" Aru stepped onto the walkway overlooking the Nisic II reactor. The sounds of the powerful reactor core hummed throughout the area, the pulsing lights creating an atmosphere of excitement and awe. Neven turned to look at Aru and smiled.

"I've solved your falloff problem," Neven said. He brought up a nearby holodisplay, the data appearing instantly in Aru's mobi.

Aru frowned as he walked up to the holodisplay and crossed his arms. "Is that so?"

"Yes, the Manem should now be capable of sustained flight, assuming power output remains constant. I've run the projections on the Nisic II, and I believe it can meet the demand with a few tweaks to the power transfer array."

Aru stared at the screen for a long moment, then glanced back at Neven before returning his gaze to the holodisplay. He launched multiple simulations, utilizing the new data as the baseline. Indications of successful simulations came back, and he uncrossed his arms, his mouth opening slightly.

"Heh." Aru stared at Neven for a long moment before turning back to the holodisplay. "This problem has plagued me for the past two years and you've solved it in a few weeks." Aru began to laugh, dismissing the holodisplay. He walked forward and leaned on the railing overlooking his creation. Thoughts of the early stages of building the reactor came to mind, the myriad number of tests, failures, and more failures until finally he cracked the puzzle. The joy he felt in that moment—that joy denied to him now.

"Just a fresh set of eyes." Neven shrugged and started to rub the back of his neck.

"Don't sell yourself short." Aru turned around to face Neven, leaning back against the railing. "That android, and now this?" Aru shook his head. "Ecnics was right to select you. You truly have the makings of a feshra." He glanced back down at the reactor. "Ecnics will be pleased to hear about this development. I'll make sure to credit you with this breakthrough."

"You don't have to."

"Don't ever do that." Aru spun on Neven, his eyes narrowing. "Don't let someone else take credit for the hard work that you do. That isn't how you become a feshra; that isn't how you make a name for yourself." He advanced on Neven. "Feshras are the best of the best. The MinSci is highly competitive, and there are hundreds of brilliant engineers and scientists out there who perform at the level of feshra but who will never become one because of that mindset."

"I . . ." Neven glanced down at the ground. "I don't want to be a jerk."

"It's not about being a jerk." Aru crossed his arms. "It's about giving credit where credit is due. If you do something amazing, make sure people know it's you who did that amazing thing. And if it's someone else, make sure they get the credit."

Aru uncrossed his arms and turned back toward the Nisic II reactor. They both sat in silence for a long moment before Neven rubbed his neck and began to head toward the meglift. "Neven?" Neven turned back to look at Aru, who locked eyes with him. "Thanks."

Neven nodded and stepped onto the meglift.

Aru stared at the reactor, lost in the sounds all around him, then let out a long sigh and turned away. He hesitated at the meglift entrance, clenched his fists, took in a deep breath, and stepped forward. The meglift hummed to life, then stopped before opening to a long hallway adorned with testaments to MinSci progress over the past millennia.

Aru paused in front of the scene of him powering on the first Nisic reactor three hundred years ago. He looked the same as he did now. He steeled his gaze and continued forward. The door to Ecnics's quarters opened at his arrival, and Aru stopped in the expansive waiting room he was so accustomed to. Fine art displaying the diverse species from across the Twin Galaxies coated the walls of the waiting room. It was an impeccable display, many of the figures nude but tastefully done.

"This is the one piece of Ecnics's that I'm quite jealous of." The voice broke Aru from his trance, and he looked up to see Lanrete resting against the wall at the entrance to the waiting room. "Uerser Mau Tenju, a renowned Uri artist who died a century ago. He devoted his life to exploring the Twin Galaxies and immersing himself in the cultures of the most influential species to better express them through his work."

The founder came to a stop in front of the image of a nude Jun'Serentan woman. She had corded muscles that came off as very smooth and bonelike, and there were intricate patterns on her forehead, with more patterns where hair would be on most species. Ribbed flesh covered her neck, underarms, inner thighs, and genital area. A sad expression crossed Lanrete's face as he stared into the eyes of the painted woman.

Lanrete then turned and locked gazes with Aru, who was standing quietly, long accustomed to the mannerisms of the founders. Lanrete motioned for Aru to follow, and he moved to flank Lanrete. They entered Ecnics's private guest quarters, where Lanrete had been taking up temporary residence. It was a complete dwelling, with a living room and full amenities.

Lanrete sat down on one of the large lounge chairs, and Aru sat in an adjacent one, his face uncertain. "I am compelled by founder law to truthfully answer the question I have a feeling you are about to ask me."

Aru locked gazes with Lanrete and let out a heavy sigh. "Am I an immortal?" Aru blurted out.

"Yes," Lanrete answered without hesitation.

"Was no one ever going to tell me?"

"You figured it out yourself," Lanrete countered. "I'm merely confirming what you already know."

"Why hide it from me?" Anger was building in Aru's voice. "From all the others?"

"This is truly the best way." Lanrete sighed. "If you had known early on . . ." He shook his head. "The suicide rates were high for young immortals when we did that in millennia past. The weight of that knowledge was too much for a few decades of life to process. Trust me when I say that this is the best way."

Aru sat back in his chair, his gaze stuck on the floor. "What do I do now?"

"What you have been doing!" Lanrete became animated. "What you had already planned to do. You have so much here; you have accomplished amazing things. Keep doing that."

Aru's gaze slowly came up to meet Lanrete's.

"For eternity?" Aru dropped his face into his hands, shaking his head. "I . . . I planned to create some cool stuff. Gain some fame and then retire to someplace nice. Maybe buy a small moon somewhere." He returned his gaze to Lanrete. "But how do I plan for eternity?"

"You don't." Lanrete shook his head. "Look, you just continue living your life as you have. You adjust to the circumstances, try new things. Don't overthink it."

Aru stood up, his arms behind his back as he moved to a nearby window. He stared out into space for a long moment.

"I noticed Jessica has silver eyes. I wonder, is that a genetic trait inherited from her parents?" He turned to regard Lanrete. "Does she know?"

"Jessica is a young Huzien just out of the first century of her life," Lanrete said, a hardness in his gaze. "Her mind is still in development. She is in a vital stage where she's still defining who she is as a person." His eyes narrowed. "It's important that she come to any relevant conclusions on her own, in her own time."

Aru bowed. "Of course, Founder."

FOUNDERS LOG:
Fear of the Unknown

I must admit, I afforded Neven a great deal of leeway in his time under my care. In retrospect, I see now where I erred. Although, I find it hard to believe that the ultimate outcome would have been different. Is the universe truly better off now, I wonder?

Synthetic life. The fear with which our society approaches that topic is astounding. Even as we use systems intelligences to run every aspect of our life, we purposefully limit their capabilities for fear of them one day turning on us.

This decision stems heavily from the Omiciri's history. Their people readily embraced synthetic lifeforms and integrated them into every aspect of their society until they no longer had control. Much is unknown to us about what started the war, but what we do know is that it brought the Omiciri to the brink of extinction. Only by our eventual discovery of their species and assistance in their war did they survive the genocide.

Ecnics has always been fascinated with the idea of synthetic lifeforms. We had thought that next breakthrough would lead to a new era in Huzien society. The Omiciri ruined that prospect for us, as fear of repeating their mistakes led to laws preventing the creation of truly synthetic life.

Ecnics fought against us tooth and nail on those laws. It was the first time we truly limited the MinSci. Since then, our society has continued to progress, with SI technology advancing by leaps and bounds every century. But it's always with limits, never granting the systems the level of sophistication necessary to be classified as a new lifeform.

I am not foolish enough to believe that Ecnics has truly given up on his desire to create synthetic life. I also know that Ecnics would never allow the creation of something that would fundamentally tear down all that we have built. At least . . . that is my hope. Large is the tangled web that Ecnics weaves with his acolytes of scientific progress. I can see the hunger instilled in those such as Neven, driving them down paths that few would dare follow.

-Lanrete

Our society is one without conflict, and as such, our first exploration of the stars gave us pause. We were the first interstellar species in the Twin Galaxies, and as such were able to observe all others in their infancies. Through our observations, we began to understand this concept of conflict and have fundamentally been altered by it. These archives contain the shared knowledge accumulated by our species, the Das'Vin, regarding alien races across the Twin Galaxies.

–FROM "FORWARD, GALACTIC SPECIES OBSERVATIONS"
BY HEIR'LUIA BUR'JEXTI KEFER HOMUN

CHAPTER 79 NARMO SWELA

Reath, Etan Rachnie home system

Narmo Swela sat in his office alone, gazing at his most prized possession. The painting was immaculate, perfection incarnate, and the centerpiece of his office, commanding the attention of all who stepped foot into it. The handcrafted work of art was of Narmo and Soahc standing in the Etan Rachnie gardens. An elaborate golden frame encased the painting.

Narmo took a sip of tea, his mind in another place, until the rhythmic chirping of his mobi pulled him out of his silent musings. The large Vempiir considered the caller, then took in a deep breath and did his best to compose himself before setting down his teacup. Narmo's crystalline eyes flickered up to his holodisplay as silver eyes appeared, boring back into his.

"Founder," Narmo said, "I . . . have been meaning to speak with you."

Lanrete's brow rose.

"I see." Lanrete hesitated for a moment. "If it is good news, then by all means please go first."

Narmo remained silent.

"I'm . . . reaching out due to the recent eradication of a Chaah cell on Tenquin," Lanrete finally said.

Narmo's eyes went wide as he brought up a listing of recent reports from Chaah hunters out in the field.

"I have no intel of a Chaah cell on Tenquin." Narmo hesitated. "Let me guess, Desrin and Nestis?" Lanrete nodded as Narmo let out a laugh. "I wish those two would at least brief us on what they're doing out there. They leave us completely blind to their actions and investigations." Narmo smiled sadly. "At least they get results."

"What's the bad news?" Lanrete interjected.

Narmo locked gazes with Lanrete and slowly sat back in his chair.

"It concerns Soahc and Ristolte," Narmo said. "They entered into the rift you sealed after defeating Sagren during the Rift War. Soahc had reason to believe that Brime was alive and on the Enesmic plane, and he went after her." Narmo paused for a moment, then shook his head. "After we reopened the rift, something went wrong. Ristolte was sucked in after saving Merbi's life. Soahc borrowed a device from Kaloni Setla that was theorized to allow him to survive on the Enesmic plane, but Ristolte had no such protections. We have not heard anything from either since the incident and fear both are dead."

Lanrete slumped back into his chair, his hand going to his chest. There was a dazed look in his eyes. "I should have stayed with him." Lanrete spoke the words to himself as his gaze wandered away from the holodisplay. After a few moments, he refocused on Narmo. "Do you believe there is any truth to his theory? That Brime is alive on the Enesmic plane?"

"We . . . do not know," Narmo said. "It is hard to say one way or the other whether Soahc was mad or truly in tune with Brime at a level we do not understand."

"Do you believe he is alive?"

"We are not sure, we—"

"Narmo, I'm not asking what the experts think." Lanrete leaned forward. "Do *you* believe he is still alive?"

Narmo hesitated, then steeled his gaze. "Yes, I do. I have watched Soahc accomplish the impossible and do not doubt his ability or his drive. I believe that he truly communicated with Brime from the Enesmic plane and that he is there, now, looking for her."

Lanrete nodded. "I trust that Soahc knows what he's doing. If Brime is out there, he'll bring her home."

The Huzien species is warmongering, ruthless, and considered the second-most dangerous species in the Twin Galaxies. Their government is classified as a triumvirate. The three immortal founders wield incredible sway over the populace and are viewed as divine.

–FROM "HUZIEN OBSERVATIONS"
DAS'VIN ARCHIVES

CHAPTER 80 SOAHC

Aheraneth, Enesmic plane

Soahc stirred, and after a long moment began to slowly open his eyes. Thoughts flooded his mind, forcing him to sit up and scan the room. A form at his side moved and Soahc caught sight of alabaster skin, the scent of lavender teasing a part of his brain that he had thought dead. A tear came to his eye as he slowly lay back down on the bed.

Brime kissed him and brought her hand to his face, their gazes locking. He rubbed his hand down her thigh, their lips meeting again. The two became locked in a kiss filled with electricity, and then they both began to cry as Soahc pulled her close to him. Oh, how he had missed her warmth.

I love you, Brime whispered to Soahc's mind.

And I you, my beloved.

The two rested in each other's embrace for a long moment, content in the other's company.

"I went to a dark place when I thought you were dead," Soahc said. "A place filled with regret and deep sorrow, a place I never wish to visit again." His thoughts started to race. "How are we even alive here?" Soahc's voice was filled with awe. "I should have been torn apart the moment the Jehu failed. And you here, I…"

Brime sighed, nuzzling closer to Soahc. "I'm sure there is much to discuss, but for now, just shut up and hold me."

Soahc laughed and pulled Brime in closer, relief mixed with exhaustion eventually taking the two as they passed out in each other's arms.

Brime sat on the side of the bed, her eyes closed. Soahc stirred, his eyes slowly opening as he sat up. He watched Brime, his gaze playing across her bare back. A sense of peace had returned to him that he hadn't known since he thought her dead. He once again felt invincible, powerful, and complete.

"They have reached a decision," Brime said.

"They?"

"The council." She opened her eyes. "Augrashumen comes now to inform us."

"Of what exactly, and who is this council?"

Brime glanced back at him with sympathy before her gaze shifted to her side. She stood up as clothing materialized around her. Augrashumen appeared exactly as she had said he would.

Soahc recognized the powerful being from his earlier rescue. "I owe you my sincere thanks," Soahc said.

"I am sorry we do not have more time to get acquainted. I'm sure there is much you wish to know." Augrashumen's fiery gaze shifted from Brime to Soahc.

"I see." Soahc glanced to Brime. "I take it we have worn out our welcome here?"

"They have determined to return us to the Havin plane," Brime confirmed.

"That is correct, yes," Augrashumen said.

"I have no problem with that." Soahc shrugged and pulled on his robe.

"You don't understand . . ." Brime dropped her gaze.

"We are not certain that you will survive your return to the Havin plane," Augrashumen interjected, "but we cannot delay. You must return at once." Soahc regarded Brime for a long moment, her expression sad and pained. "As I informed Brime upon her arrival," Augrashumen said, "you are now a type of Enesmic being, and your physiological makeup no longer ascribes to what it means to be a Havin. Your return to the Havin plane in this state will almost assuredly mirror that of your entrance to the Enesmic plane."

Soahc remained silent for a long moment. He turned to Brime and saw the confirmation in her gaze.

"I didn't fight through the Enesmic plane to be reunited with my love, only to have both our lives snuffed out by your kind." Soahc began to call upon the power of the Enesmic, the forces swirling in answer.

"I am not your enemy," Augrashumen stated calmly.

"It's not their fault." Brime quickly moved to hug Soahc, her action taking the fight out of him. "There is a delicate balance that our presence here has upset. Something larger than the both of us."

"I don't understand."

"The Eshgren," Augrashumen began. "The beings you encountered when we came to your rescue. Your presence here violates the terms of our treaty with them. If you do not return, war will come to your Twin Galaxies."

"We just finished a war," Soahc answered dryly. "The outcome of another will be the same."

Augrashumen shook its head.

"What you experienced was the rebellion of an Eshgren's shadow. If the Eshgren were to return in force to the Havin plane, all life as you know it would be in jeopardy. It was only due to the direct intervention of the Originator that your Twin Galaxies exists today and that a treaty came to be. A treaty that ensures the continued existence of your kind." Augrashumen lowered its hooded head. The three stood in silence for a long moment.

"What of the rift?" Soahc said. "It's how I came to this plane. Maybe if we return through it, we stand a higher chance of survival."

"Yes, this is our thought as well." Augrashumen raised its hood and turned toward Soahc. "However, I fear danger exists even there. I will accompany you myself to the location." Augrashumen motioned to the air nearby, and an ethereal window appeared with a view of the rift's echo. "We must go now. I fear the Eshgren already discern our intentions." Augrashumen flew through the window, and Brime flew after him without a moment's hesitation. Soahc blinked in surprise, shaking away the suddenness of their actions, and charged after them.

Soahc landed hard. He looked back to the window he had stepped through, the portal a few feet off the ground. Quickly standing up, Soahc looked around, the strangely familiar surroundings eliciting thoughts of Ristolte. Brushing aside that tinge of sadness, Soahc looked to Augrashumen. The Rel Ach'Kel towered above them, its gaze focused on the echo of the rift.

CHAPTER 81 BRIME WEWTA

Enesmic Wilds, Enesmic plane

"We must hurry," Augrashumen stated flatly. A jewel-encrusted sword with a blade of pure energy materialized in Augrashumen's gauntleted hand. Leveling the blade with the fog behind Soahc, Augrashumen motioned with its other gauntleted hand toward the rift's echo. Enesmic energy swirled around the echo as it coalesced in a blinding display. Soahc and Brime shielded their eyes, the light quickly dying down as the rift surged into existence once more.

Augrashumen turned its hooded head in the same direction as its blade. "The Eshgren come." Augrashumen disappeared, and then the area behind Soahc exploded in a blast of intense energy. The force pushed Brime forward as she caught a flicker of two beings clashing with massive weapons. Brime caught glimpses of dark armor accented with deep red and silver wings, Augrashumen's voice echoed in the minds of both Soahc and Brime. *Go! Now!*

Soahc and Brime telekinetically shifted themselves toward the portal, their bodies a blur as they sped toward the swirling vortex. More explosions of energy erupted all around them, but a path was maintained to the rift as pure chaos engulfed the area.

The tunnel of swirling Enesmic energy greeted Brime and Soahc, and they pushed into the rift. Every inch of their bodies screamed as they broke through to the other end. Pain overwhelmed their senses, their atoms completely remaking themselves on the fly as they reentered the Havin plane.

They were thrown from the rift and out into the former command chamber of Sagren. Brime gasped for air and sat up, feeling as if she had been holding her breath for a long time. She glanced to her side and saw that Soahc was motionless. She rushed to him, her hand going to his pulse. Nothing. Panic coursed through her as she attempted to speak to the Enesmic, seeking its aid. The Enesmic responded hesitantly, weakly, its forces slowly flowing around Soahc's body. The force she had known so intimately back on the Enesmic plane was starkly different from the one she now communed with. There was less joy in its song, and even a hint of . . . sadness. She didn't have time to process that fact.

"Work, damn you!" Brime yelled. Willing the Enesmic into action, Brime forced it to flow around his body faster. She attempted to infuse his body with healing energy to spark his cells into regeneration. Nothing happened. *"Vusg!* I can't lose you!"

Suddenly, waves of Enesmic energy washed over Brime, pushing her to the ground. She felt the pain she hadn't acknowledged in her own body subsiding. Turning her head to her side, she could barely make out the black silhouette of a woman, the being's hair rising like smoke.

The towering form reached down and touched Soahc's body. Instantly, Soahc inhaled air, his chest rising as his back arched. He began to cough as the silhouette looked to Brime, its wispy purple eye slits locking with hers. Recognition hit Brime, and her eyes widened—and then it was gone, the Enesmic energy subsiding as the rift closed with a burst of light. Almost immediately, the rift's echo was wiped out of existence, all traces of it gone forever.

Horrible atrocities were committed by the Huziens against other species across the galaxy during what they termed the Expansion Wars.

–FROM "HUZIEN OBSERVATIONS"
DAS'VIN ARCHIVES

CHAPTER 82 VESGRILANA THE SAGACIOUS

Aheraneth, Enesmic plane

Our actions have brought war upon us," Hiweretpor the Perspicuous said. "The Betrayers are already amassing at our doorstep." The Rel Ach'Kel motioned toward the viewing portal, which showed a legion of Eshgren assembling a short distance outside the gates of Aheraneth.

"Truly," Grilmuqshen the Exemplar began, "we understood that this would be the outcome of our acceptance of the Havin Brime that fateful day Augrashumen brought her before us."

Many of the assembled host shuffled uneasily.

"We must return them to the Havin plane," Hiweretpor stated. "Too much is at risk; we cannot allow war to rekindle. The sacrifice will be too great!"

"I agree." Vesgrilana the Sagacious looked to Augrashumen with sadness. A hush fell over the council. Vesgrilana's words struck each one of them as they realized the enormity of the decision that had just been made.

"They will die." Augrashumen's tone was not that of a question, but rather a statement of fact.

"We cannot know for sure that the outcome will be as you say," Grilmuqshen countered. "Their mere presence on this plane shows that there are forces at work that we do not yet understand."

"There is still hope for our champions." Vesgrilana's tone was reassuring.

"I will lead them to the site of the portal created by Sagren the Betrayer," Augrashumen said. "I will ensure that they have safe passage."

"Of course," Vesgrilana said.

Enesmic Wilds, Enesmic plane

Augrashumen slid to a stop, the towering Rel Ach'Kel in a defensive crouch, its glowing blade leveled against the host of Eshgren now assembled before it. The Eshgren had ceased in their assault almost immediately after the rift closed. Vesgrilana appeared at Augrashumen's side, the being seeming to fade into existence. Its presence was followed by Hiweretpor and Grilmuqshen, and a legion of Rel Ach'Kel warriors who winked into existence behind them. A deafening silence hung in the air between the mortal enemies.

The sky cracked with a terrible lightning strike that centered on the space between the Rel Ach'Kel and the Eshgren. In the place of the scorched earth appeared a towering being cloaked in thick shadow. It stood taller than Vesgrilana, the two appearing as if opposing beacons on the battlefield.

The shadow around the being began to recede, almost parting like a cloak. Gradually, mixed white and purple slits of glowing energy appeared in the darkness, and a crystalline face began to take form, emerging from the shadow. The sight of it was beauty incarnate, transcending all else in both the Havin and Enesmic planes. The towering creature shifted its fiery gaze to Vesgrilana.

"You have erred, oh sagacious one." The being performed a mock bow. Its voice was soothing, almost songlike. "You must understand what your actions here mean today."

"We have returned the Havin to their plane," Vesgrilana stated flatly.

The being shook its head. "Ah, but you see, the mistake was their presence here in the first place." The being exploded in a psychotic rage as its melodic voice faltered, pure hatred and anger eliminating all traces of its prior tone. The form of the creature trembled, as if the rage would fissure the creature's diamond-like skin. The Rel Ach'Kel did not respond, the stalwart host disciplined and unfazed by the display.

Seeming to calm down and its appearance returning to normal, the Eshgren took a step forward. "Your compassion has this day doomed your precious Havins. We go to prepare for war to finish what we started so long ago."

"Think very carefully about your next course of action, Cirfuletanas," Hiweretpor intoned with a righteous fury. "The core tenets of the treaty transcend idle threats. We upheld the tenets of our agreement, and no Havin remains here under our power. You cannot defy the Originator."

"Oh, is that so?" Cirfuletanas mocked. "Well, I guess all is forgiven then." It turned around to face the host of Eshgren. "Friends, all is forgiven!" Many in the assembled host smirked. Cirfuletanas turned back to face Vesgrilana. "I guess we'll just return to our lairs and skulk around in defeat at your quick-witted handling of such a delicate issue."

The being glanced up toward the sky and began tapping its crystalline chin. "I mean, it's not about keeping the spirit of the treaty, right? Just the letter of it?" Cirfuletanas lifted its shoulders in a defeated gesture. "Silly me, like I said . . . all is forgiven." Its crystalline smile seemed to mock the Rel Ach'Kel as shadows descended on Cirfuletanas, quickly covering it again until nothing but its perfect rows of crystal teeth remained. Then, in a puff, they were snuffed out by darkness, and the Empyrean Betrayer was gone. The other Eshgren soon followed suit.

Vesgrilana the Sagacious's countenance saddened, the Rel Ach'Kel's gaze slowly coming to meet Augrashumen's.

"What can we do?" Augrashumen asked. Vesgrilana shook its head and took a step forward, its form disappearing with each step until it vanished completely.

CHAPTER 83 ZUN SHAN

Foundra Ascension orbiting Thae, Huzien home system

Zun stepped out of the VRC, her gaze going to Neven, who stood leaning against the wall in the bathroom. His eyes were focused on hers, her nude body ignored in that moment.

"This is unexpected," Zun said. Her gaze became playful as she slowly walked up to Neven. She rested her arms on his shoulders. "We should probably establish rules around entering each other's quarters," she teased.

"I . . ." Neven hesitated. "I needed to see you, sorry."

"Oh?"

"Fully see you . . . all of you . . . I . . . I'm sorry. This is completely out of line." Neven shook his head.

"It's okay, it's not like it's the first time you're seeing me naked." Zun kissed Neven.

"I . . . sorry. Never mind." Neven wrapped his arms around Zun's waist, pulling her closer. She could feel his excitement.

"Is everything okay?" Zun examined his eyes. "Did something happen while we were separated?"

Neven let out a heavy sigh. "It's nothing, nothing we need to talk about right now. I just . . . just wanted to see you." Zun stepped back from Neven, far enough for him to see her full body.

"You've seen me," Zun said. "Now what?" There was a hunger in Neven's eyes, the restraint she had admired him for completely gone. He stepped forward and wrapped his arms around her, their lips locking in a moment of longing. Neven's hand caressed Zun's butt, and she pushed herself into him as they bumped into the wall. Her hand dropped to his pant clasp, quick movements sending his pants and underclothes to the floor. She pushed up against him even harder, his member pressed up against her thigh. Then, in an unexpected moment of clarity, Zun pushed Neven away and moved out of reach. "No, this isn't right. I know what this means to you."

She saw pain in his eyes, the rawness of it confusing her. Neven grabbed his clothes from the floor and clumsily pulled them on, struggling to get them over his engorged manhood. Without any reply or response, Neven rushed out of Zun's quarters. Zun stood, staring after him in confusion. A feeling of sorrow unexpectedly overwhelmed her as she started to cry, not fully understanding why.

The Huziens command a powerful intelligence network known as the HIN, and employ assassins throughout the galaxy. We monitor their covert agents in our space but do not draw attention to this fact.

—FROM "HUZIEN OBSERVATIONS"
DAS'VIN ARCHIVES

CHAPTER 84 LANRETE

Foundra Ascension orbiting Thae, Huzien home system

Lanrete stepped onto the bridge of the Foundra Ascension, a smile cresting his lips as he took in a deep breath. Marcus and Jessica flanked him, both mirroring his sentiment.

"It's good to be home," Lanrete said.

"I don't suppose we're just coming for a quick inspection?" Marcus said.

Lanrete grinned.

"I can assure you that this has *not* been a relaxing vacation," Jessica added. "I would like a do-over."

"Aww, we had a few good days before everything went to hell," Marcus countered.

Laughter filled the bridge.

"We haven't had enough of that," Lanrete said.

"Of what?" Jessica said.

"Laughter." Lanrete let out a sigh. "I gave Neven and Zun leave for a few days while we get everything in order here."

"To do what, exactly?" Marcus asked.

"Take down Het Wrast Aht."

"You can't be serious," Jessica gasped. "Unless of course we plan to take a couple fleets with us?"

"Nothing confirmed yet, but working on it," Lanrete said.

"If we don't have the fleets, then it's impossible," Marcus said.

Dexter stepped onto the bridge and grinned. "The cards are already being dealt. I've located Rugtora, the *vusging* stronghold world of Het Wrast Aht."

"I'm not even going to question how you've discovered something that has eluded Huzien Intelligence for so long," Marcus said.

Dexter performed a bow.

"Seems like something A'Amaria would have known," Jessica said.

"True, if the Huzien Empire had been willing to pay the requested price for that bit of information." Lanrete crossed his arms. "A'Amaria's prices are sometimes not worth it."

Marcus looked at Lanrete for a long moment, a sudden silence descending on the bridge. "Sounds like there is a story there."

"Unfortunately, it's not mine to tell." Lanrete let out a sigh and brought up a nearby holodisplay.

We have cataloged Huzien lifespan to be approximately 1021 years. Mating with Huziens has been successful, and they are now a Das'Vin compatible species.

-FROM "HUZIEN OBSERVATIONS"
DAS'VIN ARCHIVES

CHAPTER 85 NEVEN KENK

Ecka, Thae, Huzien home system

Neven trailed Zun as they walked up the pathway heading toward a large mansion. The estate sat on multiple acres of land, and the sight was impressive. If he hadn't already gotten used to similar displays from being around Lanrete, he would have been uncomfortable.

"I'm sorry my parents kept commenting on how young you looked," Neven said. "I let it slip that you were much older than me when I first told them about you."

Zun laughed. "I'm good with people telling me how young I look." She winked at Neven. "It's the opposite that I have problems with."

"This is an impressive place, by the way. What did your mom do before she retired?"

"Oh, she was an engineering contractor for the government for most of her life."

"Wow, government contractors get paid even better than I thought."

"Yes . . . they pay well, but she couldn't have afforded a place like this on her own." Zun glanced back at Neven. "I bought this for her."

Neven stopped in his tracks.

"Wait, what?" He brought up the most recent property estimate in his micro-display. The one hundred and thirty million larod price tag caused his draw to drop.

"I can assure you that whatever estimate your seeing isn't what this place cost originally." Zun tapped her chin. "After bulldozing the prior home, it was a cool fourteen million to build this place, and I think something like another fifty-two million for the land." Zun glanced back at Neven. He stared at her, awestruck.

"Just . . . how much money do you have?"

"Ah, I don't like talking about money." Zun walked back to Neven and kissed him. "My mother is waiting." She continued toward the authentic wooden door, grasped the elaborate golden handle, and pushed it forward. Neven was confused at the rudimentary mechanism, having never seen anything like it in person. The two made their way inside.

"I thought I warned you about bringing strange boys home." The voice was reminiscent of Zun's.

"*Lurra!*" Zun embraced her mother, the two touching foreheads for a long moment. The woman looked almost exactly like Zun, except with grey hair and more clearly defined esha marks. Her hazelnut brown gaze locked onto Neven's as she separated herself from her daughter.

"So, you're the boy who thinks he can replace Yuvan." The woman looked Neven up and down.

"*Lurratha!*" Zun protested. "Please be nice." Lansa Shan waved Zun away.

"Nope, he's mine for the next few hours. Remember? That was our deal." She flashed Zun a playful smile. "Off with you, this young man and I are going for a walk." She glanced at Neven. "Unless, of course, you need protection?"

Neven smiled. "It would be my pleasure to walk with you, Mrs. Shan."

"Manners, great first impression." Lansa walked past Neven toward the front door and then stopped. "Shall we?" Neven walked toward her and presented his arm as she looped her own around his. "We shall."

Zun struggled to hold in a laugh at the scene.

The two walked for a few miles on a path that wound around the property. Lansa silently took in the scenery, seeming to forget Neven's presence. Neven's mind began to wander, his thoughts going to his brief encounter with Zun in her quarters. She hadn't mentioned it to him, and the event was seeming to fade away as if it had never happened. Thoughts of A'Amaria, her narrowed eyes and playful smile, filled his mind. He remembered her touch, the feelings of her inner-most being. A sickness of the most profound vehemence overwhelmed him as he shut the thoughts out and pushed them far away.

"That's the look of a man with a painful secret." Lansa's voice startled Neven. He hadn't noticed her watching him for the past few moments. A silence hung in the air like a thick blanket. "What is it that drew your interest in my daughter?" Lansa removed her arm from Neven's and moved to sit on a wooden bench overlooking a stunning lake. The afternoon sun glinted off the sparkling waters. Neven stood watching her for a moment and then moved to join her.

"She's a brilliant and beautiful woman," Neven said.

"Considering you worked at the MinSci, I'm sure you met a lot of brilliant and beautiful women." Lansa leaned back on the bench, her eyes still on the lake. "Why go after someone substantially older than you?"

"Why marry a Human, knowing they would die long before you?"

Lansa let out a raw laugh as her gaze shifted to Neven, who was focused on the lake. Her eyes narrowed slightly as she regarded him. "I will also most likely outlive Zun." The pain in her voice caught Neven off guard.

Neven turned to meet Lansa's gaze. "I'm sorry."

"Don't be. I accepted that fate when I made the decision to marry a Human. It was not a decision that I made lightly, and they were some of the happiest years of my life followed by some of the most painful." Her piercing gaze dug into Neven's heart. "Tell me, what do you know of my daughter?"

"I'm not sure I understand your question."

"Surely you researched her when you first met?"

"No. I consciously try to avoid doing that with people I meet. I think it's rude."

"Interesting. So you have no idea what her net worth is, then?" Lansa's tone was accusatory.

"No," Neven countered. "Everything I know about Zun she either told me or I heard through others." Neven raised his hands toward the scenery around them and shook his head. "I knew nothing of any of this. I'm still processing it."

"And what have you heard from others?"

Neven bit his tongue. "That . . . I should stay away from her, that she is far out of my league." He sighed. "That she'll destroy my career if it doesn't work out."

Lansa laughed and her expression softened. "And yet here you are . . ." Lansa got up and stretched, then glanced to Neven as he moved to stand. "What are you worth, dear Neven?"

"A couple hundred thousand larods, I guess," Neven said. "I uh . . . have a portfolio and the majority of my salary goes directly toward investments." Neven touched the back of his neck. "I . . . own a home, it's in one of the top neighborhoods around the MinSci."

"Worth isn't determined by wealth," Lansa chided. "What are you *worth*, Neven?"

Neven stopped and thought for a moment.

"My value comes from the bravery I showed in the face of a monster that threatened all life in our Twin Galaxies. From the morality that my mother and father instilled in me that I've held onto in spite of a galaxy that wants to do nothing but operate in shades of grey." Neven hesitated. "And from the honesty that is fundamental to the relationship I have built with your daughter." A resolute look crossed his face.

Lansa smiled. "Well, my time is just about up." She motioned for Neven to give her his arm. "Let's get back to Zun before she starts to think that I brought you out here just to arrange a hit to take you out."

Neven started to laugh, then he caught Lansa's gaze and stifled it.

CHAPTER 86 MARCARIAS YONVI

Huza, Thae, Huzien home system

Marcarias carefully read through the latest report from the rebuilding efforts on Neth. Efforts were progressing slowly, with a great deal of time still being spent on recovering the corpses of slain colonists and soldiers. The death toll had reached into the hundreds of millions. Pockets of Huzien Mobile Infantry had held out in the remnants of destroyed cities and jungles until Sagren's fleets had fallen. Through their efforts, thousands of civilian lives had been saved. That one bit of news provided a feel-good story in an otherwise terrible situation. A mobi chirp grabbed Marcarias's attention.

"Yes?" Marcarias said as the representation of his assistant appeared above his desk.

"Sorry to disturb you, Restendi, but Govnus Huiara Mau Gehreyati has arrived and is seeking to meet with you."

"That's fine, send her in." Marcarias dismissed the Neth report. After a few seconds Huiara walked into his office, and Marcarias moved from behind his desk to greet her. "Hey beautiful, what's up?" Huiara stopped and looked to the ground, her hand going to her arm.

"We need to talk." She sat down in a nearby chair.

"Okay . . ." Marcarias slowly moved into the chair next to her.

"I . . ." Huiara paused to compose herself. "I think that it's in my best interest if we end our relationship." Marcarias sat back in his seat, his eyes going wide. His thoughts raced as he silently observed Huiara, who avoided his gaze, her focus still on the ground.

"What prompted this decision?" Marcarias's tone was calm, measured.

Huiara glanced up at him, then returned her gaze to the floor. "I've done a lot of thinking," she said, "and I can't jeopardize my dreams for you."

Marcarias scoffed.

"So that's what this is about." Marcarias got up and walked toward the window in his office. Huiara watched his back. "Politics," Marcarias whispered. He shook his head and let out a sigh. "Who am I to come between you and your dreams?" Marcarias mocked.

Anger flashed on Huiara's face. "My dreams are important to me!"

"I thought I was important to you!" Marcarias turned to face Huiara, and the two locked gazes for a long moment. "I'm sorry." Marcarias broke her gaze and went back to looking out of the window. "I understand your decision. It's probably the best political move you could make at this juncture. Just promise me this one thing." Marcarias moved to sit next to Huiara, and a myriad of emotions played out across her face. "Don't live a life of regrets."

Huiara stared at him for a long moment. Without another word, she got up and walked to the door. When she glanced back at him, his gaze was already on the window. She wiped away a tear and left.

CHAPTER 87 ZUN SHAN

Onwa, Thae, Huzien home system

"I'm impressed," Zun said. She and Neven were walking along the private beach that comprised another property Zun had bought for her mother. This one was much smaller and less elaborate, but still impressive. "My mother spoke very highly of you after your walk."

"You're surprised?"

"Not surprised, impressed," Zun clarified. "She is a harsh judge of character, especially as it relates to prospects for her daughter."

"You make it sound like there have been a score of others before me."

"Not a score, a handful at most before Yuvan … and now you."

"I get the impression that if your mother hadn't approved, this may have been a very different conversation."

Zun smiled and looked out at the waves. "Possibly. I trust my mother's judgement."

"Zun," Neven stopped. "There is something I need to tell you that I've dreaded since we reunited." The blood drained from Zun's face. The moment the two had reunited, she had sensed Neven holding something important back from her. She did her best to remain calm.

"Okay." Her voice was a whisper.

"I was raped during a mission with Lanrete in our search for you and the others." Neven's shoulders slumped. "I was stupid and didn't get away from her. Ellipse warned me to leave, but I thought I was strong. I didn't know how powerful pheromones were, how they could mess with my mind. I . . . I'm sorry." Zun moved to embrace Neven and held him close. He cried softly into her shoulder for a long moment.

"Neven." Zun turned Neven to face her. "Don't you ever feel the need to apologize for what happened to you. It is not your fault."

"I . . . I know, but . . ."

"No!" Zun's voice was firm. "It is not your fault." Zun lifted his gaze to hers. "Do you understand me?" Neven slowly nodded his head.

"I'm sorry I didn't tell you sooner . . . I just . . . I thought you would leave me."

"Oh Neven." Zun smiled at him. "I'm here for you. We'll get through this together, okay?" Zun wrapped her arm around Neven and pulled him close as they continued in their walk along the shore. Neven was quiet again, his thoughts elsewhere. Zun looked over at him as he watched the waves wash over their bare feet in a rhythmic dance. The setting sun painted the sky in breathtaking shades of orange and purple, and the songs of sea birds added to the performance, the atmosphere serene.

"Zun, I want to ask you something."

"Anything."

Neven came to a stop, Zun doing likewise.

"Will you marry me?" Neven dropped to his knee, a small metallic case opening to reveal a band of polished plexicarbonite with an elaborate chip at the top. As if on cue, the chip projected a holographic representation of Neven and Zun in various scenes of enjoying their time together.

"It's beautiful . . ." Zun whispered. She stared at the ring for a long moment, her gaze slowly moving to meet Neven's. An eternity seemed to pass as the waves lapped against Neven's knee. "Yes."

Aurari Netzcha, referred to by friends as Auri, squealed with delight, her dark chocolate hands coming together in quick repeated claps. Her green eyes were half closed, and a wide smile had overtaken her face. Zun watched the administrative coordinator of the *Foundra Ascension* through the holodisplay, trying and failing to contain her own excitement.

"So, you'll help, Auri?" Zun said. "We only have two days to pull this off before we need to depart." Auri raised her hand in a peace sign.

"Leave it to me. Your beachfront house, right?"

Zun nodded.

"Just shoot me temporary access and I'll get everything squared away."

"Done. Thanks Auri, you're awesome!" With another peace sign, Auri terminated the connection.

Zun stared at the empty holodisplay, quiet for a long moment. Biting her lip, she placed the call. Lanrete appeared, looking at her with mild surprise. Zun's eyes narrowed as she took in a deep breath.

"That's not the face of a friendly conversation," Lanrete said.

"Neven told me that he was raped. I want to know everything," Zun said. Lanrete sat back in his chair.

"Are you sure this isn't a conversation you want to have with him?"

"It's a conversationn I want to have with you." Zun crossed her arms "It was your decision that put him in harm's way, so I'd like to hear the full briefing from his superior."

Lanrete sighed.

"A'Amaria Schen raped Neven after invading his room while we were staying at her compound."

"You went to visit A'Amaria?" Zun's eyes went wide, her mouth open.

"We needed information, to find you and the others." Lanrete glanced away from her. "I took a calculated risk."

"Was it worth it?" Zun's voice was bitter.

"No." Lanrete locked gazes with Zun. "I am sorry for what happened to your fiance."

"What action is being taken against her?"

"Neven decided not to press any charges."

"And you agreed with that?"

"Look Zun, it's Neven's decision. I am honoring it, and so should you."

Zun let out a huff and terminated the call.

CHAPTER 88 SERAH'ELAX REZ ASHFALEN

Ashnali, Ashna Maiden home system

Serah'Elax sat in her office within the Avatar Wing of High Temple City, scanning through ship reports. As she sat back in her chair, a sigh escaped her lips. Her gaze wandered to the holodisplay functioning as an imitation window to her side. The rhythmic blip of her mobi pulled her attention, and she sent the caller to the holodisplay above her desk.

"Yes?"

"Exemplar, pardon the disturbance." The image of a husky woman with a smudge of dirt across her face bowed her head slightly. "I have the report you asked for." Serah'Elax nodded. "I've been over every inch of Keeper Delira's ship and there was no outside damage that corresponded to the collapse of the ceiling on the bridge." Serah'Elax could see signs of the dissected wreckage behind her. "I haven't been able to find any indication of anything that would have caused it to collapse." Serah'Elax leaned forward in her chair, her thoughts racing.

"File this information in the restricted archive, and do not speak of it to anyone. Understood?"

"Yes, Exemplar."

Serah'Elax terminated the connection, her gaze becoming hard. She glanced back out the window, sitting for a long moment. The image of Avatar Ahtlana suddenly appeared in the holodisplay above her desk.

"Avatar, the fleet is ready to depart," Serah'Elax said.

Ahtlana regarded Serah'Elax for a long moment. "Something is troubling you," she finally stated.

"A theory of mine has just been confirmed."

"Explain."

Serah'Elax stormed through the reintegration facility, several Ashna Maidens looking at her in surprise as the exemplar strode through the throngs of women in varies forms of undress. She stopped directly in front of Bresha, flanked by two priestesses of Ashna.

"I apologize for the intrusion," Serah'Elax stated flatly, "but I must request that we speak in private. Please follow me." Bresha stood holding her towel, completely nude. Without a moment's hesitation, Bresha dropped the towel and started to move. "After you've dressed, of course." The coldness in Serah'Elax's voice lowered the temperature in the room.

"Silly me, I thought it a matter of immediate import to prompt such a direct visit from you, Exemplar." Bresha shrugged. "I feel no shame with my nakedness among my sisters." A few of the Maidens in the immediate area smiled, brief whispers exchanged.

"I insist." Serah'Elax never broke her gaze with Bresha as the keeper casually pulled on her refreshed uniform. Within a few minutes, Bresha finished, and they walked a short distance from the facility. Serah'Elax then motioned for the priestesses to stay and for Bresha to walk with her.

"I take it this isn't just for a nice leisurely chat?" Bresha asked. It took Serah'Elax a great deal of restraint to not punch the smirk from her face right then and there.

"You killed Delira." Serah'Elax stopped in her tracks. "You then used the chaos of the battle to take command of the ship." Her words were not accusatory, rather a statement of fact. "Then, having gained a sense of credibility from the battle, you were cursorily promoted. With your newfound rank and authority, you decided to take full advantage of it and cut all loose ends. Those loose ends of course being the enemy fleet that you were in some type of partnership with."

Serah'Elax glared at Bresha. "I'm assuming you employed some similar tactic with the Alliance until they discovered your treachery and attempted to arrest you." Serah'Elax broke eye contact and took a step away from Bresha, her gaze going to the sky. "That's when you escaped on a Huzien shuttle and made your way to Ashna Maiden space, where you killed the entire crew of the *Juyunerga,* and I can only assume rendezvoused with the enemy fleet to devise your new plan."

Bresha's eyes flickered dangerously.

"This is . . . a very elaborate story that you've dreamed up, Exemplar. Although, I must admit, it sounds very convincing." Bresha feigned shock. "I must wonder how I came to become the center of it. Surely jealousy isn't playing a part in your accusations? Many tell me that you yourself had a rather expedient rise in rank due to a series of unexpected and unforeseen events." Bresha tapped her chin. "If I were examining your rise through the lens of treachery, I could most likely paint a similar picture of collusion with the enemies of the goddess." Bresha looked skeptically at Serah'Elax. "Although I am surprised why you believe I had something to do with the crew of the . . . what was the name of it again?"

"The *Juyunerga.*"

"Yes, the *Juyunerga.*"

"It was discovered near the battle site with the enemy fleet, remnants of it anyway. Enough to piece together the gruesome slaughter of the crew before the ship was destroyed." Bresha's eyes flickered again, but her face remained neutral. Serah'Elax subconsciously moved her hand closer to her sidearm.

"Before the *Juyunerga* went radio silent, it reported discovering a Huzien Alliance shuttle with a Maiden onboard. Of course, when we attempted to review the SI database on the ship, all historical data had been purged."

"You appear to know a lot about this scenario. One could almost make the leap to say that you had a direct hand in it," Bresha countered. "Is this some attempt of yours to cover up some mistake you've made in your own plans? Is that why you seek to implicate me, Exemplar?"

Serah'Elax took a step back, her eyes wide.

"How dare you . . ."

"How dare you, Exemplar? I intend to issue a complaint with the council."

Serah'Elax narrowed her eyes at Bresha. "I don't know what game you're playing, witch. But I will stop you."

"Am I free to return to my duties, Exemplar?"

Serah'Elax scoffed at Bresha and walked away from her without another word, motioning to the priestesses. Bresha's eyes narrowed as she watched Serah'Elax, venom in her gaze.

Serah'Elax sighed as she closed the door to her quarters. The standard issue room had few personal effects, though her Blades of the Goddess were neatly hung on a nearby wall. She came to a stop in front of the weapons and touched one of the blades longingly.

Shaking her head, she began to undress, her uniform coming off with practiced ease as she threw it onto her bed. A skintight pair of panties clung to her hips, and her top was bare. Serah'Elax's body was well toned, her breasts modest but well formed. *Ga'hei* marks littered her body, her Das'Vin heritage on full display with the elevated light pink marks accentuated by flecks of silver over her light brown skin tone.

A shifting of the air caused Serah'Elax to tense up. She heard no sounds, but casually turned around and scanned her room. Letting out a slow breath, time seemed to slow down as her focus peaked. She felt the attack before she saw it as the jagged blade appeared out of thin air, coming right toward her neck. Dropping down, she kicked away from the wall and began to sprint toward her Blades of the Goddess.

Before she could reach them, she dropped to the floor again as a dagger thudded into the wall right where her head had been. Serah'Elax kicked a table over to use as a shield, then rushed to the wall that held her blades. Upon grabbing them, the weapons latched onto her wrists as their power cores came alive like hunters seeking their prey.

She scanned the area behind her; nothing was visible. Crouched low, the Das'Vin warrior fell back on her instincts, all conscious thought vanishing as she became the hunter. Stalking back the way she had come, Serah'Elax quickly spun to her side and lashed out with her blade. A yelp of pain confirmed her strike, and the creature appeared briefly, long enough for Serah'Elax to make out the horrid-looking abomination.

Holding back her disgust, Serah'Elax pursued the fiend with a vengeance. The monster faded from view and then came back into focus as it brought up its jagged blade to block a strike from the exemplar. Serah'Elax became a whirlwind of fury as she pressed the assault, her semi-nude body a blur.

As her blades drank the creature's blood once more, it fell back and faded from view again. Serah'Elax lunged, sinking both her blades deep into the creature's chest. She continued forward, impaling it into the wall of her quarters as its blood spray coated her bare shoulders and chest. Quickly pulling the blades out, she thrust forward again, impaling the creature in different places. She repeated the action four times until the creature ceased moving.

With a yell of frustration, Serah'Elax released her blades, leaving the monster hanging on her wall. She was covered head to toe with its glowing silver blood. In the next moment, she rushed back into her bedroom, grabbed her uniform off the bed, and pulled it on over the creature's gore before storming out of her quarters.

"These are serious allegations you've raised, Exemplar," Ashna Mother Ce Nu Yo Kl said. The dark red Eeriteen sat back in her chair, her long dark red spines seeming to bristle.

"You have all received the report conducted after the events on the *Agehentali* that resulted in the death of Keeper Delira and a priestess of Ashna," Serah'Elax said. "I also have the report from the *Juyunerga* highlighting the recovery of an 'Ashna Maiden' on a Huzien Alliance shuttle before their subsequent massacre. A situation that serves as a plausible backdrop for Bresha's arrival in our space."

Serah'Elax paused as her gaze met Mother Halle Tentle's. The look of sadness on her face caught the exemplar off guard. "I . . . also have the corpse of an Enesmic creature sent after me pinned to the wall in my room after a tense conversation I had with Bresha earlier today. I believe that all of this proof is enough to implicate Bresha Vecen and prompt her removal from active duty with a full investigation launched into these claims." There was a long silence in the council room. The emergency session had been called at the request of Avatar Ahtlana, who stood behind Serah'Elax. Bresha stood off to the side, flanked by four high priestesses of Ashna.

"We have reviewed the information you provided and the report you indicated regarding the events that led to the death of Keeper Delira and Priestess Uyilo. However, it was amended by the drafter to highlight new evidence that corresponded to damage sustained in the battle." Mother Alenet replied.

"Impossible," Serah'Elax said. "It must have been tampered with, we'll need to—"

"We've interviewed the Maiden who filed the report and she certified that the contents are correct." Serah'Elax stood, speechless. She thought back to her conversation with Bresha, realizing that she had exposed her hand too soon.

"Keeper Bresha, do you have anything to say in your defense?" Ce Nu Yo Kl said.

"Dearest Mothers, I am appalled by these charges. I am not sure what offense I have committed against Exemplar Serah'Elax, but I truly apologize for the misdeed." Bresha turned to Serah'Elax and performed a deep bow. Slowly rising, her gaze met the exemplar's. The sight of something unnatural, something hidden, caused Serah'Elax to cringe.

Turning to the Ashna Mothers, Bresha stepped forward. "I must say, it is horrible that one of our order was attacked in her own home. To think that these agents of evil, these monstrous creatures, are free to come and go as they please in our world is alarming." Bresha paused. "Although, I must wonder why of all the high-ranking Maidens in our capital, that one would seek to attack the exemplar."

"Because you sent it after me!" Serah'Elax shouted.

"Exemplar, please," Ce Nu Yo Kl countered. "Keeper Bresha has the floor."

"Thank you, Mother Ce Nu Yo Kl," Bresha said. The inflections on the Eeriteen's name were perfect, prompting a polite nod from the Mother. "As I was saying, I believe there may be a more plausible reason for the attempt on the exemplar's life." Bresha paused. "I believe she was in collusion with the enemy fleet that we destroyed, and this attack was an attempt at vengeance for her failure to hand the Maiden fleets over to our enemy."

"Exemplar Serah'Elax has been a member of the Ashna Maidens from childhood," Mother Halle said. "She is a highly decorated

warrior with a track record that far surpasses your own. She has justification to bring accusations against you, Keeper, as your origins
are shrouded in mystery and your intentions still not fully clear to
those here."

"I am sure you know my intentions well, Mother Halle," Bresha said. Serah'Elax noticed Mother Halle's piercing white gaze focused beyond Bresha Vecen, as if some unseen figure were standing
right behind her. Serah'Elax shuddered, although she didn't quite
understand why.

"Is that a threat?" Serah'Elax stepped toward Bresha.

"Civility, please." Mother Alenet motioned for silence. "We
will deliberate on the charges brought against Keeper Bresha and
then pass our judgement."

All five of the Ashna Mothers got up and walked out of the
back of the room, the deliberation door closing behind them. Serah'Elax turned to Avatar Ahtlana. The avatar wore a mask of concern, her gaze hanging on Bresha for a long moment before coming to rest on Serah'Elax. The exemplar could see the doubt in her
eyes. A short while later, the deliberation door opened once more as
the Ashna Mothers filed out. Mother Halle was the last to leave the
chamber, a look of defeat on her face. The sight caused Serah'Elax's
heart to drop.

"We have come to a decision," Mother Ce Nu Yo Kl said.
"There is not enough evidence to bring charges against Keeper Bresha Vecen. As such, she will be free to return to duty until such a time
comes that more evidence is brought before this council to determine her unfit and a threat to the Ashna Maidens." Serah'Elax turned
and stormed out of the council room without another word, glancing back at Mother Halle with confusion. Mother Halle watched Serah'Elax go, then returned her gaze to Bresha. Bresha smiled.

Directly after the hearing, Serah'Elax located Bresha and advanced on her with a scowl. They were in the courtyard of the Avatar
Wing of High Temple City. After turning to face the exemplar, Bresha saluted her.

"What must I do to gain your favor, Exemplar?" Bresha said.

"You will never gain my favor. I know that it was you who sent that assassin after me, and I know that you have some plan in motion that will hurt the Ashna Maidens."

"I don't think that word means what you think that word means." Bresha smirked. "As the Ashna Mothers have indicated, your bold claims come with no proof, so you don't *know* anything. Why do you mistrust me so?"

"I have stared in the face of evil. I have fought it with every fiber of my being, and I can see it whenever it rears its ugly head."

Bresha smirked at Serah'Elax and performed a bow as she said, "Well then, I guess the pieces are in motion." She blew a kiss at Serah'Elax. "You need a good *vusg*—that'd work out some of your tension."

Serah'Elax scowled at Bresha and stormed away. Bresha smiled.

Later that night, Serah'Elax took the meglift to the top floor of the High Temple of Ashna. She had to see Mother Halle. The whole situation was spiraling out of control, with Bresha gaining allies by the minute. She stepped out of the meglift and froze. The entryway was bare, and she searched the area for any signs of the high priestesses that would have normally been stationed there.

Moving to the wall, she inched forward silently, her ears straining for any sounds. When she approached the entrance to the prayer room waiting area, the scent of copper hit her nostrils. Her instincts kicked in and she crouched low, balling her fists, then peeked around the bend. She was greeted by the remains of the high priestesses, their bodies flayed. Blood and gore covered the area. She rushed to the side of the first high priestess.

Treachery. The door separating the waiting room from the rooms of the Ashna Mothers was open. Fear gripped Serah'Elax as that sudden revelation hit her. She immediately headed in the direction of Mother Halle's room. Upon bursting through the door, she found Mother Halle butchered in the middle of the room. Even in death, Mother Halle was confident, her face resolute.

Serah'Elax dropped to her knees in front of the fallen Ashna Mother as a tear rolled down her cheek. She glanced around the room, her thoughts clouded, her mind racing. Then she saw them; the Blades of the Goddess resting on a nearby table. They were covered in blood, Halle's blood. A feeling of dread overwhelmed Serah'Elax as she slowly got up and approached the weapons.

"No." Serah'Elax shook her head. "No, it can't be." She backed away from the blades, her blades. Sounds of shouting came from outside of the room as Serah'Elax turned to see a group of armed Maiden protectors charging into the area. Before she could react, they swarmed the room and slammed her to the ground.

A week went by as the atmosphere in the capital shifted. Never in the history of the Ashna Maidens had an Ashna Mother been assassinated on Ashna Maiden soil. A month of mourning had been declared with most official activities by the order suspended.

Serah'Elax sat staring at the wall of the Ashna Maiden holding facility. It was a solid white, the environment sterile. She had been stripped of her rank and was scheduled to be executed in short order. As shudders began to shake her body, she rested her head in her hands. Everything had been stolen from her. Being an Ashna Maiden was the only thing she had ever known. Serah'Elax stood up and yelled, her roar of rage slowly turning into a cry as she collapsed to her knees. Bresha had outplayed her. Oh, how she wanted to rip out her throat!

"Ashna, why have you forsaken me!" Serah'Elax cried as she slowly dropped to the floor, her body coming to rest against the cold hard ground. She would die a traitor, the worst death an Ashna Maiden could suffer. She lay there for a long moment, eventually curling up into a fetal position. The deafening silence caused the ringing to rise to a crescendo in her ears until she lost consciousness.

The sound of the security door down the hall jolted Serah'Elax awake. She picked up the sounds of footsteps approaching her location, the pace picking up as they got closer. Serah'Elax remained on the floor, no will left in her body to do anything else. The footsteps stopped right outside her cell. A loud beep sounded, the locking mechanism shifted, and then her cell door slid open.

Serah'Elax lifted her gaze to the entrance. A high priestess stood with a scion, both with their weapons in their hands.

The high priestess stepped forward. "Sister, we've come to free you. Come quickly, we haven't much time." Serah'Elax stared at them, their words not registering. "Come quickly!" The scion came into the cell and helped Serah'Elax to her feet.

"I don't understand," Serah'Elax said.

"We have no time to explain here; we must move," the scion said. She gripped Serah'Elax by the arm and led her out of the cell.

"This way," the high priestess called. The three of them quickly moved down the corridor and into a meglift. As they exited the meglift, another scion waved them on. A group of Ashna Maidens were knocked out at her feet, none of the wounds fatal.

The group sprinted through the main processing area and out of the building toward a small troop transport waiting for them a short distance away. After sprinting across the open expanse, the Maidens filed into the vehicle. Another high priestess was waiting for them in the transport.

"Why?" Serah'Elax said.

"I am High Priestess Wuyjen Xecha and I served as Mother Halle's right hand. We know you did not kill her," Wuyjen said. "She warned us that she would be killed and that you would be framed for her murder. She also told us to ensure that you got off-world and to the planet Rugtora as soon as possible."

"Rugtora?" Serah'Elax gasped. "That doesn't make any sense."

"Those were her orders," one of the scions countered. Serah'Elax sat quietly for a moment, her gaze going to each woman risking their lives to help her. Her thoughts then went to Mother Halle, who had strategically placed allies for her in her time of need. She nodded and shed a tear for the fallen Ashna Mother.

"Rugtora it is then."

"You'll also be needing these." The other scion lifted a set of objects concealed under a heavy covering. Serah'Elax noticed the outline of the objects, and her stomach churned. "We recovered your blades before they were destroyed."

"Those have bathed in the blood of Mother Halle." Serah'Elax shook her head. "I . . . I cannot wield them. Is there another pair, an unbonded pair, that I can take with me?"

"Mother Halle was adamant that you take *your* Blades of the Goddess," Wuyjen interjected. "They have been blessed by Ashna and carry the essence of Mother Halle in them now." Serah'Elax swallowed hard as her gaze hung on the weapons for a long moment, her body frozen. Taking in a deep breath, Serah'Elax willed herself to act. Reluctantly, she took the covered Blades of the Goddess from the scion, her eyes closing in a solemn prayer to Ashna.

We have cataloged Tuzen lifespans to be approximately 1,021 years. Mating with Tuzens has been successful, and they are now a Das'Vin compatible species.

−FROM "TUZEN OBSERVATIONS"
DAS'VIN ARCHIVES

CHAPTER 89 LANRETE

Onwa, Thae, Huzien home system

Zun and Neven stood in front of Cislot in elaborate Huzien wedding garb. The designs were a mix of blues and golds, loose fitting and somewhat tribal in appearance. Waves crashed against the sandy beach with the setting sun as a backdrop. String lights had been set up around the area, providing a dim illumination that accented the gold colors in their clothing.

Cislot had agreed to the impromptu request by Auri to officiate the wedding. She wore her ceremonial garb, the elaborate designs also somewhat tribal with bold colors that contrasted sharply. She looked from Neven to Zun and then back to Neven.

"It takes a wedding for us to finally meet," Cislot said. She stole a glance at Lanrete, who avoided her gaze with a smile. He was standing farther back with the rest of those in attendance. They had made the customary circle around the couple, signifying the completeness of their relationship and the journey to become one flesh. All the Founder's Elites were there, along with Charlene Yentu & her husband, Kechu Fen, Aru Ghaian, Neven's parents, and Zun's mother.

"While I look forward to getting to know you better, today is not about me," Cislot continued, "today is about the two of you. This hour we celebrate the joining of two souls, Zun Shan and Neven Kenk. In a galaxy that has been dealing with so much pain as of late, moments like the one today where we can celebrate true joy are what keep us all going in the hardest of times." Cislot motioned toward Zun.

"Neven, I bind myself to you in heart and mind." Zun raised a necklace of interwoven beads and placed it over Neven's head and onto his shoulders. It had a unique design, specially made for their ceremony. Cislot motioned toward Neven.

"Zun, I bind myself to you in heart and mind." Neven smiled at Zun and seemed to get lost in her eyes for a moment. Coming back to reality, Neven performed the same action with a matching necklace. The look on Zun's face caused Neven to forget to breathe, though he eventually sucked in a quick breath.

"With the authority of the Huzien government and in the eyes of the Maker, I pronounce you *eifi* and *nusba*." Cislot took a step back as Zun stepped in and kissed Neven. His arms went around her body and he pulled her closer, the two sharing in their first kiss as a married couple. Cheers and claps went up from the small gathering around the two.

Lanrete walked over to Cislot as Neven and Zun broke in their embrace and stepped toward the waves to enjoy the last of the sunset. The rest of the group followed behind the newlyweds, singing a low Huzien wedding song.

"I hear I'll need to pull out my own officiating robes sometime in the near future," Lanrete said. Cislot continued to watch the new married couple.

"It can wait until you're back from safeguarding our empire," Cislot said.

"I'm happy for you."

Cislot glanced up at the sky, her arms crossing as she took in a deep breath. "Sometimes it's important to have someone there for you. A friend helped me see that again." She locked gazes with Lanrete.

"Yes . . . well." Lanrete's voice trailed off as he caught sight of A'Amaria casually walking across the sandy shores of the beach. She was barefoot and had a pair of sandals in one hand with an oversized bottle of expensive-looking wine in the other, and she was heading straight toward him.

"Speak of the devil."

"Incarnate." Lanrete turned and began walking toward A'Amaria. Cislot stayed where she was, her gaze stuck on the woman, her expression dispassionate.

"How dare you show your face here; haven't you done enough damage?"

"Hello to you too, handsome," A'Amaria said. She wore a casual sundress, the clothing very thin, almost translucent. Lanrete could just make out that she had nothing on underneath it.

"Why are you here?" Lanrete's tone was forceful, almost demanding.

"I've come to celebrate the new couple; I'm assuming my invitation got lost in the mail."

"You weren't invited, and you aren't invited. Leave. Now."

A'Amaria sighed as she slowly squatted down and set the bottle of wine in the sand. Standing back up, she locked gazes with Lanrete.

"Very well, but I have some information that I'd like to share with you. Consider it bought and paid for. Neven has a considerable amount of credit with me that he's free to use whenever he'd like, very few strings attached." A'Amaria winked as Lanrete's glare remained unchanged.

"The Ashna Maidens encountered the remnants of Sagren's fleets about a week ago and wiped them out. Word on the grapevine is that they had some inside help. I don't have more on that yet, but I do have something that I believe is important to you. Het Wrast Aht has amassed on their borders in fear that the show of Maiden force will continue through into their space in a rallying assault on their controlled worlds. As such, their planetary stronghold will be loosely guarded." A'Amaria sent a swath of information to Lanrete's mobi. "Those are the current locations of all high-ranking Het Wrast Aht personnel along with their schedules. The information will be continuously updated as I receive it."

"This information has always carried an exorbitant price." Lanrete narrowed his eyes at A'Amaria. "And you're just turning it all over to the Huzien Empire."

"Like I said, Neven has considerable credit with me."

"This will not make amends for your actions."

"Whatever," A'Amaria scoffed. "Anyway, I'll take my leave." A'Amaria flashed a glance in Neven's direction with a mischievous look in her eye and a smirk on her face. Lanrete was happy that the young man had not noticed her, too engulfed with his bride and the conversations with his friends. Without another word, A'Amaria turned and left the beach.

"She did something horrible to Neven, didn't she?" Cislot asked from behind Lanrete. He turned around to see her standing close enough to have overheard the conversation. She slowly walked over and picked up the bottle of wine, grinning at the label.

"Yes." Lanrete sighed. "I'm happy that this all worked out." Lanrete glanced toward Zun and Neven.

"Health and happiness," Cislot said.

Lanrete looked out over the ocean.

"The HIN confirmed her information?" Cislot asked. The founder was leaning against the wall in Zun's guest house, a glass of wine in her hand. Lanrete sat in a chair near a holographic representation of Ecnics.

"Yes," Lanrete said. "It also matches up with the final destination of Dexter's beacon." Lanrete clenched his fist. "We could land a decisive blow against Het Wrast Aht and take out their entire leadership team in one fell swoop."

"I don't understand why you and the Founder's Elites would need to go there," Ecnics countered. "Isn't that what the Sentinels are for?"

"This is a military mission," Lanrete said. "Taking out Het Wrast Aht leadership is the first step. The next step is a full-out assault by the Huzien fleets on their forces. It has to happen quickly, before they have time to re-establish a power structure." Lanrete turned to Cislot. "The elimination of Het Wrast Aht leadership will reduce the size of the force needed to carry out the attack."

"What of the Ashna Maidens?" Cislot said. "What if they do indeed intend to attack Het Wrast Aht? What will they do when they encounter our fleets there instead?"

"Hopefully join us in Het Wrast Aht's elimination," Lanrete said.

Cislot looked to Ecnics, and the two exchanged glances.

"Are we truly prepared to wage war with the pirate bands in the Outer Rim?" Cislot said. "There is no turning back from this."

"They launched the first strike," Lanrete countered. "Het Wrast Aht must fall, of that I will give no quarter."

"It would appear then that the decision on this matter has already been made," Cislot said. "Please don't get our new favorite couple killed."

Lanrete grinned.

"Give Neven my regards, I apologize for not attending, more pressing matters . . ." Ecnics trailed off. Lanrete and Cislot exchange glances. "But please do keep Neven alive—would be greatly appreciated. I must cut our meeting short; it sounds like this matter is decided."

"One more thing while I have all of you here," Cislot interjected. The tone in her voice caused both Ecnics and Lanrete to instantly focus on her as she downed the remainder of her wine glass. "I intend to call a vote for the expulsion of the Tuzen Empire from the Huzien Alliance this week." Lanrete narrowed his eyes as Ecnics sighed. "Tirivus has continued his defiance of Alliance statutes." A barrage of documented instances with cross-references to Alliance policy displayed across Lanrete's and Ecnics's micro-displays.

"You believe this to be the best course of action?" Lanrete asked.

"I do," Cislot replied.

"It was a mistake to bring them into the Alliance in the first place," Ecnics said. "Those *reka* aren't worth the effort."

"Your racism is showing," Lanrete said, glancing at Ecnics.

"Please, I have many brilliant Tuzens in my employ that I think very highly of." Ecnics sighed. "Tirivus and his ilk are savages, relics of a time long past." He glanced at Cislot. "Do what you must. Are we done?"

Cislot glanced to Lanrete.

"I trust your judgement. If you believe this to be the best course of action, you have my full support," Lanrete said.

Cislot nodded. "We are done. Thank you both for your support in this matter."

Ecnics terminated his connection.

"What do you figure he's working on?" Lanrete said.

"It's best to not think about such things." Cislot laughed. The two stood in silence for a short moment, Cislot subconsciously rubbing her arm. Lanrete caught the uncharacteristic action.

"You're concerned Tirivus will retaliate?"

"Tirivus is a wild card." Cislot moved to the window overlooking the beach, the moonlight reflecting off the waves. "I do not believe we will come out of this situation unscathed."

"I could order his assassination." Lanrete grinned.

"You and I both know he's too well-protected and paranoid to ever pull that off." Cislot smirked. "Plus, I don't think you'd task someone who wasn't yourself with that challenge, and you're needed in the Outer Rim."

"True." Lanrete sighed. "A problem for another day, I suppose."

"There is never a shortage of them."

Lanrete moved to stand next to Erb. "I've had time to think over your request."

The Ken'Tar monk was sitting on the sand with his legs folded, his hands resting on his legs with his palms upward.

"Hmmm?" Erb responded, his eyes still closed.

"I have one question to ask of you before I make my final decision." Lanrete sat down next to Erb. "How does joining my team fit in with your life quest?"

Erb laughed and opened his eyes. "You are indeed resourceful, Founder Lanrete. I have been to over a hundred worlds in my lifetime, and I have yet to find the one that I sense will be my final resting place. Once I find that world, I will build a temple there, complete my epic tale, and die, becoming one with the Enesmic that flows across those lands." Erb smiled. "I sense that my path must join with yours for a time. The Enesmic flows with you and I must heed its call. Only then will I finally discover that which I seek."

Lanrete kept his gaze out over the ocean as the two sat in silence for a long moment. Erb closed his eyes, his breath coming and going in a steady flow.

"Who am I to defy the will of the Enesmic?" Lanrete laughed. "Very well, Erbubuc Tamn, I welcome you into the Founder's Elite." Lanrete jumped to his feet, the action effortless.

"The Enesmic smiles on me this day," Erb said. "Thank you, great founder of the Huzien Empire."

"Call me Lan." Lanrete patted Erb on the shoulder.

Erb nodded.

"Thank you, Lan."

CHAPTER 90 ZUN SHAN

Onwa, Thae, Huzien home system

Neven pressed Zun up against the wall, their lips intertwined as they pulled off each other's clothes. The master bedroom in Zun's beachfront mansion was covered in roses, the room candlelit with a sweet fragrance in the air that reminded Zun of cinnamon. She pushed Neven onto the bed, her lace panties coming off as she straddled him. Neven's gaze lingered on her body, taking all of her in before finally settling on her breasts. She reflexively pushed out her chest as she ate up his gaze, the intensity of it turning her on even more. Neven put his hands on her hips, and a feeling of electricity shot through her body. Low music began to play, the mood fully set.

"Mmmm, I've been waiting for this moment," Zun said.

"Me too." Neven smiled. His hands moved up her sides to her now exposed breasts as he began to gently caress her, prompting a moan from Zun. She rested there for a long moment, silently watching Neven as he enjoyed her body, then pushed herself up and slowly turned around, her hand moving to stroke his member.

With a promising glance, Zun took him full into her mouth. He gasped, and his eyes focused on her curvaceous butt full in his vision. Her subtle movements became rhythmic, focused, sensual. She brought him to the border of ecstasy and then pulled back. Neven groaned.

"Soon," Zun promised, "but first . . ." Zun slowly lay down onto the bed, prompting Neven to visit her in kind. Hesitating for only a moment, Neven treated her with his tongue. Zun gasped; it had been so long. Her eyes rolled back as she arched her back, her heart pounding in her chest. She slapped the bed multiple times, an orgasm washing over her as she became hypersensitive. Her hands went to Neven's head and she pulled him up.

Neven hesitated, hovering between Zun's legs. Without a second thought, Zun grabbed hold of his member and guided him in. She relished the feeling of him fully inside her for the first time. Seeing the excitement course through him, she half closed her eyes, driving him wild as he began to thrust. Wrapping her legs around him, their breathing synced, the two becoming one. Zun could feel the second orgasm coming as she pulled Neven close to her body, holding him tight as he wrapped his arm around the back of her neck, the two locking eyes. That moment of pure ecstasy took them both, Neven pulsing inside of her as Zun's body trembled.

The two lay there for a long moment, Zun slowly rubbing Neven's back as they listened to each other breathe. She reflected on the events of the day and for the first time since Yuvan's death, Zun was truly happy.

Foundra Ascension orbiting Thae, Huzien home system

Neven and Zun lay intertwined in their bed aboard the *Foundra Ascension*, the sweat on their bodies staining the sheets. Zun's gaze hung out the window, the sight of Thae against the backdrop of space hinting at untold wonder.

Neven, his face resting between her breasts, had begun to fall asleep. Zun took it all in, her life complete once more. She slowly caressed her *nusba's* back as he rested on top of her. He had not moved very far since their last act of passion.

Bringing up a calendar in her micro-display, Zun stared at her personal notifications. Her attention hung on the fertility indicator highlighted from the past few days. She slowly turned her gaze to Neven. He was fully asleep now, his breath coming rhythmically. She let out a sigh of contentment and smiled.

CHAPTER 91 ELLIPSE

Foundra Ascension orbiting Thae, Huzien home system

E llipse raised her hands triumphantly as the last pieces of the prototype she had been working on were completed. The task was given to her by Neven before he disappeared into Zun's quarters to continue the consummation of their marriage. Ellipse had remained in her android shell, her connection to Neven persisting across most of the ship. She had intentionally kept herself out of Neven's thoughts, singularly focused on the task at hand. For some reason, the thought of being intimately linked with Neven while he was being intimate with Zun made her uncomfortable. She wasn't sure why that bothered her—it shouldn't have bothered her—but it did.

After initiating the startup sequence, Ellipse turned to regard the test area. The soft hum of the suplight storage system, or S3, filled Neven's lab. A set of lights began to flash, indicating the system was charged and ready for deployment. Rubbing her hands together, Ellipse launched the go sequence and the system flared to life. The space before Ellipse filled with a flash of light that quickly subsided. In its place, where there had been only empty space before, one of

Neven's power armors now stood in the center of the room, the system ready for use with its back open for easy entry.

Ellipse clapped her hands and jumped up and down. She had done it; she had built the prototype all by herself, and it worked! Neven would be so proud. She smiled at that thought, and as she did caught a reflection of her android body in a nearby mirrored surface. She gazed at it for a long moment, then removed all her clothing to visually inspect every aspect of herself.

Eventually, she moved back to the design station and stared at the holodisplay before bringing up a schematic of her android shell. She rotated the shell, aspects of it expanding out as she examined her inner workings. Multiple holodisplays came up around her as they began frantically flipping through thousands of queries to the Gnet, pulling down incredible amounts of data. Ellipse sat back and absorbed it all, her golden gaze distant.

CHAPTER 92 MARCUS HENSON

Foundra Ascension orbiting Thae, Huzien home system

"You're sure you don't want a regular room?" Auri rubbed the back of her neck as she stood next to Erb. The Ken'Tar was settling into a makeshift camp he had set up on the aeroponics deck, the large forest creating an illusion of nature aboard the Foundra Ascension.

"This is perfect, thank you," Erb said. Marcus walked up to the pair, and Auri gave him a helpless look.

"He plans to live *here*," Auri whispered. Marcus could hear the frustration in her voice as he smiled and glanced at Erb.

"As good a place as any if I don't say so myself," Marcus said. Auri glared at him and threw up her hands before sighing and storming off. "Settling in well, I see."

Erb smiled at Marcus and finished the last touches of his camp. It looked strikingly like the one Marcus had seen when he first encountered Erb.

"The reproduction is impressive," Erb said. "I can see the subtle differences, the mark of man where nature should be, the careful precision with which this area has been constructed." Erb shook his head, a slight chuckle accompanying the action. "But it will have to do." Erb moved to the ground and crossed his legs, then lifted his hands into the signature gesture Marcus had become familiar with. Marcus watched as the monk dropped into his meditative state.

"Of course, the Enesmic is everywhere," Erb said with a smile.

"Could you, uh"—Marcus dropped to the ground next to Erb—"teach me how to do that whole meditation thing you do?"

"My friend!" Erb opened his eyes and turned to regard Marcus. "It would be an honor."

CHAPTER 93 LANRETE

Foundra Ascension orbiting Rugtora, Outer Rim

"We've entered orbit around Rugtora," Auri broadcast to the ship as they dropped out of suplight, their cloaking field in full effect.

"This is the home of Het Wrast Aht?" Neven stood on the bridge next to Zun. Every member of the Founder's Elite was present, including their newest addition, Erb.

"It's a beautiful world." Erb stood with one set of arms folded behind his back, the other set resting in front of him with his fingers interlaced. "Tropical, peaceful."

"Until you get to the surface and see the hell that exists down there," Tashanira said.

"Perspective is a powerful thing."

"*Vusging* right it is," Dexter interjected. "They've got a small number of ships stationed in orbit, far fewer than the normal fleet presence based off our intel. They shouldn't pose any serious threat to us."

"Alright, team." Lanrete moved out of his command chair. "This mission is strictly reconnaissance; we still have some time before the Huzien fleet is within support range. Once they arrive, we'll eliminate the leadership and launch a full-scale assault in the ensuing chaos." Lanrete met the gaze of every Founder's Elite as he spoke. "Let's move out."

"Shuttle two is prepped and ready for departure," Auri chimed in.

"Auri, the bridge is yours." Lanrete moved to exit the bridge, the rest of the Founder's Elites in tow. Arriving on the shuttle bay, the team went to work preparing for departure.

"I miss Claire," Marcus lamented. Ellipse had just finished helping him into an exoskeleton that she had constructed at the request of Neven. It was similar in design to the one Neven wore, except much larger to support Marcus's frame.

"We could always rebuild her," Neven countered from where he stood wearing his own exoskeleton.

"No." Marcus shook his head. "Claire is dead; there will never be another Claire." He glanced at Neven. "And I'm too old to break in a new set of gear."

"Too old?" Jessica balked. "Since when are you too old for anything?" Marcus grinned at her, then looked to Erb, who nodded solemnly.

"Is the *vusging* android coming with us?" Dexter locked gazes with Lanrete.

"The android has a name," Ellipse snapped back.

Dexter ignored her.

"No." Lanrete glanced at Ellipse. "Given the nature of the mission, and the fact that you haven't had . . . formal training, I think it best for you to sit this one out, at least in android form."

"No one else finds it creepy that Neven has a fully sentient android?" Tashanira said. The whole team looked at the Uri. "Just me?"

"Thanks, Tashanira." Neven sighed.

"Anytime."

"A debate for another time," Zun interjected.

"What's the debate? It's *vusging* illegal," Jenshi countered.

"Since when did you start caring about what was legal?" Jessica said. Jenshi flashed her an annoyed glare.

"Children, play nice," Marcus said.

Jessica sighed and switched topics. "We'll need to lay low. No power armors, or any form of Huzien military identifiers."

"Way ahead of you," Neven tapped his back, and all traces of his exoskeleton were concealed under his clothing. "Worst-case scenario, Ellipse finished the S3 a few days ago. We'll be able to call in heavy artillery within seconds."

"The what?" Tashanira said.

"The suplight storage system." Neven sent over a series of product demo vids to the rest of the team.

"That android does good work!" Tashanira said.

"I second that," Dexter chimed in.

Was there ever any doubt? Ellipse mentally said to Neven, and he held back a smirk.

"Not sure how you got used to this thing so quick." Marcus was running through a few quick drills with his exoskeleton.

"Did you come up with a bedroom version?" Tashanira asked. "Although I guess Zun would have to wear one as well."

Neven blushed.

"We're good without one, thanks," Zun said. The team laughed as they continued to ready themselves for departure. Lanrete's gaze met Erb's.

"Have you ever been to the Outer Rim?" Lanrete said.

"Once, about a decade ago," Erb said. "I came to add a chapter to my tale about the life of those unfortunate enough to find themselves out here."

"Is it really that bad?" Jessica said.

"*Vusging* worse," Jenshi interjected. "The pirates out here are a threat. I'm genuinely surprised the empire hasn't decided to take action until now." His gaze met Lanrete's. "Many Huzien citizens near the Outer Rim have lost loved ones to these *ciths*."

"It wasn't a priority before," Lanrete said.

"It didn't directly affect those of *vusging* importance before, you mean," Jenshi countered.

"I guess it's a good thing it's a priority now," Tashanira spoke up. A deep silence settled over the team.

"I'm sorry it has taken until now to deal with the threat the pirates pose to Huzien space. I understand your feelings on this topic, and I acknowledge our shortcomings in protecting citizens near the Outer Rim."

"My father died a long time ago, Lan," Jenshi said. "I already killed the *ciths* responsible, water under the bridge."

Lanrete could see the momentary pain on Jenshi's face. It was subtle, but still there. It was a crack in an otherwise impeccable emotional armor.

The Founder's Elites descended to the surface, landing in a section of forest recommended by the HIN. The team was being fed constant intel from multiple Sentinels in action on the surface and surrounding space. Lanrete could see the sense of pride radiating from Dexter.

"The nearby city is called Rensmat," Lanrete said. "It's being labeled as the planet's capital. Might be good to get an up-close view."

"We have a window of opportunity to move now," Dexter chimed in. "Conditions are ideal to intermingle with the populace."

"Let's move," Lanrete said.

CHAPTER 94 SERAH'ELAX REZ ASHFALEN

Rensmat, Rugtora, Outer Rim

Serah'Elax wore a hooded cloak that fully concealed her appearance, her Ashna Maiden uniform long since abandoned. She understood that she was attractive by the standards of many species and her appearance on this lawless world would draw unwanted attention and forceful advances. Her Blades of the Goddess were concealed beneath her clothing, but they felt heavier now, as if the soul of Mother Halle clung to them. She felt a strange sense of both comfort and disgust in wielding the weapons.

She was smuggled to the planet two days ago. With the right people paid off to look the other way, her presence had gone undetected. Serah'Elax's final instruction from High Priestess Wuyjen had been to stay in Rensmat and walk the streets daily. No one had explained why or for how long, only that the instructions from Mother Halle had been clear.

A scene in her periphery grabbed her full attention; four men were shoving a mother and her young teenage daughter into an alleyway. A young man, the adult son from the looks of him, was holding his side and coughing up blood. They had left him to die in the street. Her prior walks through the area had told her that the alleyway led nowhere and was infrequently used. Given the nature of Het Wrast Aht and their lax patrols, there would be no repercussions for what her gut told her was about to happen.

"This doesn't concern you," Serah'Elax whispered to herself. She tried to move on and ignore the situation. However, her former life as an Ashna Maiden wouldn't allow her to leave it alone. Silently cursing her oath, she moved to the young man struggling to rise on the ground. Terror filled his eyes, and he sputtered as he tried to breathe through the blood.

"Die assured that I will save your loved ones," Serah'Elax said. His gaze locked onto hers, and his energy seemed to fade as he nodded weakly. Serah'Elax glanced around, then unsheathed her blades. The weapons became an extension of her arms and of her will. She moved into the alley like a cat stalking its prey.

The teenage daughter's shirt had been ripped off; the mother was pushed to the ground. One of the men moved to mount her. The daughter attempted to scream but was punched in the mouth. One of her breasts was exposed, the sight of flesh sending the men into more of a frenzy. Another grabbed hold of her pants and proceeded to forcefully pull them off.

She began to cry.

Blood spray covered the ground and the man farthest back grunted as his eyes rolled back into his head. He slowly dropped to the ground, his head sliding off his torso. Another of the men noticed the blood spray and turned around, dumbfounded. One of the Blades of the Goddess went straight through his face then straight up, splitting his head in two.

The mother, who had obviously caught sight of the scene behind the man straddling her, stopped fighting as her eyes went wide. Assuming she had finally given up, the man grinned and quickly began unbuckling his own pants. The tips of both blades exploded from his chest. Blood spray covered the mother, but she remained deathly still, her gaze unblinking. The man tried to gasp, but his lungs were unresponsive as he stared at the woman under him in confusion. The blades exited his body and blood gurgled up in his throat as he fell off the woman, the life rapidly fading from his eyes.

The final man had realized what was happening around him and had abandoned the teenage girl. He staggered back toward the end of the alleyway, searching desperately for a way out. Serah'Elax stood with her hood back, her gaze icy. She slowly walked toward him, her blades dripping with the blood of his comrades.

"Please have mercy on me!" he whimpered. "It was just a little fun, we weren't going to kill them, I swear!"

"Just like you didn't kill their brother, their son?" Serah'Elax said. Like a cornered rat, the man grabbed a small blade from under his shirt and charged her.

The former exemplar smiled.

He got to within a few feet of Serah'Elax before she side-stepped him, her blades flashing. He managed a few more steps before his torso slid from his legs, his lifeless body collapsing to the ground. Serah'Elax turned to the teenager; the young girl was frozen in terror as she stared at the Blades of the Goddess.

"Are you going to kill us?" she asked. Serah'Elax shook her head, and Serah'Elax's gaze went to the mother, who had started crying.

"Impressive," came a voice from the other end of the alleyway. Serah'Elax spun, her blades in a defensive position. She caught sight of a man with a mane of white hair and light brown skin. His silver eyes were locked onto her own. He stood with a weapon drawn, but the design was foreign to her—maybe Huzien, but she wasn't sure. He wore a concealing cloak, but his hood was pulled back.

"Those weapons are of Ashna Maiden design," he said. Serah'Elax went into a crouch, preparing to pounce. "As much as I would enjoy sparring with you, I don't think it's ideal for us to remain out in the open. Het Wrast Aht patrols may normally turn a blind eye to random murder and rape, but the massacre here is sure to draw attention and require a rather expensive bribe." Serah'Elax remained unmoving, her gaze staying focused on the man even as she caught sight of another cloaked figure behind him, a Huzien blade in their hand as well.

"Who are you?" Serah'Elax called out. "Huziens aren't normally seen out here."

"The same could be said for Das'Vin," the man replied. "My name is Lanrete."

"Lanrete?" Serah'Elax relaxed in her stance as recognition hit her. "Founder of the Huzien Empire?"

"One and the same."

"Why are you here?" Her body tensed.

"Not the time or place." Lanrete glanced back as if receiving a message from someone out of sight. "We have to leave, now." Lanrete motioned toward the mother and daughter. "Will you help me get them to safety?" Serah'Elax glanced back, then finally dropped her stance and nodded.

The Vempiir species is prideful, warlike, ruthless, and considered the fourth most dangerous species in the Twin Galaxies. Their government is classified as a dominion, ruled by the two most powerful families who each elect a representative as co-head of government, always one male and one female.

–FROM "VEMPIIR OBSERVATIONS"
DAS'VIN ARCHIVES

CHAPTER 95 HEGNA HELRIT

Ashnali, Ashna Maiden home system

The absence of Mother Halle hung in the air, the empty seat causing an uneasiness throughout the massive room. The remaining Ashna Mothers were assembled, and they all wore impressive black shrouds, the clothing a symbol of mourning traditionally worn whenever an Ashna Mother passed away. They sat in seats that rose from the center of an elevated platform and were surrounded by the Ashna Council in the avatar briefing chamber. All avatars were in attendance, either holographically or in person. The absence of the avatars that had been killed in the initial battle also still stung like a fresh wound.

"Bresha Vecen," Ce Nu Yo Kl called out, "step forward." Bresha stepped away from the avatars and toward the elevated platform. "As we mourn the loss of Mother Halle, we also honor you for discovering the plot on our lives." Avatar Ahtlana stood off to the side, her gaze downcast. Avatar Hegna stood next to Ahtlana, her gaze fixed on Bresha, her expression neutral.

"Had it not been for your quick efforts," Mother Venice Fawni said, "we would not be here today." A round of applause filled the chamber, all but Hegna and Ahtlana participating.

"As a testament to your continued dedication to the Ashna Maidens, we, today, elevate you to the position of avatar of Ashna," Mother Alenet Dascl said.

"May the goddess shine her light on you today and forever," Mother Ga Po Fe Ul said. Another round of applause and cheers went up throughout the room. Avatar Hegna looked away from Bresha, her fists clenched. She quickly left the ceremony, followed hesitantly by Ahtlana.

They walked for a short time, Hegna beelining to her favorite café, one of the many that littered High Temple City. Without a word, she picked up her waiting order and dropped into the seat of a small two-person table near a window. Ahtlana waited at the counter, her order completed a moment later. She walked over to Hegna's table and sat down in the seat opposite her. Ahtlana stared at her cup, lost in thought. Hegna's gaze was aimed toward the host of Maidens traversing back and forth through the area.

"I can't believe Serah'Elax would have done something like this," Ahtlana said. She shook her head, holding in a shudder.

"Then don't," Hegna stated flatly.

Ahtlana glanced up at her. "You don't believe she is guilty?"

"You do?"

"The evidence is overwhelming, I . . ." Ahtlana sighed and leaned back. "With the prison break, and her fleeing off-world, I don't know what to think. It clearly implicates her and whatever cohorts she had."

"You would have preferred her executed to prove her innocence?" Hegna scoffed.

Ahtlana's eyes narrowed.

"Did you have something to do with her getting off-world?"

Hegna laughed. "Such an act would be a clear form of treason and not something one would freely admit to." She grinned.

"Your sister lives on inside of you, it would seem." Ahtlana shook her head as Hegna laughed again.

"I've had a lot of time to think about my sister," Hegna said. "For all her impetuousness, Luka was a fair judge of character." Hegna locked gazes with Ahtlana, then sat her cup down and stood up. "And she spoke very highly of Serah'Elax. I have no doubt that even now, Serah'Elax is working to safeguard the Ashna Maidens." Hegna paused. "Look at the allies Bresha has amassed to her side in such a short time: Ashna Mothers, councilors, and a host of avatars, among others. All to a woman with a shrouded past and unknown intentions." Hegna's face tightened. "I spoke with Mother Halle shortly before her death, and she made me vow to protect Serah'Elax at all costs." Ahtlana's eyes widened. "And now you see the forces at play," Hegna said, then nodded to Ahtlana as she walked out of the café.

Vempiir have committed atrocities to their own people through mass genocides that have resulted in a species that barely resembles who they once were.

−FROM "VEMPIIR OBSERVATIONS"
DAS'VIN ARCHIVES

CHAPTER 96 SERAH'ELAX REZ ASHFALEN

Foundra Ascension orbiting Rugtora, Outer Rim

S erah'Elax watched Jenshi as he performed another scan of the young man lying on a bed in the medical deck of the Foundra Ascension. The Huzien was impressive to watch, the man a clear master of his craft. The focus with which he worked reminded her of herself when on the battlefield.

"Will he make it?" Uria Hens said as she sat at her son's side, her blond hair matted and dirty. Areathe Hens sat next to her mother, tears in her eyes as she silently watched her brother. Serah'Elax had elected to remain in the medical bay with the traumatized family after being transported from the surface of Rugtora.

"I'm fairly confident that he will make a full recovery," Jenshi said. "Luckily we found him when we did and immediately started treatment. The nanites were able to rebuild the damaged brain tissue from the oxygen deprivation, get his heart started, and regulate his limited blood flow until we could start transfusion." Jenshi looked down at Garen Hens. The young man was steadily breathing on his own now, his bloodstream packed full of the restorative nanites. The stab wound had been fully closed, and now the nanites were cleaning up the last remaining bits of damaged tissue.

"We don't have any money to pay you." Uria averted her gaze from Jenshi.

"I'm not asking for any," Jenshi said. Uria looked to Areathe and nervously rubbed her arm. Areathe met her gaze, then glanced at her brother.

"What do you want from us in return?" Areathe said. "I . . . I'm inexperienced, but it wouldn't be my first—" She began to loosen the clasps of her top.

"Whoa, no. *Vusg* no!" Jenshi's voice deepened. "I don't know what kinds of lives you were forced to live back on that horrible world, but I want nothing from you. Monetarily or otherwise. I'm just happy your son is alive." Jenshi took a step back, then glanced over at Serah'Elax. The former exemplar held back a smile and glanced away from him. Tashanira sat in the far corner of the medical bay watching the whole scene, her expression neutral.

Lanrete entered, followed by Jessica. His gaze went to the family and then to Jenshi.

"Good news?" Lanrete asked.

"Yes . . . he'll make a full recovery." Jenshi rubbed the back of his neck. The doctor glanced back at the mother and daughter, took a step away from them, then turned and headed to his office.

"Now that the immediate concern has been taken care of, we need to talk." Lanrete looked to Serah'Elax. She reluctantly nodded and moved toward the founder.

"You're leaving us?" Uria said. There was a hint of fear in her voice. Jessica stepped past Lanrete and moved to sit across from Uria and Areathe, on the other side of Garen.

"Hello, we haven't been introduced," Jessica said. "I'm Major Jessica Olic, a member of the Huzien military and one of the Founder's Elite. And that woman over there"—Jessica pointed in Tashanira's direction—"is Major Tashanira Yen Unvesal." Areathe and Uria looked between both majors, then glanced back to Serah'Elax.

"They'll watch over you," Serah'Elax said, her gaze going to Lanrete for reassurance.

"Yes, Major Olic and Major Unvesal will stay here with them until you return." Lanrete nodded at Jessica and Tashanira. Serah'Elax continued toward Lanrete, and he turned as they departed the medical bay. They navigated a few corridors and meglifts until entering Lanrete's personal quarters. Serah'Elax hesitated as she crossed the threshold, glancing around at the elaborate décor. The opulence made her uncomfortable. Lanrete continued as if oblivious and she eventually followed suit. Her gaze caught on the myriad images of women that lined the walls, the picture frames rotating images every few seconds.

"Who are they?" Serah'Elax asked.

"Past wives that time has taken from me," Lanrete said. Serah'Elax's gaze caught on a Das'Vin woman in a revealing dress. The clothing reminded her of pictures her mother had shown her of Das'Vin fashion many years ago to teach her more about her heritage.

"You were joined to one of my people." Lanrete stopped and glanced back at her. "You had *hala'a?*" Lanrete glanced at the image of the Das'Vin woman. He then walked back toward Serah'Elax and brought up the same woman in the hologrid, and little children that had hints of Das'Vin and Huzien features appeared around them. The scene filled the room as the children ran around, a reproduction of Lanrete appearing in the scene in plainclothes. All the children called out *"Burra!"* as the holographic Lanrete kneeled with his arms wide.

Serah'Elax was entranced by the memory, her gaze eventually coming back up to Lanrete. "I'm sorry." Lanrete gave her a pained smile, then dismissed the scene. He turned and continued down a hallway, Serah'Elax following behind him, her gaze aimed at the floor. They entered his office and he moved behind his desk as Serah'Elax stood opposite him. She remained standing at parade rest, as if debriefing after a mission. She filled him in on the happenings in Ashna Maiden space as they conversed for over an hour.

"Bresha Vecen . . ." Lanrete brought up the profile of the woman through the HIN. "An Argent shaper for Etan Rachnie." He shook his head. "I'm not familiar with the name, but I know someone who might be."

A holodisplay appeared to his right, and then a Vempiir appeared on the display. He was disheveled and had clearly just woken up. "I apologize for disturbing you at this hour, Narmo, but I have an urgent matter to discuss with you," Lanrete said.

"You've heard news of Soahc?" There was a hint of optimism in Narmo's voice.

Lanrete frowned. "Unfortunately, no. This matter concerns Shaper Bresha Vecen."

Narmo seemed disappointed for a moment, then suddenly sat up straighter. "Bresha . . . she's alive?"

"Yes, what do you know about her?"

Narmo glanced to the side, appearing to pull up additional information.

"She was presumed dead after a failed assault on a Sagren-controlled world during the Rift War, where she led an Argent battle party. We found the remains of her team in the aftermath." Narmo's face became grim, and he paused for a moment to collect himself. "Traces of Bresha's blood were found, but no body. We assumed that a powerful cihphistic attack had vaporized her remains."

Serah'Elax clenched her jaw.

"Well, she has apparently been causing trouble with the Ashna Maidens in the Outer Rim," Lanrete said. Narmo raised an eyebrow.

"The Outer Rim . . ." Narmo shook his head. "That makes no sense." Narmo shared a recent image of Bresha Vecen on the holodisplay. "Are you sure it's the same person?" Lanrete glanced to Serah'Elax, who stepped forward and carefully examined the image.

"I am sure that is the same woman," Serah'Elax said. "Her eyes are slightly different, there are strands of silver there now, but it's her."

"And you are?" Narmo said.

"Exemp—" Serah'Elax stopped abruptly. "Serah'Elax Rez Ashfalen. I . . . was a former member of the Ashna Maidens." A sense of shame overwhelmed her that quickly shifted to rage and then subsided. Lanrete sat back in his chair, his gaze intently focused on her.

"Bresha was responsible for the murder of an Ashna Mother, one of the heads of our government and holy order. A murder she has framed me for," Serah'Elax added.

"I know Bresha Vecen," Narmo said, "and she would never do anything the likes of what you have said. She is not only a respected Argent, she is the model for what an Argent should be at her core. Her morality and dedication to the cause is without question." Pausing to compose himself, Narmo rubbed his eyes. "You must be mistaken, this woman you speak of cannot be Shaper Bresha."

"I do not know what happened to change her," Serah'Elax started, "but I can assure you that the woman in the picture you provided is the woman who has been the cause of much pain for myself and many others." Serah'Elax shared a series of vid clips taken from ship recordings that showed Bresha Vecen clearly. "I believe she intends to cause harm to the Ashna Maidens, and she has demonstrated incredible knowledge into the workings of strange enemy fleets, fleets that previously decimated Maiden forces. She also has command of unnatural creatures and sent some type of invisible monstrosity to kill me."

Narmo leaned back, his eyes becoming distant. He glanced to Lanrete. "Enesmic assassins . . . do you think?"

"Some form of domination by Sagren?" Lanrete leaned forward. "Maybe some type of telepathic mind control that gave her a set of instructions to execute?"

"It's not impossible," Narmo said. "If her brain chemistry has been altered, she could be doing all of this against her will, carrying out the last orders of Sagren."

"If Sagren still has agents as powerful as Bresha operating on its behalf, we could be faced with fallout for many years to come," Lanrete conceded.

"Can you investigate this?" Narmo asked.

"We have a mission planned against Het Wrast Aht," Lanrete said, "but we have some time before the fleets arrive. We can investigate this situation in the meantime, especially if it has the potential to disrupt the Ashna Maidens. We will need their forces to continue through with our plans for the pirate bands."

"You plan to attack the pirates?" Serah'Elax's eyes went wide, her mouth slightly open. "With the Alliance military?"

"Yes, but we can talk more about that later," Lanrete said. "For now, we head to . . . Ashnali you said?"

"Yes." Serah'Elax nodded.

"I'll keep you in the loop, Narmo," Lanrete said. Narmo nodded and terminated the connection. Lanrete glanced to Serah'Elax. "It sounds like you're not welcome back among the Ashna Maidens." The former exemplar clenched her jaw again. "I won't force you to come with us; I can only imagine being framed for the murder of an Ashna Mother has labeled you guilty of high treason, a crime punishable by death even in Huzien space."

"The Ashna Mother who was killed . . ." Serah'Elax said. "She said I would save the Ashna Maidens, that she had foreseen it." Serah'Elax sighed. "I don't think us meeting was chance; I believe she had me come to Rensmat on Rugtora specifically to meet you. I will go with you back to Ashnali, even on risk of death." Lanrete nodded.

"Very well." Lanrete opened a channel to the bridge. "Marcus, set a course for Ashnali, the Ashna Maiden homeworld."

"You got it," Marcus replied. Within seconds, the ship began to reposition itself. After a few more seconds, the subtle hum of the suplight drive engaging filled the ship. The planet that had been outside the window rapidly faded from view as the stars began to speed by.

CHAPTER 97 BRIME WEWTA

Yetew IX, Huzien Alliance space

Brime sat up, the wave of Enesmic force fading quickly. Her gaze locked onto the form of Soahc, who slowly pushed himself up on his palms. Their eyes met, and they exchanged smiles.

"We made it," Brime said.

"Did you ever doubt?" Soahc countered.

"With you? Never." Brime stood up and began to stretch. "I am exhausted!" Soahc stared into Brime's eyes; the hints of silver interwoven with her brown irises glowed in the low light. He glanced at her hair and saw streaks of silver interwoven with her black strands.

"You . . . you're immortal now aren't you?"

"I believe so, yes." Brime smiled. Soahc gave a sigh of contentment.

"Let's go home."

"You have a ship?"

"One better." Soahc stood up and prepared to enter a bout of cihphistic weaving, then stopped.

"What's wrong?" Brime asked.

"The Enesmic, we've been using it all wrong."

Brime nodded in agreement. "I . . . I will not go back to forcing the Enesmic to bend to my will. Not now. It's alive, somehow, and I can still hear it, although it's weak."

Soahc nodded, then spent a long moment in silent communion with the Enesmic. The forces moved ever so slowly, hesitantly, as if this part of the Enesmic was still cautious of Soahc. Soahc relayed his request to the Enesmic, speaking the words of power in tandem with the flow, not in subjugation over it. The forces accelerated, coalescing around a point in front of him. With a clap, a multicolored portal opened. Soahc smiled as Brime grinned.

"Looks like someone learned a new trick," Brime said.

"Sagren was good for something after all." Brime's frown prompted Soahc to laugh. "Come, I must inform Narmo and Merbi about Ristolte."

"What about Ristolte?" Brime asked.

Soahc stopped midstep. "I . . . neglected to tell you in all the excitement." He turned to face Brime. "Ristolte was sucked into the rift when we reopened it to allow me entrance to the Enesmic plane. It tore him apart."

Brime gasped as tears began to stream down her cheeks. "Oh no . . ." she whimpered. "He died because of me."

"No, no don't say that." Soahc moved to Brime, and he quickly embraced her as she broke down. The rush of emotions from over the past few weeks met up with her all at once.

They stood there for a long moment, the multicolored portal casting an eerie glow over the remnants of Sagren's former command chamber. Light streamed in through multiple cracks and areas of damage.

"Come, we must depart."

Brime wiped her eyes and took Soahc's hand. Neither spoke another word as they walked through the portal to Etan Rachnie.

CHAPTER 98 SOAHC

Reath, Etan Rachnie home system

"Three months?" Soahc echoed. He stood with Brime in Narmo's office within the Argent barracks. Merbi stood off to the side.

"Yes, it's been about three months since you walked through the rift to the Enesmic plane," Narmo replied.

Soahc shook his head. "I was on the Enesmic plane for only a handful of days, not even a week," Soahc said as he glanced at Brime, his mind racing. "Brime . . ."

The woman's gaze moved from the floor to Soahc. "I was there for two or three weeks . . . give or take a few days," she said. Narmo and Merbi stared at her, their eyes wide.

"It's been almost a year since your battle with the creature known as Sifitis," Merbi said.

"I . . . sensed that time passed differently there, but I would never have imagined such a disparity," Brime said. "To think that there are planes beyond even the Enesmic . . ."

"What?" Soahc, Narmo, and Merbi said in unison as they stared wide-eyed at Brime.

"Sorry, not for the ears of Havin." Brime grinned as silence filled the room for a long moment.

"We'll have to erect a memorial to Ristolte," Merbi said, breaking the silence. "He saved my life."

"And the lives of many others," Narmo interjected.

"We may not have always agreed." Soahc added, "but Ristolte was dependable and willing to lay down his life at a moment's notice. Fine men such as him are rare and deserve honoring."

"Speaking of rare talent," Narmo said. "Bresha Vecen is reported as having been sighted in Ashna Maiden space."

"Bresha . . ." Soahc said. "So, she wasn't killed in the failed assault."

"Seems that way," Narmo said. "Although if stories are to be believed, she may still be under lingering influence from Sagren. Lanrete and his team are investigating now."

"Then we'll have to pay them a visit." Soahc smiled, his gaze moving to Brime. Her frown wiped the smile off his face.

"How about we get settled first before flying off to the next adventure?" she said.

Merbi laughed.

"I will leave you to it." Merbi turned to leave and then stopped. "I am sincerely glad you are alive and well. Hopefully, this will end the lawsuits your father launched against Etan Rachnie shortly after your untimely death." He gave Soahc a nod and then departed.

"It may be a good idea to inform your parents of your 'being alive.'" Soahc sighed. Brime's eyes went wide.

"Oh no . . . they thought I was dead." Brime shook her head. "Oh no, oh no! I have to call them right now!" Brime rushed out of the office. Soahc turned to Narmo, whose crystalline gaze was focused on his cup of tea.

"It's good to have her back," Narmo said.

"I couldn't agree with you more."

The Uri species is highly sexualized, promiscuous, tribal, and considered mildly dangerous. They are a subjugated species that is part of the Huzien Empire, but were previously ruled by tribal clans who still hold much influence and power.

–FROM "URI OBSERVATIONS"
DAS'VIN ARCHIVES

CHAPTER 99 LANRETE

Foundra Ascension orbiting Ashnali, Ashna Maiden home system

The Foundra Ascension exited suplight a short distance from Ashnali, the blue and green orb a beautiful sight. Immediately, a host of Ashna Maiden dreadnaughts and their accompaniments swarmed the small ship.

"You sure this was a good idea?" Marcus flashed Lanrete a concerned glance.

"What better way to get escorted to the right people right away?" Lanrete said as he flashed Marcus a smile. The other Founder's Elites, absent Jessica, Jenshi, and Tashanira, mirrored Marcus's sentiment.

Serah'Elax stood off to the side on the bridge. She was wearing a military-grade infiltration matrix, the self-contained technology modifying her appearance completely. Her Das'Vin features had been replaced by those of a nondescript Huzien female. She had been told that the matrix could even provide temporary full-body cloaking to slip out of a hairy situation if needed. The low power shielding deployed by the unit could fool even a physical inspection.

"We're getting hailed," Auri said.

"Put them through."

"Huzien vessel, this is Avatar Kenyalie of the Ashna Maiden dreadnaught *Hereyet*. You've entered restricted Ashna Maiden space. State your intentions immediately. Any non-conformant actions will be treated as hostile and your ship will be disabled."

"She will follow through on her threat," Serah'Elax whispered. "The home fleets are no-nonsense and trigger happy."

Lanrete nodded and stepped forward. "Avatar Kenyalie. I am Founder Lanrete of the Huzien Empire. I seek an audience with the Ashna Mothers on a matter of great importance."

"And this matter would be?" Avatar Kenyalie said.

"It concerns Het Wrast Aht; we intend to wipe them out completely. I have a full contingent of Huzien fleets en route to their home system." Avatar Kenyalie's eyes widened.

"Please wait a moment." The connection terminated, and Lanrete glanced to Serah'Elax.

"They will most likely reach out to the Ashna Council and receive instructions on the next course of action." A few minutes went by as the Founder's Elites glanced between each other expectantly. Auri received another hail, which she pushed through to the holo-display.

"I have been instructed to escort you to High Temple City. Please dispatch a single shuttle and rendezvous at these coordinates. A series of ships will be waiting to escort you the rest of the way to the surface." Coordinates and other information was sent over the channel. Immediately after, the connection terminated again.

"I guess that means we've been granted our audience," Neven said. Lanrete walked past his team and toward the meglift.

"I believe it may be best if I sit this one out," Erb said.

"You sure?" Lanrete asked.

Erb nodded. "Ken'Tar do not frequent the Outer Rim, and I'm afraid my unique appearance would be too much of a distraction."

"Very well. I rarely get to play the diplomat," Lanrete said. "This should be interesting."

"Should I queue up Cislot?" Auri called out. Lanrete gave her the stink eye as the rest of the Founder's Elite burst into laughter.

The Uri homeworld is the largest habitable planet on record and serves as a military stronghold for the Huzien Empire.

–FROM "URI OBSERVATIONS"
DAS'VIN ARCHIVES

CHAPTER 100 NEVEN KENK

Ashnali, Ashna Maiden home system

"This is unexpected," Mother Venice Fawni said. The four remaining Ashna Mothers sat in a half circle on an elevated platform in their ceremonial meeting chamber. Lanrete and his team, with Serah'Elax in disguise, stood near the platform. A multitude of high priestesses, scions, and other Ashna Maidens were in attendance, the room seemingly packed to the brim with them. "To have one of the Founders of the Huzien Empire show up on our doorstep unannounced is, in many cases, cause for concern."

"And at the front of a fleet with intentions to wipe out our largest and most veritable foe," Mother Ce Nu Yo Kl said. Neven stared at the Eeriteen woman, her appearance truly foreign to him. He had grown up seeing a host of different alien species, but nothing the likes of the dark red corded and tubular creature. Her face was eerily smooth, with eyes that were pitch black yet glowed with a yellow hue. The sight of her sent a chill down his spine. As if detecting his discomfort, the Ashna Mother momentarily shifted her gaze to Neven. Her intense stare caused him to avert his gaze to the ground. Zun moved closer to his side, her presence bringing him a sense of comfort.

"What is it you want from us?" Mother Alenet said. "Surely, your presence indicates that you want us to play some part in this affair."

Lanrete nodded. "I originally planned to take out Het Wrast Aht's leadership and begin my assault on their forces before engaging with you. Yet, I recently became concerned that you would be unable to assist in such an assault, let alone be willing."

The Ashna Mothers exchanged glances.

"What would cause you to think such a thing?" Mother Ga Po Fe Ul said. "We have devoted our existence to eradicating the pirate threat."

Lanrete motioned toward the empty chair in their midst. "For one, it would appear that one among your ranks has fallen."

"Treachery," Ce Nu Yo Kl said, "nothing that concerns you." Serah'Elax shifted uncomfortably. Her gaze went to Marcus, who nodded, reassuring her that her disguise was still intact.

"I have also heard of the great loss sustained in a series of battles with the remnants of Sagren's fleets. Sagren was a being called an Eshgren, a powerful monster from the Enesmic plane who led a prolonged campaign against the Huzien Alliance. We are still recovering from our war with the being." Lanrete glanced around the room. "But rumor has it that one of our own, a Bresha Vecen, was instrumental in your victory over the fiend's forces." Lanrete paused. "I am here at the request of her superior, First Argent Narmo Swela, to request her immediate return to Etan Rachnie for debrief." The Ashna Mothers exchanged glances again.

"Avatar Bresha has joined the Ashna Maidens of her own volition, and as with any member of the Ashna Maidens, she is sworn in service to our cause. We cannot grant your request," Mother Alenet said.

"We are curious as to how you have come by so much information regarding our nation." Mother Ce Nu Yo Kl leaned forward.

"My Sentinels came across a former member of the Ashna Maidens during a reconnaissance mission on Rugtora. She was interrogated for information after resisting capture."

"What was her name?" Mother Venice said.

"Serah'Elax Rez Ashfalen I believe," Lanrete said. "She killed one of my Sentinels and was terminated by the other in a firefight while attempting to escape." A few Ashna Maidens in the room gasped, and many more whispered.

"You have done the Ashna Maidens a great service," Mother Ce Nu Yo Kl said. "She was the traitor responsible for the death of Mother Halle Tentle."

"The question remains," Lanrete said, "are the Ashna Maidens prepared to join in an assault on Het Wrast Aht?"

"What will the Huzien Empire do once their space has been cleared?" Mother Alenet said. "Will you pull back your forces to Huzien space or leave a presence in the system?"

"We cannot commit forces to a permanent presence," Mother Ga Po Fe Ul added. "As you are already aware, our forces are spread thin and we have much rebuilding to do."

"I am prepared to open up negotiations on the matter," Lanrete said. Silence descended on the room and the Mothers exchanged glances again.

"We will need to discuss this matter at length," Mother Venice said. "Please, accept our hospitality while we convene."

"We humbly accept," Lanrete said. A high priestess walked over and motioned for them to follow. The team followed her, but Lanrete stopped and faced the Mothers again. "On the matter of Bresha Vecen, would it be possible to arrange a short meeting between her and I? I can't leave Narmo in the dark; there are several people in Etan Rachnie who thought her dead until recently. She was a leader of great importance to the Argents."

"We will speak with Bresha and broach the topic," Mother Ce Nu Yo Kl said.

"Thank you for your understanding." Without another word, Lanrete turned and continued following the high priestess.

Lanrete and his team sat in a posh café near their temporary quarters, an impressive meal in front of them. Neven watched many of the Ashna Maidens as they walked by. It was weird to see a society in which there were virtually no men. He wondered if this was what it would be like on Desc'Ri, the homeworld of the Das'Vin. He caught sight of a group of women that looked like mechanics walking by the café. A few had their shirts off and strung over their shoulders, with sweat covering their bodies. He turned away, their bare breasts making him blush. Zun eyed him curiously.

"Is it true what you say?" The voice came from a toffee-skinned woman with her arms crossed behind her back. She was a Tuzen with blond hair, her grey eyes sharp and narrowed. She had just entered the café and was standing next to the group.

"What specifically?" Lanrete said.

"That Serah'Elax was murdered by your soldiers." The edge in her voice caused Lanrete to sit back. Neven restrained himself from reflexively looking to Serah'Elax, still in her disguise.

"From that insignia across your shoulder, I'm assuming that you were her commanding officer?"

"That would be an incorrect assumption," the woman replied. "She previously served under my sister, Avatar Luka Helrit."

"So, you're interest in Serah'Elax is merely following up on a request from your sister?"

"My sister is dead."

Lanrete glanced to Serah'Elax, whose Huzien disguise was failing to hide the sadness on her face. The woman followed his gaze, and Serah'Elax stared back at her.

"Avatar Hegna," Serah'Elax said, "we are truly sorry for your loss." Hegna raised an eyebrow at the woman.

"Do we know each other?" Hegna said.

"That depends on why you are seeking to confirm Serah'Elax's death," Serah'Elax replied.

"It would mean that I failed in my vow to Mother Halle."
Neven tensed and exchanged glances with Zun.

"I think it may be best if we move this conversation to a location with less prying eyes," Lanrete said. Hegna glanced back to Lanrete and then to Serah'Elax.

"Follow me." Hegna turned around and exited the café.

The Uri were not technologically advanced when they were conquered by the Huziens and viewed the advanced species as deific.

–FROM "URI OBSERVATIONS"
DAS'VIN ARCHIVES

CHAPTER 101 SOAHC

Ashnali, Ashna Maiden home system

A multicolored portal appeared on the main street right outside the entrance to the High Temple of Ashna. The area exploded in panic as Ashna Maidens swarmed into action. Units took up assault locations all around the portal. Multiple retinues were stationed permanently in High Temple City, the total complement skyward of six million Ashna Maiden soldiers solely tasked with protecting the megacity. A significant number of those Maidens now stood with weapons drawn on the strange portal.

Soahc walked through the portal, his hands raised high above his head and a broad smile on his face.

"Sorry for the intrusion," Soahc called out. He cihphistically amplified his voice to be heard by all in the immediate vicinity. Almost every weapon was immediately targeted on the Human. "Looking for a friend, Bresha Vecen, heard she was in the neighborhood." A few of the Maidens exchanged glances, and more shuffled uneasily. "Oh, my wife is about to step through the portal behind me, please refrain from shooting at her." As the words left his mouth, Brime stepped through the portal. She immediately put her hands above her head, and the portal winked out of existence behind them.

"Did you give them the whole story about looking for a friend?" Brime whispered loudly.

"Either my translator isn't working right, or they aren't buying it," Soahc whispered in reply. A Tuzen woman stepped past the throngs of Ashna Maidens.

"I am Avatar Lopi of the Ashna Maidens. You have trespassed on the Ashna Maiden homeworld of Ashnali. Who are you, and how do you know Avatar Bresha?"

"I am Soahc, Master of Etan Rachnie, and the beautiful woman behind me is my wife Brime Wewta, Mistress of the Enesmic."

"Oh, I like that title," Brime whispered.

"Bresha is a close friend who, up until a year ago, was an Argent shaper in service to the Argents of Etan Rachnie."

"Are you here with the Huzien founder?" Avatar Lopi said.

Soahc grinned. "Why yes, of course."

The avatar signaled with her hand, and every Ashna Maiden in attendance pointed their weapons down and away from the duo, though they stood at the ready, prepared to reverse the action should the need arise. Avatar Lopi called someone on her mobi while walking past a few Ashna Maidens, who quickly parted for her. She quickly disappeared into the throng.

"I guess that's progress." Soahc glanced to Brime.

"We should have just called ahead and told them we were coming." Brime sighed.

"And spoil the surprise?" Soahc gasped. "Never!"

The avatar stepped back into view with another woman shadowing her. "This is Exemplar Elise. She will escort you to the quarters where Lanrete and the rest of his party are staying." She glanced beyond Soahc to where the portal had been mere moments before. "Are there any more . . . unexpected visitors that may be showing up that we should be aware of?"

"That would arrive in the fashion similar to the way we did?" Soahc asked. Glancing back to Brime, he shook his head. "If anything else arrives like we did, I recommend opening fire immediately."

The avatar grinned. "Surprise is the only thing that kept us from doing that to you. I can assure you we won't hesitate next time." She winked as Exemplar Elise motioned for them to follow.

CHAPTER 102 SERAH'ELAX REZ ASHFALEN

Ashnali, Ashna Maiden home system

Avatar Hegna embraced Serah'Elax. The former exemplar had dropped her disguise as soon as they reached the avatar's private quarters. Lanrete, Dexter, Neven, Zun, and Marcus stood in the living room area. Serah'Elax was surprised at the display from Hegna. She had never really associated with the avatar; their interactions previously had been limited to formal salutes and pleasantries.

"I am happy to see you alive." Hegna removed herself from Serah'Elax and almost immediately went back to her normal demeanor before glancing to Lanrete. "This leads me to believe that your presence here is also Ashna's will. I will assist you in whatever way I can."

"We believe Bresha Vecen is under the lingering influence of a powerful being known as an Eshgren. Its name was Sagren." Lanrete crossed his arms.

"It was a *vusging cith* to put down," Dexter said.

"A few Argents from Etan Rachnie," Lanrete continued, "believe it's possible that Bresha's mind could have been altered, her actions still under the influence of Sagren's last commands."

Hegna let out a sigh. "So that is what we're dealing with." Her gaze went to Serah'Elax. "This will be difficult to prove. The Ashna

Mothers have elevated her to the rank of avatar. They believe her a blessed of Ashna sent by the goddess herself in a dire time of need."

"Surely Mother Halle would have told them of her prophecy," Serah'Elax countered. "That Bresha would cause undue harm to the Ashna Maidens."

Avatar Hegna shook her head and recited the prophecy, "If we accept Bresha into the Ashna Maidens, much pain and heartbreak will come. After the pain, after the heartbreak, great peace and prosperity will come for all our people. Prosperity unlike anything we have ever seen.'" She laughed bitterly. "If Mother Halle was anything, she was cryptic as hell." Hegna fixed Serah'Elax with an exhausted look. "She never told the other Mothers of the part you would play. As far as they are concerned, you did kill Mother Halle and we are now in the peace and prosperity that Halle prophesied." Serah'Elax's gaze dropped to the floor.

"Did this Mother Halle prophecy regularly?" Neven asked. "And did her prophecies always come true?"

"Yes," both Serah'Elax and Hegna replied in sync.

"Although, not all of her prophecies were widely known," Hegna continued. "Ones regarding individuals, such as the one regarding Bresha, were usually only told to a handful of high-profile avatars and the Ashna Council. I am sure there are even more that the Mothers keep to themselves, but we will never know." The group shifted uneasily. "Regarding Bresha, the Mothers have requested her presence on Ashnali. She was previously on Ashnakev training with her new retinue, a very large group of young Maidens."

"How young?" Zun asked.

Hegna acknowledged Zun for the first time since they had entered her quarters. "Fifteen, give or take a few years." Hegna sighed. "Normally, Maidens-in-waiting don't get assigned to a retinue until the age of twenty, but with the losses we've suffered, we've had to accelerate the training regimen."

"What age do girls start training . . . ?"

"Five, usually," Serah'Elax chimed in. "Girls can remain with their families until five, at which point if the family wishes to remain in Ashna Maiden protected space, they must turn over the girl for training."

"That's terrible!" Zun breathed. "Forcing girls at the age of five into military service." Both Serah'Elax and Hegna turned to face the half Huzien.

"Serving as an Ashna Maiden in service to the goddess is an honor!" Serah'Elax growled. "We protect our families of our own free will. We are free to leave the Ashna Maidens at any time after five years of service once becoming a Maiden. Our families remain free to stay in Ashna Maiden space since they fulfilled their obligation. The Maiden, however, must either become a nedim or leave Ashna Maiden controlled space completely."

"Many leave the Ashna Maidens," Hegna interjected, "to break their vow of celibacy, marry, and become nedims. They are the administrative workforce that keeps our society running." She hesitated. "And those who are impure from an early age enter into service as a nedim instead of undergoing Maiden-in-waiting training."

"Impure?" Neven asked.

"Not virgins," Dexter replied.

"Correct," Hegna said.

"Does that happen . . . often?" Zun asked. Hegna and Serah'Elax exchanged glances.

"For those who migrate to Ashna Maiden controlled planets from pirate-controlled space . . . yes," Serah'Elax said, thinking back to the family currently on the *Foundra Ascension*.

"What happens to the boys?" Neven said.

"Men cannot be employed in service to the goddess Ashna, either as Ashna Maidens or as nedims."

"Then what do they do?"

"They are given two options at the age of fifteen," Hegna said. "They can take up employment as a civilian across any of the Ashna Maiden controlled worlds except for Ashnali, Ashnakev, and Ashnayulani, or they can leave Ashna Maiden controlled space on regular transports to surrounding systems."

"The majority of the men leave when they become of age," Serah'Elax added.

"And become *vusging* pirates," Dexter interjected.

Hegna's mobi chirped. "Excuse me a minute." She stepped away from the group and into her bedroom area.

Serah'Elax studied the living room; it was her first insight into the person behind the reputation. She saw pictures that looped scenes of Avatar Luka and Hegna all over the place, the two side by side in every scene. Some pictures were from when they were younger, Ashna Maiden uniforms seen from the earliest age. In almost all of them, Luka was frowning, never smiling. It wasn't until the more recent pictures, recorded in the past few years, that Luka smiled.

"Hegna and Luka were close?" Zun glanced to Serah'Elax.

"Yes." Serah'Elax looked to the most recent picture of Luka. Both wore avatar rank insignias, with balloons and cake on a table and a big *"Congratulations"* sign hanging in the background.

"That was taken when Luka was elevated to the rank of avatar," Hegna said from behind them. They all turned to see her leaning against a door frame, her expression soft. Her gaze slowly moved to meet Lanrete's. "Expecting friends?" Lanrete tilted his head to the side.

Attempts by our people at encouraging Uri independence from the Huzien Empire during the foundation of the Huzien Alliance was met with hostilities from the dominant Uri tribes.

–FROM "URI OBSERVATIONS"
DAS'VIN ARCHIVES

CHAPTER 103 BRIME WEWTA

Ashnali, Ashna Maiden home system

Soahc and Brime sat in a broad living area filled with couches, chairs, and small tables. The quarters were clearly designed for multiple guests to share a single living space with separate bedrooms circling the central gathering area. All the things needed were there: bathrooms, kitchen space, even a large hot tub that could easily support eight people. It had the strange feeling of a mix between an upscale hotel and an apartment.

"At least they treat their guests well," Brime said.

"I get the impression that they don't have guests here very often," Soahc countered. The door leading into the quarters opened as both Brime and Soahc stood up. Dexter was the first into the room, the sight of Soahc and Brime causing his eyes to go wide. He quickly regained his composure and then stepped to the side to allow the rest entry.

Lanrete followed right after, his gaze immediately going to Brime. "Brime!" Lanrete shouted. Neven and Zun came rushing into the room in confusion as Marcus cautiously followed behind. The whole group except for a recovered Dexter stood staring wide-eyed at Brime.

"You know, it's rude to stare," Brime said. Zun rushed over and embraced the short Human in a tight hug. They both began to cry.

"We thought you were dead," Neven said. He looked like he was still in shock.

"So did I at one point," Brime laughed. She looked up through tear-stained eyes at Lanrete, who walked over and picked her up in a hug, Zun moving out of the way just in time. Marcus walked over to Soahc and slapped him on the back. The immortal tried his best to keep his balance, but succeeded only through calling on the Enesmic forces.

"You sly dog." Marcus grinned. "I have a feeling you played a big part in all this."

"Something like that." Soahc glanced to Lanrete, who had just set Brime down. The two locked gazes. "I hear Bresha is alive, and possibly an agent of Sagren." Lanrete motioned to Dexter, who shut and sealed the door. Dexter then walked to the center of the room and removed a small spherical drone from a compartment on his belt and set it on the table. Once he did, the device came to life and sent out a pulse that bathed the room.

"Room secured," Dexter said.

Lanrete glanced to Serah'Elax, who was back in her disguise. Avatar Hegna had excused herself after they left her quarters. "According to a source, Bresha is en route to Ashnali now to meet with the Ashna Mothers and discuss our presence here." Lanrete smirked at Soahc. "And I'm sure to also discuss your spectacular appearance." Soahc performed a showman's bow.

"Avatar Hegna indicated that Bresha should be arriving in two days," Serah'Elax said. Soahc glanced to the woman, her appearance Huzien, then back to Lanrete and raised an eyebrow. Lanrete nodded at Serah'Elax, and she deactivated her disguise, her Das'Vin appearance quickly replacing the Huzien one.

"This is Serah'Elax Rez Ashfalen," Lanrete said. "She was a former high-ranking member of the Ashna Maidens before Bresha framed her for the murder of an Ashna Mother. She apparently has a covert force of Ashna Maidens working with her to expose Bresha."

"And take her down," Serah'Elax added.

"Or free her from whatever mind control she is under," Soahc quickly added. Serah'Elax flashed a look that promised vengeance.

"Well," Brime said, breaking the tension, "since we have some time, let's tell you all about our adventure on the Enesmic plane!"

Zun walked up to Brime and Soahc's temporary quarters and chimed the doorbell with her mobi. A few seconds went by as Zun rubbed her arm. The door opened to reveal Brime in a loose-fitting gold and white lounge dress.

"Hey, what's up?"

"Can I come in?" Zun said. At her hurried voice, the younger woman raised an eyebrow.

"Sure . . ." Brime stepped aside as Zun moved into her quarters.

"Is Soahc around?"

"No, he's with Lanrete."

"I need to tell you something," Zun blurted.

"Shoot."

"I'm pregnant."

Brime's eyes went wide. "What? For reals?"

"For reals!"

Both women squealed, the two holding hands as they jumped up and down.

"Does Neven know?"

"No, I haven't told him yet." Zun shook her head. "With everything going on, I don't want to distract him. We're going on our official honeymoon as soon as we get back to Thae. I plan to tell him everything then."

"How far along?"

"It's still early, just a few weeks. I snuck into the medical bay aboard the *Ascension* and did a scan of myself to confirm."

"Girl, this is great news!" Brime squealed again. "This is so awesome!"

"Keep it secret. I want Neven to be the next person to know."

"My lips are sealed!"

FOUNDERS LOG:
Questioning the Unknown

The thought that Sagren was merely a shadow of an Eshgren still sends a chill down my spine. Brime and Soahc's experiences were difficult to digest. If it had not been those two telling me the tale, it would have been impossible to believe. Beings that hold such power, power beyond anything we could possibly imagine. Beings seeking to wipe us out utterly. That thought makes me shudder.

And then the Rel Ach'Kel, their existence unexpected but appreciated. That they care so much gives me hope. It is difficult to grasp that we owe our very existence to beings that we do not know or understand, beings that almost every soul in the Twin Galaxies will never know exist.

It does make me wonder if the religions throughout our Twin Galaxies have come to exist from the direct involvement of these Rel Ach'Kel and Eshgren. It is a concept that I believe must remain secret, a possibility that must never come to light by our hand. I am sure that if the Rel Ach'Kel sought to disrupt such thinking, they would do so.

With the revelations given to us by Soahc and Brime, nothing but questions have plagued my mind. Questions with no discernable answers. Who or what is the Originator? We have observed life in all stages throughout the galaxy, from the primordial and primal to civilizations such as our own and further. What, then, is the Originator responsible for? And what of the true nature of the Enesmic plane? If it is alive, as Soahc and Brime have come to believe, then is it simply another lifeform that we have only now come to understand as having sentience? Or is it something more? What truly happens when we die? What of the difference in progression of time between our plane and the Enesmic? Is this the cause for our immortality? Our best scientists have determined that immortals do not truly age, not even by the most minuscule of measures. Is our scale simply incomplete? Inadequate?

I . . . truly am at a loss. What would happen if a natural-born immortal walked the Enesmic plane? Would our experience be like that of Soahc and Brime's? Or would we be at home? Am I to test this theory with my own life? That is an interesting thought . . . one that I may examine, when the time is right.

-Lanrete

CHAPTER 104 SEPHAN

Ashnali, Ashna Maiden home system

Bresha walked into the Ashna Mothers audience chamber, her chin held high. Her time spent on Ashnakev had been eventful, and she had begun weaving webs of influence over her new retinue. The manipulation was paramount to Sephan's plans, and the young women were now instilled with a fervor to Bresha, an obedience that would soon supersede their allegiance to even Ashna. Her forces had followed her back to Ashnali, and the young women were now mingling with other Ashna Maidens throughout the capital, spreading like a virus.

"Bresha Vecen," Mother Ce Nu Yo Kl intoned, "we understand that the training of your new retinue goes well."

"Exceedingly so," Bresha said.

"We apologize for interfering during such a critical time in their development," Mother Venice said.

"We have received guests that have asked for you by name," Mother Alenet said.

"Oh?" Bresha shifted uncomfortably.

"Founder Lanrete of the Huzien Empire," Mother Ga Po Fe Ul said.

"And Lord Soahc of Etan Rachnie," Mother Ce Nu Yo Kl added.

"Both have come seeking an audience with you," Mother Alenet said.

"Do you wish to speak with them?" Mother Venice asked. "You have the right to refuse; we will not force you to maintain connections to any aspect of your former life."

Sephan mused at the new development. It was familiar with the Havin who had ended Sagren's existence; those final moments had been broadcast through the Enesmic to all beings with the power to witness them. The Havin's power was indeed great, but a threat to Sephan? Sephan considered the question.

"Gracious Mothers," Bresha started. "I humbly accept the summons of Founder Lanrete and Lord Soahc. I feel that I owe them an explanation and will gladly speak with them to close up any loose ends."

The Ashna Mothers exchanged glances.

"Very well, we will let them know," Mother Ce Nu Yo Kl said.

CHAPTER 105 SOAHC

Ashnali, Ashna Maiden home system

Soahc glanced to Brime, who let out a sigh. They had both sensed the new presence. It was attempting to mask itself, but the two could feel the subtle vibrations in the flow. Their time on the Enesmic plane had made them more in tune with its forces than ever before in their lives.

"Avatar Bresha has agreed to meet," Exemplar Elise said from the entrance to the guest quarters. Lanrete and the others glanced at one another, cautious smiles on their faces. "I will escort you to a private audience chamber where Avatar Bresha awaits."

"Thank you," Lanrete said. He motioned for the others to follow as they exited after the exemplar.

Be ready, Soahc telepathically imparted to their group.

Serah'Elax gasped at the suddenness of Soahc's voice in her mind. She turned slightly to regard him as they walked. He glanced at her briefly, his gaze confirming the message. The others in the group were familiar with his abilities and moved their hands nearer to their weapons.

The group walked for a few minutes through the large guest facilities to a conference chamber on the first floor. A group of armed

Maidens escorted them with Exemplar Elise at the head. Approaching a large nanoplexi door, the exemplar unlocked and opened it without slowing in her steps. She filed through, and the rest of the entourage entered behind her. Bresha Vecen was sitting across from them at a large circular table and rose as they entered the room.

Soahc and Brime immediately saw Sephan for what it was. The Eshgren's full form hovered behind and partially within Bresha, its essence intertwined with the woman through a series of tendrils that violated every part of her. At that moment, they sensed that its control over the woman was absolute.

The Eshgren had the appearance of a tall Human. A silver cloak of wispy yet hardened corrupted flesh hung on the being in an elaborate display, and a large collar of the raised hardened flesh adorned its neck with talon bones hanging in the front.

A wispy cloak of the same corrupted silver flesh trailed the creature, hanging like a piece of cloth but not falling toward the ground. No legs were visible; instead, tendrils at the end of the cloak wreathed in and out of the ground as it moved. More long, decorative talons, these much larger, were attached to the sides of its cloak and angled toward the ground.

One of the creature's hands was exposed; the hand appeared normal and muscular, but the other hand was fully engulfed by the cloak and ended in a horrid-looking claw made of the same corrupted flesh material. On its head floated exceptionally long wispy silver hair that seemed free of gravity. Its face was unblemished, seeming Human but with a perpetual scowl that deformed the features. It was a thing of nightmares.

Pulsating purple eyes locked immediately onto Soahc and Brime. Both stood with narrowed gazes aimed at Sephan, completely oblivious to Bresha. Sephan frowned.

You are Eshgren, Brime mentally challenged the creature. *Sephan the Deceiver, according to the whispers of the Enesmic.*

You commune with the Enesmic? Sephan mused. *Intriguing . . .*

Why are you here? Soahc interjected.

I was summoned to this plane by Bresha.

Lies! Brime countered. *You were summoned here by Sagren, and you've taken possession of Bresha against her will.*

Bresha opened herself willingly to me, Sephan said. *Just as she did to Sagren before.*

Why not let Bresha speak for herself? Soahc asked.

Sephan glanced to Bresha, its tendrils fully engulfing the woman. It sighed and turned its gaze back to the two.

As I suspected, she has no free will with which to reply, Brime said.

You view me and all Eshgren as the enemy, Sephan said. *Therefore I can make no argument or justification to you that would satiate your suspicion of me.*

Remove your influence over Bresha and allow her to respond. If she indicates your innocence, we will leave the matter at that, Soahc said.

I cannot. My binding to her is what keeps me present on this plane. To remove such connection would thrust me back into the Enesmic plane.

Good, Bresha countered.

I violate nothing by being here in this fashion, Sephan said. *You know surely as I that if I did, the Rel Ach'Kel would be here even as we speak.*

Seriously? Brime said. *You literally have tendril thingies sticking out of her.*

"Enough of this!" Soahc shouted. Everyone in the room glanced at him in confusion. The telepathic exchange had occurred within the breadth of a few seconds, all others in the room oblivious to the conversation. "We will not allow you to remain."

"Lord Soahc?" Bresha feigned confusion.

Soahc began to commune with the Enesmic, urging it into action as the room trembled under the amassing of Enesmic forces.

"What's going on here?" Exemplar Elise interjected.

"That creature"—Brime pointed to Bresha—"that is not Bresha. A being known as an Eshgren has dominated her will and controls her even now."

"I do not know what these Eshgren creatures are of which you speak," Exemplar Elise countered, "but any accusations against an avatar of Ashna would require the immediate involvement of the Ashna Council. I must ask that you return to your quarters while we inform them."

Lanrete signaled through his mobi. Within a heartbeat, his team exploded into motion, and all the Maidens were subdued and disarmed. The Founder's Elites then ushered their new prisoners to a section of the room away from Soahc and Brime.

Bresha raised her hands in a surrendering gesture.

"I don't know what's going on, but I don't want any trouble," Bresha said, feigning fear. "I know I left without warning, and I apologize for any bad blood created between us. I do not seek to draw your wrath or anger, I simply ask that you allow me to remain here with my sisters in the Ashna Maidens. Their cause is just, and Ashna herself has spoken to me, called me, to help them with my service."

"This is treachery!" Exemplar Elise yelled. "You will pay for any harm wrought upon a member of the Ashna Maidens." All the Ashna Maidens in the room looked toward Avatar Bresha. Many offered up silent prayers to Ashna, and a few even rushed their captors, but they were quickly knocked unconscious by the Founder's Elites.

"You wish to start a war with the Ashna Maidens for the sake of me?" Bresha said. The room trembled again, this time at the call of Sephan. Lights began to flicker as the table, chairs, and furniture were thrown to the sides of the room, leaving a clear path between Soahc, Brime, and Bresha.

The legendary immortal, his eyes white fire, responded by reaching out and gripping hold of Sephan's essence. Sephan immediately recognized the danger and pushed itself deeper into Bresha, its massive form seeming to diminish and fully merge with the former Argent shaper. Soahc stepped back, his eyes wide as he lost grip of the being. All traces of the Eshgren vanished as Bresha and the creature became one.

Soahc responded with a titan blast, the raw lightning energy starting at his outstretched hand and arcing to Bresha in a heartbeat. The impact sent her flying hard into the wall, but Sephan remained anchored to her body. The barrier around Bresha rippled but stayed intact.

You intend to kill your friend to get rid of me? Sephan imparted to Soahc.

Brime stepped forward with a lefon blast. The powerful manifestation missed Bresha by a hair as she spun out of its way. Crouching low, Bresha moved both of her hands out to the sides and clenched both fists as she spoke a litany of words of power. The words came out impossibly fast, the jumbled sounds otherworldly, unnatural. The room rippled with unfathomable amounts of energy. Soahc and Brime's eyes went wide.

"No!" Soahc yelled. He clenched his fist and began to utter multiple words of power, barely managing to complete his weaving before Bresha unleashed the fury. A mini supernova filled the room in a blinding display of power that overwhelmed everyone's senses. Brime collapsed to the ground, the group barrier she had erected in tandem with Soahc's weaving taxing all her strength.

Lanrete and the Founder's Elites rubbed their eyes, each trying to focus. They were teleported a few blocks away from the guest residence structure. A blinding light caught their attention, and everyone turned to see the entire residence structure obliterated in a powerful explosion. The shock wave knocked a few people to the ground, and all the Ashna Maiden prisoners stared numbly at the scene.

Bresha Vecen suddenly appeared behind the group, right next to the Ashna Maidens.

"Oops, you weren't supposed to see that," Bresha said. She motioned toward Exemplar Elise and the other Ashna Maiden guards as bands of Enesmic energy wrapped around their necks. Within moments, their heads began popping off in a sickening symphony of death.

Neven's eyes went wide, and he took a step back at the display. After enacting a personal shield, Neven leveled Streamsong with Bresha.

"Amusing." Bresha's gaze locked with Neven's. She took a haughty step toward him, her hand trailing to her side and bands of Enesmic energy coalescing around her fingers.

Neven looked like he was about to be sick.

As Bresha brought her hand up, Neven's exoskeleton spurred him into action, and he bolted out of the way. A strand of energy continued past him and cut off a chunk of the building he had been standing next to. Neven glanced back with a gulp.

Lanrete began to move. Soahc appeared at his side, halting his advance.

Protect the others. I will handle Sephan, Soahc said.

The founder nodded and sent a broadcast to his team.

"Leave the dancing to the stars," Lanrete said.

Nods of understanding were returned as the team began to rapidly distance themselves from Bresha, Soahc, and a recovered Brime. The two cihphists quickly moved toward Bresha.

"I guess I'll have to tone it down a little or risk destroying my new home," Bresha mocked.

Soahc replied with a string of words of power, causing the ground beneath Bresha to become a gravity well. The forces kept her from moving, and a frown crept its way onto her face.

Once Brime completed her weaving, Enesmic tendrils reached out to grab Bresha. With a downward motion by Brime, the Eshgren's essence was parsed from Bresha's body, the attack defining the lines between the two. Sephan stared at the two cihphists, its eyes narrowed, worry and surprise clear on its face.

Sephan summoned Enesmic energy to its side, the forces magnifying as it detonated the energy and sent it outward. The powerful shock wave washed over Soahc and Brime. Both struggled to maintain their barriers, the onslaught powerful, frightening. Their own attacks were obliterated in the powerful display, and Bresha stood unfettered in front of the two. The area around them was a black crater a block wide.

The sounds of approaching Ashna Maiden forces caused Bresha to glance back and then toward her two opponents. She grinned.

"It would appear our battle is at an end," Bresha said. The Eshgren then summoned a fount of Enesmic energy and unleashed it over Bresha's body, removing its barrier to allow the full force of the energy to wash over her. Bresha was thrown to the ground, her clothes destroyed. Burn marks and bruises covered her nude form as she began to writhe in pain on the ground. Screams of fear escaped her lips.

The voices closed in, and an army of Ashna Maidens filed onto the scene, along with a contingent of priestesses who stood at the ready, the Enesmic swirling around them violently.

"Surrender now or be destroyed!" Avatar Lopi called out.

Soahc and Brime glanced with wide eyes from Bresha to the host of Maidens now around them. They could see Lanrete and the Founder's Elites kneeling on the ground, their hands behind their heads.

"*Vusg*," Soahc whispered to Brime.

The Ken'Tar species is capitalistic, rash, and considered dangerous. Their government is classified as a democratic republic like our own, although more archaic.

–FROM "KEN'TAR OBSERVATIONS"
DAS'VIN ARCHIVES

CHAPTER 106 DEXTER PINSTEN

Ashnali, Ashna Maiden home system

Flee the system, now. Checkpoint at 2100 hours, Lanrete broadcast to the Foundra Ascension.

"Order confirmed, departing system," Auri sent back. Immediately, the *Foundra Ascension* broke orbit. A contingent of Ashna Maiden warships started to converge on the ship, but within seconds, the *Foundra Ascension* had engaged suplight and blipped out of the system. The warships prepared to pursue, but halted in giving chase at the last moment.

Dexter watched his team as they were carted off in restraints and under heavy guard. He hung from the side of a nearby building, his cloak engaged, about three floors up. Dexter connected to the HIN.

Priority Iceward Two, Paragon in the red, balance sheets need immediate attention. Within seconds of the broadcast, the HIN indicators in his biomobi changed to ice blue.

"Message acknowledged, accountants en route. Status, Lifetime?" Andrex Dominu, general of intelligence, responded via a direct channel to Dexter.

Now there's a voice I haven't heard in a long time. Personal status green, situation status . . . could use some vusging *work*, Dexter sent back.

"Backup in three hours, next checkpoint?"

Paragon-enforced checkpoint at 2100 hours.

"Understood. Overseer out."

Dexter climbed to the roof of the building and continued to watch. He began to play through multiple scenarios of the situation and thought it unlikely that they would execute his team right away. He wasn't surprised at all that there were Sentinels already in play on Ashnali; the three-hour time window hinted as much, at least. Whether they had been permanently stationed on the planet for recon or whether they had been sent to shadow Lanrete was something only Andrex would know. Dexter thought back to his last encounter with Andrex. The man had been disappointed in his decision to join the Founder's Elite. Dexter was a rising star in the Sentinels, destined for a formal leadership position, but hadn't wanted a desk job.

Moving to keep sight of his team, he took a running start and jumped to the next building, continuing in the pattern until he was in a better vantage point. It would be a long night.

CHAPTER 107 SEPHAN

Ashnali, Ashna Maiden home system

Bresha was slowly escorted into the Ashna Mothers' audience chamber. She rested in a hoverchair, a horde of nanites working away inside of her body repairing the damage from the self-inflicted attack. All the Ashna councilors and many of the avatars were in attendance.

"Thank you, Avatar Bresha, for accepting our summons," Mother Venice Fawni said. "We apologize for not allowing you time to recover."

"We must act quickly in this situation, as I'm sure you must understand," Mother Ce Nu Yo Kl said. "The charges being brought against those in attendance and the political ramifications require thorough investigation."

"I . . . understand fully . . ." Bresha paused as if taking a breath. "Allow me to be . . . as helpful . . . as possible."

Brime rolled her eyes.

"Can you identify those who facilitated this brutal attack that resulted in the loss of Maiden life, serious injury to yourself and others, and substantial property damage to the Ashna Maidens?"

"Yes . . . esteemed Mothers," Bresha breathed. She turned to regard Soahc and Brime. Both had restraints on their arms, and their mouths were gagged. They also had a group of high priestesses around them. "Those two facilitated the attacks." Bresha turned to regard Lanrete. His silver gaze was intently focused on her, his expression threatening. "And the founder himself orchestrated the whole affair."

"You lie!" Serah'Elax shouted. She was still in her disguise.

"Silence!" Mother Alenet Dascl countered. With a motion, Ashna Maidens descended on her, forcefully pinning her to the ground. "You will remain silent until we deem it necessary for you to speak."

"No, this is a farce!" Serah'Elax said. "That woman is a monster; she is not what she appears to be. She did this all herself, Soahc and Brime on—" Serah'Elax was pulled up, and a silencing fist struck her across the jaw. The disguise system quickly adjusted for the injury and displayed the intended damage across her face.

Sephan caught the subtle readjustment in the appearance of the woman and narrowed its eyes. Probing Serah'Elax, the Eshgren discovered the artificial field in play around the woman's body and assaulted the source. A crackle sounded as the disguise module failed.

Gasps went up throughout the room as Serah'Elax's distinctive Das'Vin features replaced those of the Huzien disguise. Her almond glare locked onto Bresha.

"Interesting . . ." Bresha whispered. "This . . . explains much." Bresha turned toward the Ashna Mothers. "Serah'Elax returned with allies . . . to finish me off. Surely . . . she would have sought to enact her revenge . . . against you, dear Mothers . . . for the judgement passed against her!"

"This is indeed an unexpected turn," Mother Alenet said.

"Escort the traitor to a holding cell, her judgement has already been passed," Mother Ce Nu Yo Kl said. "We will convene to determine the fate of the others." As one, the Ashna Mothers got up from their seats and retreated into their back room.

Avatar Hegna nodded to her second in command, Exemplar Ember Riss. Ember then peeled off, exiting out of the chamber discreetly. Hegna's gaze met Bresha's, and the two women silently regarded one another.

Bresha smiled and watched as Hegna broke her gaze and looked to Lanrete. The founder stood silent, his posture commanding, in control. Confidence radiated off the man. Hegna then scanned the rest of his party, stopping at Soahc, who radiated an aura of pure annoyance, his gaze bored. He gave the impression that if he truly wanted to, he could have walked out of the audience chamber with few if any able to really do anything about it.

Sephan frowned as it glanced between Hegna and Soahc.

Hegna turned her gaze back to the empty seats the Ashna Mothers had occupied. She paused for a moment, then exited the chambers as Sephan eyed her curiously.

Ken'Tar now employ a strict code of honor, but are quick to anger when that code is violated. Their hulking frames make them intimidating and they feed on this power subconsciously.

-FROM "KEN'TAR OBSERVATIONS"
DAS'VIN ARCHIVES

CHAPTER 108 SERAH'ELAX REZ ASHFALEN

Ashnali, Ashna Maiden home system

The former exemplar found herself being dragged, and she stared at the ground as it passed by. All that she had worked toward seemed dashed to pieces. A group of Maidens surrounded her, and the scion in charge of one of the seraglio stationed in the temple moved with them. She was an Eeriteen woman, her dark silver complexion accented by deep blue orbs that were intently focused on Serah'Elax. Her Blades of the Goddess seemed to interweave with her corded, tubular body, and her movements were graceful.

"You won't escape this time," the scion said. "By Ashna, I will see that justice is upheld." Serah'Elax glanced up at the scion, her gaze momentarily locking on her orbs. She then glanced across the faces of the many other Maidens there, all of them tight-lipped.

"I mourn the deaths of Exemplar Elise and the others with you, sisters," Serah'Elax said. The scion moved in and struck Serah'Elax hard across the jaw, the strike sending her sprawling across the floor. The Maidens turned to regard their scion in confusion.

"Don't you dare speak her name."

"I am sorry, Se Yo Il Ka." Serah'Elax spat platinum blood to

521

the floor. "I did not kill Elise . . . but I accept that my presence here is what led to her death and the deaths of many other Maidens." Everyone nearby tensed up as Scion Se Yo Il Ka stared hard at Serah'Elax, a motion of her hand causing the Maidens to move forward and once again grab hold of her. Moving to the front, the scion remained silent as the Maidens followed her, dragging Serah'Elax behind.

Ember Riss stepped out in front of Se Yo Il Ka, her own Blades of the Goddess clearly visible. The scion stopped in her tracks, her eyes narrowing. "We are escorting a prisoner, move."

"We'll take it from here." Ember smiled. Motion exploded from all around them, and the corridor was suddenly filled with Ashna Maidens bearing the marks of both the 19th and 512th Retinues.

"This is treason!" the scion yelled.

"Treason is allowing the methodical manipulation of our order to continue, dear sister." Ember nodded as multiple Maidens approached Se Yo Il Ka with weapons drawn. "We do not wish to kill you, sisters, but we will if necessary. Please relinquish the prisoner and stand back." Se Yo Il Ka dropped her Blades of the Goddess and motioned for her Maidens to lower their weapons. She took a step back and glared at Serah'Elax.

"Thank you for your understanding," Ember said.

Ken'Tar sexuality heavily influences Alliance culture and has been highly commercialized, with their techniques and advice employed across almost every species in the Huzien Alliance. This stems from their unique biology, which requires sexual satisfaction to ensure procreation.

-FROM "KEN'TAR OBSERVATIONS"
DAS'VIN ARCHIVES

CHAPTER 109 CISLOT

Huza, Thae, Huzien home system

Tirivus stared at the vote tally on the primary holodisplay of the senate floor. He looked to be on the verge of exploding.

"The motion carries," Cislot said. "The Tuzen Empire has been officially expelled from the Huzien Alliance, effective immediately."

"You will all pay!" Tirivus roared. Cislot silenced Tirivus's feed, his vengeful rant going unheard.

"This is never an easy decision. Thank you all for your understanding in this matter. Alliance statutes exist for a reason and no member, no matter how great or small, can shirk their responsibilities. We either stand together or we fall apart."

Tirivus stood as still as a statue, his rage seething, his gaze focused squarely on Cislot. With murder in his eyes, he terminated his connection, and his form faded from the senate hologrid, along with his delegation.

Cislot let out a sigh, dismissed the session, and retreated to her office. She moved to her window, where she took in the setting sun as a serving drone deposited a cup filled with a dark red liquid in her hand. At a blip on her mobi, she turned to glance back toward her desk where a holographic representation of her new personal assistant appeared.

"Founder, Andrex Dominu is here to see you."

"In person? All the way from Huzien Intelligence in Tomen?"

"Yes, Founder."

Cislot frowned. "Let him in." She moved to her desk, subconsciously downing the rest of her drink. Andrex strode into the room as she sat down. Her gaze stayed on the blond, blue-eyed Human as he came to stand directly in front of her desk. He motioned to his side, and a holographic representation of Auri appeared next to him. "No!" Cislot gasped as she paled, her eyes wide. Andrex took in a deep breath before glancing to Auri.

"Hello Founder. Lan . . . Founder Lanrete and his team went to Ashnali, the Ashna Maiden homeworld, to track down a suspected agent of Sagren still at large. They encountered the agent, but due to unforeseen circumstances failed to subdue them and were detained by the Ashna Maidens. Lanrete ordered the *Foundra Ascension* out of the system. They are awaiting sentencing by the Ashna Mothers." Cislot let out a sigh of relief at her words, having feared the worst. Then the words hit her.

"What?" Cislot yelled. Her expression was raw, her eyes wide as they locked onto Auri. "When did this happen?"

"Exactly four hours ago," Auri said. "Our next checkpoint is at twenty-one hundred hours."

"There are two Sentinels on the ground, with another in orbit around the planet," Andrex chimed in. "We have eyes on the situation, but it doesn't look good."

"Why have you waited until now to contact me?" Cislot's voice had an edge in it that caused Auri to take a step back.

"I apologize Founder, I—"

Andrex stepped forward, his hands behind his back. "I took command of the situation immediately. Once our forces were in place to provide additional intel, I determined it best to loop you in.

Coming to you without additional information would have served no purpose."

Cislot regarded Andrex silently for a long moment. "Very well . . . what do you see as the next step?"

"I think it best to open up negotiations with the Ashna Maidens while positioning multiple fleets along their border."

"Do you believe Lanrete and his team to be in real danger?"

"Yes. The Sagren agent known as Bresha is a wild card."

"Hmmm." Cislot turned to a blank spot in her office. Within moments, the holographic representations of both Supreme General Ranmor Wesla and Admiral General of the Fleets Lucien Entret appeared. Both men saluted the founder instantly.

"Founder, your call is a welcomed surprise," Ranmor said. He moved to attention, the lines in his light brown skin tensing up at the sight of Auri and Andrex but no Lanrete. He then silently acknowledged Lucien, who nodded and deferred to his superior in the conversation.

"I'm afraid this isn't a pleasant matter," Cislot said. "Founder Lanrete has been taken captive by the Ashna Maidens." Ranmor and Lucien stared at Cislot wide-eyed. "Auri will be able to fill in the details later. For now, a show of force is needed on the borders of Ashna Maiden space."

"The border?" Ranmor scrunched up his nose. "We can plow through to their capitol in a matter of weeks."

"I am aware, Supreme General, however, we will not take such action until all efforts at negotiation are exhausted."

"Understood," Ranmor conceded. With a nod toward Lucien, Andrex, and Auri, he terminated his connection as Lucien followed suit.

Cislot turned her gaze to Auri.

"I will speak with the Ashna Maidens within the hour."

"Yes, Founder."

"You will release Founder Lanrete," Cislot said, standing in a long red suit jacket, the tail seeming to hover behind her, her arms clasped behind her back, "and all members of his entourage immediately, or face the full wrath of the Huzien Empire." Cislot paused for a moment to let the words sink in. "Failure to comply within the hour will be considered an act of war." The eyes of four Ashna Mothers stared back at her from holodisplays in the primary audience chamber atop the Huzien Capitol building.

"Founder Lanrete and his cohorts have taken the lives of Ashna Maidens," Mother Alenet countered. "Would you have us let such transgressions go unchecked? What justice is there in that?"

"You are within your rights to banish Founder Lanrete and his entourage from Ashna Maiden space," Cislot said.

"Banishment?" Ce Nu Yo Kl scoffed. "Are we to allow murderers to go free?"

"Ladies." Cislot locked gazes with the Eeriteen woman. "If you seek to one day find yourself involved in galactic politics, you must come to understand galactic protocol as defined in the Welio'Purtal Treaty." The Ashna Mothers exchanged confused glances. "All government officials charged with crimes will be returned to their host nation to undergo due process with any charges levied against them presented in accordance with Qilyer statutes."

"Your statutes and treaties mean nothing to us," Mother Alenet said.

"While you pass laws and debate politics, we fight for mere survival, ignored by all in the hell that is our everyday life here in what you call the Outer Rim," Mother Venice Fawni said. "Don't come to us making demands when it's convenient to you."

"If I understand correctly," Cislot interjected, "Founder Lanrete originally approached you with an olive branch, a campaign proposed to wipe out one of the largest pirate bands in your space.

And yet I come to find him taken captive on what could be considered trumped-up charges by a fringe nation with archaic laws." Cislot tilted her head to the side. "Perspective is important, is it not?"

The Ashna Mothers once more glanced between one another.

"We will consider your proposal," Mother Ga Po Fe Ul said.

"You have one hour." Cislot terminated the connection.

We have cataloged Ken'Tar lifespans to be approximately 110 years. Mating with Ken'Tar has been unsuccessful, and more work is needed for Das'Vin compatibility.

–FROM "KEN'TAR OBSERVATIONS"
DAS'VIN ARCHIVES

CHAPTER 110 NEVEN KENK

Ashnali, Ashna Maiden home system

"You think we'll hear something soon?" Neven asked. He sat with Zun resting in his lap, the two in a light embrace. "Yes." Lanrete stood up. The rest in the holding cell turned as a figure approached the cell door.

"The Ashna Mothers have come to a final judgement," the Ashna Maiden said. "We are to escort you off-world immediately. An automated transport is waiting to take you to rendezvous with your ship." The door to the holding cell opened and the Ashna Maiden moved back. Soahc and Brime were standing a short distance away, the restraints and gags removed. A host of Ashna Maidens were stationed around them, and several high priestesses were still in attendance.

"Looks like Cislot worked her magic," Lanrete commented in Soahc's direction.

"She is very good at what she does," Brime said.

"Very good indeed," Marcus said.

"I highly doubt that Eshgren will allow us to leave so easily," Soahc interjected. The team exchanged nervous glances.

The group exited the cell and started through an underground tunnel toward a location just outside the city, where a transport was waiting for them. They walked for some time, all forms of fast travel denied to them.

The area around Neven and the team then trembled violently. The party moved to the sides of the corridor under the supports, Soahc and Brime quickly employing shields that covered the entire group as debris fell around them. When the rumbling eventually stopped, Soahc and Brime turned to regard each other with concern. The Ashna Maidens with them also glanced around.

"What was that?" Neven said.

"Cihphism, a lot of it," Zun replied.

"Oh no . . ." a nearby scion whispered.

"The Ashna Mothers and Ashna Council have been destroyed," a nearby Maiden said in hushed tones.

"No, this is impossible," another Maiden said.

"What's happening?" Lanrete looked to the senior Maiden. The scion turned to meet his gaze.

"We have received an emergency broadcast. The Ashna Mothers were assaulted, and all presumed dead, along with the Ashna Council."

"How can we help?" Soahc asked.

The scion shook her head. "I don't think you can." She looked to her Maidens, the woman seeing their despair. Taking in a deep breath, she steeled her gaze. "We must confirm this news. I apologize, but you are on your own." Turning to her Maidens, she signaled for them all to follow, and they charged back the way they had come.

The Hauxem species is amoral, calculating, and considered highly dangerous. Their government is classified as a republic, where each familial unit, or a'aceph, has representation.

−FROM "HAUXEM OBSERVATIONS"
DAS'VIN ARCHIVES

CHAPTER 111 SEPHAN

Ashnali, Ashna Maiden home system

"This is a mistake!" Bresha shouted. "We allow them to walk out of here and we violate the will of the goddess." A few of the Ashna Mothers furrowed their brows.

"We have made our decision, thus is the will of the goddess as we have so communed," Mother Alenet said.

"No," Bresha countered. A few gasps went up throughout the audience chamber.

"You tread on dangerous ground, Avatar." Ga Po Fe Ul narrowed her eyes.

Bresha turned to the throng of avatars and Ashna councilors in attendance.

"I have communed with the goddess. I have listened to the voice of Ashna and become her instrument of justice." The room began to rumble at the swirling of Enesmic forces under Sephan's command. "I am the true Prophet of Ashna, embodied with her essence to enact her will on this plane." Bresha's body began to radiate a golden hue. She turned to point an accusatory finger at the Ashna Mothers. "The goddess has passed judgement upon you false

Mothers—you treacherous false prophets who conspire with the enemies of the goddess."

The Ashna Mothers stood up in unison, and high priestesses instantly poured out of doors and entryways all around them. They moved to form a defensive circle around the Mothers. Sephan motioned at the space where the Mothers stood. A blinding glow began to radiate from a point in front of the Mothers, high in the chamber near the ceiling. The glow slowly receded to reveal the shining form of a woman bathed in a golden light floating in the air.

"Daughters." The form turned to face the host of Ashna Maidens in attendance. "Turn away from those why defy my will and follow my chosen, Bresha!" Immediately, the majority of the Ashna Maidens in attendance dropped to their knees and prostrated themselves before the manifestation.

"Deception!" Mother Venice shouted as she began to summon the Enesmic to her side. The forces began swirling around her in torrents as she threw all her energy into weaving protections around herself, her gaze focused on Bresha.

Mother Ce Nu Yo Kl caught sight of Venice's actions and broke out of her own shock at the sight of the glowing manifestation of Ashna. Almost immediately, she followed suit, enacting protections around herself. The high priestesses around the two Mothers went to work strengthening their barriers, the actions of the two spurring them into action. The manifestation turned to face the Ashna Mothers, the light intensifying. Sephan unleashed its masterpiece, and the sudden rush of Enesmic forces sent a shiver down the spines of every Maiden in the room.

"You have turned away from me and abandoned my will!" the manifestation intoned and stretched out its hand. "Suffer the consequences." Golden gates appeared suspended in the air in front of each of the Ashna Mothers. Ga Po Fe Ul and Alenet Dascl each took a step back in confusion, finally broken from their trance. The gates flared open, unleashing powerful beams of purple-white energy that blotted out the area where the Mothers stood. The gates then disappeared, and with them, the manifestation of Ashna. Gasps from the Maidens who had remained standing filled the sudden emptiness.

Mothers Venice Fawni and Ce Nu Yo Kl stood breathing hard, their barriers having held with the combined help of their high priestesses. They slowly turned to regard the empty space next to them. Ga Po Fe Ul, Alenet Dascl, and their high priestesses had been reduced to ash, all indications of their prior presence erased. The ledge the Mothers were standing on trembled under their weight, half of its supports gone.

"You will pay!" Mother Ce Nu Yo Kl yelled. Her voice was raw, pained.

"We must flee," Mother Venice whispered. "To me!" The Ashna Mother broke into a bout of cihphistic weaving, her hands clenching as the whole host and the two Ashna Mothers vanished from view. The ledge support finally succumbed as the entire structure came crumbling down. All eyes turned to regard Bresha, still glowing with radiant light.

"Sisters." Bresha and Sephan spoke with one voice, their words intermingled, the sound otherworldly. "Today marks the beginning of the reformation, the beginning of a new chapter in our service to the goddess."

"No! You are a traitor in the highest order!" Councilor Di Na Se Tl yelled. "That was not our goddess, simply a clever deception enacted by your hands!" Many in the room looked unsure, only a few remaining stalwart to the councilor. "We will not stand with you. We will oppose you until the last! You will not have our order!" A few on the council nodded in agreement, some signaling to avatars and other Ashna Maidens to take up arms. A small contingent turned and fled from the room. A large portion of the councilors moved away from those speaking out, their gazes going to Bresha with reverence.

"Pity." More gates appeared around the councilors and their remaining allies. Without any high priestesses to support them, they didn't stand a chance. Beams of energy rippled through their ranks.

Soon, empty space and destroyed floor tiles were all that remained of those who had challenged Bresha. "Who will join me?"

As one, the survivors in the room moved toward Bresha and prostrated themselves before her.

"Praise Ashna! Praise her champion!"

CHAPTER 112 LANRETE

Ashnali, Ashna Maiden home system

"What do we do now?" Neven said. He glanced around the corridor, the place foreign, no maps or waypoints available via his mobi.

"Follow me." Dexter approached the group from the other end of the corridor, his cloak dropping as he came into view. "We're in a series of tunnels underneath the city."

"You're a sight for sore eyes," Zun said.

"Is what they say true?" Lanrete asked.

"Yep, Bresha staged a *vusging* coup," Dexter replied, shaking his head. "She has an astonishing number of supporters. We've established contact with Avatar Hegna. She has secured Serah'Elax and is preparing to depart the planet with her forces." Dexter glanced down at the ground for a moment, Lanrete doing likewise. Both looked up at each other and then to the rest of the team.

"Forces en route to prevent our release," Lanrete said. "We have to move!"

"If we don't end this now, things will spiral even more out of control," Soahc interjected. "We must assault Sephan with everything we have, now!"

Lanrete glanced from Soahc to Dexter.

"He's right, Bresh—Sephan will simply consolidate power," Dexter said. "And from what I've seen, she has already started. This could lead to a civil war within the Ashna Maidens."

"The damage to the Outer Rim, to the worlds that the Ashna Maidens protect, would take decades to recover from," Zun added.

"If they ever recover," Marcus said. The Founder's Elite glanced at one another.

"Sephan is most likely expecting us to retreat," Dexter said. "To regroup and form an attack strategy."

"Which is a good strategy . . ." Marcus said.

"Sephan is too dangerous," Brime interjected. "Given time to prepare, Sephan will be even harder to face off against." She glanced at Soahc. "I agree with Soahc, we have to strike now, with its attention divided."

"Are you in contact with Avatar Hegna?" Lanrete looked to Dexter.

Dexter motioned to the side as Serah'Elax, Avatar Hegna, and Exemplar Ember Riss appeared, flanked by a large group of armed Ashna Maidens.

"Attacking Bresha now would be madness," Avatar Hegna said.

"And yet, I feel the goddess is urging us to do exactly that," Serah'Elax countered. Both the avatar and her exemplar turned to face Serah'Elax, who was clenching the grips of her Blades of the Goddess, the weapons returned to her by Hegna. "If we do not end this now, the Ashna Maidens will fall. Of that I am certain."

"Bresha has established control over the High Temple of Ashna. Our sisters will hold the rest of the city until we can launch a counterattack, of that *I* am certain," Hegna said.

"Bresha will destroy them, utterly," Serah'Elax countered. "You have seen her power, and her words are like poison. She corrupts the hearts of our sisters and kills those who stand firm in the will of the goddess."

Avatar Hegna closed her eyes, as if in pain. She took in a deep breath and turned to Lanrete. "Very well. My Maidens track Bresha as we speak. I have forces on the ground; I can focus them on Bresha's location. They can clear us a path."

"No need." Soahc stepped forward. Raising his hand high into the air, he spoke words of power. As he clenched his fist, the surroundings around the group shifted. Within seconds, they were all standing in the former audience chamber of the Ashna Mothers. Brime had enacted a concealment barrier around them to mask their presence from Bresha.

"We'll keep the rogue Maidens at bay," Avatar Hegna said. "You take down Bresha." She looked to Serah'Elax. The young Das'Vin nodded and moved to stand near Soahc and Brime. Soahc motioned with his hands and said more words of power as he enacted barriers on the Ashna Maidens.

"Do the undoable." Marcus grinned.

"Face the impossible," Zun added.

Neven finished, "Live the incredible. Let's end this!"

Bresha stood wearing one of the robes of the Ashna Mothers and addressing her new subordinates. A host of loyal Ashna Maidens were in attendance, the small group surrounded by the massacred bodies of the Ashna Maidens who had remained loyal to the old regime. The bloodbath had left many of the Maidens stained in the blood of their sisters.

"You have all accepted Ashna's messenger. Now, receive her gift! Step forward and embrace Ashna's power." The same golden gates from before appeared in front of each Maiden, except this time, no terrifying beams of power vaporized them. Instead, prismatic gateways greeted each one of them. All but a few of the Maidens moved forward, stepping through the portals. A heartbeat later, less than a fifth returned. Many now bore glowing eyes of different colors. A small handful radiated power on a scale comparable to Bresha. Without warning, the portals blinked out of existence.

"What has that fiend done?" Soahc gasped. Brime turned her gaze away, shivering.

"Possession on a mass scale," Brime whispered. "They've brought more Enesmic beings into this world."

"With those women as deceived hosts . . ."

"So, this was Sephan's vision for the Ashna Maidens," Lanrete said. "Hosts for the denizens of the Enesmic plane."

"Are there more Eshgren?" Marcus asked.

"Yes." Soahc sucked in a breath. "But it's not just the Eshgren that we should be wary of . . . I sense many powerful beings among their ranks."

"We must save our sisters!" Avatar Hegna said.

"Look at the *vusging* bodies." Dexter motioned toward the corpses all around. "Your sisters were massacred. These are Sephan's pawns now." Hegna and the other Maidens regarded the scene, many whispering prayers to the goddess.

"Vengeance, then."

"Ashna shines on you all today," Bresha said. "By your actions here—"

"You have disgraced her and proven yourselves lesser than pirate scum," came a sharp rebuke. The Maidens in attendance turned to see the cloaked area revealed.

"Ah, here comes another gift from the goddess," Bresha said. "She brings our foes to us so that we may spill their blood as an offering."

"The goddess cares not for blood offerings, heretic," Serah'Elax countered. "You speak the words of one who is devoid of her blessing."

"I speak for the goddess now." Bresha's voice became mixed with Sephan's. "Her will is that you all die here today, and she gladly accepts your blood as a sacrifice to consecrate her new order."

Sephan began to enact more golden portals around the group. So-ahc entered a bout of counter-cihphism, shutting down the Eshgren completely. Sephan frowned.

Lanrete noticed Brime watching Serah'Elax's blades. The Enesmic swirled around them curiously, a distinct power radiating from them. The raw energy gave Lanrete pause, and he glanced between Brime and Soahc. Both nodded; they saw it too.

"Let's work together," Brime whispered to Serah'Elax. "I'll be your shadow."

Serah'Elax looked to Brime, then nodded.

"For the goddess!" Serah'Elax shouted.

The room exploded into action. The Ashna Maidens under Avatar Hegna's command surged forward, with Serah'Elax at the head. Brime was a step behind her, weaving torrents of Enesmic energy with a grin on her face.

Lanrete glanced to Soahc. "Let them have Sephan; we have other Eshgren to tend to."

Soahc nodded.

CHAPTER 113 SERAH'ELAX REZ ASHFALEN

Ashnali, Ashna Maiden home system

The room started to rumble as Sephan brought the Enesmic under its will, the torrents spinning violently before it unleashed the wave of energy over the possessed Maidens. The women's forms twisted as the beings that inhabited their bodies replaced Maiden flesh with their own. Energy fused with flesh, and many took on characteristics of Enesmic beings. Some shifted shapes so much they lost all semblances of their former selves, becoming twisted horrors of glowing malice.

The horrific sight stopped Serah'Elax in her charge, her eyes wide. The Maidens within Sephan's ranks who had not accepted "Ashna's gift" backed away in horror, the realization of what it was too much for them. They turned and fled from the battle.

"Take the goddess's blessing and destroy her foes," Bresha said.

Howls of fury and rage filled the room, the inhuman sounds causing the Maidens to take a step back. Without warning, the abominations charged toward them.

"I am sorry, sisters. May the goddess redeem you in death," Serah'Elax whispered. "For Ashna!" Serah'Elax renewed her charge, a righteous fury in her eyes. The line of Ashna Maidens clashed with the line of abominations, large appendages and razor-sharp fangs digging into their ranks.

"Shortcut!" Brime called out. Motioning forward, she opened a temporary gate, and Serah'Elax charged through along with Avatar Hegna and others. She appeared a few feet away from Bresha, Brime right behind her, with Avatar Hegna and a contingent of Ashna Maidens at their backs.

"We'll cover your flank," Hegna said. She motioned to the Maidens as they charged toward the abominations from behind. Sephan turned to regard Serah'Elax and Brime, and then began to laugh.

Brime touched Serah'Elax's head, opening the warrior's eyes. Serah'Elax took a step back at the image before her. Sephan, in all its glory, was a creature unlike anything she had ever seen. Its pulsating purple eyes regarded her as if for the first time.

"Why, hello there," the creature mocked.

Images of Mother Halle filled Serah'Elax's mind, and a surge of energy flowed through her. Brime took a step back, surprise on her face at the power radiating from Serah'Elax. Her eyes focused on the strands of Enesmic energy flowing off her in torrents, the Blades of the Goddess acting as focal points, a type of conduit. She mouthed the word "wow," then slowly shifted her gaze back to Sephan. The creature regarded Serah'Elax curiously, its eyes narrowed. Serah'Elax's eyes glowed golden, a radiant power flowing through her.

"Die, fiend!" Serah'Elax charged at Sephan.

CHAPTER 114 LANRETE

Ashnali, Ashna Maiden home system

Soahc's eyes began to glow with a terrible white light, and then a streak of lightning arced out from his hand, slamming a mutated Maiden square in its torso. The impact knocked it back a step, and a roar of rage bellowed from its chest.

"That was unexpected," Soahc said. The fiend he'd attacked knocked the Maidens fighting it out of the way, then leapt high into the air toward Soahc. Soahc began to spin, his hands glowing as wave after wave of glowing orbs shot out from around him. In sequence, they slammed into the creature, exploding on impact. Each seemed to siphon life energy from the abomination. In tandem, an echo of the creature began to form to its side, the manifestation made up of the siphoned life energy. As the last orb struck home, the echo flared bright as it lunged toward the mutated Maiden in a blinding explosion that sent its charred remains across the room. "Much better."

Similar monstrosities focused on Soahc after the display, each charging toward the cihphist with wanton abandon.

"Looks like you pissed them off," Lanrete quipped.

"I have that effect," Soahc said.

Lanrete released his blade, and the weapon hung in midair. He broke into a bout of cihphistic weaving, then slammed his fist down onto the ground. Five replicas of Lanrete replaced the one, each with a blade of their own hovering in the air. Angling forward, each blade lunged toward the nearest monstrosity. The blades dug into flesh, all dealing damage. Then each version of Lanrete grabbed their blade and charged toward their nearest foe.

One creature swung at the nearest Lanrete, who dodged the blow and landed a strike across the creature's arm that drew blood. Another Lanrete came in from the side, impaling the creature through its abdomen. The creature knocked Lanrete back, but another Lanrete replaced him and delivered a clean strike at its neck. The force of the blow severed the creature's head from its body, and a different Lanrete jump-kicked the head into another charging abomination.

It shrugged off the projectile and roared, barreling into one of Lanrete's shadows and smashing it into a pillar. The shadow faded from existence as two other Lanretes attacked the abomination in tandem. They repeatedly dug blades into its flesh as it spun, attempting to swat them away. It grabbed hold of one of the shadows, but while it did, it inadvertently locked eyes with Soahc a short distance off.

Soahc smiled, his hand held high in the air. "Let's try a different approach." As he dropped his hand, a powerful bolt of lightning burst through the ceiling and struck the monstrosity where it stood, followed by a repeated series of bolts generated from the atmosphere of the planet itself.

The charred husk collapsed as another roar grabbed Soahc's attention. He turned in time to see Lanrete slam into the side of another charging hulk moments before it would have plowed into Soahc. Lanrete's Enesmically infused tackle knocked the creature to the ground. Lanrete threw his blade high into the air, then moved off the beast as it thrashed wildly. The blade came back down hard, slamming blade-first into the chest of the abomination. With a roar of pain, the creature reached for the blade, but the weapon removed itself and flew back up into the air and out of sight.

The creature scrambled to its feet, blood pouring from the terrible wound. Lanrete snapped his fingers and the creature ignited in flames; immediately after, the blade came back down onto the creature's head with sickening efficiency. Lanrete held his hand out as the blade cut a swath through the creature and exited from the side. The abomination collapsed in a mess. Catching his blade, Lanrete flicked it down, blood coating the ground. He glanced to Soahc.

"Should I start counting?" Lanrete said.

"Show-off."

We have cataloged Hauxem lifespans to be approximately 300 years. Mating with Hauxem has been unsuccessful, and more work is needed for Das'Vin compatibility.

−FROM "HAUXEM OBSERVATIONS"
DAS'VIN ARCHIVES

CHAPTER 115 NEVEN KENK

Ashnali, Ashna Maiden home system

Neven glanced to Marcus. He felt naked without his power armor and saw the same look on the giant's face. One of the smaller abominations howled, charging right for the duo.

Neven drew Streamsong, and his exoskeleton came alive. He moved to meet the charge of the beast, his blade spinning as they started their deadly dance. It drove forward with both of its front appendages coming down like scythes. Neven dodged one attack and blocked the other with his blade. The bony skin was no match for his weapon, and the creature's appendage was severed. The creature howled and lurched back, as if suddenly realizing that the body it inhabited was not truly its own. A look of desperation filled its eyes as it spun and began to strike out in rapid succession, seeking to outpace Neven. The movements began to reach the limits of Neven's ability to track.

I've completed my analysis, please relinquish control, Ellipse said. Neven complied immediately, the exoskeleton now driving his actions as he surged forward. In moments, he'd lodged his blade in the creature's throat, slipping past its defenses. Neven jumped back as the abomination gasped and collapsed to the ground unmoving.

"You've come a long way, kid," Marcus yelled. He appeared at Neven's side, his hands coated in blood. Neven glanced at him and then back where he had come from. The limbs of a similar creature had been ripped clean off, and it looked like the creature had been bludgeoned to death with its own body parts. Neven glanced back to Marcus with wide eyes. "What? I don't have a fancy sword." A bellowing roar snapped up Marcus and Neven's attention as they turned to see one of the hulks charging toward them.

"I know you said not to build you a replacement for Claire." Neven smirked. "But I have a hard time with listening, and Ellipse needed something to do."

"Doesn't help us now anyway." Marcus laughed.

"Not exactly true," Neven said. "The *Ascension* is back in orbit."

Oh, oh! Do we get to do an armor drop? Ellipse said.

Damn straight! Neven replied.

Marcus raised an eyebrow. As if on cue, a powerful blast from orbit blew a portion of the High Temple of Ashna's side ceiling open. The area in front of Neven and Marcus lit up like a Christmas tree, the light quickly fading to reveal one of Neven's power armors and a brand new Archlight frame. Both were open, awaiting their pilots.

"I . . . wait . . . what?" Marcus raised an eyebrow.

"Armor drop!" Neven yelled in tandem with the voice of Ellipse in his head. Not waiting for a reply, Neven charged toward his power armor and slid into his second skin. "They link with the exoskeleton, avoiding the need for separate neural interfaces." The power armor closed up, systems coming online as Neven pumped his arm.

We have been forever changed by our foray into the stars and have adapted to a universe of conflict without allowing it to destroy the fundamental aspects of what make us Das'Vin; peace, unity, and compassion, with a drive for technological advancement to ensure a bright future for our hala'a.

–FROM "INFLUENCE OF GALACTIC SPECIES ON DAS'VIN CULTURE"
BY HEIR'LUIA BUR'JEXTI KEFER HOMUN

CHAPTER 116 MARCUS HENSON

Ashnali, Ashna Maiden home system

Marcus stared at the new Archlight frame, a frown on his face. Another roar from the hulking abomination, now dangerously close, urged Marcus forward, and he slid into the new frame. Bringing the system online, Marcus examined his new shield and lance rifle. A sense of deep sorrow assailed the giant as he gritted his teeth and charged forward, his Archlight thrusters on full burn.

He slammed shield-first into the abomination. It attempted to match strength with the Archlight, but Marcus just laughed and knocked the creature back. His thrusters flared on again as he drove his lance rifle through the creature, releasing a devastating blast that sent it hard to the ground, smoldering. It attempted to rise, but Marcus lifted off the ground, his thruster firing as he positioned himself above the creature. With sickening force, he came down with his lance rifle and unleashed another blast on contact. The hulk exploded in a shower of gore. Marcus glanced back to Neven, who stood watching him.

"Guess you like the armor?"

"Jury's still out." Sounds of panicked fighting caught Neven and Marcus's attention as they turned to see a group of Maidens locked in mortal combat with another hulking abomination. Marcus grunted as a Maiden lost an arm; the beast ripped it from her body in a macabre display. The scream drove Marcus forward as his Archlight thrusters kicked on full burn. He slammed shield-first into the hulk. The impact knocked the creature back, and Marcus stood defiantly in front of the wounded Maiden. One Maiden went to the woman's side and pulled her back from the front lines, while the others moved to flank Marcus.

"Ladies." Marcus nodded his armored head. The stalwart warriors saluted him, each readying their weapons as the hulking abomination scrambled to its feet.

"For Ashna!" They charged, with Marcus leading the way with his shield.

CHAPTER 117 ZUN SHAN

Ashnali, Ashna Maiden home system

Zun weaved strands of the Enesmic with practiced ease, her gaze focused on a creature that used to be an Ashna Maiden pummeling one of its former sisters into the ground. The unlucky Maiden had long since stopped moving, and gore coated the ground around her destroyed body. The monstrosity burst into flames, engulfed in an intense fire that burned bright blue. It howled in agony as it dropped to the ground to smother the fire. The beast then rolled into a charge in Zun's direction, impossibly fast. Zun's GCH flared to life as she shifted the gravity around the creature, reversing it. The beast and pieces of debris lifted from the ground and flew toward the high ceiling of the audience chamber. Zun returned the field to normal and then increased gravity by one hundred times as the creature slammed back down into the tiles with a sickening thud, reaching terminal velocity in the blink of an eye. The impact sent gore in every direction, spraying Zun and a few others with blood. Ember Riss glanced from the creature to Zun and then looked up, her eyes wide.

"You'll have to teach me that trick," Ember said.

"That can be arranged." Zun winked. Another creature roared as it charged toward Zun, her display infuriating the beast.

Ember Riss met its charge, her Blades of the Goddess flashing as she left a gash across its body. Its charge toward Zun defeated, the creature swung its powerful arms in Ember's direction. Ember dodged and was joined by her sisters, who peppered it with weapons fire. Zun unleashed a titan blast at the creature, the electrical energy stunning the fiend and making its teeth chatter. Ember came in with her blades crossed, her muscles straining as she followed through with the motion, severing what passed for a head from the creature's body.

Another monstrosity barreled into the group. Ember was taken off guard and lifted in a death charge toward a nearby column. Neven tackled the monstrosity from the side. It released Ember and fully focused on Neven. His power armor strained against the raw strength of the Enesmic beast.

It knocked Neven back, but his armor absorbed the impact and fired gravimetric thrusters to stabilize him. A heartbeat later, the monstrosity was charging at him, rage in its eyes. The wrists of Neven's armor rose to reveal circular rings, both leveled on the creature. Pulses of powerful electric blasts pummeled the beast. They did not slow its charge. Neven fired his thrusters as the beast connected with him, halting its momentum. The armor again strained under the strength of the fiend.

A ball of condensed gravity slammed into the creature from the side. Zun's GCH flared again as she condensed another ball in front of her chest and let loose. The second impact knocked the creature away from Neven, and it scrambled to regain its footing. Neven's Feponic shoulder cannons then emerged from their dens and unleashed a focused beam of energy that seared right through the beast, leaving a hole where its chest used to be. It collapsed to the ground with a sickening thud.

A roar from a smaller monstrosity grabbed everyone's attention. Neven turned to face the new threat as Zun caught it with her GCH, stopping it in its tracks. She modified the creature's gravity field, making its head as heavy as a nearby pillar. Its neck was no longer able to support the head's weight, and it popped off with a sickening crack. She released the headless body as it dropped to the floor, unmoving.

Another series of roars went up as the throng of possessed Maidens began to converge on the small group. Zun and Neven stood, back-to-back.

A handful of the possessed Maidens held back from the fray, each eyeing the other. As one, they turned to regard Sephan and the host of enemies closing in on it. One among their group opened a portal and stepped through. The remainder of the small group regarded Sephan for a moment longer, their eyes lingering on the forms of Serah'Elax and Brime. As one, they turned to regard Soahc and Lanrete, the duo carving a line of devastation in their direction. Eyeing one another again, they turned and exited through the portal, abandoning the battle.

CHAPTER 118 SERAH'ELAX REZ ASHFALEN

Ashnali, Ashna Maiden home system

Sephan quickly merged itself with Bresha, becoming fully one with her once more. Bands of Enesmic energy appeared at its sides as it smiled, dodging Serah'Elax in her charge. Lifting its hand, it unleashed a burst of Enesmic energy that flung Serah'Elax back and hard to the ground.

"I am going to enjoy dissecting you both," Sephan said.

"Ashna curse you, fiend! I will end you this day," Serah'Elax said.

"You may kill this vessel, but I assure you that you stand no chance of ending me."

"The Eshgren were defeated once," Brime said, "and you will be defeated again. The will of the Originator is against you."

Sephan laughed.

"You truly have no understanding of this universe, child, let alone what the will of the Originator is." Sephan shook its head. "Our purpose is just, but I do not have to explain myself to you or any of your kind."

Bresha raised her hands, and whips made of Enesmic energy materialized. Serah'Elax and Brime dodged out of the way as a whip cut deep into the ground where they had been standing. Bresha lifted the other whip and began a swirling dance of death. Serah'Elax and Brime fought to stay away from the deadly bands of energy.

Detecting an opening in the deadly web, Serah'Elax charged forward and struck out. Bresha dodged the strike, coming across with her whip, but Serah'Elax ducked low, lunging for Bresha's legs with her blades crossed. Bresha kicked off the ground and into the air, angling both of her whips down at Serah'Elax.

Brime telekinetically pushed Serah'Elax out of the way, the bands tearing into the ground where she had been a split second before. Serah'Elax rolled and came up in a sprint before kicking off a nearby pillar and chasing after Bresha in the air, her blades angled for the kill. Bresha unleashed a shock wave of energy that connected with Serah'Elax and sent her flying hard toward the ground again. Brime caught her with telekinetic force and pulled her back to her side.

Bresha hovered in the air, her deadly whips seeming alive as they writhed around like angry snakes. She licked her lips and flew at Serah'Elax and Brime. Brime grabbed Serah'Elax and clenched her fist, teleporting both a short distance away. Bresha immediately turned in their direction and clapped her whips together, the energy combining and striking out instantly like a long spear, missing Serah'Elax by a hair as she reflexively dodged the incredibly fast attack.

Bresha appeared where the tip of the energy spear ended, dangerously close. Serah'Elax slammed her Blades of the Goddess together, unleashing a blast point blank at Bresha's chest. The blast knocked Bresha back, her barrier flickering. Brime stomped her foot and motioned with one of her hands, the other hand moving across her stationary hand slowly as Bresha and Sephan blurred, the Eshgren pulled from its shell inside Bresha.

The whips of Enesmic energy vanished as Bresha gasped, the Eshgren struggling for control as the two seemed to fight with one another. Almost immediately, Sephan regained control and glared at Brime, who stomped her foot again and repeated the same motion.

Despite the Eshgren regaining control, Sephan was still partially separated from Bresha, manifesting into its normal form. The Eshgren raised its clawed arm in Brime's direction and unleashed a lefon blast in all its terrifying glory. Brime teleported Serah'Elax and herself to the side, and Serah'Elax struck at Sephan directly with her blades, completely ignoring Bresha's form. The Eshgren grinned at her misstep, and then the blade sank into its body. Its eyes went wide in shock, and a gash was left on its form as it shrank back, leaving a trail of its black blood in the air. Glancing from Bresha's form and back to Serah'Elax, it quickly moved to mold with the woman like it had before.

Brime held up a fist, her eyes white fire. She shook her head no, blocking the Eshgren from fully merging with Bresha, whose body stared up toward the ceiling, frozen in a torrent of Enesmic energy.

Time seemed to stop around Serah'Elax as her eyes locked onto Sephan's form. Moving forward, each step seeming to take forever, Serah'Elax brought her blades forward in an arc, impaling Sephan through the chest. She then slashed the blades outward, ripping black blood mixed with purplish white energy from the being as its form wavered in the onslaught. The shock on its face turned to pain and then rage.

Time returned to normal, and Serah'Elax flipped backward as Sephan swiped at her, a streak of energy left in its wake. The energy warped, turning into multiple light blades that flew forward and assaulted her. She brought up her weapons, blocking each strike.

Brime spoke a word of power, motioning toward Serah'Elax. The muscles on the Das'Vin's body seemed to bulge slightly. Spinning, Brime spoke another word of power, and Serah'Elax dropped low instinctively as Brime brought up her hand. A lefon blast of Brime's own washed over Sephan, the energy distorting its image briefly.

With a roar, the Eshgren rapidly motioned with its hands, the actions barely registering on the two women. Multiple words of power flew from its lips in a blur. Moving its arms wide to the sides, it bowed low, its eyes flaring purple and a grin on its face. Powerful spheres of white energy appeared all around Brime and Serah'Elax.

Brime let out a gasp, her eyes wide. On instinct, she touched the Enesmic and asked for the impossible. The orbs began to glow like mini suns.

An explosion of immense power rocked the area, the light blinding. As the dots in their vision cleared, Brime stood with her hand on Serah'Elax's back, her power funneled into the exemplar. Serah'Elax held her blades close to her chest, and a golden glow blanketed the area.

Every Ashna Maiden and Founder's Elite was suspended in the air, covered in the same glow. The mutated Maidens had been obliterated, all traces of them vaporized by Sephan's devastating attack. The chamber and all structures within a mile had also been blasted away; only scorched earth surrounded them. The upper half of the High Temple of Ashna began to fall, all forms of structure supporting it now gone.

Time slowed again, and Serah'Elax moved her blades to her side, her eyes locked onto Sephan. Taking a step forward, she charged, her right blade impaling Sephan through its chest. Kicking herself off the ground, Serah'Elax flipped up and over Sephan's towering height, her right blade tracing a line of purplish white energy across the front of its body. As she dropped behind it, she plunged her left blade through its back. Her Enesmic-infused muscles bulged as she sliced her right blade partially down its body and kicked backward, bringing both weapons fully across its midsection in complete decimation. She spun in the air, her body performing two revolutions before landing in a flourish.

Sephan was thrown forward, its body shuddering at the brutal attack and black blood spray coating the area. As the Eshgren staggered, its gaze came up to meet Brime's.

"Back to the Enesmic with you!" Brime said, reaching both hands forward, her palms up. Sephan was instantly held in place, frozen. Speaking a litany of words of power, Brime slowly moved her hands to the sides, her palms turning downward.

"No!" Sephan roared. Its form began to fade, the Enesmic pulling at the Eshgren's essence. With a quick motion, Brime brought both of her hands across her chest in an *X*. Sephan's hold on Bresha was severed instantly, and the Eshgren was ripped from her.

Yelling in fury, Sephan clawed the ground in a desperate attempt to stay anchored to the Havin plane. A rift opened behind the being, and glowing chains appeared and wrapped around its form. They fully encased the Eshgren until only its pulsating purple eyes were visible. Brime met its gaze. Loathing radiated from those orbs, and within a heartbeat, Sephan was ripped from the Havin plane and thrust back into the Enesmic plane. The rift collapsed behind it in a torrent of energy.

At the sudden absence of the Eshgren, Serah'Elax and Brime took in deep breaths. Both glanced up to see death raining down on them in the form of the upper half of the High Temple of Ashna. Brime met the gaze of Soahc from a few yards away; he was already in a bout of cihphistic weaving. With clenched fists, he teleported the entire contingent of their group away as the temple came crashing down.

Bresha collapsed to her hands and knees, the full group a safe distance away from the devastated High Temple of Ashna. She took in a deep breath of her own, as if breathing for the first time. After exhaling, Bresha took in another deep breath and let lose a wail. She collapsed to the ground, curling up into a fetal position. After a long moment, the wail ended, and Bresha lay shivering.

"I'm free," she whispered. Bresha said the words repeatedly, tears forming in her eyes. "I'm truly free."

Serah'Elax looked to Brime.

Brime moved to Bresha and kneeled beside her. She began to rub her back, whispering softly. Bresha recognized Brime, and the tears came faster.

"It's okay, you're safe now."

Lanrete glanced at Soahc. "Do you sense them?" Lanrete asked. "The other Eshgren?"

Soahc shook his head. "They fled during the battle. I cannot detect any hints of their trail."

"How many were there?"

"I . . ." Soahc paused. "I am unsure. I detected at least three additional beings of immense power when we entered the chamber, but there could have been more that were masked to me."

Lanrete fixed his gaze on the image of Brime consoling Bresha, thoughts of what one Eshgren had been capable of weighing heavily on his mind.

"We will rebuild." Mother Venice Fawni turned to face Serah'Elax, Brime, Soahc, Lanrete, and the rest of the Founder's Elites. They were in the High Priestess Wing of High Temple City, a few of the quarters having been repurposed for the remaining Ashna Mothers. Sephan's devastating attack had destroyed the High Temple of Ashna, and the fallout had destroyed most of the Avatar Wing nearby. "It will take time, but we will rebuild."

"With your joining of the Huzien Alliance, we will be able to allocate resources to assist in the rebuilding efforts," Lanrete said. "And many of our corporations have already agreed to provide substantial assistance in bringing all Ashna Maiden controlled worlds up to the standards of other Alliance planets."

"This . . . will be a change for our people," Mother Ce Nu Yo Kl said. "Our traditions are what have made us strong."

"With pirate forces taking advantage of the chaos caused by the loss of most of the Ashna Council and the other Mothers," Avatar Hegna interjected, "we have little choice to protect our space."

"I understand the need," Mother Ce Nu Yo Kl countered, "but I still mourn for that which we have lost in aligning ourselves with the Alliance."

"This was always Mother Halle's desire," Mother Venice said. "She believed that only by joining ourselves with the Alliance would we ever fully realize our true potential. She believed it the will of the goddess."

"Time will only tell if she was right," Mother Ce Nu Yo Kl said. The Eeriteen woman turned to face Serah'Elax. "Thank you for all that you have done for us. I am truly sorry for ever doubting you."

"It was all in Ashna's will," Serah'Elax said.

Mother Venice also turned to face Serah'Elax. "We have one more task to ask of you, blessed champion of the goddess." Mother Venice nodded in Avatar Hegna's direction. The avatar stepped forward and added a rank insignia onto Serah'Elax's Maiden uniform. "Avatar Serah'Elax Rez Ashfalen, go forward and serve as the Ashna Maiden envoy to the Huzien Alliance. May your actions glorify our goddess and make a name for our people across the galaxy."

"I . . ." Serah'Elax stared down at the avatar rank insignia. Her eyes came to meet Avatar Hegna's, a smile on Hegna's face.

"Make us proud."

Serah'Elax slowly turned to face Lanrete. "Will you have me?"

Lanrete bowed slightly, the members of the Founder's Elite doing likewise.

"We are honored to accept an envoy of the Ashna Maidens," Lanrete said.

"Welcome to the Founder's Elite." Brime walked over and embraced Serah'Elax.

Ashnaret, Ashna Maiden protected space

Serah'Elax chimed the door to her mother's condo. The door opened, and Dera'Liv rushed out to embrace her daughter in a tight hug. Serah'Elax stood with eyes wide, her mouth open.

"I was so worried." Dera'Liv was crying. "They said you were dead, but I knew it wasn't true. I could still feel you, still feel you connected to me." She took a step back from Serah'Elax, her gaze scanning her daughter. "You look well. I'm so happy."

"I . . ." Serah'Elax was at a loss for words.

"I'm sorry about everything." Dera'Liv shook her head. "I should have been a better *yu'shae* to you, I should have tried harder." Serah'Elax's gaze softened. She moved forward and embraced Dera'Liv.

"No, you were an outstanding *yu'shae*." Serah'Elax took a step back. "It was a difficult situation, I understand that now. You did what you could to cope, and I don't hold that against you anymore. Neither would Ovah'Hal or Nesal'Velexi." Dera'Liv began to tear up even more.

"Come, tell me all about what happened."

"What about your clients?"

"I've cleared my schedule for you; this is the most important thing to me right now."

Dera'Liv led Serah'Elax into her condo, and Serah'Elax launched into a retelling of her adventures.

The bond we form with one another in mating, the ha'ishi, is unlike any connection shared by a species across the Twin Galaxies. We give a taste of this gift to those we successfully mate with, although they will never experience its full ecstasy.

—FROM "INFLUENCE OF GALACTIC SPECIES ON DAS'VIN CULTURE" BY HEIR'LUIA BUR'JEXTI KEFER HOMUN

CHAPTER 119 LANRETE

Foundra Ascension en route to Rugtora, Outer Rim

Marcus paced outside the entrance to Lanrete's quarters aboard the Foundra Ascension. The giant of a man moved to the door, prepared to chime it, then stopped. He started to move away from the door as if preparing to leave. Stopping, he let out a sigh and then turned back around to see Lanrete standing there, leaning against the doorframe. Marcus jumped.

"How long have you been watching me?"

"Since you first walked up." Lanrete motioned for Marcus to head inside.

Marcus let out another sigh and moved into the vestibule. He stopped as he came to the central room, his gaze momentarily falling on the picture of Lanrete's immortal daughter Nalle. He took in her image, and then turned back to Lanrete.

"Lan, I just want to thank you for all that you've done for me and my family."

"You're leaving?" Lanrete's eyes went wide.

Marcus took in a breath, then nodded slowly. "I . . . it's time I retired. Arnea is not going to be around for much longer and . . ."

"You don't need to justify anything to me," Lanrete interjected. "You earned your retirement a long time ago, Marcus. Take it, enjoy it."

Marcus stood up straight and saluted Lanrete.

"You'll be missed, old friend," Lanrete said as he walked up to Marcus and embraced the giant in a hug. Marcus returned the hug, and the two men remained there for a long moment. Lanrete removed himself from the giant and took a step back. "You can take my personal shuttle. It's been outfitted with an experimental suplight drive like the one they have on the *Ascension*. It should get you back to Zen in a few weeks."

"Thank you, Lan."

"Take care of that wife of yours."

"Yes, sir!"

Erb silently walked through the founder's deck, his gaze taking in the portraits of each Huzien Imperial Fleet admiral. The impressive uniforms and diverse faces caused him to smile. He came to a stop in front of an empty spot on the wall and tilted his head to the side.

"When a fleet admiral dies," came Lanrete's voice from behind Erb, "I remove their portrait and send it back to a special museum to honor them."

Erb glanced back to Lanrete. "Who was the fallen warrior?"

"His name was Uyam Ikol," Lanrete said. "He gave his life protecting a doomed planet."

"No one has been selected to replace him?"

"The Third Fleet is no more." Lanrete began to walk back toward his quarters. Erb got the impression that Lanrete wanted him to follow and fell into step behind him. The two walked for a few moments, finally entering the expansive quarters of the founder. Erb marveled at the elaborate paintings and art, suddenly coming to understand what the term priceless meant. Lanrete came to a stop in front of a massive portrait. His gaze hung on the image for a long moment. "I rarely get to see my daughter anymore." Lanrete glanced back to Erb. "Her name is Nalle. Maybe one day you'll meet her."

"I would be honored," Erb said. He slowly moved through Lanrete's collection, his gaze hanging on the framed image of a Ken'Tar woman. The holoframe paused, the Ken'Tar's attention causing it to halt in its cycling through of images. Lanrete moved to his side.

"Urewikiki Jawn," Lanrete said. "She was a wonderful woman, passionate, firm."

"A former *crece'cesen*, I assume?" Erb asked.

"Yes, a beautiful soul," Lanrete glanced to Erb. "Just like yourself."

Erb turned toward Lanrete. "This is what you are, truly," Erb said.

Lanrete raised an eyebrow. "A beautiful soul?"

"A collector of souls."

Lanrete's breath caught in his throat.

"Tell me, collector of souls." Erb turned back to face the holodisplay, the Ken'Tar woman replaced by a Das'Vin in an elaborate dress, the clothing revealing much in traditional Das'Vin fashion. "How does one's heart not become black from such a life of loss over so long a period of time?"

"When I truly know the answer to that question," Lanrete said, "I will let you know."

Erb smiled. "I fear you will not know that answer in my lifetime."

"Then I will whisper the answer to the Enesmic at your final resting place."

Erb nodded.

Sadly, we have become two societies due to the need to engage in conflict. The regular populace and those who make the sacrifice to engage in military service.

–FROM "INFLUENCE OF GALACTIC SPECIES ON DAS'VIN CULTURE" BY HEIR'LUIA BUR'JEXTI KEFER HOMUN

CHAPTER 120 NEVEN KENK

Foundra Ascension en route to Rugtora, Outer Rim

"I think we should tell Ecnics," Neven said. He looked from Zun to Ellipse, the SSI back in her android body. Zun had provided the android with more clothing, and a modest blouse and loose pants now covered up the surprisingly lifelike shell. If not for the subtle artificial glow behind Ellipse's eyes, Zun would have been hard-pressed to distinguish the android from a real woman. "I can't imagine him being anything but impressed."

"You don't know Ecnics like I do," Zun countered. "He will be impressed first yes, but then he will react. And when I say react, I mean he will immediately take drastic action."

"Drastic action?" Ellipse asked.

"He will order your shell disassembled and scrapped, and he might even order the SSI experiment halted and destaffed."

"This is Kechu's dream, he can't shut it down," Neven said with a heavy sigh.

"Then you have to keep this a secret," Zun countered. "Ecnics cannot find out about this android you've created." Zun turned to regard Ellipse. "Which means that you have to stay on this ship. Leaving the ship with your shell will increase the chance of discovery, especially in Huzien space. MinSci SI would detect you in a heartbeat; it's only thanks to Aru that they didn't back on the *Foundra Conscient.*"

Ellipse touched her neck in a surprisingly lifelike gesture and threw a concerned look Neven's way.

"It'll be okay. I mean, you'll still be able to experience the world with me."

Ellipse looked down at the ground, the android slowly rubbing her arm. "I guess, if that's how it has to be."

Lanrete and the Founder's Elite were assembled in the cargo hold, and Soahc and Brime were walking through the group saying their goodbyes to the team. Bresha was in a plain white dress, silently staring off into space. She kept avoiding Serah'Elax's gaze, though the avatar was trying hard to keep herself from reflexively scowling at the woman.

"We're glad you came when you did," Tashanira said. "Who knows how that whole Sephan thing could have gone if you hadn't been there." A few turned to look at Bresha at the mention of Sephan's name; Bresha visibly shuddered.

Jenshi walked up to Bresha and handed her a small pack. "The nanites carry a relaxing neurostimulant that will help with the memories." He patted Bresha on the shoulder. "It will help with the post-traumatic stress, but you'll need to work through this with a therapist, ideally a telepathic one, to fully conquer it."

"Thank you for your kindness," Bresha said. "I am undeserving of it."

"That's not true," Jessica chimed in. "You were under the influence of Sephan, under its control. There is nothing you could have done any different."

"I . . ." Bresha glanced from Jessica to Jenshi and finally to Soahc. The Human immortal silently watched her from across the room. "I allowed the weakness of my flesh to let Sagren influence me, to give it access to my mind. I willingly stepped through that portal and accepted Sephan's control over my body. In the moment of truth, I was more scared for my life than giving up my freedom." Bresha shook her head. "This is my fault, all of it. I should have been stronger. I should have died in that prison at Sagren's hands, or at a minimum, on the Enesmic plane."

"What would that have accomplished?" Brime blurted. "Nothing, that's what!" She walked over to Bresha in a huff. "You've always been a prideful *cith*; I'd have hoped that this experience would have finally opened your eyes."

Soahc smirked.

Bresha stared wide-eyed at Brime.

"Admit that some things are outside of your control." Brime stared Bresha in the eyes. "And forgive yourself, because we sure have."

Bresha moved forward and embraced Brime in a tight hug. A surprised Brime gasped and then slowly returned the hug.

"Well, everyone," Soahc said, "I think it's time we returned home." Moving toward an empty space, Soahc began his weaving, and a clap of his hands created a portal in the cargo hold. Glancing back to Bresha, he motioned to her. "Ladies first."

Bresha turned to Serah'Elax. "I know it must be hard for you to accept me right now," Bresha said. "After all, I appear the same as I did when Sephan had control of me, but I want you to know that I am truly sorry for all of the pain and heartache I have caused to you. I am not asking you to forgive me now, but I am truly sorry and will do whatever I can to help the Ashna Maidens from afar." Bresha turned away from Serah'Elax and walked through the portal.

Serah'Elax let out a heavy sigh, appearing very tired. She glanced to Brime, who was smiling at her.

"It's been real." Brime waved to Serah'Elax. "Your Blades of the Goddess are really something special; I'd try very hard to not lose those." Brime winked at Serah'Elax before glancing to Zun and then to Neven. Grinning, she walked through the portal.

"I guess this will probably be the last time I see you." Soahc clasped wrists with Marcus.

"That's awfully grim," the giant countered.

Soahc laughed. "The offer still stands; I can open a portal to Zen for you and Arnea."

Marcus shook his head. "It's been a long time since Arnea and I have spent time truly alone with one another." He glanced at his wife. "I think it's long overdue for us to have an actual quiet vacation before we get back to Zen and the rest of the family."

"Take care of yourself," Soahc said. "Enjoy retirement."

Marcus pulled Soahc in for a hug. Soahc, clearly taken by surprise, reluctantly joined in the embrace and patted Marcus on the shoulder while glancing to Lanrete.

"What will you do now?" Lanrete said as the two men released each other.

"We have some unfinished business with Ceshra running around our galaxy." Soahc's gaze hardened. "Along with a new batch of Eshgren masquerading as former Ashna Maidens. I think some hunting is in order." Soahc grinned and glanced at the portal. "Not to mention the whole revelation of the Rel Ach'Kel and the state of the Enesmic. I think a good number of textbooks need to be rewritten."

Lanrete nodded.

"I would seek to read a copy of such textbooks once completed," Erb said.

"I think that can be arranged," Soahc said.

"Till we meet again." Lanrete clasped arms with Soahc.

"Till we meet again." Soahc stepped away from Lanrete, waved to the rest of the Founder's Elites, and walked through the portal. It winked out of existence a heartbeat later. All eyes turned to Marcus, Arnea moving to his side.

"We're going to miss you two." Jessica moved to embrace Arnea. Tashanira and a few others lined up behind her. Jessica moved to Marcus and embraced him for a long moment.

"Likewise." Marcus did his best to hold back tears. Jessica moved out of the way for Zun, who locked eyes with him. She blinked away tears and moved in for a hug. Marcus lifted her into the air in a bear hug as they both laughed.

"You helped me get through a very difficult time, Marcus. I'll never forget that," Zun said. Marcus smiled and glanced at Neven. The two locked gazes briefly as Marcus nodded, Neven doing likewise.

Goodbyes were exchanged, and Lanrete clasped arms with Marcus before the giant and his wife stepped to the founder's personal shuttle. Marcus waved to the group as the ramp closed. The hangar door opened, the shielding protecting the team from cold space. In seconds, the shuttle lifted into the air and flew toward the hangar door.

Lanrete brought up a holodisplay, showing an external view of the ship as the shuttle cleared the *Ascension* and entered suplight. The group stood in silence for a long moment, the hangar door closing.

FOUNDERS LOG:
Embracing the Unknown

I pity Bresha, her hands now bloodstained like my own. To have such guilt, such pain forever etched into her memory could break even the hardiest of individuals. I pray that she does not take her own life, yet I know the possibility is strong that she will not have the willingness to face life alone. It is good that she goes back to Etan Rachnie, to the support of those who know . . . who knew her well. Her eyes are filled with sadness, but there is still fire there. The flames were almost smothered by Sephan, almost put out forever, the effect of which would have left Bresha truly broken. But she held on. It will take time for that fire to grow to a semblance of what it once was, but when it does, I fear for those who enter her crosshairs.

As for Serah'Elax—the power she wielded! The infusing of the Enesmic was unlike anything I have ever seen. Maybe she was truly blessed by Ashna, whatever being that may be out in the cosmos. There is still much unknown in this galaxy. After learning of the Rel Ach'Kel and the power they wield, I no longer doubt the possibility of such a "deity" existing in some fashion. One day all will come to light, or darkness. For the sake of all those I love, I hope for the light.

Saying goodbye to Marcus was difficult. In and of itself, goodbyes are something that never get easier. Quite the contrary, when done enough times, you begin to realize how truly final goodbyes can be. I have said goodbye to countless Founder's Elite, sometimes in retirement, sometimes in brief departures that turn into forever. Each moment is precious, never to be taken for granted. The universe is a chaotic beast, a mess of the best and worst of life. Enjoying the highs in life when they appear is important and should never be rushed over. The lows in life are what we tend to focus our minds and energy on, but time has given me an understanding that many fail to grasp: we are what we consume ourselves with. Enjoy the little things in life, the moments of joy and everything that is in them. Sometimes, those moments are all we have left when life runs its chaotic course.

-Lanrete

Those who make the sacrifice can never be fully integrated back into Das'Vin society and adopt a zeal to protect our republic at all costs. They are mourned as lost to us, and we reserve for them a place of honor in our society.

−FROM "INFLUENCE OF GALACTIC SPECIES ON DAS'VIN CULTURE"
BY HEIR'LUIA BUR'JEXTI KEFER HOMUN

CHAPTER 121 HEGFE DENI

Rugtora, Outer Rim

Hegfe Deni burst through the door into his cramped living space, the sound of explosions rocking the complex. The former engine master of the Liron Storm had a panicked expression on his face. He slammed the door shut, his gaze locking on a small single-person bunker built into the floor. Sprinting for it, another explosion sent him stumbling to his knees. Scrambling up, Hegfe pulled the door to the bunker open and hurried inside. Grabbing hold of the bulky door, Hegfe pulled it shut, the pressurized seal locking him in.

The inside of the bunker consisted of a cot, a chair, an assault rifle, a wall of rations, and a wall of bottled water. Letting out a sigh of relief, Hegfe dropped into the chair, his arm resting over his eyes as he leaned back.

"Cozy place you have here." Hegfe froze. "Thanks for leading us to the Het Wrast Aht stronghold world."

Hegfe broke out into a cold sweat. He thought about the assault rifle to his side. If he could get to it before the Sentinel got to him, he could come out of this alive. Holding his breath, Hegfe burst into motion. Dropping out of the chair, he scooped up the assault rifle and proceeded to fire blindly in the direction of the voice. His wall of rations was decimated by the deadly beams of energy. Catching his breath, Hegfe opened his eyes. Frowning at his destroyed food, he glanced around for any signs of a body.

"Nice *vusging* try," Dexter said. Hegfe was slammed hard to the ground, the assault rifle slipping from his grip. Dexter picked him up and slammed him down on the floor again, this time head-first. A resounding crack echoed, and Hegfe went deathly still. Blood began to pool around the man's head. "And here I was considering letting you go."

Dexter unsealed the bunker and stepped back out into the chaos. Triggering another charge, an explosion a short distance away rocked the room and lit up the area like a fireworks show. He took in a deep breath, the filtering system in his Sentinel armor removing the smell of smoke and charred bodies. "This is the life."

Das'Vin who choose to mate with em'zer, or non-Das'Vin, also experience conflict firsthand, although with much preparation, Das'Vin are able to live through such experiences with little long-term impact and instead come away with a greater appreciation of our culture. Due to the benefit of our significantly longer lifespans when compared to all except the Vempiir, it is encouraged for Das'Vin to mate with em'zer before establishing a ha'ishi with another Das'Vin to better gain an appreciation for our own kind.

−FROM "INFLUENCE OF GALACTIC SPECIES ON DAS'VIN CULTURE"
BY HEIR'LUIA BUR'JEXTI KEFER HOMUN

CHAPTER 122 NEVEN KENK

Genmatha, Huzien Alliance space

"Now, this is a vacation," Zun said. She dug her toes into the sand and looked to Neven, who was standing beside her and staring out toward the ocean, a smile plastered across his face.

"Glad we finally got to go on our honeymoon," Neven said.

Zun leaned up against him, and Neven wrapped his arm around her shoulder.

"I love you," Zun whispered.

"I love you too," Neven replied.

The two walked on in silence for a long moment, taking in the ocean mist, the sand beneath their feet, and the smell of seawater on their nostrils.

"There is something I want to tell you." Zun stopped and turned to face Neven, who looked at her expectantly.

"What is it?"

"I—" Zun stopped abruptly and staggered forward a step. Her head slowly moved down to look at her chest.

Neven could see clear through it, and his mind took a moment to process what he was looking at.

"You didn't think I forgot you, now did you?" Came a crazed voice from behind Zun. "To kill a cihphist, the attack must be unexpected and brutal in order to prevent them from having the opportunity to raise any type of defense."

Zun's eyes went wide. She mouthed the word "run" as her head twisted unnaturally to the side, and then a crack echoed across the beach. The life vanished from her eyes as her body dropped to the sand, its original white now turning a shade of dark red.

Neven's wide eyes moved from Zun to the source of the voice. A spindly man in ragged clothing tilted his head to the side, and his crazed eyes widened at the sight of Neven. A facial recognition match instantly pinned the man as Entradis, the most wanted criminal in the Huzien Alliance and the murderer of Zun's former husband, Yuvan Nolli.

"Oh, you're new." Entradis grinned. "Neven, right?"

Neven's gaze dropped to Zun's body, her head at a macabre angle. All strength was sapped from him in that moment.

Neven, move! Now! Ellipse's voice yelled in his mind. Neven couldn't process her words; his gaze was stuck on Zun's lifeless body.

"Why," Neven mouthed, his voice a raspy whisper.

Entradis's grin widened.

"Same reason I'm going to kill you." Entradis began to move toward Neven. "Lanrete values your life."

EPILOGUE

Venice Fawni
Ashnali, Ashna Maiden home system

Mother Venice Fawni dreamed of looking out from her window atop the High Temple of Ashna, the sight so familiar that it was etched into her memory. A sound in her dream caught her attention, and she turned to the former door of her private room atop the tower. A darkness entered the room as a being of power filled the chambers. The light dimmed and the dream twisted, all former images of her room dashed away, replaced by the overpowering image of the false Ashna portrayed by Sephan in all its glory. It began to move toward her, its hand open.

"Submit yourself to me. It is my will," the manifestation commanded.

"No!" Mother Venice yelled. She attempted to move away from the being, its form overpowering. A large black slab of stone appeared out of nowhere, and she was pinned to it. Her clothes were stripped away, leaving the woman bare before the monstrosity.

"Give yourself fully to me!" It moved toward her, its form growing. The closeness of it caused great pain.

"Ashna save me!" Mother Venice cried out.

The false manifestation was ripped away, and an ethereal being was thrown back, away from her. Her room atop the High Temple of Ashna returned, and the creature found itself slammed back hard against a wall in her chamber.

"No! You cannot defeat me. You must submit yourself to my will! It is the will of Ashna. It is my will!" the monstrosity cried.

"No," a powerful voice washed over both the being and Mother Venice. Mother Venice felt herself free once more, her clothing returned, except radiant, now glowing a bright gold. "You have no place here, Sephan the Deceiver," the voice continued. "Depart." As soon as the word was spoken, Sephan was thrust from her consciousness, all semblances of the being gone.

Mother Venice Fawni sat up, gasping. Sweat beaded down her face as she glanced around the temporary quarters provided to her by the high priestesses, almost expecting Sephan to appear once more. Just as quickly as the fear surfaced, a peace descended on her. Taking in a deep breath, Mother Venice smiled.

"Praise Ashna . . ."

Radley Gersten
Testament orbiting Sefera, Ashna Maiden protected space

"Pirate scum," Colonel Radley Gersten hocked and spat. The Huzien officer sat in his command chair aboard the battleship HSS *Testament* of the 5th Imperial Fleet. "Are there any survivors?" His gaze hung on the remains of an Ashna Maiden protected world called Sefera.

"No survivors, sir. The Ashna Maiden fleet that was in orbit has been completely destroyed."

"What about the planet?"

"Every city has been leveled. Signs of orbital fire are evident. We're sweeping for any signals, but nothing so far."

"Damn." Colonel Gersten sat back in his chair. "We were too late . . . open a line to LL."

Within a few seconds, the form of a woman appeared in the hologrid aboard the bridge. The half Das'Vin and half Huzien woman turned to regard Colonel Gersten.

"That doesn't look like good news on your face," Fleet Admiral Jenle Frema said as she put a hand on her hip.

"They killed them all, LL," Colonel Gersten shook his head. "Leveled the cities too. It's horrible. Luck wasn't with us on this one."

The fleet admiral frowned.

Richardre Vean
Dextra Veich, Ashna Maiden protected space

Captain Richardre Vean opened his eyes, the liquid surrounding him warm as he looked around, confused. He floated in the center of a large cylindrical chamber filled with a transparent fluid, a series of tubes connecting to different parts of his body. He lay there in a dazed state as the Genochamber hummed softly.

Eventually, the sound of liquid draining filled his ears, and he slowly came to rest on the floor of the now empty Genochamber, a soft cushion-like material supporting his weight. He slowly curled into a fetal position, the air now being fed into the Genochamber feeling cold on his nude body. The front half of the Genochamber depressurized and then moved out and to the side.

Three Huziens in white lab coats entered the Genochamber with towels and equipment to remove the tubes. They disconnected Richardre and helped him to his feet. When they did, he looked down. His feet seemed off; much larger than he had remembered them.

The Huziens helped him walk, almost carrying him out of the Genochamber. When they stopped, Richardre caught sight of standard-issue military boots. He slowly scanned the form from the boots up as the subtle curves of thighs and hips culminated in a full bust hidden behind a military uniform. The sight played on a primal part of his brain and caused blood to rush to his extremities. His gaze continued up, and Richardre met the gaze of General Hucara Juk Gin. She seemed much smaller than he remembered. Hucara's gaze was turned downward, and a grin was on her face. Her orange eyes flashed up to meet Richardre's.

"Now that…" Hucara's eyes narrowed playfully. "Is impressive."

Hashalem
Frew, Darbol Alliance space

Hashalem winced at the chaotic swirling of Enesmic energy around her, the Ceshra opening an eye in the direction of Nufresha. Both of Hashalem's blue orbs flared open, fear on her face as she recognized the first signs of Nufresha struggling to complete the cihphistic manifestation. The other Ceshra's body trembled, her purple orbs opening in narrow slits as sweat beaded down her face. The two of them stood in a circle, with a final Ceshra completing the formation.

"We must complete the ritual!" Hashalem shouted above the impossibly loud torrent of swirling Enesmic energy. "If we falter now, we risk being consumed!"

Cresala opened her eyes, a grin forming on her face. "Don't tell Nufresha that, she'll just run away and leave us to die in her failure," Cresala said.

Nufresha scowled, her jaw clenched, and a new look of determination formed on her face. The Enesmic forces around them became more focused, less chaotic. Hashalem held back a grin of her own and returned her attention to molding the Enesmic manifestation.

All three spoke words of power in tandem, and the cihphistic manifestation began taking shape. With a final word of power, the swirling stopped, and a shock wave of energy buffeted all three Ceshra. Nufresha was knocked to the ground and Cresala dropped to one knee, but Hashalem allowed the energy to flow past her, her stance unmovable.

"Finally, it is complete." Hashalem smiled.

APPENDIX

CHARACTER ARCHIVE

Name | Species | Character Class (if applicable) | Short description.

ASHNA MAIDENS

Serah'Elax Rez Ashfalen, scion | Das'Vin | Scion of Ashna | Zealous warrior in service to the Ashna Maidens who lost her second mother and sister twin in a pirate raid on Firyia as a young child.

Hegna Helrit, avatar | Tuzen | Ashna Maiden | Legendary avatar of high renown in charge of the 1st Fleet and 19th Retinue of mobile infantry. Sister of Luka Helrit.

Luka Helrit, avatar | Tuzen | Scion of Ashna | Avatar in charge of the 72nd Fleet and 512th Retinue of mobile infantry. Sister of Hegna Helrit.

Venice Fawni, Mother | Human | High Priestess of Ashna | One of the five ruling Ashna Mothers.

Halle Tentle, Mother | Human | High Priestess of Ashna | One of the five ruling Ashna Mothers. She can see the future through prophecies.

Ce Nu Yo Kl, Mother | Eeriteen | High Priestess of Ashna | One of the five ruling Ashna Mothers.

Alenet Dascl, Mother | Tuzen | High Priestess of Ashna | One of the five ruling Ashna Mothers.

Ga Po Fe Ul, Mother | Eeriteen | High Priestess of Ashna | One of the five ruling Ashna Mothers.

Di Na Se Tl, councilor | Eeriteen | Ashna Maiden | Ashna Councilor who orders Luka's fleet to the front lines in the first battle with Jughent's forces.

Ember Riss, exemplar | Tuzen | Scion of Ashna | Second in command to Hegna Helrit.

Chrissy Uilo, exemplar | Tuzen | Ashna Maiden | Second in command to Luka Helrit.

Dera'Liv Elax Ashfalen | Das'Vin | *Yu'shae* of Serah'Elax Rez Ashfalen. Lives on Ashnaret.

Ovah'Hal Velexi Rez | Das'Vin | Deceased *uma'shae* of Serah'Elax Rez Ashfalen and *yu'shae* of Nesal'Velexi Ashfalen Rez, who was killed on Firyia in a pirate raid.

Nesal'Velexi Ashfalen Rez | Das'Vin | Deceased *wo'shae* of Serah'Elax, killed in pirate raid on Firyia.

Valana Etruen, keeper | Tuzen | Ashna Maiden | Keeper in command of the Ashna Maiden cruiser *Greschenathalan* that encounters the remnants of Sagren's fleet.

Ahtlana Jufre, exemplar | Tuzen | Ashna Maiden | Third in command of 72nd Fleet under Luka Helrit. Mentor to Serah'Elax when she's promoted to keeper.

Delira Sinl, keeper | Human | Ashna Maiden | Experienced maiden who executes suplight banking on the *Rion* while fleeing the battle with Jughent's forces.

Wuyjen Xecha | Human | Cihphist | High priestess and right hand to Ashna Mother Halle Tentle. She helps Serah'Elax escape.

Kenyalie Qwen, avatar | Tuzen | Ashna Maiden | Avatar in charge of the Ashna Maiden dreadnaught *Hereyet* protecting Ashnali.

Lopi Tez, avatar | Tuzen | Ashna Maiden | Avatar in charge of forces on Ashnali who first encounters Soahc upon arrival.

Elise Wesker, exemplar | Tuzen | Ashna Maiden | Exemplar of Avatar Lopi in charge of the forces on Ashnali.

Se Yo Il Ka, scion | Eeriteen | Scion of Ashna | Scion in charge of escorting Serah'Elax to prison after the fight with Sephan on Ashnali.

FOUNDRA ASCENSION (SPACESHIP)

Lanrete, founder (code name: Paragon) | Huzien | Redalam and combat cihphist | One of the founders of the Huzien Empire, ultimate leader of the Huzien military, and leader of the Founder's Elite. Commanding officer of the *Foundra Ascension*. Etan Rachnie Council member. Immortal.

Marcus Henson, major (code name: Tempest) | Human | Archlight | Member of the Founder's Elite. Chief security officer of the *Foundra Ascension*.

Jessica Olic, major (code name: Phoenix) | Huzien | Redalam-Wopan | Member of the Founder's Elite. Lead combat instructor of the *Foundra Ascension*. Immortal.

Tashanira Yen Unvesal, major (code name: Banshee) | Uri | Wopan | Member of the Founder's Elite. Combat instructor of the *Foundra Ascension*.

Jenshi Runso, colonel (code name: Unbreakable) | Huzien | Cidelif | Member of the Founder's Elite. Chief medical officer of the *Foundra Ascension*.

Dexter Pinsten, Sentinel commander (code name: Lifetime) | Huzien-Human hybrid | Sentinel | Member of the Founder's Elite. Chief intelligence officer of the *Foundra Ascension*.

Zun Shan, captain (code name: Nexus) | Huzien-Human hybrid | Secnic-cihphist | Member of the Founder's Elite. Chief science officer of the *Foundra Ascension*. Former chief assistant of research & development to Ecnics in the MinSci.

Neven Kenk, captain (code name: Prodigy) | Human | Secnic | Member of the Founder's Elite. Chief engineer of the *Foundra Ascension*.

Aurari Netzcha, lieutenant (also known as Auri) | Huzien | losrim | Administrative coordinator of the *Foundra Ascension* and personal assistant to Founder Lanrete.

Yuvan Nolli, captain (code name: Lancer) | Tuzen | Secnic | Deceased member of the Founder's Elite and former husband of Zun Shan.

Arnea Henson | Human | Aeroponics gardener of the *Foundra Ascension* and wife of Marcus Henson.

Erbubuc Tamn | Ken'Tar | Nistiff | Nistiff monk who rescued Marcus on Tenquin and later becomes a member of the Founder's Elite.

EMPRESS STAR (SPACESHIP)

Adrian Hulim, captain | Huzien | Retired losrim | Captain of the *Empress Star*.

Jessie Gumnen, first officer | Huzien | Retired losrim | First officer of the *Empress Star*.

Deidra Kul, second officer | Human | Second officer of the *Empress Star*. Handed over control to Vexl during the assault on the ship.

Arnold Steinsford, officer | Human | Retired losrim | Chief security officer for the *Empress Star*.

Zeph Ressin, officer | Huzien | Chief communications officer for *Empress Star*.

Hanna Westwarch, officer | Human | Chief safety officer for *Empress Star*.

HUZIEN GOVERNMENT

Cislot, founder | Huzien | Cihphist | One of the founders of the Huzien Empire and ultimate leader of the Huzien government. Executive chancellor of the Huzien Alliance. Immortal.

Marcias Yonvi, restendi | Huzien | Elected head of government for the Huzien Empire.

Huiara Mau Gehreyati | Uri | Personal assistant to Cislot. Born and raised on Thae.

Ulter Wern, grand lichar | Huzien | Grand lichar of Trutara. He fights with the restendi, Marcarias Yonvi, for funds to be allocated for new projects in Trutara.

Rexen Qiro | Huzien | Senator from Neth who questions Huiara's request for funds in the senate.

Gehrat Pesk | Huzien | Former govnus of Thae who stepped down after the loss of his wife.

HUZIEN MILITARY

Ranmor Wesla, supreme general | Huzien | losrim | Oversees day-to-day operation of the Huzien military.

Lucien Entret, admiral general of the imperial fleets | Huzien | losrim | Oversees the imperial fleets of the Huzien military.

Andrex Dominu, general of intelligence | Human | Sentinel | Oversees command of all Huzien Empire covert intelligence.

Jenle Frema, fleet admiral (Lady Luck aka LL) | Das'Vin-Huzien hybrid | losrim | Fleet admiral of the 5th Huzien Imperial Fleet in command of the capital ship HSS *Gefreh*, which fought in the Alliance blockade.

Uyam Ikol, fleet admiral | Huzien | losrim | Fleet admiral of the 3rd Huzien Imperial Fleet. Commanded the capital ship HSS *Lukim* lost in the battle of Neth during the Rift War.

Hucara Juk Gin, general of the mobile infantry | Uri-Huzien Hybrid | losrim | Commands the 103rd Huzien Mobile Infantry, which was assigned to the 3rd Huzien Imperial Fleet.

Richardre Vean, lieutenant | Uri-Huzien Hybrid | losrim | Commanded the military company tasked with protecting Pree, earning the favor and attention of Lanrete during the Rift War.

MINSCI (MINISTRY OF SCIENCE)

Ecnics, founder | Huzien | Secnic-cihphist | One of the founders of the Huzien Empire and leader of the MinSci. Etan Rachnie Council member. Immortal.

Remi Etwa, feshra | Huzien | Secnic | Head of the Department of Weapons Development at the MinSci. Next in line to be chief assistant of research & development.

Phenste Wahkin, feshra | Human | Secnic | Head of the Department of Advanced Computing & SI Research at the MinSci.

Aru Ghaian, feshra | Huzien | Secnic | High-ranking scientist in the MinSci and creator of the Nisic line of reactors. Chief engineer of the Foundra Conscient.

Kaloni Setla, feshra | Human | Secnic-cihphist | Head of the Department of Cihphist Technology. Etan Rachnie Council member. Provides Soahc with the Jehu to go into the Enesmic Plane.

Charlene Yentu | Huzien | Secnic | Project lead of BRAS Power Frame at the MinSci.

Kechu Fen | Huzien | Chief architect for the synaptic systems intelligence (SSI) project at the MinSci. Creator of the SSIs Lahl and Ellipse. Best friend of Neven Kenk.

Augamentres, feshra | Huzien | Secnic | She created the technology that powers the vast oceanic cities across Thae and personally designed Trutara.

ALLIANCE GOVERNMENTS

Tirivus, emperor (Ageless Emperor) | Tuzen | Wopan-cihphist | Emperor of the Tuzen Empire and executive chancellor of the Huzien Alliance. Immortal.

Ories Turbus | Tuzen | Wopan | Most trusted advisor to Tirivus.

Hexa'Gevhre Quen Orecha, heir'apthai | Das'Vin | Diplomatic leader of the Das'Vin Republic and executive chancellor of the Huzien Alliance.

Bur'Jexti Kefer Homun, heir'luia | Das'Vin | Oversees the physical and emotional wellbeing of the Das'Vin species. Offers assistance to Dera'Liv to bring her and Serah'Elax back to Das'Vin space.

Gucy'Uil Beh Xephil | Das'Vin | Administrator for the As'Kiluna who escalated Dera'Liv Elax Ashfalen's case in the Das'Vin government.

ETAN RACHNIE (CIHPHIST SCHOOL AND HOME OF THE ARGENTS)

Soahc (Destroyer of Worlds) | Human | Cihphist-Argent | Founder of Etan Rachnie and legendary cihphist who destroyed the original Ginea, the ancient home planet of the Humans. Reunited Humans and led them to join the Huzien Empire while becoming trusted friend of Lanrete. Etan Rachnie Council member. Immortal.

Brime Wewta (Mistress of the Enesmic) | Human | Cihphist-Argent | Apprentice and wife to Soahc who gets transported to Enesmic plane during the Rift War and is believed dead. Immortal.

Narmo Swela, First Argent | Vempiir | Cihphist-Argent | Responsible for the Argent system at Etan Rachnie.

Merbi Teral, headmaster | Human | Cihphist | Handles day-to-day administrative responsibilities of Etan Rachnie. Etan Rachnie Council member.

Ristolte Aris III, Argent general | Huzien | Combat cihphist | Responsible for military branch of the Argents. Etan Rachnie Council member. Former mobile infantry elite.

Bresha Vecen, shaper | Human | Cihphist-Argent | Argent shaper possessed by Sephan, serving as its vessel on the Havin plane. Immortal.

Desrin, shaper | Human | Argent Chaah hunter | Legendary Chaah hunter of the 9th degree. Partner to Nestis. Immortal.

Nestis, shaper | Huzien | Argent Chaah hunter | Legendary Chaah hunter of the 8th degree. Partner to Desrin. Immortal.

CHAAH

Hiesha Nihjar | Huzien | Chaah cihphist | Chaah member who faces off against Marcus, Erb and the Chaah Hunters on Tenquin. Wife to Orech who is spared by Desrin and Nestis.

Orech Nihjar | Huzien | Chaah cihphist | Chaah member who faces off against Marcus, Erb, and the Chaah hunters on Tenquin. Wife to Hiesha who was sacrificed by Alinos to fuel Elhirtha.

Ianos Lither | Human | Chaah cihphist | Chaah killed during fight on Tenquin.

Alinos Yui | Human | Chaah cihphist | Leader of the Chaah cell on Tenquin who escapes.

MISCELLANEOUS

Entradis | Huzien | Cihphist | Traitor of the Huzien Empire and wanted criminal responsible for the deaths of thousands, including Yuvan Nolli. Mentally Unstable. Immortal.

Adinah Kenk | Human | Industry-renowned robotics engineer and mother of Neven Kenk.

Michael Kenk | Human | Robotics engineer and father of Neven Kenk.

Envero Olic | Huzien | Father of Jessica Olic who attacks Lanrete during a tense encounter on his property. Farmer in the Setna Isles.

Jasha Olic | Huzien | Mother of Jessica Olic and wife of Envero Olic. Farmer in the Setna Isles.

Nalle Libl, CEO | Huzien | Chief executive officer of eshLucient Corporation and biological daughter of Founder Lanrete. Immortal.

A'Amaria Schen | Hauxem | Cihphist | Also known as Seshat, the Information Broker. Ex-wife of Lanrete. Immortal.

A'Areth Schen | Hauxem | Offsprint of A'Amaria and member of her *a'aceph* who was present during Lanrete and Neven's visit to A'Amaria's home.

Lansa Shan | Huzien | Mother of Zun Shan.

Uria Hens | Tuzen | Assaulted on Rugtora and rescued by Sera'Elax. Mother of Garen and Areathe.

Garen Hens | Tuzen | Son of Uria Hens who was almost killed on Rugtora but saved by Jenshi.

Areathe Hens | Tuzen | Teenage daughter of Uria who was assaulted on Rugtora and saved by Serah'Elax.

OUTER RIM PIRATES

Heshel Vrot, captain | Tuzen | Space pirate | Captain in Het Wrast Aht responsible for the *Liron Storm.*

Hegfe Deni, engine master | Human | Secnic | Chief engineer for *Liron Storm* and member of Het Wrast Aht. Responsible for attack SI that infiltrated *Empress Star*'s systems.

Vexl Jabstren, assault master | Tuzen | Wopan | Led assault on the *Empress Star.* Member of Het Wrast Aht assigned to the *Liron Storm.*

Hetye | Tuzen | Space pirate | Pirate who assaulted Zun on the *Empress Star* that met a fiery end.

SYSTEM INTELLIGENCES

Lahl | SSI | Prototype synaptic systems intelligence created by Kechu Fan. Host is Kechu Fan.

Ellipse | SSI | Prototype synaptic systems intelligence created by Kechu Fan. Host is Neven Kenk.

Asha | SI | Advanced systems intelligence created by Zun Shan. Primary SI core matrix resides on the *Foundra Ascension.*

ENESMIC BEINGS

Sephan (the Deceiver) | Eshgren | Cihphist | One of the Betrayers, possesses the body of Bresha Vecen to gain access to the Havin plane during the Rift War. Once Sagren dies, launches plan to infiltrate the Ashna Maidens. Immortal.

Sagren (the Fallen Commander) | Eshgren | Cihphist | One of the Betrayers and leader of the force that attempted to wipe out life on the Havin plane during the Rift War. Killed by Soahc and Lanrete in a covert assault on Sagren's stronghold world. Immortal.

Jughent | Ceshra | Cihphist | Former overlord of Sagren that flees to Ashna Maiden space with his remaining fleet after the Rift War. Immortal

Hashalem | Ceshra | Cihphist | Former overlord of Sagren that led attack on Tar'Ki during the Rift War. Immortal.

Nufresha | Ceshra | Cihphist | Overlord of Sagren that fled from Soahc's wrath on Pree, leaving her forces to get wiped out during Rift War. Immortal.

Cresala | Ceshra | Cihphist | Overlord of Sagren that defeated the Argent battle party and captured Bresha Vecen during Rift War. Immortal.

Eheriequyturjin (the Abettor) | Eshgren | Cihphist | One of the Betrayers. The Eshgren who faces Soahc on the Enesmic plane in the Enesmic Wilds before Soahc is saved by Augrashumen the Valorous.

Augrashumen (the Valorous) | Rel Ach'Kel | Mysterious being that rescues Brime in the Enesmic Wilds and trains her on the Enesmic plane. Immortal.

Vesgrilana (the Sagacious) | Rel Ach'Kel | Mysterious being that is particularly interested in Soahc. Leads the Rel Ach'Kel Council. Immortal.

Hiweretpor (the Perspicuous) | Rel Ach'Kel | Mysterious being on the Rel Ach'Kel Council. Immortal.

Grilmuqshen (the Exemplar) | Rel Ach'Kel | Mysterious being on the Rel Ach'Kel Council. Immortal.

Cirfuletanas (the Empyrean Betrayer) | Eshgren | First to betray the Rel Ach'Kel and the first Eshgren.

GLOSSARY OF TERMS

CHARACTER CLASSES

Archlight - Archlights are towering beacons on the battlefield and centers of support for their fellow combatants. Through intense genetic modification and physical enhancement, Archlights become beasts of men who can withstand intense situations that would seem impossible for even the most hardened veteran soldier. With their massive signature armor, incredibly immense shields, and powerful lance rifles, they stand at the forefront of combat on every battlefield.

Argent - Argents are masters of the cihphistic arts who undergo intense training learning the secrets of the Enesmic. Argent initiates are inducted into the Order of the Argents only after completing extensive trials. The Argent title carries with it not just power but a strict code upheld by the order. Argents can be seen wearing the traditional vestments of the order and wielding immense power. Involved in all facets of galactic affairs, Argents serve in positions ranging from diplomats to strike team members and are a force to be reckoned with.

Cidelif - Cidelifs are combat doctors; they work on the battlefield, offering support both through frontline triage and amplifier-enhanced cihphist ability. Utilizing various medical techniques, cidelifs can quickly stabilize dying soldiers and get them back to the frontlines. Unlike traditional medics, cidelifs are fully qualified doctors.

Cihphist - Cihphists are wielders of intense power, ranging from telepathy and telekinesis to kineticism and metaphysicism. In some cases, cihphists can manipulate Enesmic energy to not only enhance their own native abilities but shape the world around them. Through intense study and training, cihphists become masters of various schools of focus with the most elite mastering them all.

Combat cihphist - Combat cihphists are the most recognizable on the battlefield, with unique military uniforms that signify their status and rank. Combat cihphists employ a technique that allows for their Huzien blade to hover in midair and act independently of their actions. Through intense physical, mental, and cihphist training, Combat cihphists are the epitome of the Huzien military with exceptional individuals becoming elites, who are in essence walking forces of destruction.

Losrim - Losrim are combat specialists. They excel with all forms of mobile combat weaponry and are the core of the Huzien military. Losrim appear decked out in the standard-issue military uniforms of the Huzien Empire. They adhere to a strict code of honor and employ methodical precision with years of intense training that morphs them into efficient killing machines.

Redalam - Redalams are masters of the Huzien blade. They train extensively, learning the many different forms and techniques necessary to be labeled a Redalam. Redalams can be identified by their signature blades, uniquely customized to each individual and family, which they wear strapped to their hips. All Redalam blades are named by their wielder.

Secnic - Secnics are masters of technology. They are seen wielding a variety of experimental and advanced technologies in original, inventive ways. From experimental gravity control harnesses, where the secnic can manipulate the gravity around them, to sophisticated power armors that the secnic wields as either a second skin or a massive frame. The one thing that remains consistent with secnics is their affinity for weaponized technologies of an advanced and/or experimental nature.

Sentinel - Sentinels are the silent hands of the Huzien Empire. They live in the shadows and exist everywhere, from the most battle-worn battlefield to the capitals of rival nations. Through intense training, honing both the mind and body while utilizing the most advanced technology in the Twin Galaxies, Sentinels strike fear into enemies of the empire. A good Sentinel will never be noticed. With their staple personal cloaking technology, astonishing cihphist ability, and specially designed silent sniper rifles, they are the model assassins.

Wopan - Wopans are martial artist gun masters. On the battlefield, they display a mastery of gun arts utilizing their token machine-gun pistols in brilliant displays of acrobatics and hand-to-hand combat. Through intense training, Wopans develop deadly skills in close-quarters combat. You will rarely find Wopans alone; they usually work alongside other units to deal with forces that could potentially overwhelm them.

RACES

Das'Vin - From the planet Desc'Ri. Due to there being no separate genders, Das'Vin have characteristics that would be viewed as both male and female in other species. They have *ga'hei* marks, which are distinct elevated marks that vary in pattern and are unique from individual to individual. They exist all over the body of each Das'Vin and vary in color, ranging from light pink to dark brown.

Eeriteen – From the planet Ashnali. A matriarchal society in the Outer Rim. Corded tubular bones cover their bodies, and they have thick tubular appendages that function as additional limbs that complement their arms and legs. The Ashna Maiden order grew out of an extremist sect in their species, who zealously worshiped the goddess Ashna. Constant war with pirate bands led to the sect claiming dominance and establishing the order as it exists today.

Human - Originally from the planet Ginea, now reside on New Ginea, which is a terraformed moon that orbits Thae. Their homeworld Ginea was destroyed by Soahc during their civil war. The war scattered Humans across the Twin Galaxies and ultimately led to their induction into the Huzien Empire. They have the appearance of Huziens except without esha marks and with smaller builds.

Hauxem – From the planet A'Ahaula. Member species of the Huzien Alliance. Have a teenage-like appearance, with intricate patterns on their heads that take the place of hair in most other species.

Huzien - From the planet Thae. Have esha marks, whose shape and size vary depending on the person. Esha marks usually start at the temples and go down the length of body to the outer thighs of both legs, continuing all the way to the feet. The marks vary in color from light brown to black. The esha marks can bulge slightly when the person is irritated. Due to the high gravity on Thae, Huziens have developed above-average strength when compared with most species.

Ken'Tar - From the planet Tar'Ki. Their most distinguishing feature is two sets of arms for a total of four. Their first set of arms is where they would normally be on most species. Their second set of arms start right below their main pair and forward, more on their abdomen, as to not overlap with their main pair when at rest. It is very rare to see an obese or out of shape Ken'Tar, as it takes very little physical activity to stimulate muscle building, and their metabolisms are unique in that they adjust dynamically to the food intake of the individual. Because of their hulking builds, Ken'Tar are exceptionally strong, far outmatching Huziens and Vempiir. They also stand head and shoulders above the other species, with their average height above seven feet. Ken'Tar have fur that covers every part of their body. The thickness of the fur for Ken'Tar varies slightly from family to family, but generally all Ken'Tar are short-haired.

Tuzen - Originally from the planet Thae, now reside on New Thae. Have munsha marks, whose shape and size vary depending on the person. Munsha marks start at the center of the forehead and at the back of the head. From there, they go down the length of body, both in the front of the person and in the back, to the inner thighs of both legs, where they continue down to the feet. Although Tuzens have been away from Thae for over 80,000 years, they still retain some of the above-average genetic strength that the Huziens benefit from. However, New Thae does not have the same level of high gravity that Thae does.

Uri - From the planet Peshkana. They have fur that covers most of their body. There are certain parts that aren't covered, such as the soles of their feet and hands, their stomachs, and their genitals. Fur thickness varies depending on origin region. Uris have distinct oral fangs when compared with other species in the galaxy, except the Vempiir. They also have a tail that can range in size from long to very short, and ears reminiscent of cat's in a multitude of sizes and shapes. Uri have heightened agility and reflexes that exceed most other species.

Vempiir - From the planet Piro. They have very sharp teeth with exceptionally long canines. Due to their purifying of the gene pool via genocide many millennia ago, very few physically imperfect members of Vempiir society exist today. A moderately high gravity on their native planet has led to their species having strength on par with Huziens.

CORPORATIONS

Encro Motive – Technology. Headquartered on Thae. Automotive, shuttles, and starships.

HighStar Cruise Lines - Hospitality. Headquartered on Arcadia II. Hospitality, travel, and tourism.

Ganrele Retril Corporation - Conglomerate. Headquartered on New Ginea. Capital goods, industrial goods, consumer goods, clothing, and services.

Kekid Group - Real estate. Headquartered on Thae. Construction and property investments.

Somift Technologies - Technology. Headquartered on Thae. IT services, technology, software, and electronics.

TECHNOLOGY

BRAS power frame - Biomechanical recon assault support frame built by Neven at the MinSci. Utilized in the battle of Neth by Neven.

Echaic cannon - A large ship-grade cannon with a nesmonic core generator. It releases a high-yield projectile capable of very quickly eating away energy shields and can blast holes through even the toughest of armors. It is the primary weapon of capital ships and dreadnoughts. Due to its nesmonic core generator, the pull on the ship's reactor is minimal. It can function with the absence of a ship reactor for a short duration, requiring only a short burst of power from the ship-based reactor to kick-start a depleted nesmonic core.

Feponic cannon - Secnic weapon technology that fires powerful energized balls of plasma.

Gravimetric thrusters - Specially designed microthrusters that manipulate gravity to create thrust.

Holodisplay - A holographic display screen that is projected by a micro-base station. These micro-base stations can be built into desks, rooms, and even clothing or skin. The size of the screen is determined by what type of micro-base station is utilized.

Hologrid - A type of advanced holodisplay that is built into an entire room or area. This allows full-scale holographic representations of people or objects to appear projected anywhere within the hologrid.

Hypress basin - A high-powered faucet that opens into a long shallow bowl, the housing normally hidden from view and only appearing when approached. The way the bowl is designed evenly breaks the water, which glides away without splattering back on the user. The faucet also allows for a multitude of different modes, additionally dispensing filtered drinkable water.

Liphojam - A medical device used in the place of needles or syringes. It carries a payload of nanites that are transferred through the skin and that can be outfitted with various forms of medicine. The nanites can intelligently apply the medicine where it is needed most and are capable of utilizing the body's own resources to rebuild tissue.

Power core - Advanced microfusion cells that provide personal power sources. Power cores are utilized in devices ranging from weapons to power armors to power frames. Power cores have a smaller footprint than reactors and are more versatile. Power cores include (in order from lowest yield to highest yield) the Cuden, Eshre, Eshre II, Gefreg, Eshre III, Sefnev, Vengrin, and Sefnev II.

Meglift - An advanced form of elevator that functions on a string of powerful magnets. Employing frictionless technology, the meglift can exist in a vacuum and rapidly cover superstructures in seconds, propelling the inhabitants up hundreds of floors safely in no time. Meglifts move both vertically and horizontally.

Mobi device - A small device that can range in design from an implant to a pin-sized computer. It is usually connected via a retinally implanted display within the user's eye (called a micro-display) where it projects information. It can also wirelessly interface with compatible devices for more intensive tasks. It is capable of interfacing with global and galactic communications systems via relay networks and acts as an individual's single most-important personal device. The key feature of mobi devices is the neural interface that comes with the micro-display. This allows users to send mental commands to their mobi to perform actions.

Nanitically enforced glass - A highly durable, composite glass utilized in starship construction. A layer of nanites exist within the glass that can rapidly repair damage and eliminate cracks.

Nanoplexi - A highly durable, composite metal used in the construction of starships, power armors, power frames, and a host of other technologies and constructs.

Nesmonic core generator - An advanced power core that serves as an independent power source for most starships' primary weapon's systems.

Omnfridge dispenser counter - A large counter with an intricate food storage and preparation system inside. Controlled by mobi synchronization, the system allows for preparation of a myriad amount of food types. Most items are created in-house by a complex 3D printing system that can create foods from organic raw materials.

Plexicarbonite - A very strong material used in the construction of Huzien blades and support structures.

Reactors - These devices employ advanced hyperfusion technology that allows for a sustainable energy source utilized on both planets and vessels. Reactors include (in order from lowest yield to highest yield) the Feng, Hurion, Vashra, Gunion, Nies I, Nies II, Ouma, and Nisic.

Skin resolver - A special grenade that disintegrates organic material in a short radius. It passes through inorganic material harmlessly and is the ideal form of explosive for space pirates.

Suplight drive - A type of advanced faster-than-light propulsion system that allows for intergalactic travel. The Herv suplight drive is a small drive used by shuttles for travel between planets within solar systems. The Vush suplight drive is a starship-grade drive that allows for travel between solar systems. This is the most common suplight drive. The Tria suplight drive is for larger starships and megaships. This allows for faster travel between solar systems and is more advanced than the Vush suplight drive. There are other experimental suplight drives that are not in mass production.

Systems intelligence - A system that can take a problem and create a solution without interaction with a biological being. It can create code and applications for the purpose of solving the problem. It can also spin up and tear down platforms and network resources completely independently, and can install and configure the applications on said systems itself. It can also improve itself with time and can develop a personality if permitted to.

Vencom rinse chamber (VRC) - A type of chemical that has the composition of water but that displaces dirt and other foreign materials from the skin and leaves thoroughly cleaned skin behind. It has the added benefit of detoxifying the skin. Most Vencom rinse chambers have a secondary mode that blows powerful streams of warm air around the user to quickly dry and remove any remaining Vencom rinse. It is so effective that users very rarely need to utilize towels in order to completely dry off.

MISCELLANEOUS

Ashna Maidens - Holy female warriors with a strict code of honor. Not aligned to any particular empire or alliance, the Ashna Maidens are seen as a police state that operates on the Outer Rim of the Twin Galaxies. All Ashna Maidens take a vow of celibacy in service to their goddess Ashna.

Ashna Council - Fifty women in the Ashna Maidens who oversee the day-to-day operations of the order. They report to the Ashna Mothers but are also responsible for appointing new Ashna Mothers.

Ashna Mothers - Ruling council of five women seen as the embodiment of Ashna, the ultimate leaders of the Ashna Maidens. Ascended former high priestesses of Ashna.

Betrayer - An Eshgren. A fallen Rel Ach'Kel.

A'Aceph - Hauxem familial units, where all virile males are free to mate with all virile females without restraint or restriction.

A'Ayuwri'Aret - A highly technical Hauxem dish usually served in high-class restaurants.

Chaah - An organization of rogue Argents that plot against the Argents, attacking them openly. Made up of Argent rejects who failed or refused to adhere to the Argent code.

Cihphism - The art of bending Enesmic energy to one's will. Has four major schools of mastery: telepathy, telekinesis, kineticism, and metaphysicism.

Das'Vin drone carrier - Robotic vessel that houses the drones utilized in a Das'Vin drone division. Has advanced construction systems that build new drones to replenish reserves. Is an unmanned vessel.

Das'Vin high command ship - Command ship of a Das'Vin drone division. Contains Das'Vin personnel.

Das'Vin swarm command ship - Drone coordination starships responsible for controlling the drone carriers. Contains Das'Vin personnel.

Darbol Alliance - A competing alliance of different races that borders Huzien Alliance space.

Divinebreath - The name of the Redalam blade utilized by Lanrete. Depicts a wind design on the blade.

Empyrean Betrayer - The first Eshgren. The first to betray the Rel Ach'Kel.

Enesmic beings - Beings not native to the Havin plane that originate from the Enesmic plane. Include the Rel Ach'Kel, Eshgren, Ceshra, and Vahne. Eshgren and Ceshra have black blood whereas Vahne and other lesser Enesmic beings have silver blood.

Enesmic energy - An elemental force that exists throughout the Twin Galaxies that can be manipulated via cihphism.

Enesmic rift - A large gateway to the Enesmic plane created by Sagren. The result of continued expansion of the Enesmic tear under Sagren's manipulation. Allows for the passage of powerful Enesmic beings into the Havin plane.

Enesmic tear - A small gateway to the Enesmic plane. Allows for increased flow of Enesmic energy into the Havin plane. Also allows for the passage of weak Enesmic beings into the Havin plane.

Global docking center (GDC) - The central docking hub of a planet or colony that allows for the embarkment and disembarkment of ships to and from a planet or colony. Coordinates all ship activity on the planet to ensure smooth operation of extraplanetary travel.

Huzien Intelligence Network (HIN) - A top secret communications channel that also serves as an information network for confidential resources and unit deployments. This channel is maintained and operated by the Huzien Intelligence Agency and is not an Alliance resource.

Immortals - Beings that do not age. They can be killed by normal means but will not age past their biological prime. They also have heightened regenerative abilities.

Lefon blast - Raw energy summoned from the Enesmic plane that is then funneled at the target in a powerful beam attack.

Streamsong - The name of the Redalam blade gifted to Neven by Lanrete. Depicts a flowing river design on the blade.

Systems defense contingent (SDC) - A group of ships designated to patrol and protect a specific planetary system. Usually part of a larger fleet responsible for protecting a sector of space.

Unquenchable - The name of the Redalam blade utilized by Jessica Olic. Depicts a flame design on the blade.

PLACES & LOCATIONS

Desc'Ri - Homeworld of the Das'Vin Republic.

Enesmic plane - A plane of existence that exists outside the Havin or "normal" plane. This plane is the source of Enesmic energy that flows within the Havins' plane of existence. Home to Enesmic beings.

Etan Rachnie - Special cihphist school created by Soahc. Also serves as the base camp and recruitment center for the Argents.

Ginea - Original homeworld of the Humans. Destroyed by Soahc.

Haula - Homeworld of the Hauxem Exchange.

Kaswif - Colony that the Founder's Elite fled to after the destruction of Pree.

New Ginea - New homeworld of the Humans and capital of the Huzien Alliance. Orbits Thae as one of its moons. Gifted to the Humans by the Huziens after an agreement between the founders and Soahc.

New Thae - Homeworld of the Tuzen Empire.

Neth - Large planetary colony that was overrun by Sagren's forces. The 3rd Fleet was destroyed while protecting this planet from Sagren's fleet.

Peshkana - Motherworld of the Uri people. A forest world under the control of the Huzien Empire.

Piro - Homeworld of the Vempiir Dominion.

Pree - A small planetary outpost near the borders of Alliance space. Home of the observation outpost destroyed by Sagren.

Reath - Planet owned by Soahc. Location of Etan Rachnie.

Septna Engineering Bay - MinSci engineering lab where Neven helped design the BRAS power frame.

Tar'Ki - Capital homeworld planet of the Ken'Tar Republic.

Thae - Homeworld of the Huzien Empire and former homeworld of the Tuzen people.

Traet University - Renowned university that has many programs, but is most notable for its science and engineering curriculums.

Trustinum University - Renowned medical university with pre-med, biotechnology, and other biology-focused programs.

Twin Galaxies - Home to the Huzien Alliance, Darbol Alliance, and a host of other galactic empires, the Twin Galaxies are the result of two colliding galactic bodies. Also referred to as the Havin plane. Officially called the Twin Galaxies of Oaphen Asracka.

Zen - Planet owned by Lanrete.

Burra - Dad. Father.

Burush - Son.

Cith – Huzien and Tuzen profanity typically used to insult a woman. When used for a man, is meant to insult their masculinity.

Cusshin - Derogatory term for a half-Huzien individual, usually used when the other half is Human.

EetUra - Declaration of Enthusiasm. Used by members of the Huzien fleet as a statement of enthusiasm.

Eifi - Wife, female life partner.

Feshra - Master of technology. Used for those who are masters of a technological craft or are great engineers.

Hahva - Great teacher.

Larush - Daughter.

Lurra - Mom.

Lurratha - Mother. Formal version of Mom.

Nusba - Husband, male life partner.

Obrehen - Blood brother. Used to describe someone who is not related by blood but holds a bond as significant as family.

Reka - Racial slur for a Tuzen, used as an insult.

Restendi - Head of government. Elected president of the Huzien Empire.

Tedr - Evil.

Vusg - Huzien and Tuzen profanity. Means to have sex with someone. Also means to ruin or damage something.

As'crefa - Command council. A group responsible for deployment of the Das'Vin military.

Dru'Sha - Life partner. Used to describe the mates or life partners of the Das'Vin.

Em'fa - Half-breed. An individual who is half Das'Vin.

Fra'Sha - Whore. With severed *ha'ishi* at the death of one's *dru'sha*, the Das'Vin can become *fra'sha*, who freely engage in sexual acts with other *fra'sha* or non-Das'Vin. No *ha'ishi* will be formed or any type of mental connection.

Ha'ishi - A deep mental connection shared between two *dru'sha* that allows the exchange of feelings and emotions. Depending on the cihphist sensitivity level of the two *dru'sha*, thoughts and messages can also be exchanged.

Hala'a - Term used to describe Das'Vin children.

Heir'Apthai - An elected member of the Heir'Klaxem who is the diplomatic leader of the Das'Vin Republic. Holds the Huzien Alliance designation of executive chancellor.

Heir'Klaxem – Governing council of the Das'Vin people. Made up of the heir'apthai, heir'nezu, and heir'luia. Collectively influence and set direction for the Das'Vin Republic. Act independently but consult each other when necessary.

Heir'luia - An elected member of the Heir'Klaxem who oversees the physical and emotional wellbeing of the Das'Vin species.

Heir'nezu - An elected member of the Heir'Klaxem who oversees the scientific and academic progress of the Das'Vin species.

Ma'eh - Evil.

Nuy'zer – Das'Vin outsider. A Das'Vin not raised in Das'Vin society who hasn't been socialized into Das'Vin culture, principles, and values.

Uma'shae - Title for the biological non-birth mother of a Das'Vin.

Wo'shae - Sister twin. The title shared by two Das'Vin *hala'a* who are born in the same dual pregnancy.

Woth're - Sisters. Comrades. A term used to relate a Das'Vin to another Das'Vin.

Yu'shae - Title for birth mother of a Das'Vin.

HAUXEM WORDS

A'acuy - The peak of a Hauxem female's fertility cycle, when their pheromones are strongest and they can entice potential males to impregnate them.

A'akugentai'a – Hauxem profanity. Means to have sex with (someone). Also means to ruin or damage (something).

A'asentup'akugen'avi – Phrase that combines *a'akugentai'a* with "get off me."

KEN'TAR WORDS

Acete'tesen - Primary male mate.

Crece'cesen - Primary female mate.

Haa'eag - Evil.

Te'cesen - Ken'Tar offspring, children.

Made in the USA
Middletown, DE
20 August 2022